## PRAISE FOR
# *THE BOOK OF LOST SAINTS*

"Older's **SPELLBINDING** novel is a fever dream full of magic and loss, wickedness and grace, faith and love, spirit and power."

**—MARLON JAMES,**
Booker Prize–winning author of *Black Leopard, Red Wolf*

"A **LYRICAL**, **BEAUTIFUL**, devastating, literally haunting journey of assimilation, resistance, and family. Older just gets better and better."

**—N. K. JEMISIN,**
award-winning author of the Broken Earth trilogy

"Older's **MASTERWORK** . . . should launch him into the company of American literary greats . . . **EPIC** and **INTIMATE**, conjuring laughter on one page, tears on the next."

**—TANANARIVE DUE,**
American Book Award–winning author of *The Living Blood* and *Ghost Summer*

"A moving, startling, **BOLDLY DRAWN FAMILY SAGA** that is equal parts mystery and ghost story, with details sharp enough to cut and characters who surprise at every turn."

**—LEIGH BARDUGO,**
worldwide-bestselling author of *Ninth House* and the Grishaverse novels

★"Thoroughly transportive. This moving story of family and freedom is **SURE TO CAPTIVATE READERS**."

**—PUBLISHERS WEEKLY**, starred review

"With lyricism and atmosphere, Older skillfully emphasizes tone . . . Haunting, melancholy, and **UNDENIABLY INSPIRING**."

**—BOOKLIST**

"A **GRITTY**, **COMPELLING** look at love and war and the ways past actions reverberate down through the generations."

**—SHELF AWARENESS**

"A thoughtful, intense, and resonant family saga . . . **UNFORGETTABLE** and well worth your time."

**—ALEX SEGURA,**
acclaimed author of *Blackout* and *Dangerous Ends*

*For Brittany, with all my heart*

A Feiwel and Friends Book
An imprint of Macmillan Publishing Group, LLC
120 Broadway, New York, NY 10271

Originally published in the United States of America by Imprint

Library of Congress Cataloging-in-Publication Data

Name: Older, Daniel José, author.
Title: The book of lost saints / Daniel José Older.
Description: | New York : Imprint, 2019. | Summary: The spirit of Marisol,
who vanished during the Cuban Revolution, visits her nephew, Ramón, in modern-day
New Jersey, and her presence prompts him to investigate the story of his
ancestor, unaware of the forces driving him on his search.
Identifiers: LCCN 2019002414 (print) | ISBN 9781250620910 (paperback) |
ISBN 9781250185822 (ebook)
Classification: LCC PS3615.L37 B66 2019 | DDC 813/.6—dc23
LC record available at https://lccn.loc.gov/2019002414

Our books may be purchased in bulk for promotional, educational, or business use.
Please contact your local bookseller or the Macmillan Corporate and
Premium Sales Department at (800) 221-7945 ext. 5442 or
by email at MacmillanSpecialMarkets@macmillan.com.

Book design by Ellen Duda

Feiwel and Friends logo designed by Amanda Spielman

First paperback edition, 2022

1  3  5  7  9  10  8  6  4  2

Si le quitas la cubierta a este libro, cuidado que no te caiga un rayo encima.

# THE BOOK OF LOST SAINTS

## DANIEL JOSÉ OLDER

[Imprint]
MAKE YOUR MARK

NEW YORK

*"Dos patrias tengo yo: Cuba y la noche.*
*¿O son una las dos?"*
*"Two homelands have I: Cuba and the night.*
*Or are they one and the same?"*

~José Martí

# Part One
# TIRAR

# CHAPTER ONE

His name is Gómez.

He carries a butcher knife in one hand, a chicken in the other. The chicken doesn't flap, doesn't tremble, just waits, watching everything. Back. Step back. The blade is sharp but the face is kind, hardened but kind, and the blood splattered on the apron is old.

*Isabel sent me*, says a little girl's voice—my voice.

Gómez scrunches up his face, as if he's a giant and I—she?—we are one of the little people they speak of that live in the forests outside of town. (Town? A town on the outskirts of a big city, a confluence of voices nearby. A market . . .)

*Her sister*, Gómez says. He nods. *I see it now.* Then he turns, holds the chicken down on the counter and *thwunk* beheads it, and the blood gushes then trickles onto the floor. Then he angles his body just so, after a conspiratorial wink down at us, and does something to the chicken.

It takes him a few minutes' worth of sweating and mumbling *carajo* and adjusting his shoulders, and all the while the sound of a heart beats languidly around us: *Ga-gung!* It had somehow been there all along and now just gets louder and louder. It is gigantic, so big it must belong to the whole world.

Finally Gómez turns back around and hands us the paper bag, already wet from the newly dead bird and heavy—too heavy.

He doesn't notice the heart that beats through the plaster walls of his shop, the tiny interruptions on the surfaces of puddles out in the street, the way the whole universe rattles with each *ga-gung*.

*Careful out there*, he says, watching us struggle with the weight of the bag. But of course we'll be careful—the streets are full of soldiers and walking bad dreams.

When we look down, the thunder of that heart bursting through us, blood has already dripped onto our pretty . . . new . . . shoes.

*

"¡Ramón!"

A gruff and familiar voice, it yanks me forward along the pathway of that slow beating heart, away from those tiny bloodstained shoes, into a small ugly room with only a couch. On that couch, a gigantic man sits up, blinking awake.

"¡Ramón! ¡Te toca a ti!"

That is not my name.

I have no name. I have nothing, am nothing.

But I know that voice, and, distantly, I know the face of the man in front of me, who now rubs his eyes and glances around, bemused. Stubble from a few days without shaving crescents the bottom of his light brown face; his mouth hangs slightly open as he blinks away the fluorescent glare from above.

I know him, knew him once.

Once, when I was whole.

Shreds of it echo back to me: an old book, hurled across a cluttered office. A tower blocking out the sun. The smell of the ocean. A few indistinguishable splinters of voice, the creases of a face. Gunfire and the pound of wood against flesh.

That's it. The fractured puzzle pieces. Useless really.

I have been here all along. Whatever happened to me, I lingered. I held on and remained, as my body turned to dust and my mind rejoined the swirl of whatever it is that minds swirl up into. At some point I must've become we and the little parts of me scattered into a great pulsing collective of minds. And we watched.

We watched.

We watched and we waited, processing, sometimes judging. Sometimes we dithered inwardly or sneered, that faraway crinkle in the fabric of the world you sense. We cringed when everything goes wrong, or exalted in some sweet conflagration.

But now I've been spat back out. Pulled, really. A second chance?

If I existed, if I'm more than just a nameless thread in some ghost tapestry, then I must know why I've been released, why I came back.

I must know everything.

Ramón puts both hands on his knees and grunts but doesn't get up.

He is, let's be honest, a lug.

Maybe it's because he just woke up . . . but no, that's a charitable lie. He shakes his head, looks around a second time, and I want to yell: *Again, Ramón? Have you not already seen this pathetic little room enough times?* But I can't yell, I can't wave, can't sing—I am nothing.

He cracks his neck, sickeningly, then scratches his balls, yawns. The entirety of me, whatever that is, each simmering phantom speck, feels ready to blow. Maybe I should just let myself be enveloped back into the ether and be done with it, if this is what being back among the living consists of.

Finally, he rubs both hands up his face and into his wild black hair. "¡Ya voy!" he bellows. Then Ramón rises and suddenly the room seems smaller. He's not fat so much as just large in every direction. He's got some belly sag, sure, and arms like great napping iguanas, but it's his height that seems to dwarf this tiny waiting area. He has to crane his neck to not crack the fluorescents.

He hunches his shoulders up and down a few times, then looks up, directly at me, and freezes.

A hundred seconds seem to fly past as Ramón slowly leans forward, squinting.

He sees me.

I am nothing, but he sees me.

And, taking his face in for the first time, I see him too. Recognition tugs at the edges of my memory, the first piece fits into place.

I know this. His beating heart beckoned me, his blood summoned mine, or whatever remnant of a lineage is left to me.

Ramón is family.

And he sees me. Face still squeezed into a fist, he cocks his head to the side, then reaches up and slicks back an unruly cowlick.

I whirl my attention to the part of the room behind me, and there is Ramón again, this version somewhat mustier and blocked by stickers.

I release something from myself—a sigh, I realize. It is long and exasperated and perhaps it comes with the slightest of sounds, a gentle whoosh of air, because Ramón pauses his mirror preening and glances around with a furrowed brow.

Then he shrugs and steps directly into the empty space I occupy and I gasp. The world becomes a press of fluid and organs, meat! All shoved up against each other, against me, and saturated with billions of thoughts, dreams, memories, lies, meandering, impossible threads all tied in knots and strewn through each other, through Ramón's interior, through me.

I can read him, know him, this man.

He is my nephew.

My nephew—he freezes again and this time I know it's because something really has registered, some part of my shimmering, impossible presence has made itself known to this flesh-and-bone behemoth.

He does not see me—I am within him, after all—but Ramón feels me. Of that I am sure. I know because I feel him feel me, sense the icy slither of my presence work its way through his consciousness.

"¡Ramón!" that haunting, smoke-stained voice hollers again, and the moment is broken, the body lurches forward and I release it, watch the back of my nephew's shaggy head duck and disappear into the darkness of a corridor.

And me—I breathe in and out in my long, impossible breaths, grasping desperately for my faraway phantom memories, and remain.

✳

Until it seems like I can't anymore.

Because I am vanishing further, becoming even less than the barely there that I already am. It doesn't seem possible, but this most fragile of holds I have on reality is about to give—I feel its tender fibers stretched to shatter point. It's as if the collective mass of ether I emerged from has

4

already swamped me with those heavy coils of emptiness, will soon drag me back into that nothing.

I don't have much time, and I don't know what it is I'm here to do, but I know it starts with finding out who I am, was, and the only key I have to that just lumbered out the door.

I flush forward; the room blurs past and then the dank corridor and then a resounding boom hammers through me, through everything, and I wonder if we're under attack somehow; people are screaming. Then another follows, louder, and I'm turning in circles in the darkness, tangled in my own panic, lost between point A and B, a disaster.

Bright lights reach me in a flickering crescendo from down the hall. Not the hideous fluorescents—these splatter a rainbow of flashes across the peeling posters on the walls around me. As another clattering roar blasts out, the lights shimmer to match it. Forward. Forward through the corridor and out into a magnificent, pulsing world awash in sudden brightness amidst the shadows and writhing bodies, and that sound!

That sound. It rages at first, a hellish screech—no, many screeches intermingling like a tangle of lost souls stretching upward into the night as the steady thud of some war drum pounds and pounds beneath. But the notes seem to find each other, to slide into formation and sweeten, sparkle. I warm to this music, or it warms to me. And I move, over the heads of these squirming, fussing bodies, up into the darkness. We are in a converted warehouse of some kind. Below, the dancers unleash and there, on the stage, a single figure moves between different tabletop setups, controlling it all.

Ramón.

I hurl down toward him, fascinated, and the music grows and bursts around me: a church choir. Horns. Some high-pitched whistle I have no reference for. Beneath it all that burning beat, relentless.

I circle Ramón. His hands move from a keyboard to a turntable, back to the keyboard, then another turntable. He moves without thought, fear, doubt. He just moves, and every time he does, something happens in the air around us: The wall of sound falls away as suddenly as a crashing wave, and then we're left with just that pounding rhythm that rises; now crashes and shimmers, disperses. And then all that's left is the high clacking of two sticks.

*Dak . . . dak dak . . . dak dak . . .*

The crowd erupts into first cheers, and then claps. Not applause, though—they clap in time with those sticks: A hit, a breath, then two more, a pause and then two that seem to answer the first three.

*Dak . . . dak dak . . . dak dak . . .*

There is something so simple, so elemental about that easy call and response and the fact that everyone knows it, that we know it.

We.

A hundred schoolkids clapping at the same time, laughing, but holding the beat, that pulse beneath, and somewhere, I am among them in that smiling sea of cheeks and foreheads and black-brown hair. Somewhere.

But what matters is: I have a place, a place that knows me and I know it. It has a rhythm, a people. A we beyond that impossible ethereal mass.

The world around me becomes that much crisper, like someone adjusted the focus on it.

Each of Ramón's wild strands of hair reveals itself in perfect detail, the dandruff on his black T-shirt, the beads of his bracelet, the tiny buttons and lights on his setup. Ever so slightly, I inch forward, feel the squishy embrace of all that muscle and flesh. I allow myself to be enveloped in it, in Ramón, and then I am with him, fully, a part of his cellular machinery, his mind and memory.

It's still just the clacking of sticks ringing out—*dak . . . dak dak . . . dak dak*—and the whole club clapping along, but all of Ramón rocks with the deep downbeat below it, that pulse that hits before and between and through each clack. It moves silently through me too, as I move through him, and then it's very suddenly not silent anymore. I feel it coming a half second before he moves: A hunger erupts in him for that space to be filled and then with the flick of a wrist the record he'd been holding spins free and the beat quakes through the club as the dancers burst back into motion.

Ramón pushes more buttons; sends more rhythms booming and popping into the mix. I feel each one rattle through me just before it falls into place, feel the hunger become anticipation and then satiate with something real. Something you can move to.

No wonder Ramón is such a slug: He is exceptionally good at something and it comes easy to him. It always has, that much is clear. These machines surrounding him are extensions of himself and he works them as such.

Across the rage of this sound, the perfection of these chattering rhythms, more pieces fall together.

None of them make much sense: a place I am from, scattered shards of terror, yearning, rage. A flicker of something else: love, maybe.

But the butcher shop, with its heavy secrets inside the corpse of that chicken—that memory belonged to me. That much I know, and if I accessed it through my passage here, along the thought lines of this big strange man, then he will be my ticket to salvation; he will be the catalyst and through him I will find myself.

The music pounds on into the night, and deep within the warm, pulsing world of my nephew, I simmer, remain, and conspire.

# CHAPTER TWO

A family portrait.

Nilda at the door, halfway out of it really, carrying her satchel full of music partiture, on the way to some piano lesson or choir practice or whatever bobería she's chosen to fill her weekends with this time. Long and slender and aggressively fragile; her thin eyes narrow further at the sight of me, the unusually heavy chicken bundled in my arms along with one of my ever-present books—a novel, I'm sure—and my heart lurches. I know I carry a secret; I don't know what it is. But Nilda can see through me, knows everything, is forever unimpressed, and godly powers lurk in her stern cynicism.

But she's in a hurry, so she lets me know with a glance that she'll be back and have questions, and then she's gone. And half of me is disappointed, because I'd wanted to lord it over her that I knew something she didn't and then hopefully we could play some games; but the other half is relieved.

Isabel in the front room, waiting with creased brows. The oldest of us three, somehow the sweetest in spite of being made to pull the most weight around the house and at school, looking out for Nilda and me. She's wide where Nilda is just a thread, and always has open arms and cheek kisses when Nilda would rather not. I know she wants to say something, ask me how it went with Gómez, since she's the one who sent me, but she's not alone, so we can't talk yet.

Cassandra, the ancient housekeeper, rises from the big living room chair as I enter and starts fussing—the mud I've tracked in, the door not closing fast enough, the mosquitoes, the birds, the whole world a cruel and festering antagonist trying to invade through any open space available. But we all know damn well it'll be Isabel, not Cassandra, who cleans up the mud and swats off any other intrusion from beyond.

Cassandra's job is to fuss, and she does it with panache, when she's up to it. Mostly, we take care of her.

*You got what I sent you for?* Isabel asks without a trace that it's anything irregular, and I'm impressed, because if it were me I'd have been wiggling my eyebrows like a fool.

*You were at Gómez's?* Cassandra asks. *What for? Are we having company tonight? Is he still selling those skinny sides of ham? I can't do anything with those hams; it's a travesty, really, but I suppose he's all we have right now.* No one answers her, because she's never really asking a question, just rattling off a list of random thoughts and complaints. She sighs and finds her way back to the chair to put her feet up. *Ay, mi madre.*

I just nod, not trusting myself not to wink at Isabel, and head quickly to the kitchen, trying to ignore how that heaviness in my arms feels like it's dragging me toward the floor.

❋

An ugly splatter of drum hits brings the ceiling, then a fancy telephone device into sudden focus. The shock of waking and then a familiar name across the display screen: *Nilda* and in parentheses, the word *mami*, and though I have no body, some part of me cringes somehow. A deep-down recoiling of the soul.

My sister. I don't know where this wrath comes from. I don't have a why, but I can imagine my hands sliding around her neck and the image is a familiar one; it rises within me the way an old friend walks into your house and makes himself at home.

This man of flesh and tendon, blood, bone, and hair, he reaches across the slight woman sleeping beside him and somehow makes the phone go quiet.

Aliceana, her name is. She showed up at the club toward the end of his set, and the immediate ease between them spoke of many delicious nights and words that didn't need to be said. She tipped up her chin, eyebrows wiggling; he gave a couple sultry shoulder jigs in response. Their eyes barely met from that moment on, but it was as if they'd silently created a tiny, cozy world for themselves in the space between them. She posted up at the bar with a tequila and quietly murdered every nascent attempt at small talk as Ramón closed out his last song.

He lies back down with a grunt and then the dream seems to surface; its steamy tendons haven't released him yet, and the impossible weight of that chicken lingers, and so do I.

Then a brown hand slides along his brown shoulder and he turns, a sly smile on his face, and she lets him know with a nod that she is ready, woke up that way, and a few moans and familiar maneuvers later he is inside her.

Ah.

You think I shouldn't speak on or even notice such things.

I'm beyond considering your judgment, though, lucky for you. I couldn't give a damn, after all I've been through. After whatever I've been through.

The weight of it is with me. It's an unusual, disconcerting weight, like the chicken in the dream; something is not right.

And this man, he will help me find out what, even if he doesn't know it yet.

So I remain.

Through the arching backs and frenzied grabs at air, the whole room becomes hot around us, lit with her expanding orgasm, and I remain. Watch, even. Stop. I'm sure you would too. She's a slight thing, gorgeous in her way, but from what I've gathered, one of God's more mediocre creatures. Perhaps she matches my strange nephew in that way.

They certainly do click. In the club, they'd faced outward to the bustling world, and each carried the simple and unspoken trust that the other was there, present in that space in between that they'd made. Now, closer than close, their bodies entwined and breath filling the room, their eyes meet and they teeter toward something much bigger than either of them, something that feels very much like an abyss.

Then her gasps peak. She collapses over him like all her bones suddenly disappeared and a few pumps later he explodes too.

I remain.

And here, as they lie there panting, is where the wonder of what's left unsaid runs out. They have no title, I realize, so in a way, they are nothing. Everything and nothing, but in these moments, as that magic breathlessness fades, there are words that want to be spoken. They linger in the air, garbled, unmanifested. They cloud up the room, complicate the sweet simmer down.

He's about to speak; doesn't. Maybe for the best: The words aren't coherent for him anyway, not yet, so he'd probably just make a mess of them.

And anyway, it's dawn and she's going to be late, so she disentangles herself and wipes some sweat off and prances toward the shower.

Ramón waits, breathes, then rises. Sitting on the bed edge, he rubs the sheets over his dick a few times till it feels dryish and then cracks his neck and reaches for his cigarettes, which aren't there because he quit three days ago. He executes a somewhat ridiculous body roll across the bed, grabs Aliceana's light blue scrubs, and fumbles with them till her pack falls out, frees a cigarette. Lights it.

Now, I believe, is when he senses me. Or perhaps all along, but now now now this moment, with the girl showering and the curl of smoke from his lungs, the January day creeping to life through the half-opened blinds, the still groggy glow after a righteous fuck—now my presence eats up just enough of the emptiness in the room to warrant some attention, and he looks sharply up from his abuelo's easy chair. The sheets drape over one shoulder like he's about to address the Roman senate and one thick eyebrow rises and the smoke curls up from the cigarette and the day grows a shade brighter, and the shower shushes, but none of it lets loose any clue as to what that feeling is that suddenly crept over him.

I remain. Perfectly still. Breath bated. A shadow in the shadows. Tingling with a new sense of power, I wait. Wonder. Should I, right now? Is there time? Could I? I feel myself solidify ever so slightly within his gaze, a dizzying thrill.

Any second the shower will stop shushing and the girl will emerge.

But for a precious and dangerous moment, I think, to hell with it—al carajo, actually—and I begin. Ramón takes a pull on the smoke and watches the air around him. His eyes scan back and forth; he's sitting up straight, almost smiling. That almost smile, it's all I need to know, I decide, and I stop.

Which is good, because just then Aliceana bursts out of the bathroom, mumbles something passive-aggressive about her cigarettes and him quitting as she pulls on her scrubs and then flits out the door with a quick kiss.

And still, I remain.

❋

His coffee's cold and he's not smoking, but his breath comes out in steamy gasps that roll and then stretch up into the gray sky above the hospital. I hover just behind his head, a passing glint of nothing, a cold flash. Those great big shoulders sag forward just so—not a full slouch, but you know: The ground seems to pull him toward it. And sure, he shows up at work every day, and he has this night gig with the music, but really, he gets by on the bare minimum and that'll just have to do, for all he cares.

And that would be all well and good, but I need him. Specifically, I need his internal drive to not be in a constant sputter. I need forward motion.

Instead, here we are again, outside the hospital for yet another non-cigarette break. He puts the mostly empty cup on a trash can lid and wraps his arms around himself for warmth, gazes out at the traffic.

"Diiiime," a familiar singsongy voice drawl-whines through his cell phone, and again I convulse with that deep-down soul cringe. I hadn't even noticed him take it out and flip it open—these things are so small now.

"Hey, Mami, you called this morning? I was still, uh, sleeping. Everything okay?"

"Ay, sí, mi amor," Nilda chirps electronically. "No, no, todo bien aquí, tú sabes."

There are things I'm sure I never knew in life that are clear to me. The simple physics of emptiness and the thick lines around it offer up whole libraries of information I never could've imagined—histories, both banal and grand, and the flow and sweep of emotions that trail behind each of us in elegant, phosphorescent capes. I understand the great movements of people across oceans, the rise and fall of kings and tyrants. But I cannot fathom what it is about this woman, this woman who was my sister, that calls forth such a rage within me.

Who knows what can tear two sisters apart in this world? There are so many things, really. I know her voice, can conjure up the lines of her face. I can see the three of us beside each other: Nilda in the middle, Isabel at the far end even though she's the one I was closer to. Each of us in our bleached white school uniforms with those ridiculous blue bows tied at our necks. But that's it.

"Okay, Mami," Ramón says. "Do you want to have lunch this weekend?"

Still, I trust myself. Surely there is a good reason.

"¡Claro que sí!" she says, enthralled, but there's an edge in her voice. They've had this conversation before.

"Maybe we could grab something from Valentino's on Clark." He says this, I realize, knowing it won't happen, wondering why he bothered trying in the first place.

"Ay, m'ijo." Not an answer, but in a way, the only answer he'll probably ever get.

"Mami."

"Es qué . . . tú sabes, Ramón. Ay teroristas por allí, y . . . ay, no sé."

"Terrorists? Mami, nine-eleven was three years ago. And nobody cares about suburban Jersey. No terrorist is trying to blow up Benigno's, I promise."

"¡Pero no digas esas cosas, Ramón!" Nilda scolds. "¡Por favor!"

"It's just—"

"Y además tu papá me necesita," she explains, as if Ramón had just conceded the point and now she's clinching it with this new bit of info.

"Papi is a grown man," Ramón says. "And healthy to boot. I just . . ." He shakes his head, dangling somewhere between sympathy and utter exasperation. "I worry about you, Mami. I want you to get out. It's not healthy, you being cooped up all day and night like that."

"All that fat and hair and you're still cold?" Derringer materializes next to him and lights a Marlboro. "That's, like, such a waste."

Ramón glares down at him.

"¿Qué?" Nilda asks over the phone.

"Nothing, Mami. Te veo pronto, ¿okay? I'll come by the house."

"Ay, te quiero, mi vida."

"Y yo a ti," Ramón mumbles, still eyeing Derringer. I know that face: It means he's swallowing a curse-out. Derringer knows it too and he chuckles and then coughs something wet up and swallows it back down.

"All that rotting ass gunk building up in your lungs and you're still alive," Ramón says. "A medical motherfucking miracle."

"Ah, you're just salty you quit and the rest of us are still having fun."

Ramón scowls and tugs on the fur-lined earflaps of his hat. "Have fun dying."

"Hey, we're all dying. Anyway, I saw on your Myspace page that you're spinning tonight," Derringer says after another coughing fit.

Ramón nods. "If Inspector General Jackass lets me off on time I am."

"Alright, I'm gonna try and make it this time, big guy."

"Shall I put you down as minus one like all the oth—" Ramón doesn't finish his sentence because a short, naked man in a cape flashes past them and gets hit by a car.

"The fuck?" Ramón bellows, launching into traffic. He throws his big arms out in either direction, feels more than sees or hears cars pulling to a halt around him. The guy is laughing when Ramón reaches him. His teeth chitter-chatter and he's sprawled out on the blacktop, writhing and cackling. The cape turns out to be a hospital gown, tied around his neck. It's one of the telltale bright yellow psych patient ones, and the guy is all tangled in it.

"What the hell, jackass?" Derringer demands, panting and irritable from the sudden exertion. The driver hops out of his car, wondering the same thing in a much more colorful way. Then the psych patient is up again and about to make a dash for the park across the street.

"No you don't." Ramón snatches the guy up by the back of the neck and then he and Derringer begin wrastling him toward the ER bay.

Ramón's coffee waits on the trash can. I linger over it for a few seconds. I become my breath and let my breath become the breeze, inhabit the empty molecules just within the rim, take in whatever's left of the flavor. It's not bad. He got it from the Dominican spot around the corner and they made it right: strong with a swirl of sugar. For a few minutes, as the carnival of body parts and angry curse-outs cavorts past, I just stay, and breathe, and stay. And breathe.

A sister I want to kill who won't leave the house. Another who is gone, as gone as me. Vanished and dead, I'm sure. Parents long gone. I am orphaned of family and body alike, this boy-beast my only tether to the world.

And still I fluctuate between a gathering strength and that creepy fade. Like right now, as the brittle wind sweeps past, it seems to whisk off more of my shadowy self. I am less and less and less and finally, hungry for something I can get a fix on, I swoop around and enter the hospital.

# CHAPTER THREE

I flush into the stale, cramped exam room as Aliceana stands on her tiptoes to get a good gape at the scratch marks crossing Ramón's shoulder. "What the hell did that guy do to you?"

"It's fine," Ramón says, but you can tell he doesn't mind the attention. I move toward him, then breathe and enfold myself within. Ramón, I am surprised to discover, is nervous. This man who can command a crowd with the flick of his wrist for hours on end, he is suddenly somehow undone and doesn't know why. And neither do I.

"It's not fine," Aliceana chides. "He probably had all kinds of hideous bacteria under those nails." She climbs up on the stretcher behind him and dabs at a scratch with gloved fingers.

"Ow! Fuck. Is that the medical term? Hideous bacteria?" He plays it off well; I wouldn't have known from the outside. But that racing heart, the tiniest shiver of his hand. I don't know why, what subtle twist in the fabric of this particular day or moment did it—maybe it's the way she cares for him, that studious attentiveness as she gets all up into his scratch—but something huge and full of light is rising slowly within Ramón. It is terrifying.

"Yes. When was your last tetanus shot?"

"Aliceana."

"When? If you don't remember it, we should just—"

"Aliceana." Ramón executes an impressive swivel, only scowling a little, and pushes his hips forward. Unable to process his own nervousness, he resorts to something he does understand.

"¡Ramón!"

"The door's closed."

"Ramón," she laughs. She's considering it though. You can see the memory of this morning's lovemaking dash across her eyes as her mouth opens slightly, as if to accept his looming kiss. Instead, she puts a finger up and shakes her head. "Someone'll come in."

He scootches back. "First of all, I locked it. Second of all, so?"

She just looks at him. The look says: *You know it, don't make me say it.* It's never been said, but it's written all over both of them. Shame and the shame of shame. A double whammy, ricocheting back and forth between them in some cruel echo chamber. The night they first began, she'd run up to him at the club to compliment his DJing. And she didn't recognize him, he'd realized immediately. It vexed him at first, and then much less so when they'd found themselves naked in each other's arms a few hours later.

But then he'd watched her expression when he told her they work together. It was inscrutable actually, but he imagined in it a whole web of crisscrossing concerns. He wasn't too far off the mark, but none of the concerns were enough for either of them to forgo more sheet-grabbing, so they kept at it and kept quiet, only exchanging brief nods when their paths crossed at the hospital. And Ramón accepted early that his dreams of some telenovela-style storage room sexing were probably fleeting at best.

*Just say it*, he almost blurts out. *Say you don't want anyone to know you're banging security.* The words stay in his mouth and get bitter there. He frowns and turns back around on the stretcher. "Last year at Rutgers."

"What?"

"My tetanus shot."

"Oh. Alright, I guess I'll just—" A throttle of drumming erupts from Ramón's belt, cutting off Aliceana. He pulls out his phone, cringing, and flicks it open.

"Another one of your adoring teenybopper fans?" Aliceana asks.

Ramón nods. "Who else calls me?" But both Aliceana and I can tell he's lying. She scowls behind his back. Ramón shrugs and pockets his phone. It's not a girl though, but someone named Alberto, whom Ramón fervently wants nothing to do with.

"Alright, rock star, I'll be back with some antibiotic crap for your naked cape guy gunk scars."

"Gracias."

"Shut up."

✳

They came in boats and airplanes, armed with false documents and holy terror and a grinding wariness of what they would find. They came and breathed sigh after sigh of relief, closed their eyes, and put trembling hands to foreheads. They came and settled into these flashy modern digs, cursed at the atrocious weather, renamed streets without English's sharp consonants, erected bakeries and memorials and three-star restaurants that reminded them just enough of home not to trigger nightmares.

They came and left behind family members clutching photographs, and promises to send money and frequent letters and powdered milk or vacuum cleaners or whatever was impossible to find that year. They left behind true loves and mistresses and streets pulsing with memories. Each brought along a cord that stretched all the way back to the island and when they slept, each prayed the cord would send along news from home until slowly, each one came to call this place home and the cords wavered beneath the weight of the present tense.

They came and made Miguelitos and Carlitos and Anitas and Selinitas. And they told the little ones stories, tried to remember as best they could but always came up with folktales; no matter how hard they tried, their stories always felt like lies. They cringed at half-learned Spanish and pan-Asian vegetarian takeout, and then they tried it and didn't mind so much, and life rumbled along with new updates now flashing across computer screens instead of pulled from weather-worn envelopes smelling of the past.

They came and made new lives, and me? I got lost in the shuffle. Somewhere in between. Became a part of that great semi-sentient we and disappeared. I don't know. I'm still piecing it all together.

But those strands, those many lives, I feel them. They are obvious to me, as clear as words scrawled on a notebook page. A place speaks, and maybe to you it's just the ambient chugalug of everyday life, the buzz of a light fixture, the hum of a power generator, the occasional blurt and sputter of traffic. To me, each place carries stories and they sometimes whisper and sometimes yell.

People too, of course, just walk around with all their stories hanging around them like so many chattering birds.

It's just past sunset and snowing when Ramón gets to his front door. Not the graceful dancing kind of snow, but a soggy drenching mess that sloshes out of the night sky and becomes instant brown crud in the streets. Even I feel it, a shudder that ripples to my source, and I find myself lingering closer to Ramón as if to soak up some of that good flesh-and-blood warmth.

So alive, this useless boy-man. All his cluttered organs and gushy pumping liquids, all that life! A waste, really. No one who has it knows the true meaning of inhabiting form. We, we watch silently as you lumbering chunks of skin and fat trundle through existence striving for meaning, and we chuckle and moan at the irony of it. But you who inhabit those mortal bags—you guys just don't get it. Well. Ramón's face tightens with the uncertain sensation that he's been defeated before he realized he was playing. His fists clench in his pockets, yes, from the cold, but also from some undescribed frustration that lurks.

See? Useless.

He fumbles for his keys, fingers stiff from the cold.

I could soothe him. But this is not the time, nor is it my purpose. The culmination of all my work and travel is not to brighten some behemoth's foul mood on a winter night. Even if the behemoth is my nephew. No. Timing is everything. If I get sloppy now, I risk it all.

The apartment building is dull. White tile hallways and fluorescent lights. Plaster walls. It looks very much like the building next to it, in fact—a semi-suburban pocket of mundane similarity in the shadow of the hospital. He slouches up the stairs and down the hall;

the shadows grow across his face as he goes. Key in lock, the familiar squeak of the door, eyebrows raised as he peers inside. The place is dark though; Marcos and Adina are out. Ramón can't decide if he's relieved or annoyed. He's in and naked and in the steaming shower within minutes, gingerly lathering up the long day's scratch marks.

He only has an hour or so before he has to head out to the club, but instead of plopping in front of the TV or jacking off, Ramón sits at the cluttered desk in the corner of his bedroom. He roots around for a piece of paper, finds something even better: an almost empty notebook he'd bought a couple months back for keeping track of what songs he played. The first three pages have messily scrawled setlists. The fourth has two paragraphs of a—let's be honest—pretty inarticulate letter to Aliceana, and the rest is blank blank beautiful blank.

He flips through the empty pages and I eye them hungrily from over his shoulder. Empty pages. A whole story to tell. A whole world to unravel. If he does what I hope he will, and if my skills are on point and I can build on what I've begun . . . well. Well. We shall see.

Here is where I require just the slightest bits of forward motion from this water-treading giant. I'm not asking for mountains to be moved, just a small step toward me, now that I've come all this way. I don't know the details of my journey, but I know it has been a long one, and I know I've come through some hell. I suppress the urge to call out, name my sudden burst of hope with a joyful yelp. I am patient though. I am a thing beyond the petty politics of hope and fear.

Usually.

I strive to be anyway.

Then, as if to reward my restraint, Ramón turns to the first blank page, clicks out his pen, and writes: *His name is Gómez.*

# CHAPTER FOUR

Isabel.

She is plump, nervous, sweating, peeking out of the shadows. Whatever this is, it's something real, important. I can't remember Isabel ever looking this unsettled. She's got that ever-present notebook tucked under her arm and the other hand curled into a tight fist.

She hides in the walk-in cupboard, just where she said she'd be. Waiting for me. She's so vivid when she's not faded black and white, so alive. And so terrified. Her eyes keep jumping back to the doorway and she'd let out a tiny yelp when I first entered. It's a game to Little Me—we're excited, puzzle pieces in a great mystery, something gigantic and terrible and so much better than any stupid hopscotch or marbles or anything else. And my favorite part: Nilda doesn't know about it. Even better: She suspects. What good is a secret with your older sister if the middle one has no clue about it? No. It's much better this way—her gut tells her something's off, there's a conspiracy afoot, but her mind can't wrap around what it could be. I giggle a little at the thought of it.

My high-pitched laugh startles Isabel and she swats me hard across the arm. I have to stop myself from crying. Isabel's never hit me before, barely even raised her voice. Because I'm her favorite, of course. Nilda may be older than me, but she's such a pain and is always playing by the rules, always doing exactly what Mami and Papi tell her and trying to make sure we do too. But Isabel and I, we have our own thing, so when she slaps me it hurts my heart even more than my arm.

*You have it?* she whispers, softening some because she sees I'm close to tears.

I don't speak, just offer it up to her. It takes both arms because it's so heavy. Isabel's stronger than me though, and she easily lifts it and puts it on the counter and tears it open.

She's selecting one of Mami's big knives when a knock comes at the front door and I have to stifle a shriek. Isabel glances at me, teeth clenched, then whispers, *Come on*, and I follow her out into the den and watch as she opens the door.

The big toothy grin of Enrique Gutierrez awaits us, and I'm positive we both roll our eyes at the same time.

*Nilda's not here*, I say, one hand on my hip.

*Who said I was looking for Nilda?* Enrique demands, grin gone.

*Go*, Isabel says. *We're busy.*

*What are you so busy wi*—he starts, but I cut him off.

*I have to tell you a secret*, I say, leaning forward so he leans forward too. *You have too many teeth and not enough face.* Then I slam the door before he can respond and, giggling, we hurry back into the cupboard.

I watch, praying she doesn't make me leave. I watch while she removes the chicken carcass and then pulls a knife off the rack on the wall and cuts into it. I hear the clink of blade touching metal and then Isabel stops and throws a glance at the door. Nothing happens. No one comes. It's quiet. I think she's going to make me leave then, and my heart is beating so fast it's probably going to burst at any second.

There's a wet, nasty sound when Isabel plunges her hand into the chicken and I cringe but stare in fascination as she digs around, unperturbed by the gunk all over her. Finally she smiles. I love Isabel's smile with all my heart, but I mean the real genuine one, not the one she shows when the abuelos come to visit. It's the real one that happens now when she adjusts her position and then pulls a paper bag out of the chicken. She strips it away and holds in her hand a pistol. A real one, not a toy. There's another bag with the balas in it, and she puts it on the counter.

She's not smiling anymore when she looks down at me, holding the pistol in one hand and a notebook in the other, and tells me to clean up the mess while she hides the gun. And I do, I do because I love her and I'll do anything for her, and there are guerrillas in the mountains outside of town, and at night sometimes we hear the cracks and low rumbles of their war against the government. And this war is a noble one, according to the whispered stories Isabel fills me with late at night as Nilda snores. And even though it's only been going on a few years, it stretches back whole centuries, as generation after generation has risen up to throw off one form of oppression or another, and maybe now, maybe this time, we stand on the precipice of the whole world changing forever. And somehow, we're part of that change, and because Isabel is there with me, and I know we can do anything if we do it together, I close my eyes for a second and brace myself for all that is to come.

✳

Ramón wakes, the dream still with him, the world still strange and hazy with the heat of our Havana suburb, the shock of a much colder, grayer city outside the window. And I hover just above him, feeling empty and even more barely there than before.

It drains me, this cruel gift of my memories that I give. It takes something small and immeasurable from me. I know I'll replenish, can already feel the damage begin to undo itself as I strengthen. But if memories are all that make me, there can't be an endless supply. Even re-energized, something is gone. There's only so much of my life I can give.

And everything feels different now that I'm on a first-name basis with that seeping, vanishing sensation: my undoing.

The notebook lies open on the bedside table beside him. In it, the tiny event of my trip to the butcher, my return home, is scrawled out in his sloppy handwriting. Ramón eyes the pen, considering adding this strange new chapter, but it's time to leave, almost past time, and he has to make it to the club to set up.

He hurls himself into a sitting position and stumbles to his feet, and for a second I think he's going to dash off out the door and be on his way. He is about to be late, after all.

But this is Ramón, of course, and so instead he ramóns his way through that unintelligible sequence of yawns, grunts, eye rubs, and crackling joints. Then he stands perfectly still for a few moments, and at first I think he's fallen back asleep. I venture closer, allow myself to merge with him.

Music.

It ripples through him like light on a lake: just the rough sketches of melodies that rise and fall and cut suddenly short, chortling waves of notes that crash into each other and then cycle back toward some vaguely defined one; sudden blasts of harmonies that diminish and then are gone. But mostly, there are rhythms: the fanciful and abrupt lullaby of the guaguancó. That loving, familiar side dash of the bolero, the high clack of the clave, which waits, and then lands on each beat, then waits again and slips between them.

And now, Ramón opens his eyes.

He is ready.

❋

Here's how I died, since I'm sure you're just salivating to find out: fast footsteps on pavement, a frantic run, the pursuit not far now. Yells in the distance, closing. An impossible clutter of crossroads, alleyways, storefronts. Some unfamiliar neighborhood, and the gnawing sense that one of those streets surely leads to another that leads to another that will bring me to some part of this haunted city by the sea that I do know, somewhere familiar, safety. But no: Instead, the approaching boots get louder and the yells to stop feel like they're right in my ear and I know what's coming so instead of stopping I run harder and then and then and then: nothing.

I don't know if it was the fallen regime or the one that replaced it. Does it even matter? They all start to look alike from here.

I don't remember the bullets ripping through me. Or the sudden wreckage my face became beneath their clubs.

I need to know the whole truth of it though. Because somehow, it will make me whole.

❋

Cold weather kept the crowd slim tonight. The folks who are here bop in perfect time to Ramón's thumping beats, form circles around each other, and take turns contorting themselves and head spinning. Marcos showed up around two with his congas and now punctuates the hip-hop beats with a sultry guaguancó.

"Aliceana?" Marcos says as Ramón segues into a thickly synthesized trance section.

Ramón shrugs. "Same, I guess. Neither here nor there."

"What's it been, half a year now?"

"Nah. Just three . . . four months."

"Maybe you should consider some side slice."

Ramón shrugs again, not even convincing himself. "Hard lookin' for side slice when the slice you got ain't in the middle."

"Maybe you should look for some middle slice and make Aliceana the side."

"If it's the middle, it's not a slice. It's a half. Or something."

The layered drone rises and falls in waves of guttural, electronic sound. Strobe lights catch the dancers in millisecond freeze-frames of movement, now turning, catching each other's gazes, now reaching, eyes closed, mouths open, backs arched, skin glistening, designer clothes damp. Ramón and Marcos take in the scene without speaking for a few seconds and then Ramón asks Marcos if he's seen Alberto.

"Ugh, that comemierda? Fuck no. Why would he show his face around here?"

"Dunno."

"Ramón?" Marcos prods.

The drone becomes a pulse, bass so deep, the bones of the dancers must rattle in time, and they rally to it knowing that soon the beat will drop back in and cue a precise explosion of movement.

"Ramón, if you think Alberto would be here . . . Why would you think that?"

"I . . . it doesn't matter." Ramón doesn't drop the beat; he keeps building layer on layer of synth drone, and the room becomes thick with sound. The crowd writhes in expectation.

"¡Oigan muchachos!" It's Luis, an older gentleman who holds court at one of the far corners of the club most weekend nights, dishing out advice and favors and keeping folks generally in check. He's thickly built with a thickly built mustache, and something about those hard, bright eyes belies a kinder man than his harsh voice and thick hands—fighting hands—would have you believe.

"¿Qué bolá, asere?" Marcos says, exchanging a pound with Luis.

Ramón nods and looks back at his turntables.

"Ramón, Alberto is outside looking for you."

"Shit," Ramón mutters.

"Yo, what the fuck?" Marcos demands.

By way of an answer, Ramón finally lets the beat fall, a static-laced bass drum that pounds away as the snares clack back and forth their sudden, maniacal conversation. The explosion comes, the dancers burst to life, and Marcos rolls his eyes and launches in on the congas.

❋

"What do you want?" It's pelting icy chunks and it's just past four a.m. and the sky will be getting light soon. Ramón is trying not to fixate on Alberto's menthol.

"Just to say hi to an old friend. Is that so weird?"

I know this kid. Well, no. I know the angle of his jaw. His slim eyebrows and the trace of red in his light brown hair. I know the grin that is sinister and cautious all at once, the glint in his eyes that can charm or offend. The smell. I never knew the boy, but I know from whence he came—two generations back, actually: Enrique, who was always stopping by looking for Nilda.

Anyway, the boy is three rum and Cokes deep and it's got him even sloppier as he tries to look tough and see through all that alcohol and sleet.

"It's weird that you've emailed me four times and texted me twice in the past two days."

"Well, you didn't answer." Alberto rattles the ice in his paper cup and grins. "Try, try again and shit, no?"

"No."

"Ah c'mon, Ramón. We're basically brothers." He swings an ungainly arm out to pat Ramón's shoulder, but Ramón steps back. Alberto regains his balance and frowns.

"No," Ramón says. "My mom being your madrina doesn't make us brothers. Not even godbrothers. It just makes my mom your madrina."

"Damn, man," Alberto sulks, but I can tell they've been through this before, that this isn't the first time he's pulled the godmother card.

"You bring any of your gangster friends this time?" Ramón asks.

"No, man. Look, I forgive you for being an ass before. Okay? I'm cool with it. I swear. I really don't even give a fuck."

Ramón just looks at him.

"But look, my, uh, abuelo needs to talk to you."

"Oh?" Ramón says. He looks genuinely surprised. As he should.

Alberto glares down at the slush, puts one foot forward and then pulls it back. "Yeah, I mean . . . yeah."

"'Bout what?"

"I dunno, man. Just come up to the house tomorrow and we'll talk about it."

"No."

"What?"

"I said no. What makes you think I want anything to do with your abuelo, let alone that I'd go up and talk to him about nothing in particular just because he asked. No."

"You're an asshole, Ramón," Alberto seethes. "You know that?"

"Thanks for dropping by."

Ramón turns to go back into the club, trying not to look rattled.

"Fuck you and your whole fucking family," Alberto mutters. Then, quietly, as if as an afterthought: "Except your mom."

Cadiz, the six-foot-four bouncer, is glowering in the doorway. His frown says he's considering using Alberto's face to shovel snow, but he keeps still. Everybody knows who's who, and anyway, the picture is painted in the smell of sweat and frustration pounding through the air, the rage of Ramón's heart in his ears, the way Cadiz hesitates, his fists clenched tightly into themselves: No one's dumb enough to put a finger on a Gutierrez, least of all the beloved grandson, heir to the ugly empire. Ramón exchanges a nod with Cadiz, puts away all the violence threatening to burst out of him, and walks back inside.

# CHAPTER FIVE

It's so quiet.

Ramón and Marcos are still on the way home. Adina—the third and, let's be honest, best resident of apartment 3C—sits at the kitchen table, clacking self-righteous lawyerly things onto her laptop. She's having a moment, so all the other lights are out and she has headphones on, probably with some heartbroken diva bleating through them, but I try not to make assumptions. I'm in Ramón's room, quiet. Quiet because I'm gathering myself.

I must've carried the freezing rain inside with me—I'm chilled and permeated with something else . . . loneliness? I'll be honest with you: I'm more lost than I seem, only grasping at memories, barely making sense of the present, let alone the past.

Slowly, slowly, pouring all my concentration, all my breath, all my being into my hands, I lay them on his bedside table. Yes. It's shaky, but there is a solidity to me. I'm encouraged and lean into it a little too hard, slide forward and through the wood, its solid form prickling against my nothingness.

From the top.

I didn't get this far by giving up. I don't think.

(Then again, maybe it's exactly what got me here . . .)

I rally, chase off disappointment, allow the slathering, almost solid slices of rain against the window to lull me back to calmness. Release the chill I've been carrying. Re-center myself on my fingertips. The edge of who I am to the edge of the wood, and stop, our molecules meeting; sweet resistance means I'm good and I'll stay slow, stay focused.

All known and unknown factors considered, I'm still just moving toward the light. And the light seems very, very far away right now. I have no map, no plan, just the fierce knowledge that this is a piece of the puzzle, this is how we get to the next part: He has to see the me that once was, he has to know how close I am to him. I will show him. And I know that if I fail at any tiny piece here, if I misstep or lose patience, give up that holy swagger I've managed to click into, it won't just be a matter of the puzzle getting tougher to beat: There won't even be a me to beat it.

So I keep my breath focused forward, my energy charged to the very limits of myself, my fingertips wrap around the wooden handle. Pause. Breathe. Breathe. Pause. Prepare, and pull.

✳

Laughter and irreverence from the kitchen.

Adina, roused from her reverie by the return of the boys, puts on music, some pretty atrocious rock/salsa mix that Ramón only tolerates because he's tired of offending her.

I make my flowing, elegant way out of the bedroom and into the warmth of the kitchen to sit among them. I'm sure I once carried on like this, with friends, with Nilda and Isabel, surely, though the memories have been torn from me. I'm sure we reveled in the impossibilities of life and topics we weren't supposed to cover. Surely.

"I'm saying," Ramón retorts to some smirk from Marcos that I didn't bother listening to, "it's not like you're some magician of the pussy yourself, sir."

Adina struggles not to spit out her coffee. Ramón turns back to the dishes he was washing.

"I do alright," Marcos says. No one's convinced though. Adina hums to herself, which the boys correctly interpret to mean she's getting more pussy than both of them combined.

Marcos puts his elbows on the table and rests his chin on his fist, eyebrows raised. "Alright, then, bushmaster, what's the big secret?"

"First of all," Adina says, closing her laptop and grinning ear to ear. "Patience. Y'all penis packers are in such a damn hurry all the time."

Ramón finishes the dishes and swats the dampness from his hands.

"We are patient." He pulls up a chair. Gray spreads through the sky outside. The chorus of birds has started up. "We waited for you to finish your sentence to disagree with you."

"Fine. If you don't want to understand, don't ask."

"No, no, go 'head," Marcos says, waving his hands defensively. "We'll shut up." He punches Ramón's shoulder. "Shut it, man. Let her finish."

"Men"—Adina speaks very slowly; each word comes carefully picked—"tend to be in a fucking hurry." She looks back and forth at them, waiting for a challenge. "To get to the magic pussy."

"I mean," Marcos starts. Ramón returns the shoulder punch and he shuts up.

"Especially young men like yourselves. I shouldn't even have to say this, but if you want to know why I bag so many women, even confirmed signed sealed and delivered straight ones, even born-agains, for Christ's sake, it's because I know a thing or two about the P. In fact, I have one of my own. And there's very few things that pussies have in common, but one of them is this: If you don't know what the fuck you're doing with it, it doesn't like you. Any questions?"

Ramón and Marcos glance at each other and sip their coffees.

Adina rolls her eyes, laughs. "Actually, never mind. How was the crowd tonight?"

"Not great but not terrible," Ramón says. "But for a freezing nasty night, I ain't mad."

"And Alberto was there," Marcos adds. Ramón glares at him.

"Gutierrez? That piece of shit. Why?"

"Wanted to talk to this guy." Marcos thumb-points across the table. Adina glares at Ramón. "He doesn't want to talk about it."

"I don't. I already did, anyway. He said his granddad wants to talk to me."

Marcos raises his eyebrows. "You didn't say that before!"

"Enrique?" Adina asks.

"That's the only one I know of."

"Why?"

"He didn't say. I wasn't interested. I don't want to talk to that old bat."

"Probably he wants you to smuggle guns into Cuba or something," Marcos suggests.

"No," Ramón snaps. "Why would he want me of all people? I disrespected his stupid seed more blatantly than anyone has ever dared to that night and I still haven't paid for it." Collectively, the three sitting around the table let out a kind of resigned chuckle at the memory of some wild party that had gone awry, a lingering irritation finally expressed by Ramón in the form of a stinging rebuke; Alberto's shocked face. I don't know exactly what happened, don't care much, but they certainly all enjoyed it. "More likely he wants to intimidate me into apologizing or something, because stupid Alberto is too pathetic to ask for it himself."

"Or something worse," Adina says. It's almost a whisper and she really means it.

They both look at her. "Like what?" Ramón asks.

"He has virtually unlimited resources and the local police in his pocket. And he's wrathful like a scorned storm. And you fucked with his favorite grandkid, as you say. So no, I don't think he'll ask you to smuggle arms, since he can get any fulano to do that and already does, and I don't think he just wants to idly threaten you into apologizing, because that's pointless, really."

"So?"

"So surely he has some truly dirty work he needs done and since you already know that with a flick of his finger, your life is a fuckpuddle, he doesn't *have* to threaten you. Don't you get it? The threat is implicit in the fact that he wants to meet you. We all know who he is, what that means. So he can be as sweet an old man as he wants to be and you'll still know he means business."

"Clever bastard."

"The power of people knowing you have power means you don't have to use it."

"Until you really, really want to," Marcos says.

"Yeah, well." Ramón has nothing to say to that, he realizes after he's opened his mouth. He stands up, pours the dregs of his coffee down his throat, and rubs his eyes. "I'm going to bed. Thank you all for that inspiring pep talk about my future."

"Any motherfucking time," Adina says, flipping open her laptop.

✳

The coffee did nothing to Ramón. He's Cuban, after all, and was probably raised on the stuff, knowing Nilda. The day and a half of work drags him down, every hour another anchor that guides him toward the bed. Maybe he'll just pass out and that'll be that; message left unattended to till he wakes later today and then maybe not at all. He lumbers forward, shedding clothes as he goes, collapses like a slow-motion blimp crash onto the mattress. It's dawn and the light is growing inside the room, so he fumbles a long arm up, grasps the string on the third try, and pulls it just so and lets go. The shade snaps down and the room is dark enough.

I'm afraid he's about to pass out, rending all I've done pointless, when he rolls back over and makes a face at his nightstand, gathers himself up onto one elbow, leans over it.

Yes.

It is the family photo album. Yes. How strange, I'm sure. And open. He sits up a little more, looks around the room. Could it have been Adina? But that's almost as absurd as it *not* being her. No, none of it makes sense. And surely he didn't leave it there himself. Hasn't looked at the thing in a decade. He clicks on the reading light and runs his fingers along the pages. No, he's not dreaming.

The photo album is there, opened because *I* opened it.

There's Abuelo and Abuela, looking young and dignified, serious in that way people used to when they were getting their pictures taken. And there's Cuba, behind them. Las Colinas, specifically, that outskirts of La Habana, the corner of the house we grew up in and the palm tree that Isabel fell from and shattered her humerus when she was nine.

There's the sidewalk, cracked and filthy. There's Conchita the dog with the most Cubanest possible name, unreasonably tiny and looking somehow offended, always. There's Tío Angelo and Miguelito the neighbor nobody liked. And there's Isabel and Nilda, both smiling, and there, serious as ever and pouting in my quinceañera dress, am I.

# CHAPTER SIX

He's going home.

I knew this would happen. Willed it even. He woke up and shook his head. He wrote down the dream about Isabel from yesterday evening, glancing at the photo album. Then he dressed and shuffled out the door, headphones on. It'll be the moment that puts all my work to the test, seeing her.

There are wide swaths of nothing, blanks I don't think I can fill in by myself. But while the details are murky, I do know the rage. It still swells inside me after all these years, threatens to drown me when I get complacent.

We swish through the winter streets. I hardly notice.

A bus across town. Suburbs turn to slums. A brief spin through the towering financial zone. Blessedly brief, because I can barely fight off the killing rage and take in the sudden everything that is a city all at once. I'm like a walking warhead right now, and it takes every bit of my concentration not to let go of the trigger and take this city bus out with all the holy, hungry intensity trying to blow out of me. But other things want my attention, a million molecules, a million different crisscrossing lines of communication and chaos. I can see the old man on his way to the clinic get uncomfortable, shift in his seat at the teetering energy. A middle-aged Chinese lady scowls out the window, clutches her ten-year-old son close to her.

I find my center. Send wave after wave of emptiness against the rising tide. For a few seconds, I don't know what will happen. I teeter. And then the air eases. We're leaving the chaos of downtown, turning down a quiet street, with no pulsing electrical currents, no screaming advertisements, no towers. No towers that always watch. I gently let myself shatter, collect the pieces, and slide into a dark corner beneath Ramón's seat.

Where I remain.

I remain until the bus screeches to a halt on Andover and Thirty-Fourth Avenue, a few miles outside of downtown, a neither here-nor-there burb called the Grove that feels queasily familiar. I scowl at the somewhat cared-for lawns and decent two-story houses. Mediocrity and the American dream. A treacherous thing.

It all happens so fast: Ramón is up the front steps and ringing the doorbell and the door is opening and there's Nilda. She looks . . . old. It's been over thirty years, so, of course, but there's only hints of the girl she used to be. Of course, of course, but still. All those years of living, all that life, surely she's done her own work to stave off the clawing regret, and it shows all over her face. Gravity seems to be winning, like her skin wants to roll off and glide away and all she can do to stop it is apply more eyeliner, more rouge, more everything that's not her in the hopes of keeping each piece more or less in place.

"Ay, Ramón," she gasps as if he never ever comes over and she hadn't spent the last two hours preparing for his visit. She puts her hands all over his face, reaches up to kiss his cheeks, envelops him in her thick perfume cloud until he says, "Ya, Mami, okay, yo también te quiero, pero coño . . ." and she steps back shrugging and frowning like she's been accused of something terrible and ushers him inside.

And I'm left here on the steps with my rage boiling over. There is a thing we say sometimes, a way we are playful with words, because the difference between *why* and *because* is just an accent and a space. An accent and a space and that upturned ending that denotes a question. See: ¿Por qué? Porque. And when we're really on a roll explaining something, it becomes a pivot: *This and that and the other*, we say, getting more and more excited, the truth and importance of what we're getting at building, and then: *¿Por qué? Porque this and that and the other* and away we go.

But here I am with just the question. The Why lingers, sears through me; the Because is nowhere to be found. Still, reason or not, the rage remains.

But I won't kill her.

Don't even know if I could, but I know I won't try.

Somewhere inside me there's an oath not to. I swore it once—I must've. Or maybe it's some weird familial tie. But it is binding and I will abide. Still, the urge persists.

Of course everything is perfect inside the house: each knickknack placed just so, an entire room of couches and coffee tables not to be touched, only seen and appreciated. And then another room, slightly less just so but still, just so. And here Ramón finds a seat, grudgingly accepts the crackers and guava spread and less grudgingly a cafecito, and when Nilda finally, finally stops fluttering around and twittering on about things even she doesn't care about, Ramón pulls the photo album out of his satchel and opens it.

Good man, Ramón.

Nilda straightens her back. She looks so small in that big pink plush chair. Its vinyl cover amplifies every squirm with a squeal and a groan. Above her, Jesus Christ takes in the world from his miserable perch and a single dollop of blood hangs from his thorny crown, perpetually about to drop. "Ya tú sabes que no sabemos nada de esas cosas." She shrugs with panache, head shaking. "Pero nada."

Deny deny deny until you disappear. This is the strategy. And it's worked for so long, why stop now? We don't know nothing. Not a thing. But nothing. That emphatic gusto that is a Cuban's first language as much as Spanish is. You can see in her eyes she doesn't believe it. She always trembled, but it's more pronounced now. She won't lift that tiny coffee cup because it'll spill everywhere.

*Where has Isabel gone?* I remember asking once, after being stonewalled over and over by our parents. Little Nilda glared down at me firmly, as if by sheer will she could bend the world to be the one she wished it was, one where Isabel hadn't left and the country wasn't falling apart around us. Her shaking head became a shrug, and though she said she didn't know, swore it, what she really meant was *How dare you ask? Who are you to demand these answers of me? To make me lie to you?*

"Mami, mira, sé que . . ." Ramón gives up on his second language with a shake of his head. "I know you don't know what happened but . . . I just . . . I never asked you much about it because you never spoke much about it, and—"

"I never espoke about it because I don't know anything about it, m'ijo." She's deflecting so hard I'm afraid she might turn inside out. That lipsticked mouth droops all the way down at the edges, and she leans back, crosses her arms as if closing the matter.

Ramón, who hates it when she interrupts him, has to catch his own flash of anger before he can speak again. "Look, I know it's hard to talk . . . about Las Colinas and—"

"You have no idea, m'ijo."

"Mami, por favor," Ramón growls. "Let me finish."

Heavy frown, fluttering eyes. "I am sorry," she says, pronouncing it extra carefully, that *oh* hyperannunciated, and looking like she's the one who should be accepting an apology, thank you very much. I know that face. Any minute now, she'll hurl all that trembling denial outward in the form of wrath and this conversation will be over before Ramón can even catch his breath.

"No, I don't have any idea what it was like or how hard it is to talk about it. I don't. But that's just the point. I want to know, Mami. I . . . it feels like something's missing inside of me. A whole part of who we are. And then I was looking through the album and I saw the picture and I just thought. I . . . don't know. I mean, they're, they were family. No?"

The dreams. Inwardly he flails for words to explain what he's seen but none of them work.

"Of course, Ramón querido. But we can't live in the past. They're gone. Dead. So why go crazy? I'm sure it killed your abuelos, the grief. First Isabel and then Marisol. And I won't live my life a victim of someone else's disappearance. Do you understand? This all happened so so many years ago, Ramón, why are you trying to dig up things now?"

They keep speaking but everything stopped for me at the mention of my name.

Marisol. The sun and the sea.

I have a name. It fortifies me. Luz Marisol Caridad Aragones. A name is also a prayer, the most personal prayer there is. Without even meaning to, I solidify ever so slightly. I'm sure if Nilda were looking at the empty space beside her son instead of rubbing her eyes, she'd see a flicker of flesh. Surely she'd chalk it up to her nerves and go back to trembling and carrying on. Surely.

But none of that matters.

Marisol.

The one-word poem my parents chose for me, and not something plain like Nilda. And then I'm full of sorrow that they're gone. They're gone, and somehow I'm sure I never said goodbye.

I have to get myself together. My emotions have been bettering me all day. I center again and tune back into the conversation. Nilda wants to end it, so she's drifting deeper into melodrama, threatening Ramón with the passive-aggressive wrath of her tears. "Ramón, I just, I don't understand . . ." Voice trembling, eyes wet. And in case he missed her shaking hands, she goes ahead and lifts her tiny cup, sends cascades of sweet black coffee down her fingers onto the plate. "Ay coño," she snaps. "You see?" There it is. She half stands, but Ramón's up first, sitting her back down, long-stepping to the kitchen for some paper towels.

The matter is dropped. And he has to get to work anyway. Ramón retreats, and I with him, both of us confused but not defeated.

# CHAPTER SEVEN

It's early afternoon, still gray gray gray from the pavement to the sky and occasional bursts of rain. I'm exhausted and when Ramón goes to work, I take refuge in his room. First I do nothing. I do it carefully though, specifically. Nothingness: such a blessing. Doing nothing is a prayer too, when you do it right, and I make sure each of my impossible, semi-existent cells finds rejuvenation in my stillness. It's hard, keeping still. Also, I'm Cuban, so even harder. But I have practice, and I settle in after not too long, quiet the torrential arguments blasting through what's left of my mind (or is my mind what's left of me?) and the goodness soon takes me over.

Adina's home early from work. Her phone call gradually takes shape through my meditation. She's pacing and it's a very sad one, the conversation. "No," she says, again and again, but it's gentle, not defiant, a tired chorus of defeat. "No. It wasn't . . . no. Not like that, certainly. No. Babe, please, listen . . . no." I slip in and out of consciousness and the nos weave through my thoughts, sad, loving, and lost.

Surfacing again, I understand. Adina is a lover. More than a lover: She's a romantic. A desperate one at that. She's *in* love, actively. You can feel it through the wall, all that love. And it's long-distance and over-complicated; harder than either thought it would be.

"Baby, baby, sweetheart, please." Cooing now, sinking to the floor, fighting tears. I slip under the crack of the door and find the girl curled around herself, looking somewhat ridiculous because she's still in her fancy lawyer slacks and blazer and frowning from the inside out. I can't help myself; I wrap around her.

"Baby, look, listen, just . . ." Words with no meaning. The girl on the other end is crying too. Now that I have a name I am stronger, I can give more of myself and not risk fading away forever.

40

If Adina registers my presence, she doesn't show it. Her brain might be too lawyered up to notice. It doesn't matter though. Maybe it's more for me than her anyway. The phone call ends and the phone drops to the floor and Adina lets out a wail so earnest, so raw and rending that I feel it too, I feel it deep in me and I wrap tighter around her and together we breathe and breathe and breathe.

✳

At some point during those passing moments, I begin to fade again. That gradual, growing lack, that emptiness, it gnaws at me.

And part of me wants to just let it; part of me is dizzy with terror.

It's so slow and subtle I don't notice it unless I make the conscious effort to take stock of myself, a little less, a little less. But then it seems to slow and then suddenly there is more again, and more, and then I am whole, with no reason or explanation except the shifting winds of this impossible world.

"How was work?" Adina asks when Ramón walks in the door.

If Ramón were paying attention, he'd notice her red eyes and ruffled clothes. He'd realize that even the mild strayaway from her usual immaculate self speaks to an hour plus of crying in a little ball on the floor. Instead he dejackets and plops down at the kitchen table with a sigh and says, "Terrible. Aliceana wants to *talk*." Little bunny ears indicate the true terribleness of the word: It means *talk* in that most profane, overexplaining misunderstandings way.

"Oh?" Adina starts to sit, reconsiders, then goes to the cabinet and gets the bottle of Havana Club her best friend Miguel brought her back after his trip. "Tell me."

"Man, I dunno." Ramón reaches his long arm to the dish rack behind him and retrieves two glasses. "Things are just okay, you know? Like, they been okay since we met. Fantastic sex, basically from go and, like, we have a really good time together even when we're not having sex, like playing Halo and talking about work and it's kinda like we're really good friends and also have really great sex?"

Adina pours. "So? Or rather, but?"

"Well, I was thinking about it today and yesterday, because, you know, she won't fuck me in the hospital . . ."

"Wait, what?" Adina allows a real smile to surface. It's such a sharp contrast to her seriousness that Ramón just looks at her for a second, maybe finally realizing she has her own shit to deal with. "What?"

"You alright, Adi?"

"I'm fine." Blatant lie. I'm sure Ramón can tell, but he's not sure how to push her without being pushy, so he just nods. "Why you mad you can't get any hospital ass?" She passes him his glass.

"I mean, no, it's not that I think she owes me hospital ass, it's just . . ."

"You had your hopes up."

"Right. Not unreasonable, I think." He shrugs and throws his hands up.

"Isn't it?" she scoffs. "You of all people have seen the nastiness that goes on in that place. Why would you want your uglies bumping amidst all that mess?"

Ramón gives a noncommittal shrug.

"And anyway, it's unprofessional. Maybe she wants to keep her job. And anyway anyway, so what? And anyway anyway anyway, have you asked why?"

"'Aliceana, why won't you put out in the on-call room like all the doctors do on TV?' No, I haven't asked."

"Well . . ."

"Because maybe I kinda sorta don't wanna know."

"Why not?"

"Because I might not like the answer?"

"That a question?"

Ramón sighs and swishes his rum around. "I guess?"

"Here," Adina says, raising her glass. "Al carajo."

Ramón brightens and clinks with her. "Al carajo."

They drink and Adina pours another round. "Thing is," Ramón

says, "I think . . . I think, and don't tell anyone this, please, but I think I really like her."

"Uh-oh."

"Like, *like* like."

"But . . . why? I mean, I like her too. She might be my favorite of your little friends."

Ramón scowls at her and raises his glass. "To all of our little friends."

"Except Kat. I hated that little hussy."

"Damn, Adina."

"I never told you she hit on me?"

"No!"

"Oh. Well, yeah." She goes to clink, but Ramón pulls his glass back.

"Did you . . . ?"

"No! Ramón! Coño . . ."

"Well, I mean . . . You're you, after all."

"Right, I'm me. Loyal before lover, hard as that might be to believe, jackass. No, I did not sleep with stupid Kat." They clink and gulp back the rum.

Despite being huge and a semi-regular drinker, Ramón has no tolerance and he's getting sauced already. "Thing is, I couldn't tell you why if you asked. It's not one moment or another that makes her . . . likable, to me, I just . . . it's something about the way she looks at me, I think. She sees me. I'm babbling."

"No, it makes sense," Adina says, clearly trying not to let it resonate as much as it is. She pours some more and they sip as they speak.

"I just, even though we rarely speak on deep stuff, she appreciates me in a quiet way. Took me a while to understand, ya know? But I was just starting to see it in the small shit she'd do; wait up for me when I was out late just to say good night and then fall asleep right when I crawled into bed, which used to annoy me until I realized it was her way of having that little second with me and that it actually meant a lot."

"I see."

"Or the way she catches my glances in the hospital. Like, no, we don't fuck in the on-call room, but every once in a while I'll catch her looking at me, and you know, it's like, better'n fucking in its own kinda way. Know what I mean?"

Adina nods, looks away.

"Anyway, I don't think it's over over; she probably just wants, I dunno, something or other. But I haven't done anything to fuck this up, and we've been pretty alright, so I don't see . . . Bah, I'm not making any sense."

"Only barely," Adina says. "But I'm just saying, if you really truly—"

*Sweat!* Ramón's phone screams, followed by a frantic hip-hop beat. *Sweat!* He picks it up before the horn section kicks in. Adina looks relieved.

"Oh, cool," Ramón says, but it sounds like whatever he just heard is definitively the opposite of cool. He puts down the phone. "Aliceana's downstairs. I didn't realize she meant this soon when she said she wanted to talk."

"Oh." Adina frowns. "Cool."

"I might be drunk."

"Go get 'em, cowboy."

✳

Aliceana looks somehow beautiful in the hideous lighting of Ramón's entryway. Or maybe that's Ramón thinking, not me. She's wearing a big navy-blue winter jacket. The fur lining the hood makes a fuzzy halo around her pretty, dead-serious face and the neon hallway shine gives those cheeks swirled highlights. She's also wearing the pilot hat with those silly earflaps that Ramón lent her at work earlier because she forgot hers. It's either sweet or manipulative, depending on how things play out, but either way, her little face peering out of all that winterwear is hard not to find adorable. Even for me.

That—that thing that began rising within him back at the hospital yesterday: It hasn't gone anywhere. It's gotten bigger than he knows what to do with, but I know it's there.

44

They say each other's names at the same time. Ramón laughs while he cringes and Aliceana seems to retreat a few inches into her jacket. She's about to speak but Ramón cuts her off. "Look." He snaps both his hands out in front of him, palms facing each other like whatever he wants her to look at is all explained within the empty space between them. She looks.

"I mean, listen: I was just talking about you to Adi. Upstairs. And . . ."

"Ramón."

"Thing is, I really, really like you. I know I haven't said it before, and I'm not really exactly sure why. You just come over after my shows and we have this great sex and play video games and then we catch each other's eyes at work but there's a whole other something going on between us that neither of us know how to explain." He pauses to let his mind catch up with everything he just said.

"Me, I mean. About the not having the guts. If that was the case, it was me I was referring to. Not you. I don't know what the thing with you was, maybe you were just waiting for me to go ahead and take things somewhere else, beyond all that just being, just existing but not growing or moving or anything, just being. Which is cool and all, in a Zen kind of way, I guess, but also maybe it's just that we could do so much more. We could—"

"Ramón." Finally, she puts enough authority in her voice to shut him up.

"Yes?"

"I came here to . . ." She pauses and her bottom lip trembles and I know what she's about to say, even if my inebriated nephew doesn't. ". . . to break up."

"Oh."

"I mean . . . I . . . Not that we were a couple exactly anyway, but . . ."

"No. I . . . understand. I think. I'll just be . . . leaving now."

"Ramón?"

It's too late though: He's already out the door and down the block, not running exactly but moving fast, carried along by the waves of

Havana Club and too many emotions to keep track of. He's oblivious to the passing traffic and blinking lights around him, doesn't hear her call after him, doesn't care about the fact that he's only in his T-shirt and work pants and fails entirely to pay any mind to the crisp January air prickling against his bare skin.

He also doesn't notice the two men walk up behind him, one with a retractable nightstick. It even takes an added second or two to register when the nightstick cracks against the back of his head. He sees an explosion of whiteness and stumbles a step forward before regaining his footing. Turns around, rubbing his scalp.

"What just happened?" he asks one of the guys who seem to have appeared out of nowhere.

I'm in a frenzy, trying and knowing I'll fail to rally myself to do something useful. I'm just barely there, but there must be some way . . . I send my everything outward toward my fingertips, just like I did with the photo album, but it all takes time, time I don't have. Turns out, I didn't need to though, because my nephew is gigantic and unstoppable all by himself. Also, wasted, which surely helps at this moment. Having absorbed the hit, he just stands there. The men glance back and forth at each other trying to figure out why Ramón hasn't collapsed and readying their next move.

"Did something fall on me?" Ramón looks up, then back at the men. I think it's dawning on him now; he takes a step back, wavers slightly. "Oh. Oh shit."

I have a name, dammit! Marisol. Luz Marisol Caridad . . . Luz Marisol . . . Coño. The men close in on Ramón and he's about to turn around again, which is surely not the right move, when a voice calls out. "I said be easy, goddammit! He's practically my brother!" Alberto hops out of a double-parked car and runs toward them. "The fuck is wrong with you two?"

The men exchange uneasy glances. "Well, he didn't drop," complains one of Alberto's guys.

"I don't give a fuck. We can't drag him up there all black and blue

46

because you dickheads couldn't control yourselves. We're not even sup-posed to have laid a hand on him at all, and you wanna biff him up for real."

"Um . . ." Ramón ventures. "Can I go now?"

"No, goddammit!" Alberto growls. "Get in the fucking car."

A tense moment passes. Ramón may or may not be weighing his options. Finally he puts up both hands and shrugs. "Don't have much choice, do I?"

"A well-thought-out decision," Alberto sneers. He nods at his guys and they all pile into the car and drive off as I labor to catch up to myself, to everything that's just happened, to whatever is yet to come.

# CHAPTER EIGHT

Mami and Papi.

They sit on the pink couch and hold each other like they come in a set: jimaguas, the twins. So stern you'd think they're ancient trees, their feet becoming roots that claw into the ground as the world changes faster and faster around them. It's been so heavy around here since Isabel "disappeared." I mean, everyone knows she joined the rebeldes. Always impossible to shut her up, it's all she talked about right up until she didn't and then her silence was all we needed to know that something had changed. Even self-absorbed Nilda noticed—now her songs all seem slightly off; the minor key tiptoes a jangly danzón through the empty rooms, its helter-skelter sweeps and swerves sending us all into a quiet stupor.

I guess I first knew it when she took that smuggled gun out of the chicken carcass. It started as a slow trickle of strange events only I knew about. More bullets. Messages. An army uniform. All passed through our doors and then vanished away to somewhere else, the mountains surely.

But I never thought she'd leave for real. And if she did, I was sure she'd take me with her. This thing, this revolution, was ours. She had brought me into the fold when she sent me to Gómez's.

But then one day she was gone. And everybody knew where.

Las Colinas sits on the edge of the city, nestled into the beginning of the wilds, el campo, where the little people plot their mischief, where Jorge Sincabeza gets his revenge on unfaithful wives and where the sounds of beautiful, mournful singing accompanies the tambores late into the night. Also, the rebeldes.

When I look out my bedroom window, past the beat-up old shack and puddles across the street and out toward the mountains, I imagine

Isabel out there, dancing to those tambores with the little men and Jorge Sincabeza and whatever other forest ghouls haunt el campo. And of course, Gómez, the butcher, who disappeared at the same time along with Irma Caridad, the lady who runs the library; Manolo Sanpedro, who lives three doors down; and a teacher at my school, Carlito Delgado. All gone, all rebeldes. Heroes, traitors. Whatever.

And the truth is: I'm jealous. I'm sure she's going through all kinds of impossibilities I can't even conceive of out there, but she's part of something huge, the whole world changing, a rupture in history, and I want in.

At least I did when I was imagining it. But now, now Batista's men are raining their fists down on our front door and it doesn't seem so grandiose or romantic; it's just terrifying. Nilda's fingers freeze on the piano. Old Cassandra is bawling in the corner and Mami and Papi are both looking like their heads might pop. Papi's fists are clenched. I can see him go in and out of panic, trying, trying not to let it rule him. He's a giant and carries fire inside, a walking volcano, and he knows, I know, we all know, if he loses it now it'll be the end: the end of everything.

Mami touches his fist and I notice for the first time the veins in her hand are starting to show in that way only old people's do, like Cassandra. And I think on top of everything else, how sad that this is the first day of being old for Mami.

*Abre la puerta*, Papi says, but no one knows who he's saying it to because his eyes are closed, he's concentrating so hard on keeping the volcano fire inside.

*¡Cassandra!* Papi bellows, when it's clear no one's about to take up the order just for the sake of it. *¡Abre la puerta, coño!*

Cassandra whimpers and makes her slow, arthritic crawl toward the foyer. We hear the door creak open and the soldiers' demands and then their boots in the hallway and then there they are. There's three of them and they're just boys, eighteen at the most and skinny. It would take another two to match Papi's weight. If he lets loose it'd be over for them, but then soon after it'd be over for us, for Papi especially, so I know he'll hold back. He loves Jesus Christ, who watches wearily from his cross on the wall, and he loves his family and he loves Cuba and Las Colinas and because of all these things he loves he won't lose it, I know he won't.

*Buenas tardes, caballeros*, my father begins. *¿Cómo podemos ayudar?*

As if we all didn't know what they wanted. As if anything was ever a secret. The guy in the middle just has a wisp of a mustache and he sweats, looks slightly off to the side when he demands to know where my sister Isabel is.

Papi tells them he'd like to know himself and he in fact filed a missing report with the policía municipal just yesterday. Then Wispy says some words that I'm not even allowed to think without getting slapped and I see Mami wrap her newly old hand tighter around Papi's big meat slab of a hand. I think of Gómez the butcher and the hanging carcasses in his shop and what will happen to all that meat now that he's run off to join the rebeldes, who will make sure it doesn't just rot in the hot Havana sun?

I feel suddenly queasy and I think I might throw up, and how horrible that would be on a day that the Guardia Civil came pounding on our door and Mami became old and Papi had to not be a volcano.

I'm trying to breathe slowly the way Cassandra told me to do when I don't want to throw up, when suddenly Papi stands. He's even taller than usual, and he makes the Guardia Civil guys look like toy soldiers, like he could sweep his arm across the room and knock them all over. And for a second I think maybe he will and I forget I have to throw up, because we're all just standing there, even the soldiers, staring empty-eyed at the giant monster that is my daddy.

He doesn't bellow though. He says *Váyanse de mi casa* in the quietest, most horrible voice I've ever heard; the voice God uses when He's speaking the magic words that turn whole cities to dust. I don't care how many guns or tanks I had, I would leave if Papi told me to like that. I think Jesus Christ would too, right at that moment.

The soldiers walk backward out the door, clutching the pistolas on their belts and frowning. And we've won the hour but we've lost,

50

we've lost, we've lost the war, because that was the moment everything changed, and none of us need a crystal ball to know it.

✳

Overwhelmed by fear, alcohol, and emotion, Ramón has managed to fall asleep in the back of Alberto's SUV on the way to the old man's house. He wakes up drooling and haunted by another dream I've sent him from my childhood. Not the best moment to reach him, I suppose, but I don't have time to have good timing. Not the way things are going.

I don't have time and now I am weakened again from expelling another shard of who I was into Ramón. These expensive gifts. I don't know how many I have left. What's worse: The past is mostly a phantom haze with occasional bursts of clarity slitting through like lightning against a dark sky.

Each moment unlocks itself as it arrives. Sometimes I can choose, and sometimes the memory just shows up, unbidden, and all I can do is bear witness as it ekes forth, through me and into him.

As they roll deeper and deeper into the elite Cuban Jersey suburbs, the houses become more grandiose and obnoxious. Do my countrymen realize that no amount of gaudiness can heal a broken heart? Surely by now they do, but it's much too late for all that. Luxury is a drug as foul and taxing as heroin, and it sucks you into its very heart and spits you back out emptied of all your insides, all you hold sacred. And then you either climb back up into the ranks of the living or suffer in silence till you fade away, long-lost loved ones looking on blankly from the foot of your fancy deathbed.

Well. Maybe it's not all that bad. I wouldn't know. Just how I imagine it all. Anyway, the mansions come complete with spiraling cupolas and high walls with guard posts, something out of the embassy-lined avenidas of Miramar.

"He awake?" Alberto asks from the passenger seat.

Alfonse, the well-dressed thug sitting in the back, peers over at my nephew. Ramón is staring glumly out the window. Alfonse nods at Alberto and Alberto turns back around, shaking his head.

The SUV brings us up a hill, down a tree-lined driveway, and through an impressive perimeter fence. I'm still trembling from the flash of that memory-dream, and it takes some effort to wrench myself back into the present.

Ramón is trembling too, trapped in the uncertainty of the moment, the frustration of confinement. He gets out of the SUV without a fuss, exchanges some glares with Alberto's men, and then follows them inside the mansion. It's obscenely decadent, from the chandeliers to the marble pillars. Blood money, all of it. Birthed from and bound for blood. We parade through an elegant front hall, past a stairwell, through the kitchen—slightly less over-the-top now that it's officially out of guest view—and down a darkened corridor. Alberto taps three times on a door, says "¿Abuelo?" and then opens it.

Enrique Raul Gutierrez is ill. He wears a perfectly pressed light blue guayabera and creased maroon slacks. His hair is coifed just so, his gray mustache trimmed with precision. But there's something wrong with him, I tell you. The lean he has isn't just from his age. His belly sticks out like any self-respecting Cuban man over thirty-five, but there's a gauntness to his face; his eyes are sunken in and glassy behind the shaded lenses. What little hair he has left is quickly on the out and out.

Briefly, I merge with him, feel that fragile warmth of his core surround me—his pulse doesn't call me like Ramón's does, and it's an uncomfortable place for me, like I'm not supposed to be here. It is a grim, collapsing world inside Enrique. Vital organs droop, gray and rancid, like abandoned cobwebs from the corners of his carapace. His life force flickers, faltering toward oblivion with each rattly breath. His heart keeps shivering with useless fibrillations between every couple of beats.

It was probably a mistake, getting this close to him. I'm startled to find myself feeling sorry for the man. He has, after all, just kidnapped my nephew, to top off a list of general ugliness and federal crimes. But, he is dying. And once, a very long time ago, he was my friend. He doted on Nilda, but then, when we were thrown together by war, it was me he held tightly while I came, and then cried to when it was his turn; he fell asleep while I lay beside him and listened to the forest breathe, and he woke up groggy and demanding but still with a certain sweetness.

How Nilda ended up being the godmother to his only grandson, well, I'd rather not know, honestly. But I can only imagine it involved an amorous advance gone sour and a guilt trip.

"Ramón." The old man plants a hand on either arm of his chair and stands with some effort. Around him, framed pictures adorn the wood-paneled wall: laughing soldiers with their arms around each other in the forest; Donald Trump and George Bush, all dignity and rehearsed smiles beneath their scribbled signatures; Henry Kissinger, not smiling; a family photo from the mid-eighties, terrible hair and gigantic glasses. Awards from various social clubs and affinity societies. A framed picture of the two towers, a faded American flag behind them and the words *Never Forget* in horrific, illuminated script across the sky. Enrique makes a grand gesture of hugging Ramón and kissing his cheek, sits again with a loud groan and a sigh, and orders coffee to be brought.

Ramón, struggling to walk the line between unimpressed and polite, makes a half-smile and rubs the sizable lump on the back of his head. "Don Enrique, you have an elaborate way of inviting someone up to your beautiful house."

"Did those little motherfuckers hurt you?" Enrique opens his mouth with shock, and I'll say this about the old warrior: He's a terrible liar. "Alberto!"

Alberto emerges from some dark corner he'd been lurking in and they exchange a quick tiroteo in rapid-fire Spanish. Alberto withdraws, looking surly, and Enrique turns back to Ramón. "You have my most sincere apologies, Ramón. I promise you that I will keep my grandson on a shorter leash when it comes to his dealings with you."

"Thank you," Ramón mumbles. "May I ask what is so important that you've demanded I come up here?"

Enrique lets out a rhonchal laugh and I flood with memories. It's more cluttered with decades of shit building up in his lungs, but the man's laugh is still what it once was: fierce, unrestrained, genuine. He couldn't lie worth a damn, but Enrique was nothing if not a charmer.

Ramón doesn't really see what's funny and he says so. Adina's words of warning are still hot on his forehead.

Enrique gets solemn, weary of overplaying his jaunty old man routine. "You know I care deeply for your family, right, Ramón?"

Hmph. Indeed.

"Uh," Ramón says. "I guess?"

"How's your mom, by the way?"

"She's fine."

"She is . . . has she been . . . ?" *Leaving the house.* The words sit between them, unsaid but loud anyway.

Ramón shrugs a *no*.

"I've always carried an especial place in my heart for Nilda. She is a beautiful woman, your mother." We know, Enrique, we know.

"Uh . . ."

"And I've always told my comemierda of a grandson that if he ever disrespects his godmother, I will strangle him myself." He holds up two trembling hands. "With my own hands, ahahaha!" More coughing.

"That's really sweet, thanks."

"Well, anyway, stories for another time. I'll get to the point. I'm old now, but I have one more term in me, you know. There's still so much work to be done before we see a free Cuba and I know I may not see it in my lifetime, but I do want to do everything in my power to make it happen. I want to die knowing I have given it my all, Ramón. And the best way I know to do that is to keep doing what I do now."

*Running guns and passing outrageous laws in the state senate that mean nothing?* Ramón is clearly thinking but doesn't say.

"Used to be," Enrique continues after a small coughing fit, "no corner of this county didn't know my name. Used to be my influence reached into every bakery, club, and corner store within a hundred miles. But this is a new era, I know it as well as any. And my beloved Consuela isn't with me anymore." He nods at a picture of an enormous woman with purple hair and an unfortunate smile. "What I'm saying is, I need your help."

Ramón makes a noise; something between a laugh and cough. "I have no idea what I could possibly do to help you, Don Enrique."

"Of course not," the old man laughs. "How could you? That's why I invited you here: to tell you! I have no pull with this new generation of Cubans, Ramón. First of all, we've got a whole influx of recién llegados, an unknown quantity, of course, so there's that, and then we've got dominicanos, colombianos, ecuatorianos. All of them, coming in droves. And of course, they've heard of me . . ."

"Of course."

"But it's not the same. But you, Ramón, you have something I don't have."

"Oh?"

"Access. You have access to the youth, Ramón. I had my people do a Google on you."

I don't know what this means, but from Ramón's blank stare, I can tell Enrique barely does either. "How'd that work out?"

"You have quite a following, it seems, Ramón."

Ramón is getting a sense of where this is going and he doesn't like it. He shifts his weight in the vinyl chair, remembers he has a coffee waiting, and sips at it, frowning. "I got some people."

"You are . . . alarmed maybe? That I was checking up on you so extensively?"

Ramón shrugs off the question. "What is it you want, exactly?"

"A series of campaign events, parties really. You throw them, you set them up, use your mailing list, your Friendlier—"

"Friendster."

"The Myspace, all these things. We do it at the club, but I come to you, Ramón, because your friend Luis and I . . . we have some bad blood, you know?"

"I don't, actually."

"Back in the ugly years. He was a mischief maker. We had him watched. He rabble-roused. It's all here in my files, if you want to see." The old warrior nods toward a cabinet beside his desk. "If you wonder what your friend was up to in the bad old days, all you have to do is ask."

Ramón declines with a wave of his hand and a frown.

"But I didn't bring you here to resuscitate old beef. No. I heard about what you did last year at the Mirabella Festival. I know you can bring the masses, get them excited. Because they haven't heard anything like you before, have they? You espeak to them. I know."

"I don't know if I'd say all that really. I play music, people like my music, they come to see me perform." A tiny image of Aliceana flickers around Ramón's head and the memory of their conversation echoes through him. *It's over*, he realizes again, and then she's gone. I wonder, though. Within him, I wonder. He shakes his head. "That's it. I'm not moving masses at my command."

"Ah." Enrique flicks his hand in the air. "Nonsense, Ramón, estop. Look . . ." He throws a weak, fat-addled arm toward some black-and-white photos in an upper corner of his wall. "Political prisoners, Ramón, all of them. Men and women that suffered for the cause of freedom." And I know why we're here. Not in the small way. In the small way it's obviously to fulfill this small man's big dreams. But in the larger, *the Lord sent me* type way, now I know how this all fits. "I know it's a hard thing to understand," Enrique goes on, laying it just thick enough to not sound canned but still get his point home. "This life we have now, these beautiful things we have. It's hard, in the United States, to understand what it means to really struggle for something we believe in. Here, we have everything."

*The fuck you mean* we? is written all across Ramón's face, but he keeps it contained.

"There, he took it all away. He crushed our spirits, killed our families. He tortured us, Ramón. Raped our sisters and daughters, slaughtered our fathers and brothers, left us broken, enslaved, castrated." He's working himself up into a righteous, possibly rehearsed frenzy. He even rolled the *r* in *castrated*.

My picture's not on the wall, thank God, but I can see the seed of the question germinate in Ramón's mind. If only Enrique would calm down enough for him to ask. "And still, young people—*your* generation!—they go to Cuba on these vacations and school trips and to find their families, as if their families weren't traitors and every dollar they spend doesn't go toward propping up a murderous regime! Una locura."

Ramón doesn't mention it—wisely—but even as the old warrior rails on, a vista of old stucco buildings and the thundering sea opens up within my nephew, this child of exiles. He has no reference points except old pictures, family horror stories, and whatever lies the history books tell. The smell of the air, the way that Caribbean sun embraces your skin, seeps into each cell, the terror of soldiers coming down a block to uncover all your long-hidden secrets—none of that is available to him.

He wonders, not for the first time, what the music sounds like as it wafts along through curtains that rumba gently in the afternoon breeze, what it would feel like to fall in love with the reality of a place you've never been but always dreamed of.

"And then Elián," Enrique snarls, oblivious, unable to read the room. "That was the final insult, no?"

"That was like four years ago," Ramón says, but clearly there's no stopping this train.

"They took that poor child away from us! To become who knows what in that pit of hell that man has created. And after that, now . . . what we need is a victory! A cultural victory, yes? That will be in the papers, that the world will see."

"I don't know, Enrique."

"Look," the old man says, suddenly comely, defeated even. He fumbles on the counter for a pill bottle and slides two into his mouth, swallows them with a gulp of warm water, and then sips his café. "I get excited, you know. What I am asking is simple, Ramón. This younger generation of Cubans, your generation, doesn't know what we fought for, what many of us died for. They are concessionists. Easily accommodated by their cellular devices and social medias. They don't understand yet that to even bend a little bit, to even deal with any of those traitors who remained behind, is an act of tyranny. That we cannot give up now that we've come so far. But I need to espeak directly to them. I need to *make* them understand."

Ramón, mostly distracted by his dreams of Cuba, raises his eyebrows. "Well, it seems like you've really got a handle on that already."

Enrique chortles. "You see? Sarcasm! That's what I am talking about. You understand."

Ramón scowls.

"You understand what I don't understand. You speak this language, the language of these children. I need you to bring the message to them."

"What message?"

"That we will never give in to these rat commie hijos de putas comemierdas que nos arrancó toda la libertad de nuestra querida isl—"

"¿Mi amor?" A woman's voice calls from another room. "Tranquilo, mi amor. Tranquilo."

Enrique cringes. "I get, you know, excited sometimes. Emotional. I want the children to know what we fought and died for. That after the first revolution went to hell because of that man, there was another revolution, a forgotten one, and it continues to this day."

Revolution. A word so deeply perverted by men like Enrique it's become meaningless. I know he once fought passionately for something he believed in, but now he's just become a withered clown, funneling money to fund useless terror stunts by a dwindling group of paramilitary exiles, begging for more CIA cash and still trying to punish the Democrats for Kennedy pulling air support during Bay of Pigs.

"Did you know my tía?" Ramón says suddenly.

And there it is: Enrique's face curls into itself like he's about to cry. Instead he relaxes it, takes a breath. "Isabel? Ah, a brave, sad soul. Qué pena . . ." An artful dodge, but I doubt worth the trouble.

"No, I mean Marisol."

"I knew her, of course," Enrique admits with a shrug. "You know I've always loved your family, Ramón. Especially—"

"She disappeared? Marisol?"

"Another of his victims, Ramón. That is two of your family that he has their blood on his hands. This is why—"

"But I mean, how?"

"Ay, chico, you know an old man doesn't remember every tragedy that has befallen our people." Bullshit. He knows. He remembers. He won't meet my nephew's eyes. A beat or two of unpleasant silence passes as Enrique tries to let the unanswered question evaporate. I want to scream into the silence, but I don't know that my rage won't somehow disturb the flow of air, cause a distraction that Enrique would then use to change the subject. I hold it in, that scream, and it churns. "You will do this thing I have asked, Ramón? For the political prisoners of Cuba, those who have died and been forgotten, for your family . . ."

I feel myself deflate some. He doesn't need a distraction to change the subject. And how much can Ramón be expected to pursue him on this? The old man levels a long, hard stare at my nephew.

"I . . . I don't know," Ramón says. "I'll think about it."

"Don't think too long." More groaning and sighing as Enrique lifts his tired, plump body up from the chair. "I need your help. They need your help."

# CHAPTER NINE

The dark New Jersey streets slide past. I see Ramón is as muddle-headed as I am, frowning out the window, wrapped in a carousel of thoughts, worries and fantasies that I wish I could strip away from him forever. But that is not our path. He'll have to learn on his own how to quiet that raging mind.

I stay lost in my own imaginings all through the gasps of relief and asphyxiating hugs from Adina and Marcos. When they've talked it all out and moved on to other topics and slurped down several bowls of reheated rice and beans and more than a few Coronas, Ramón hugs them both and comes in the room. He keeps all the lights off, flips open his laptop, and scrolls mindlessly through some emails.

*¡¡¡¡Asere!!!! begins one, and I see Ramón smile like he's just bumped into an old friend. I'm sending a track for you to make into another absurdly fucking amazing work of art to post on your Myspace. Seriously. The people here are getting pirated CDs of your shit como nada. But are we getting paid? Ni un centavo chavo como dicen los pavos. But all my guys on the black-market routes keep selling more and asking me what else you got.*

*This one track I'm sending is old as the sun: a singer named María Teresa Vera, the godmother of Cuban music, my friend. "Veinte años." Do what you feel with it: I'm positive it will be magic. My guy Catabalas digitized it just for you.*

*Also attached is a rap by one of my other hermanos—we put it on a click track that should line up with whatever you decide to do.*

*The crew sends love and listen: When the fuck are you bringing your ass down here? Everything is in place for a grand production. Say the word and I roll it out.*

*Un abrazo bien fuerte, 'mano.*

*KACIQUE*

I already know what this track is, and what's going to happen—is already happening—as he prepares to play it. My dress shoes clacking on the linoleum kitchen tiles, my little hands in Isabel's, both of us looking kind of irritated because Nilda is telling us what to do. But in a tiny, secret chamber of my heart, I'm thrilled because this means Nilda is about to play piano.

"Adina!" Ramón bellows so suddenly it makes me lurch backward from his shoulders and send a tiny, breeze-like adjustment rippling through the air. Ramón raises one eyebrow and looks around the room.

"Whatsup?" Adina appears, brushing her teeth and wearing some stylish black silk pajamas.

"What's this mean?"

Adina leans over and frowns at the screen. "*Chavo* is Mexican for *kid*, I think. Kacique has Mexican friends?"

"I guess?"

"So: Not one penny, kid, like the turkeys say?"

"I know that, thank you. I'm saying, what does it *mean* mean?"

"Oh." Adina straightens, brushes, thinks. "I dunno. Just an expression, I guess. He sent you a María Teresa Vera track? My mom used to . . . listen to her." Adina's spontaneity and ease with the world disappear whenever she mentions her family. You can barely make out the last few words of what she says.

"Oh? I'd never heard of her."

"Yeah." She's standing, wrapping her arms around herself even though the heater is cranking away. "Old-timey guitar-playing songstress. You gonna make a track from it?"

"That's what Comandante Kacique has requested, so yeah. Why not? You wanna hear it?"

"Sure," Adina says, but it sounds more like a whispered moan.

Ramón frowns and clicks his mouse and the room is suddenly full with that scratchy, white hum of a very long time ago. The guitar sounds like it's playing from underwater; a tumbling construction of shaken notes resolves into a suave, confident vamp.

"Wow," Ramón says. Inside him, the crooked nostalgia churns, the one that took over his mind in Enrique's mansion. Each scratchy note brings with it an image of that imagined island: the corny palm trees and plazas, sure, but there is something deeper there too—the sense of loss, the impossible reach toward a family before it was shattered. Ramón has never seen Cuba, but he longs for it.

Adina just nods, eyes closed.

And we begin again: My dress shoes clack on the linoleum kitchen tiles and Isabel's hands squeeze mine as Nilda's notes ring out from the old piano. Her fingers stretch expertly across the keys, and she makes that opening riff feel dramatic, majestic; it's what falling in love must feel like, and then, my favorite part: Her left hand joins in, and the bass tumbles along beneath the melody. I imagine a manly lover sweeping into the room with wiggling eyebrows, sliding through the sly sensuality of those tinkling high notes with his thick vibrato strut, and the two voices gallivanting through the air above us, dipping and diving and pulsing.

My sister is a whole orchestra! I can't even concentrate on the steps, Nilda's music is so enthralling.

Here in New Jersey, the voices sweep in: a woman's louder, firm and impassioned but somehow vulnerable, demanding. The man's a softer undercurrent beneath it, barely there. *¿Qué te importa que te ame?* and the guitars dance along in mocking echoes.

"You okay?"

Adina shakes her head.

"You wanna talk about it?"

Another shake.

"Should I turn it off?"

"No."

"Okay."

*Si las cosas*, the duo croons, and silently, I croon too, *que uno quiere, se pudieran alcanzar*, and it's perfect, the feeling like the words and the music were created in total unison with each other and meant to be sung just like that, in this very moment. *If the things we wanted / could* be reached . . . *tú me quisieras lo mismo / que veinte años atrás.* I remember this version of the song too; there was an era when it was done a thousand times over by every conjunto in the club or fool with a guitar on the Malecón. *You would still love me / as you did twenty years ago.* Smoothly tragic, like all great boleros: a total emotional train wreck, perfectly harmonized and squeezed into a three-and-a-half-minute ditty.

But none of that compares to Nilda's fingers stretching across the piano as Isabel and I try pathetically to keep up on the linoleum kitchen tiles.

"It's a habanera!" Nilda yells, bringing the song to an abrupt crashing halt. "Not a waltz! You have to do it with *passion*!"

I giggle and Isabel rolls her eyes and then Nilda inserts herself between us, sweeping me up in a ridiculous dance as I squeal, and then dipping me so my head hovers just above the tiles. "Like this!" she says. "Passion!"

"I'm going to go to bed," Adina whispers when the song winds to a close.

Ramón stands, not sure what to do with his body. "Okay. Good night."

And she's gone.

Ramón shakes his head, irritated at what a giant awkward mess he can be in the face of his friend's sorrow and the whole ridiculous mess that this night has been and everything else. He plugs a spectacular pair of giant studio-style headphones into his computer, puts them on, and clicks the song back to life.

On his back, the room dark, New Jersey sleeping and frozen outside the window, Ramón allows the song to stretch out in his mind. The notes expand and coalesce around the pulse, the voice, guitars, ambient hums lose all meaning and become interwoven strands of sound. Our dress shoes against the linoleum kitchen tiles. *Es un pedazo del alma . . . It's just a piece of the soul . . .* A beat could drop, a drone, a clack . . . *Que se arranca sin piedad . . . torn away without pity.* A pause, a shimmying rattle breaks the silence, cueing the sudden relapse of sound . . . *es un pedazo del alma . . . que se arranca sin piedad.*

# CHAPTER TEN

Padre Sebastián, carrying a prayer book and, of course, a yo-yo.

He flips it down, not even bothering to look, and it hovers there, some magic thing, antigravitational because his wrist has willed it so, and then it zips back up, disappears into his palm. He has such a young face. Well, he is young, I suppose. All of us loved him from the second we saw him. Only kind of in that carnal way that's supposed to be so wrong. I mean, yes, definitely that way, in so much as our young hearts could manage, but also in some other way. We loved that smile, slightly mischievous and knowing, a touch of self-effacement and so much ease in his stride. We wanted to make it ours somehow, not even knowing what that meant, we wanted the smile to shine for us and us alone. He'd catch us snickering about something during catechism and instead of telling on us or glaring like Padre Eugenio, Padre Sebastián'd just make a mean face so we know he'd seen us and roll his smiling eyes, and it worked because we'd stop talking and pretend to pay attention.

My first orgasm ever was dedicated to Padre Sebastián. I mean, he never knew, of course, but when I got home after receiving Communion one morning, and disappeared into my room while Mami was preparing lunch and Papi chatting with the neighbors and Isabel and Nilda playing rayuela out front, our room belonged to me and my body belonged to me. And I thought about it belonging to him, him putting that wafer on my tongue and me taking his finger in my mouth and then rising up like an angel over him and the whole congregation disappearing around us in our passion and his hands all over me and my hands all over me and Christ watching from his cross above us, smiling slightly in that Mona Lisa way and then explosions, explosions all around me, rising up inside me and I'm done, wake up still in my church dress flat on my back on Nilda's bed smiling and sweaty and flushed and Mami calling me for lunch.

If he ever knew any of us hungered for him so, he never let on, never flirted back, never even remotely made it seem like we would have a chance. When Isabel started spending more time with him as the revolution swept around us, I had a brief fury thinking he'd finally caved and it was my sister of all people who had coerced him out of his vows and not me.

But no. That's not what this is about. It never was. Isabel has been gone almost a year now. I don't even know if she's alive and my house has settled into a steady, tragic clockwork of daily life, which I guess is better than the constant crying and hand-wringing of the first three months. She's gone. She's not coming back.

But now I'm sitting in Padre Sebastián's broom-closet office and he's yo-yoing and his brow is furrowed like he's trying to pick what words to say. Padre Sebastián loves words, and his love of words is like a tornado—it swirls around him and widens and then catches you up in it and soon you love words too and you're not even sure why. At least, that's what happens to me. Padre Sebastián treats language like a lover; he caresses it and wonders about it, turns it over and over in his mind, lets it change his whole world as he explores it deeper. I didn't give a damn about learning English or Latin until Padre Sebastián started comparing them to Spanish and showing how much could be gleaned from bouncing one language off another.

All of which is to say: The father is rarely at a loss for words, and when he is, people pay attention. At least, I do.

❋

There's Christmas decorations everywhere; the fake snow is like a joke in the burning tropical sun, but everyone's sense of humor was sucked into the vacuum of civil war, constant explosions, plots, rumors, executions, disappearances. We are a tired people, and, somehow, excited. "We've never been here before," Isabel whispered before she disappeared. "This is something brand-new. Something the whole world will feel." And little that I knew, I knew she was right, that every word she spoke was true, and something gigantic was in the works, that a regime would fall, and if it did it would be a long time before the dust would settle. Every day, the newspaper would lie about how the government was winning battle after battle, and every day the radio station the rebels had pirated would say the opposite: Victory at La Plata. A breathtaking escape in the Battle of Las Mercedes. And it wasn't just that we wished it was true, these daring revolutionary escapades—it was that we *felt* them to be true, felt them in our breath and our bones. The whispers around town spoke of an imminent counteroffensive by the rebels, that any day now they'd sweep down from the Sierra Maestra with all the weapons they'd captured from government troops and flush across the countryside. And now the whole country feels like that moment of chaos before a song resolves back to its one chord, and Isabel's part of that dissonance, a tiny reminder that we've never known harmony, it's just now we've reached fever pitch and everyone craves that tipping point, after centuries of Spanish rule and then yanqui rule by proxy and never freedom, just the veneer of it, but it still hasn't happened and now we're all wondering if it ever will. And I was so proud of her, for being part of that change—it made her somehow just as much a giant as the change itself. To me anyway.

And I want in. That's the truth. I want to see her, and I want in. Because what good is it admiring someone from afar when your country is falling apart and soldiers' fists are slamming on your front door just for having a sister who disappeared and anyway the whole tide of history is sweeping in with a roar and the distant rumble of explosions in the mountains—what damn good is it?

Why admire when you can *be*?

I read all the books Isabel left for me a thousand times, but mostly Martí. Martí with his faraway hairline and elegant mustache. Martí, who hated empire in all its forms and organized abroad before sailing heroically back to Cuba to fight for freedom, much like some of these bearded men storming through the countryside. The yanquis have their hands as deep in our pockets and our personal business as the Spaniards did, and the echoes of one long-ago brutality resonate all the way to today.

And I can be a part of something. Something bigger than me and my little whims and crushes, my petty fights with Nilda.

Finally, Padre Sebastián puts down the yo-yo, slides a folded piece of paper across his desk at me.

An address is written on it, it's in Vedado, the middle of the city. He stares at me for so long I think I might shatter. He puts one finger to his head, then points to the paper, points to my head. I look at it again, print each number into my brain, and then nod and Padre Sebastián brings the paper over to one of the white candles and we both watch it turn brown with the sizzly glowing edges before it disintegrates into ash.

※

Ramón rises early on this cold January morning, and I wait, recovering slowly from the toll of that dream.

I've become so impatient, a casualty of our awkward coexistence. But it's not without cause. All these games are cute, but with each memory I fade, and even if I manage to recuperate some of that lost strength along the way, it's the not knowing how many I even have left that wracks me. That I could simply be gone again, for real and for good this time—that's what surges through me every time Ramón seems to stall out.

Like right now.

He sits on the bed once again, rubbing his eyes and thinking, and all the while the dream I have so carefully crafted slips slowly away beneath the tide of banal thoughts about the day ahead.

The notebook of my life is open beside him, the pen beside it.

The events of the night before circle through him and his head pounds at the memories.

That dream, my life, becomes vague, a ghost like me.

Padre Sebastián is the key to so much, that I know. He is part of this, one of the pillars of who I was, my young life. He did . . . he did something important. I need him there, his name, his actions, and irregularities, in that book.

Ramón stands and, just as the seething wrath in me is about to boil over, he glances down at the notebook.

Makes a face.

I wait.

He sits. Picks up the pen.

I simmer. Churn.

He breathes. Writes: *Padre Sebastián.*

Something in me feels like it's about to break. When it doesn't, I disperse myself, torn between shame and relief, and let myself cool to the sound of Ramón's scratching pen.

# CHAPTER ELEVEN

Aliceana is ignoring him.

Technically, they're ignoring each other. Which is also technically not any different than what they do every day. Except now you can see the sadness radiating off Aliceana. Well, I can anyway. It's all over her when she steps out of the doctors' lounge, passes Ramón without smiling, and disappears into the ER: She's devastated.

Ramón watches the ebb and flow of body aches, asthma attacks, and minor injuries. None of it touches him. It hasn't for a while, but even less so right now. At noon, ambulances bring in an old man. They're pumping on his chest, squeezing oxygen into a tube coming out of his mouth, but he's quite dead. Been dead a while and surely isn't thrilled about such an invasive goodbye party to the world of life. He'll get over it. Ramón steps out of the way as they rush the gurney through the bay doors and into the crash room.

"S'amatta?" Derringer asks.

"Nothing."

"Man . . . I'm bored. At least let me live vicariously through your obviously chaotic and at least vaguely interesting life."

Ramón looks down at Derringer, who seems to always be squinting for no apparent reason, and shakes his head. "Nah, man, I ain't in the mood."

"I'm saying, though—"

Ramón's phone bursts to life, depriving us all of any more of this awesome conversation. "Hello?" he says, flipping it open as he steps out into the cold.

"¿Diga?"

"Um . . . ¿hola?"

"Yes? Who is this?"

"You called me . . . wait a minute." Ramón looks down at the number. North Jersey. "Tío Pepe?"

"¿Jes?"

"It's Ramón. I called you earlier."

"Who?"

"Ramón, el hijo de Nilda."

"¡Ah! ¡Ramón! ¿Cómo andas, m'ijo?"

"Bien, Tío. ¿Y tú?"

"I'm okay, papi. Everything okay."

"Listen, Tío, I wanted to ask you some questions about the family and stuff, that alright?"

"¿Okay?"

Ramón looks up at the sky, then closes his eyes. "Was that a yes?"

"¿Sí?"

"Tío Pepe, I'm going to drive up by where you live. A tu casa, Tío, esta tarde. Hoy. Okay? I want to ask you about the family. And about, um, ancestors? I remember you talking about Santería once. Just some questions. That okay?"

"Okay, m'ijo. Como quieras."

"Okay, Tío." Ramón shakes his head, clicks the phone back onto his belt. Says a quiet prayer to no one in particular and walks back inside.

✳

I remember Tío Pepe. He's technically Ramón's great-uncle, my mami's brother, but who's keeping track? He was a semi-big-deal businessman under Batista, had a chain of grocery stores, a few houses. Everything came crashing down around him after the revolution and he retreated into himself for a few months before showing up one day at a family dinner, all back slaps and corny jokes like he used to be, and the next day he was gone. At first we all thought he'd gone underground, like rebellion was a family trait that polluted all of our blood. I saw the thin veneer of *everything's fine* start to crumble in my mom's trembling hands and Papi's day-long bouts of silence.

Then a letter showed up from Miami, all smiles and abrazos a la familia and land of liberty bullshit. We celebrated: Tío Pepe wasn't dead and he wasn't going to show up one day getting his insides splattered against a wall on our television; he was alive! And in yanquilandia, coño . . . Papi got out one of his favorite wines, now contraband, and we sat around the table, but there was still an empty chair where Isabel was supposed to be and everyone knew I was sneaking out every night and no one could fathom any reasonable end to this sudden reign of terror we'd plunged into.

A twenty-foot concrete wall surrounds the little cluster of houses where Tío Pepe whiles away the last years of his life. It's tall enough to prevent any invading communist hordes, I'm sure, and gives the sense that you've somehow stumbled onto the first Cuban-American moon colony.

Inside, cookie-cutter one-story houses huddle close together, their front doorways turned in toward the narrow corridors that separate them. Gnomes and flamingos populate the azalea and orange blossom gardens. There's a family of cats, an occasional passing opossum or squirrel for them to eat or get thrashed by. A few brown chirpy birds do battle around a feeder someone has dangled from an evergreen. It's all very quaint.

"This is creepy," Adina says as she directs her beat-up Volkswagen past the guardhouse and onto the main road of Miramar Villas.

Ramón scowls out the window. "It really is. Thanks for driving, Adi."

"Bah, it's nothing. I needed a break from the city anyway."

The about-to-be-sunset sky's streaked with bright orange and barely there blue. Dirty snow splotches the edges of some of the lawns and a lonely wind chime is tinkling away in the January early evening breeze. "You been alright, Adi?"

Adina scrunches up her nose. "Not exactly."

"You wanna talk about it?"

"You wait till we roll up on your great-uncle's united suburban military compound to ask me if I want to talk about it?"

71

"So that's a no, okay."

"Obviously I haven't been alright, Ramón, since I don't normally stand perfectly still like a zombie because you put on some old song and you don't usually come home to find me with puffy, red eyes because I was crying for three hours straight in a little huddle on the floor."

"I . . . I didn't realize."

"Of course you didn't. I'm not trying to snap at you. I mean, a little, but whatever. It's this one?"

"One-eight-seven? Yeah."

Adina parks and turns off the engine. Some crooning Spanish ballad gurgles along quietly on the radio, all synthesizers and drum machines. For a few moments, neither of them says anything. Slowly, it dawns on Ramón that he needs to take the initiative.

He throws his hands up. "I'm sorry."

Adina blinks at him.

"Wait," Ramón says. "That sounded angry. Or sarcastic. It wasn't meant to. I was frustrated at myself for being so obtuse and I made it sound like I was frustrated at you for making me apologize. Let me, uh, let me try again."

Adina bites her lips and nods.

Ramón takes a deep breath. "I'm really sorry I haven't been there for you or a good friend to you. I've been caught up in my own shit, which is an explanation not an excuse, and . . ." All of it, all of me, is right there, waiting to come out. *I've been seeing my dead aunt's life every time I go to sleep and what a fucked-up life it was* . . . but instead he just shakes his head. "I've just been going through a lot of stuff too and I don't even know how to talk about it."

Adina blinks a few times, nods again. "Thank you. And I'm sorry you're going through stuff. I'm here if you need to talk. Like about whatever weird family mission you've got me driving you around for."

Ramón almost laughs—what would he even say?—but catches himself. Shakes his head instead. "Just following up on some stuff for . . . you know, the family."

"Look at you being proactive! How does it feel?"

He snorts. "Weren't we talking about your messed-up family, not mine?"

She concedes the point with a shrug. "Yeah, yeah, I just . . . I miss them," Adina says. "I hate them for kicking me out and I miss them at the same time. It'll be three years on Monday and all I get's an email every now and then from my sister and the sad feeling that my mom misses me almost as much or more than I miss her but is too proud to reach out and it just sucks is all."

"You reach out?"

"I send a card at Christmas and sometimes I email. At first I'd call but I'd always hang up after a ring or two. Not because I was afraid of rejection; I was afraid of what I'd say. You're already familiar with the fire this mouth can spit."

Ramón nods, perhaps a little too enthusiastically, but Adina lets it go.

"I didn't want to make things worse. If my dad picked up I'd . . . I wouldn't hold back. But they're attached at the hip. She doesn't even have a cell phone, so there's no way to reach her without maybe reaching him and . . . Yeah, I just gave up. What's the point anyway? They made their decision. I'm living my life."

"Your awesome life full of beautiful women that want to fuck your brains out."

"Yeah." Adina looks out the window. "All except one."

"Oh. Corinna? Thought that was over."

"It is."

"Oh."

"Again."

"Ah."

"C'mon." She shuts down the car and steps out into the chilly evening air. "Let's go talk to your weirdo tío."

※

A pretty middle-aged woman opens the door. She's wearing scrubs and has on rubber gloves and a lot of makeup and a huge smile. "Ramón!" she squeals, and hugs him, careful not to touch the gloves against his shirt.

"Hey, Teresa." Ramón smiles, leaning down so she can plant her cheek kisses, and steps inside.

"And this is?" Teresa takes a good hard look at Adina. "¡Pero qué bonita!"

Adina blushes and goes in for her kiss. "That's my friend Adina," Ramón says. Teresa wraps around Adina and holds her tight. For a second, I think Adina might break down, she looks so startled to be embraced like that. Then she eases into it, a serene smile crosses her face, and she lets her head rest on Teresa's shoulder.

"Y qué buen espíritu," Teresa murmurs quietly. "You'll be alright, mi corazón. Don't worry." Adina nods her head and they release their hug as Ramón looks back to see what the holdup is.

"Your uncle is so excited you're coming, Ramón." Teresa bustles past him, into the kitchen, and starts taking down plates and cups. "Can you reach that for me? The bowl with the little bananas and flowers painted on it? Esa, sí. Gracias. Yes, he's putting on his nice clothes now and he'll come out in a minute. Sit, sit, sit."

From the look of the place, Teresa must wage constant war to beat back the masses of collected junk. Hundreds of magazines, videos, and books are squished into a series of bookcases lining the walls. Antique lamps cast scant light on a huge multimedia system that takes up a full quarter of the little front room. Towering speakers stand guard on either side and a flat-screen TV sits on a whole blinking mess of devices.

Ramón is halfway into an ancient easy chair when Teresa calls out from the kitchen: "Ramón, mi amor, would you bring me the sugar from the cupboard, por favor?"

"Of course." He sidesteps around the velvet couch, dodges Adina's sweep kick at his knees, and walks around the counter into the kitchen.

"¡Coño, mi sobrino! ¿Cómo tú estás, chico?" a voice blurts out from the bedroom. I remember him as a giant, Pepe. Of course, I was a kid and he was in his heyday; he was like a clock tower above me; I thought he could see the whole world from all the way up there. But this little man? He's all crinkled over like he was some piece of paper that life was discarding. A gnome. If I'da met him back then I would've thought he was one of the little forest people.

"Bien, Tío. ¿Y tú?"

"Okay, ya tú sabes." He's wearing a slick little button-down shirt, military style with a pocket on each side of the chest, and gray slacks. He hobbles forward, cane first, and wraps a trembling little arm around Ramón. "Ay, chico. Hace rato."

"It's true, more than a year, no?"

"No, ¿ju know the last time I saw ju? At Ysenia's quinceañera ¿no?"

"Yes! I think so. That was a beautiful party."

"¡Bah!" Pepe swipes the very idea away from him with disgust and hobbles into the sitting room. "It was freezing cold that day! ¿Ju don't remember? Coño, pero qué frío . . ."

"I mean, yeah, it was February, Tío, but the party itself was—"

"Hello, mujer bonita de mis sueños más profundos!"

"Hello, sir." Adina stands, straightens her dress, and kisses Pepe on the cheek. "Adina. Amiga de Ramón."

"So I see." Pepe shoots a wicked wink at Ramón, who just shakes his head. "¿Teresa, café?"

"Ya está hecho," Teresa hums from the kitchen. "Siéntate."

Pepe eases himself onto the couch next to Adina, and Ramón helps Teresa bring in the tray with coffee and snacks. They banter back and forth through the required pleasantries, slipping easily between languages, Ramón never quite sure which to use and Adina or Teresa occasionally interpreting Pepe's more obscure Cubanismos. Finally, Pepe signals he's ready to get down to it by settling back into the couch and lighting a massive cigar. "Cubano," he points out, grinning. "I know we are not supposed to, but at this point, I am old. And jus' don't give a fuck anymore, ¿ju know?"

"I kinda do, actually," Ramón admits.

"Ahora, ¿what is it ju wanted to ask me?"

I swing down in a long arc through the stale air of Tío Pepe's cramped apartment, center myself, and listen.

"My tías . . ."

"Isabel and Marisol." At the mention of my name, I shudder. Pepe says it correctly: a poem. Mar y sol, the *ee* sound extended just ever so slightly for maximum effect and then resolving into that gentle *el* ending. Marisol. My name. Me. "Teresa, el libro."

Clearly, he'd been preparing for this moment. Perhaps for a while. He opens the photo album that Teresa passed him and beckons Ramón over. "Allí están, las tres."

Ramón stands and peers over Pepe's shoulder. Adina looks. Teresa looks even though she's seen the picture before, I'm sure. Me? I don't. I can't. My heart is already shattered across the world. Why would I pound another nail into it? What could that picture show me except a fantasy of what might've been but wasn't. A tantalizing quizás, if only, but alas. No thank you. No indeed.

"Wow," Ramón says. "That's Mami in the middle."

"Claro, those eyes. Always had very beautiful eyes, your mother."

"And Isabel, the oldest. And that's Marisol."

"Sí, señor."

I want to look. I do. It is me after all. Besides that one photo from my childhood, I haven't seen me in . . . decades probably. Me with a body, a face. Me: more than just this ethereal nonsense, where it takes all of my concentration just to be, just to have some feeling at the tips of my not-there fingers. Mierda. To have a body. The me in that picture is before all the terribleness came tumbling down. Maybe just before. Maybe after Gómez gave me the package but before Isabel disappeared. A hundred paths lead out of that image but only one is what happened, and here I am: gone.

"Eran tan bonitas, ¿no?"

"Claro que sí," Teresa says, leaning over from the back of the couch.

I don't believe in regrets. Even after so much, after everything. I don't believe in regrets. I don't. I detach myself from the shadows, move across the room. To see myself. Avoid the bodies—they're so warm and full, so heavy and solid, so different from me. I don't want to send a shiver down anyone's spine, don't want to complicate the moment by having to cringe and disperse myself until their uneasiness passes. I just want this to be simple. So I glide in between the warm, pulsing bodies, sweep over the surface of the couch, and peer over Pepe's crumpled old shoulder. And there I am, staring right back at me through the long veil of history, wide, serious eyes, dark and earnest and oddly defiant.

Dios mío, I was so young once. My skin was smooth except for a few pimples I couldn't seem to get rid of. My fingers so slender wrapped around that copy of *A Thousand and One Nights* that I used to covet like a Bible, my face wide open to the world. I'm trying to look tough. The other two are trying to look sweet, but my chin is up, my mouth forced into a frown, my eyes ever so slightly narrowed just to prove I don't care. The hand not holding the book rests on Nilda's shoulder, which is odd because I'm quite sure by that time I already couldn't stand her, but I probably just did it to cause trouble in one way or another.

I am beautiful, back then. So young and pulsing with the certainty of God's love and all my tiny inventions, my ever-unwinding imagination of how things will turn out, all lies, broken fantasies ripped from all those books I kept my nose in. I think this was the year I began to realize how hard things could be; the shadows had started tiptoeing around the edges of our house, but they hadn't taken over yet.

"How did they die?" Ramón asks. I don't know if I want to hear Pepe's answer.

"Ay, chico," he sighs. Teresa retreats back to the kitchen. The question threw a shroud over the room. Adina looks into her little coffee cup, then closes her eyes.

"There is a building in Vedado," Pepe says. "They call it el trampolín de los muertos."

"The trampoline of the dead?"

"Eso. De allí, se tiró Isabel."

*Tirar* is a powerful word. She didn't just jump, she hurled herself, she shot, projectiled, from the building. You tirar una pistola. And, if you're Isabel, you tirar yourself. My sister could never do anything halfway. This was a truth I have carried with me, somehow. The knowledge doesn't land with any surprise; it is simply a fact about Isabel I've always known. Se tiró.

Gulping back a sob, Pepe uses one hand to demonstrate a body falling, watches it, and then, instead of smacking it into his other hand the way things probably happened, he makes it flutter up and away. Then he sits there frowning for a few seconds in silence.

Then: "They never tell ju, Ramón?"

Ramón shakes his head, looking broken. "I kind of knew. But never how. They don't talk about it. Ever. What about Marisol, Tío?"

"Ay, esa se mató." The hand gesture is different, a wrist-flick and then another one, his old head nodding back and forth, eyebrows raised. A deep frown.

This is a complicated answer. *Se mató* can either mean she killed herself or she was killed. That *se* is a question mark, but I doubt Ramón has the capacity to get at that nuance.

"¿Se mató?" Adina asks, slicing one hand across her wrist.

Pepe half shrugs. "She loved her sister though, Marisol. Even when they were little, Marisol always chased after Isabel, always looked up to her, followed her everywhere, never left her side. She loved her sister. Entonces . . ."

I see. That's what they all think: I loved my troubled sister, chased her lost soul over the top of some other building, somewhere where I wouldn't be recognized, or the ocean perhaps. Desaparecida. Gone.

Makes sense, I suppose, as much as any tragedy can. I'm Tío Pepe's fluttering hand, all my parts dispersed in the wind. And really, just one of so many, so so many souls lost in those first terrible years.

"Nobody knows?"

Pepe makes a noncommittal grunt. "I was already gone, by then. Everything . . . fell apart. So quickly."

"Poor Mami," Ramón says. "Two sisters gone . . . like that."

Again that recoil. Nilda . . . a ferocity rises in me that I don't even have a name for. Hatred, maybe, but it feels thicker, more intimate. But of course Ramón would think of his mom. He can't see the past, doesn't know how far apart the world flung us, even before Isabel se tiró and Nilda se fue.

"Sí," Pepe says with a sad nod. Then he grimaces and makes another fluttering gesture near his head. "She is, ya . . . no." *She's never been the same*, he means, and the whole of Nilda deteriorating self is somehow encapsulated in that shaking hand. *She's barely there*, he means, conjuring images of my sister sitting in the darkness of her perfectly maintained house, barely leaving, collapsing within, forever collapsing in slow motion within.

And she might be barely there, but I'm the one who's gone. Isabel is gone. Poor Nilda, but she's the one who made it out.

No one knows what to say for a couple of moments. The possibilities of what was just said playing over and over in all of our imaginations, I'm sure. I think Pepe's teetering on the edge of bursting into tears. He rallies though, finds a smile for Ramón. "¿Algo más?"

"What?"

"Something else. ¿Ju had another question? ¿La Santería?"

"Ah yes, I wanted to ask . . ."

"Ay, pero ya estoy cansado, chico." The old man stands and everyone else stands around him.

"I'm sorry, Tío, I wore you out. Bringing up all those memories. We should be going."

"No."

"No what?"

"I am going to bed. It's past an old man's bedtime. But you have questions about la Santería, you can speak to the expert." He quickly embraces Adina and Ramón and then disappears into his bedroom, chuckling.

"Who . . . ?" Ramón asks.

Teresa, standing in the kitchen, coughs into her hand.

"Oh. You?"

"Mhm. Come, jovenes, estep into my office so we can talk."

# CHAPTER TWELVE

This, then, is how I died: It's cold, the wind blowing in from the ocean wraps around me and I pull my shawl close and the city is a rippling splatter of pastiche and crumble around me. Down on the street uniformed men swarm like ants, building to building, and when they get to my apartment and bash in the door they just find a cup of coffee on the table, still warm, and a cigarette half smoked in the ashtray and the screen door leading to the balcony open, wide open, and the cool ocean breeze making the curtains dance like spirits in the empty room.

I can see it all like it happened right in front of me; it's all right there: crisp and achingly true.

※

Teresa's "office" is a little side room, probably used for storage in a normal apartment, but Pepe treats his whole place like a storage bin, so this room is free for Teresa's little setup. It's not much, just a fold-out table with a nice cloth over it and a stool. There's a Tarot deck and some fancy crystals and one of those seven-day white candles you can get at the bodegas. A long stick is propped against the wall behind her and a bunch of framed black-and-white family photos cluster on the ground around it. Her ancestor shrine, I presume. She lights a cigar and settles on the stool.

"Nice setup," Adina says when they walk in through the beaded curtain.

"Gracias. Now, siéntense, chicos. Make yourselves at home. My dingy little side office es tu casa."

"You do readings and stuff in here?" Ramón asks, trying to fit himself into the folding chair.

"Your tío and I negotiated it as part of my home health aide pay.

Works out well actually, plus he gets his own in-house spiritual counselor gratis."

"Not bad," Ramón admits, though I'm sure he's thinking that neither of his parents would be thrilled to hear about the arrangement.

"What did you want to ask, mi vida?"

"Well, I was wondering . . ."

"Estop." Suddenly serious, one hand raised, eyes closed. Ramón clams up quick. Teresa turns to Adina. "I know it's not for you that Ramón has come asking, but you're hurting. I don't need to pull a card or drop a shell to know it."

Adina nods. I get the sense she's not used to being this fragile; the tears keep creeping up on her and she has to sniffle to hold them back.

"It's okay, mi amor. You don't have to estifle all of that feeling." Teresa passes a tissue across the table and Adina dabs at her eyes, still refusing to let the flood come. "I know this looks like a lot of magic, a lot of brouhaha, as they say, but really, it's just so much science. Very precise." Ramón raises his eyebrows and Teresa winks at him. "I don't expect you to understand, don't worry. Adina, you've always been a warrior, and now you are learning that the true warrior is also very vulnerable on the outside, the pain has become so great that it is impossible to act tough anymore."

Nods. Eye dabs. Sniffles.

"I know it's impossible to see right now, but this is a very beautiful thing, mi amor. Cherish it. It's the moment when you are most alive, most in touch with your warrior spirit. Don't fear it. Don't be ashamed of it. Wrap love around even the most broken parts of yourself, because they are what God has given you to remind you how strong you are."

Someone said something like that to me once. Once when I was broken. His voice was gravelly and whispered; he was broken too. But he reached inside himself and found some words very much like those and he laid them at my feet like a pilgrim placing an offering. It was a world full of darkness and it was all I had. Adina hasn't known the pain

I have. I pray she never does. But she's deep in her own dark place and I can see that what the santera says is a tiny glimmer of light to her too.

"Okay," Adina sniffles. "Okay."

"Now, Ramón."

Ramón's kind of flabbergasted, I see. At least he knows when to shut up and be amazed by a powerful moment happening between two women in front of his face. He takes a second to get it together and then says: "I was wondering about the dead."

"Ah yes, ancestors. Egun, we call them in Lucumí." She nods back at the photos on the floor around the stick. "They give us life, you know. In so many ways. We owe them so much and thank them so rarely." I see she's placed some coffee down there for them and I half consider taking a sip just to mess with everybody. But let me stop. Let me focus.

"You don't have to worry about the dead," Teresa says. "They don't mess with you." Okay, well, I'd been impressed up till now, but Teresa clearly has some training to do. "Some people have the dead all over them like lice. Some people have a good relationship that they have cultivated with the dead; they help each other out. You? This is not a concern for you."

Ramón looks disappointed. I am too; I'd had high hopes for this one. "But, when the dead do show up in people's lives, is it, I mean, is it like in the movies, where they want something, you know, some unfulfilled thing?"

Teresa laughs for a long time. It's a beautiful sound—deep and uninhibited and straight from the gut. Then she enjoys a few tugs from her cigar while Ramón squirms. "Short answer? Sure." A shrug and she releases a cathedral of smoke into the small room. "Sometimes. Sometimes they are hungry for things they didn't get in life—affection or attention or some material silliness. The dead see things we don't. They have, how you say? Like, worldview. They can see through things, no? Into the essence. So when they're around, they can get frustrated, that we don't see things. They want to show us. Or they have agendas, yes. Sometimes they left something somewhere. Death can come suddenly, can cancel all the best-laid plans, you know. So, yes, maybe if the dead are around it's to get the living to help them do something, but I warn you: It's rarely so simple, Ramón. Death is like life, laden with problems of power and impossibilities. Usually, all the dead want is to evolve. Just like us, no?"

"I see. Kinda."

Teresa smiles. "You don't, but that's okay. I'm sure you will." She stands. The session is over.

Ramón and Adina stand too, Ramón fumbling with his pockets. "Can I . . . ?"

"No, shush, m'ijo. Don't be silly. You are family."

"I am?"

"Close enough. Go. Don't forget what I told you."

A few kisses and hugs later, they're outside, pulling off, waving through the Volkswagen windows, smiling and slightly puzzled. They drive home in silence.

# CHAPTER THIRTEEN

Isabel.

Answers the door to the address Padre Sebastián gave me with a pistol pointing out and she has her glasses on and she's still the same Isabel but skinnier, so much skinnier, like the time away has sucked her very body into near nothingness, cheeks sallow, eyes wide and afraid. When she sees me and wraps around me, it really is her; her smell is all over me; I'm submerged in it and then I'm crying and crying into her arm and she's pulling me inside before I make a scene and putting down her gun and holding me while I cry and cry and cry.

She doesn't though. The old her maybe would've. I've seen her cry; once when Papi got into a fight with Big Fernando up the street and we watched while they went at it and once when she first got her period and stained her favorite dress and Nilda scolded her for not being prepared.

But now she doesn't cry. She says, *How did you*—and then shakes her head, because she's put the pieces together herself. And you can see the weight lift off her, my sister, the rebel; her first thought upon seeing me was that she'd somehow been caught.

That's when she finally smiles, and it's so wide and toothy I have to believe it. The apartment is small, cluttered with crates and papers and canned food and clothes. There's a table by the far end of the room and then the balcony and then the bright Caribbean open sky over La Habana and I've never been this high up before, never seen Vedado like this: There's the Hotel Presidente, El Nacional, and there beyond all those rooftops is the Capitolio and the old city stretching around it and out to the sea. And I say, *It's so beautiful* and Isabel just nods, like she's just now realizing that yes, it is quite a view. I start tearing up again because of that faraway look in her eyes, and Isabel relents a little; she lets a layer of wall crumble and asks me if I want anything to eat, any coffee, anything. Before I can answer she's asking about Mami and Papi and, with a laughing roll of her eyes, Nilda, and all of her friends and finally there it is, before I can even get out the first word, finally she breaks, shatters even, and then she's in my arms and she's sobbing and sobbing and I hold her and watch the clouds ration sunlight across the rising rooftops below.

*I miss you*, she says, sniffling.

I just shake my head because all along I thought I was the one missing her and she was just out in the world, living this amazing life without me. Why would she miss me? There was a war to be fought. That's when I start crying, and then she's holding me, we're holding each other and kind of sob-laughing.

*I miss you too, boba*, I moan. And when everything calms down some we're still holding each other and I say, *I want to join up too*, into her shoulder. *I want to fight.*

My eyes are closed because I know what she's going to say next and then she does: *No, Mari.* And when I shake my head, crying again, she adds: *Not yet.*

*Why?* I try to keep the whine from my voice, because I already feel like a little girl.

She holds me a little bit away from herself so she can look at me. Frowns. *There will be plenty for you to do, believe me.*

And I do believe her, but I'm not sure what she means because there's a heavy rain cloud around her words and I can't put my finger on it.

*And anyway*, she says, smiling now even though her eyes aren't, *it's almost over. This part anyway.*

Over canned pineapples and cold coffee, she tells me about months and months of dodging the secret police, passing messages between the guerrillas in the Sierra Maestra mountains and the leaders of the Student Directorate in the city. Terrible nights waiting for the door to burst in, trying to look innocent, showing falsified papers to guardia officers that would harass her on the street. She tells me she gave up her body more than once to get away with things, rubs her eyes and I wonder if it's to try and shake away the nightmare memories that keep rising, but when she looks at me, her face is even, not broken, just concerned. There's no tell I can find to match my worst fears about what she's been through, what it's done to her. I shake my head, trying to wrap my mind around it but not wanting to, trying not to imagine what that really means. Put my hand on hers and hold it tight. She's still there, still strong, in spite of it all. There's still light in her eyes when she looks up at me. She's still so alive.

In the morning she tells me it's all happening, and the radio is bursting with frantic transmissions. It's almost New Year's; the three fronts are converging in Santa Clara, Ché's troops will sweep away the last battalions of government fighters and it will send a devastating shock wave all the way to La Habana and into Batista's corrupt little heart, and then he will know, finally and without any doubt, that the people have risen against him and defeated him at every turn, even though outnumbered and living like animals in the mountains, the people have risen. And the victory will echo across the world, the very seat of empire will shake, a resounding answer to the question asked centuries ago. The yanquis won't own our sugar anymore, won't own us anymore, and they'll have to rewrite all the history books to sing about our victory. She sounds like the propaganda the rebels leave scattered around town, but she believes it, it's real on her lips, I feel it in my own heart, my gut. But there's something else too: She's afraid.

I realize now it's not just the fear of the bursting-in door; there's a deeper, more sinister menace lurking in her nightmares and she doesn't even have words for it. I can tell because even as she narrates all the things that are about to happen, all swollen with revolutionary glory and patriotic fervor, her voice trembles ever so slightly, and she doesn't smile, she's not excited, she just sees it, says it, and then she's quiet.

And a few days later, while I'm still staying at her apartment in Vedado, that's how it happens, just like she said: The three columns of revolutionary fighters converge, and while Batista's men destroy one, the other two sweep through the streets of Santa Clara, with a revolutionary fervor that crushes the undertrained, underpaid, and afraid soldiers and keeps rolling all along the dark countryside highways and into La Habana, up the palace steps and into the ear of the dictator, who nods silently, eyes closed, and knows in his twisted little heart that after years of pushing back against the rebels, cracking down and executing, torturing and cursing and waiting and fighting, he's finally lost.

And he flees.

And then the streets flood with hundreds and hundreds of people, Cubans, my people, yelling, cheering, screaming, throwing flowers, shooting rifles, being alive and in love and spontaneous and free free free suddenly free. Isabel and I make our way through the writhing crowds, through the living streets, past the waves crashing against the Malecón, along the edge of the brand-new city in the brand-new world. Up ahead stands a group of rebels, beautiful, uniformed men with beards and machine guns, all yelling and cheering and watching up the road, waiting for their savior to sweep through and herald the dawning of a new day in Cuba.

They embrace Isabel, flirt with her, laugh with abandon and scream at all they've been through, and Isabel whispers to me that I'm not to leave her side, not to disappear for any reason at all no matter what, to stay close, and she cracks a smile and plays along, and the men are kind to me, although I see them keeping me in the corner of their eyes and minds, their pretty rebel girl's pretty young sister. I feel them see me and it is one part terrifying, two parts invigorating. These powerful men, I wonder what power I could hold over them, whether these conquerors would fall over themselves to win me, like they do on TV.

A line of trucks passes us by, more bearded rebels hanging off the sides and yelling and shooting into the air. They pass and suddenly there are people all around us, the whole city of La Habana has emptied out into the streets and everyone is screaming at once, the whole city is screaming, years—no, centuries, generations of tension, fear, mourning suddenly explode into one outrageous outpouring, unrepentant, unafraid, alive.

Truck after truck passes, then a few tanks and smiling rebels jogging alongside. I wonder where Mami and Papi are and if this finally means the end of all our terror and whether Isabel will come back home now, and if this explosion of life will carry us along through time into sustained peacefulness, some kind of freedom. Then Isabel tugs on my sleeves and points at one of the men passing on a tank; he's bearded like the rest of them with a childish face, all cheeks and forehead, and he's waving and smiling, surrounded by the black-and-red flags of his movement; the light blue, white, and red flags of our country; his fighters and his people. You can see he's on fire with the glory of it, all that it means and all the future has in store.

And then he's gone and we're swept up in the parade, all rebel green and black and red. Beards and smiles and eyes wide open with excitement. A moment, a moment if only just a moment of total enthrallment. A whole city, a whole country, this beautiful island that is my home wide awake and hurling into the future with an open heart and a mouthful of hope . . .

❉

Ramón has the day off and, having scrawled out the dream in his journal, he's making beats. I wonder if all this history-giving is too much. There are no experts to consult, or the ones there are, like Teresa, don't even recognize my presence, so what good is that? It's a purging, like vomiting but beautiful somehow, and when it's done I am diminished and weak, but I am clean. Does that mean Ramón is dirty? Have I made him into a waste bin for my memories, our diseased past? I can only hope this process will get him somewhere better, that his ignorance is perhaps its own form of filth, that knowing, however painful, will be its own cleansing.

When his eyes close and his mind goes I glide just above him, then give over to his flesh, allow myself to dissolve into that solidness and so we merge. Then, I remember.

When I have the choice, I choose carefully. There's only so much time and space, even with the odd out-of-proportion dream state. He needs to be able to retain it, at least the important parts, when he wakes, so I can't pour all of La Habana into his sleeping mind. So I craft, form, fix, and then I give. Some of it clicks into place so easily; he already knows what the house in Las Colinas looked like; he's seen the pictures. He has stored away images of Mami and Papi, his own mother when she was a child. Other things, I have to paint as gracefully and honestly as I can so he sees it the way it was. He sleeps and I give, empty myself, and as I give I grow. My own past unrolls through the act of showing it, and so I become, ever so slightly, more real. Less a sprinkling of displaced air currents, more a living memory, a participant in the world, however shadowy. I live.

No one's home, so he has the speakers on and María Teresa Vera's voice pouring out of them. He woke up early, scribbled the whole winding dream saga as best he could remember it in his journal as always, and then made his coffee and got right to work. Now he flips back to the beginning of the song, plays it out once—those guitars dancing together, building into the now familiar opening line—and then stops. A messy collection of bass beats burps out of the speakers until he finds one he likes and throws it on top of a ticking metronome with some snares and cymbal crashes. It's all very cursory, I see; he's trying to get a sense of what can be done, eschewing precision for progress, mean mugging the screen, sipping coffee, rubbing his stubbly face.

This is why I'm not worried: Ramón is not a closed circuit. Yes, it's a lot that I give him. A heavy load to carry, all that history, and someone else's to boot. But we all walk with history, whether we know it or not. It was there anyway, the hints of it at least—the collected lies, aversions, and half-truths my sister told him. The filled-out story only becomes meat on the bones, something he can sink his teeth into. But it doesn't sit heavy in his cells, doesn't metastasize or gather like plaque and turn malignant. He pours it out just like I do, wraps around these halting beats and basslines he makes.

He hits play and watches the song scroll by in dancing waveforms. Takes a swill of coffee, leans in, and lines up the beginning of a measure to the tallest spike, squinting. He's not thinking about Gutierrez or the crowded streets of La Habana or Aliceana or old Tío Pepe. He's lost in the beat and happy.

So I leave him there, squinting happily at his screen. I have a theory to test.

# CHAPTER FOURTEEN

See, this is what I mean about Aliceana: The apartment is completely bare. There's a table with a chair, wooden and dull as daytime television. There's a TV in the living room, a couch—just a couch. In her room: a simple bed, a desk, and a bookcase. No clutter on the desk, not even a knickknack, dammit. One photo: her parents, hugging each other and smiling in the pale winter sunlight outside their house in North Jersey. A stereo takes up one of the shelves of her bookcase with one of those fancy new music-playing devices plugged into it. In her bathroom there are tampons, aspirin, toothpaste, a toothbrush, contact lens solution, a little holder. Shampoo. I'm falling asleep just looking at it.

She didn't get to say everything she'd wanted to that night. Ramón ran out quick when things didn't seem to be going his way and I could see his speech caught her off guard. My stories may not stay and get stagnant, but unspoken words? Emotions left in limbo? Deadly. So after my cursory tour of the empty apartment, I wait. The lighting is nice in here, I'll say that. The day progresses and the sun sends window-shaped squares of light across the wall and occasional cars pass and occasional neighbors yell back and forth to each other.

The daylight softens into moody orange and then the door clicks open and Aliceana comes in. She wears no expression as she shrugs off her courier bag and strips out of her long winter jacket, out of her scrubs, and disappears into the shower. She's a blank to me, and part of me wants to call it quits. Maybe that's all I needed to know. Maybe I'm looking too hard for something that's not there. But I wait. It's what I do, so why not do it some more? Anyway, I'm still curious. She comes out of the bathroom naked with a towel turban wrapped around her head, walks to the stereo, and punches something into the little player of hers and suddenly the whole room is full of sound.

It's the slow intro to some club mix. A series of throbbing synthesizers overlap as horns fade in and out and a voice I can only imagine is exalting God in some language hollers out into the immenseness of the music. I hadn't realized that Aliceana had also set up speakers in the upper corners of her room and in the living room. The sounds pours in from all around and when the beat drops, it rumbles through me, reckless.

Aliceana pulls on some sweatpants and a sports bra as the song builds. She looks up, face twisted like she can't place a smell. The phone! I didn't even hear it beneath all the clamor. She goes tearing across the apartment, displaces pillows, hurls clothes to the side, opens drawers before finally coming up with an apparently rarely used cordless and blipping it on.

"Hold on! Hold on!" she yells, and then runs back over and offs the stereo and sinks to the floor panting. "Hello?"

She smiles. "Hey, Mami." The Tagalog small talk rambles on for a few minutes, Aliceana nodding, agreeing and repeating that she's fine at least six times. Then she says "Okay," waits, and then "Hi, Papa." You can hear her voice change—she leaves each pause longer to give him time to answer, pouting in spite of her forced-cheerful voice. There's not much coming from the other end; occasional croaked monosyllables that may or may not have anything to do with the simple questions she's asking. "I love you," she finally says when everything else seems to fail. "Bye."

There's no reply and eventually her mom gets back on, sends love from both of them, and hangs up. Aliceana sighs and absentmindedly sticks the phone on the second shelf of her bookcase where she's sure to not be able to find it. She rises, reaches her arms up over her head and arches her back, and then clicks the music back to life.

I'm so unprepared when Aliceana leaps up into the air and comes down headfirst that I almost, almost, fling into sudden physicality and try to stop her. She lands miraculously in a handstand (and on beat), touches her head down lightly, then sets herself off into a furious spin, kicking her feet out to gain momentum. What I thought was an absurdly plain carpet is actually a mat of some kind, used to facilitate not cracking open your skull during such endeavors.

You wouldn't even call it dancing at first, because it just seems like the natural movement of a body in time with the pulsing beat—free of intentionality, decision making, self-consciousness. It is, of course, dancing, but in that blissful, uninhibited way you rarely see outside of people's private little worlds. The spontaneously choreographed equivalent of a diary entry.

I have been hasty. Cruel even.

I took a quiet disposition and made it into not-much-going-on. I'm usually pretty accurate with my assessments, but maybe I'm slipping. Or maybe bias has gotten the best of me, as I said. And, since we're being honest, Ramón isn't exactly the great communicator either. Neither of them has said much, and somehow their feelings grew anyway; grew and got hurt. She had plenty of reason to think she was in over her head and want to step out, and I still wonder what she would have said that night if he'd given her the chance.

Once again, I am fading. Barely there and fading. This was what I came to find out, and here's my answer. Something in Ramón anchors me. Perhaps it is the blood, perhaps a deeper element, one I'll never understand. But the fact remains: When I'm away too long, that is when I am weakest. That's when each second begins to take its toll. This is as far as I've been from him. The hospital is only a block away from his apartment. Even there, I feel it in small ways on the days I don't follow him to work, that gradual fade like the passage of time. But here, across town, I know I won't be around much longer if I linger.

I am tethered to my nephew, and without him I will vanish.

I leave Aliceana to her wild dancing.

The night suddenly feels impossibly dark and dangerous, and I wonder what I was thinking trying such a reckless experiment. Perhaps it's our shared blood that fortifies me, and whoever is in charge of these things knew better than to have me attached to Nilda.

I enter the frosty New Jersey sky as the end of day fades at the horizon. Bland apartment buildings rise around me. I sense memories trying to creep in. Painful ones; not the kind you reminisce over with friends and a swill of rum.

An empty chair.

Its emptiness carves something out of me, breaks me.

No. These are memories that wait for you to be having an off moment and then come settle into your bones, wrap their tentacles around your arteries and veins and creep along toward your heart, poisoning everything they touch.

But this is my struggle. My memories are my salvation. In their slow unraveling, I become whole again.

I'm lost. The New Jersey night seems so far away and these shards of memory so close. But without Ramón's dreams to filter them, it's hard to make them make sense. The chair is a familiar one—it's from our kitchen table. Someone should be sitting in it but they're not. There's a green cushion on its seat with a slight indentation on it. The wood is old, scuffed. That emptiness keeps carving me up. There are people nearby, but none of them know what I'm feeling, the depths of this loneliness.

I wonder if I'll ever come back, so flimsy is this curtain between my two worlds, the past and the present. And again, I am there. And again I am lost.

Something touches me. Moves me. It's jolting, a flicker of sharp light inside all my weighty depths. I look up from the empty chair and see the sky. The sky is flecked with dots of white. It pours down on me, numbers beyond comprehension, the whole night, the whole city, everything, steeped in it. The snow has nowhere to be, no memory. I'm wrapped in it, even as it passes through me, slowing slightly. I'm alive in it, even as I'm nothing of the sort. I'm awake, fully, inside the moment, and what I've left behind is no less real, still a part of me but far, far away. Snow. Everywhere. And somewhere beyond it, the ongoing footsteps of my nephew's heart thumping along, guiding me home to him.

Fading, I hurtle through the snow-speckled sky, back to Ramón.

# CHAPTER FIFTEEN

Isabel.

Not her but the empty space where she's supposed to be. That chair she always would sit in at the kitchen table, the one with the green cushion.

And maybe that's the first sign that something's not right: She's still not back.

And even though it's a brand-new day—just a few fragile months into a new year, since a whole new Cuba began dawning around us—it seems very dim somehow. Mami still sits idly at the piano, tinkling *boberías* while Papi watches image after image of the bearded men swarming across our capital and it's not so ecstatic anymore. It's a little creepy, like we've all fallen in love with a beautiful prince but it turns out he's not a prince at all, not even a person, just a beautiful sack of skin concealing a billion squirming maggots.

Nilda's been even more prickly and impossible than usual; I can't remember the last time she played music. We barely speak these days because nothing is really worth the aggravation of another stupid argument.

And while Mami's making no discernable melody on the piano keys one day and Papi's locked in his room and Nilda's off with her friends, they kill the first man on TV. We know because Cassandra starts screaming and on the television the men are saying *Paredón paredón* like it's some kind of game. We run into the room, Mami and I, and Cassandra's standing there transfixed, her mouth open. There's a blurry little shape, pale face, little mustache, dark suit, and he's standing against a wall and the voices are speaking more and more frantically, saying horrible things that he's supposed to have done, juicing up the audience, I'm sure, trying to make us thirst for his blood—but I can't distinguish between what they're saying he did and what's about to happen; it all just seems like spilled blood to me. And Mami's getting older by the second, like she can see the future and I think if we stand here any longer she'll be all hunched over and crinkly like Cassandra. Then the *pop-pop-pop* sound bursts from the television and the man crumples. He doesn't fall, he crumples, but his shadow stays upright on the wall behind him and then I realize it's his blood, not his shadow, his blood and his insides.

I'm staring at the screen and it's all just so many gray and black dots and then it re-forms into a man on the ground and he's moving still. He's living the last seconds of his life far away from his family and in front of the whole nation. Cassandra collapses into a chair, gasping, and Mami just walks away, mumbling. And Isabel's nowhere to be found, she's gone, an empty spot at the table, not there to wake up late at night when I'm feeling broken or terrified, not there to make fun of Nilda for making fun of me. Gone.

Isabel knew something.

Mami won't speak to me, too wrapped in her grief, so I walk out the door, yell something nonsensical because I don't even bother lying about where I'm going anymore. And it's one of those warm Cuban afternoons in Las Colinas just after the rain, the sun is close to us: A friend, not some distant space thing, and it paints sparkly light shows across the puddles in the torn-up pavement where the tanks passed through.

Isabel knew this was coming. It was written all over her face that day: While the rest of the country thundered with bliss, she held back. She'd always been a little reserved, but then, the moment of our greatest collective triumph, as soldiers streamed past and the whole of La Habana poured into the streets around us—for her to be so quiet. She saw something, during those long nights sneaking from building to building, hiding out, and running for her life. Something more than what she told me.

I have to find her again.

No one else understands, we're all too shell-shocked, but Isabel and I shared something that January day and she needs someone she can talk to. Or I need to be talked to. Either way, I have to find her. The need is sudden and certain and it overtakes me. School's been out for months while the revolution reorganizes itself into a bureaucracy, no one's checking on anyone except everyone's checking on everyone. Already, people are careful what they say around each other, you can feel it, something in the air.

Without realizing where I'm going, I find myself in front of the cathedral and I wander inside. Padre Sebastián, of course. He found her for me once, surely he can do it again. Anyway, he always knows how to make sense of things that don't, always has that calm Go With God easiness about him. But when I walk into his office, the books are all down from the shelves, the pictures down from the walls, and Padre Sebastián himself is standing on a chair, trying to unscrew the great white Christ on the wall behind his desk.

Padre Sebastián sighs the word *mierda* and slumps his shoulders.

*¿Padre?* I say. He turns around and gives me a look so raw and heartbreaking I think I might burst into tears right then and I have no idea why. Then he carefully gets down from the chair and says, *No.*

*What do you mean,* no? I demand. I'm in no mood to be told no. I'm furious, in fact, suddenly in full angry adolescence and that simple word has sent a fire welling up inside of me.

Padre Sebastián sees it and smiles, puts up two conciliatory hands, palms out and sits. *No Padre,* he says. He's not a priest anymore. There are no priests anymore. No church, no religion. No God Almighty, thanks to our brand-new revolution. For a second I think Padre . . . No. Not-Padre Sebastián might cry, but then he smiles instead. Then he asks me what's wrong. He looks tired. It's the first time I've seen the man with a five-o'clock shadow and his eyes have bags underneath them.

I tell him I want to see my sister and he laughs. It's a hoarse, terrible laugh that says Sebastián is fighting harder than he ever has had to to beat back the bitterness. I frown. My whole body must be frowning, because when he looks up at me he looks startled, stands back up, crosses over to me, and hugs me. At first, I admit it, I think something might be about to happen. *Something* something. He is, after all, not a priest anymore.

There's no more God, no religion, so: no rules. Right? So, break open the gates of hell and let the sinners and saints rejoice as one, no? So, perhaps my afternoon finger grinding had been a prayer all along, and just before God became nothing He saw fit to send me the answer to my prayers, literally. Maybe to make up for all this other horrible shit He's sent our way.

Or maybe the answer to my prayers was really just the most tightest, most genuine hug I've ever gotten from a man that I love in a way I could never explain. I suppose God gives you what you need, not what you want, but still . . . I'm halfway through all those thoughts when I realize Sebastián is crying, just a little bit. He gets it together before he pulls out of the hug though, wipes his eyes and apologizes and I shrug it off because really, I'm moved to the point of not knowing what to say. Then he says he wants to see Isabel too, that she always knew how to make sense of this terrible world and this world is about as terrible as he's ever seen, but still—he doesn't want me to get involved. And it occurs to me that they were pretty good friends somehow, that Sebastián was in deeper with the resistance than I'd realized.

*You do know where she is, don't you*, I say before I can stop myself, and I realize I'm furious.

He blinks at me and his silence is a yes.

*Then why?* I yell, and we both cringe, because no one yells anymore. Not unless they're at a rally. Yelling, any loud noises, draws attention, and surely, one way or another, you're breaking one of the new edicts of this freshly born Triumphant Revolution, which is so all powerful that even the tiniest infractions apparently can collapse it, so we all must be so vigilant, which means we all must be as quiet and unobtrusive as possible.

*Why*, I say again once it's clear no one is about to barge through the door. I say it more quietly this time but also more emphatically. *Why won't you tell me where she is?*

*I . . .* he starts.

*She's my sister!* A shrill whisper.

He looks around that half-packed office and scratches his thick black hair. Picks a book out from one of the boxes—*Las vidas de los santos*—and hands it to me.

I've seen this before. No. I devoured it, more than once. I know exactly where it used to sit on his shelf. It was within grabbing distance of the chair in front of his desk and there are pictures, so when I would be in here waiting for him or wasting time, it's what I would grab. Half-naked bodies writhe and contort and anguished eyes glare at the heavens. Spears, arrows, swords puncture pale, muscular limbs. Loose cloths barely conceal breasts, penises, butts. They imply, perfectly, they suggest. And I surged through the pages—one of the only books I cared more about the illustrations of than the words—and I imagined and wondered and imagined more. Sometimes with Padre Sebastián's face.

Sometimes I'd read the stories as well, but honestly they took too long to get juicy compared to the pictures. Those beautiful, suffering men and women, offering up their agony and those firm, supple bodies as an obscene kind of gift. *What kind of God demands such oversexual acrobatics of his acolytes?* I wondered. And then I imagined some more.

But now I have no time for theology or desire, and no interest in Sebastián's well-meaning sermons, so I hurl the book at him and scream, yes scream: *¡Me cago en los santos, coño!* And he jumps out of the way maybe a little too fast, because he ends up crashing into a stack of books and they crash into another and then Sebastián is looking up at me from a pile of tattered Bibles on the floor.

There is a pause in which I can't believe what I've just said, what I've done. And then we both burst out laughing. We're also crying some by the time we finally stop and I feel terrible but also amazing for the first time in so long, and I'm about to ask him what it is he wanted to tell me about the saints when he brushes himself off, whispers a curse, and tells me to come with him.

We hop in his old putt-putt car—the church's actually but Sebastián's the only one who knows how to drive and anyway, I suppose it belongs to the revolution now, whatever that is.

We speed through La Habana, along the Malecón and into the old city. There's soldiers everywhere, everywhere and a group of them flag us down outside the Gran Teatro. Sebastián's tense, and I wonder why, considering we're not doing anything wrong, but then I think back on what he'd said earlier and I realize we may very well be carrying some contraband. What if he's already joined the counterrevolutionaries and so has Isabel and he's bringing her arms? And is it still called a counter-revolution if the revolution wins? Doesn't it just become a revolution then? Does it matter? The rebels, or soldiers, or whatever they are keep asking Sebastián the same three questions over and over, who he is, where he's going, and who I am, and each time they ask it like they've caught him in a lie even though he's said the same thing each time. I'm trying to ignore them, playing games with the impossibilities of language and revolution in my head, but the questions get louder and louder and I can feel them looking at me, their eyes on my bare legs beneath my skirt and I want Sebastián to just speed away even though I know that means they'd kill him, kill us both probably, so instead I just look out the window and wonder if something could be a counter-counterrevolution and what color uniforms they would wear and where they'd hide . . .

Finally it seems like they're going to let us go but then the head guy asks to see what's in the trunk. Sebastián hesitates for a split second and in that moment I know, I know, I know that yes, there are weapons in the trunk, which means we're both going to die, probably on TV, our insides splattered in a dark gray across the wall and the voices of a hundred angry witnesses screaming *Paredón* fading in our ears.

The soldiers see it too and they hurry around to the back of the car without waiting for an answer, because really, that moment's hesitation was all the answer they need. I realize I'm clenching my whole body, every muscle I have, as if I could somehow crawl into myself and disappear. Sebastián's just staring straight ahead and I close my eyes and hear the trunk pop open and cringe deeper into myself and wonder if they'll arrest us or just shoot us right here and now, which I think I'd maybe prefer, and then they walk back around to the window and say, Okay, we can go on, buenas tardes.

And we putt-putt off and I exhale what feels like my entire life in a single breath. When my legs finally stop shaking a few minutes later, I look over at Sebastián but he doesn't say anything, doesn't look back at me. He just looks angry, angry like he wants to kill someone angry, and I think if he speaks fire will come out, enough fire to even topple a mountain like Papi and keep burning, burning till the whole city is leveled and smoldering.

❉

Ramón rises, writes the sprawling dream out over five scribbly pages in his journal, and then makes a hearty breakfast. He's off work for the second day in a row and I can see his whole mind is music, the beats churn through his head as he finishes his scrambled eggs and sausage. He's not looking at anything in particular, occasionally mumbling a line from the María Teresa Vera song and then beatboxing, stopping, repeating.

"You're sort of like an idiot savant," Adina announces. She's standing in the kitchen, looking fresh and regal in those silky black pajamas and staring at Ramón.

"How long have you been standing there?"

"Like, an hour, man."

"No!"

"Okay, maybe five minutes, but still: dude."

"Yeah. I'm trying to get that piece finished by tonight so I can play it in my set. At least a demo."

"The one Kacique sent you?"

"Yeah."

"You sure that's a good idea?"

"Yeah. Why not?"

"You bringing that coffee or nah?" a voice calls from Adina's room.

Ramón perks up. "Oh. Don't let me keep you."

"Wouldn't think of it," Adina says. She fills two cups from the cafetera and disappears. A sultry R&B song bumps out from behind her closed door and Ramón rolls his eyes, grinning to himself. He picks up his own coffee, brings it with him to his own lady-in-waiting, albeit a colder, grayer one, and is about to settle in when his cell phone blips to life, all flashing lights and manic drumming. It's a blocked number.

"Yes?"

"Ramón, Alberto."

"I don't remember giving you my phone number."

"You didn't."

"I see. Perhaps that was for a reason."

"Well, anyway, I'm well, thank you for asking. I'm calling on behalf of my grandfather."

"How nice for you."

"He wants to know if you've considered his proposal."

"I have."

"And?"

"And what?"

A pause, where Ramón and I both imagine Alberto to be silently cursing and gesticulating violence at his phone. "And what did you decide, Ramón?"

"Oh, I haven't yet."

Another pause. Slightly more ominous for no discernible reason. "I see," Alberto finally says. He sounds exhausted suddenly, like he can't even be bothered with all these games anymore. "Well, he'd like to have an answer by tonight. Someone'll be in touch, Ramón."

And the call cuts off before Ramón can muster up a comeback. He rolls his eyes, puts on his headphones.

I pass several hours being perfectly still, watching Ramón fidget and fuss with the rhythm strips and dancing guitar riffs, while a few more Cuban tracks download at an achingly slow pace. Those old-time recordings are tricky, I'm sure. Seems Señorita Vera played in her own time signature, pausing and slowing slightly down whenever she felt the song called for it, so Ramón has to get meticulous to make it all click. I remember Nilda pausing dramatically at the end of each chorus as the final couplet repeated itself and we'd all sing it together, then fall out laughing.

Sometime around two he walks out into the kitchen for lunch and finds Corinna sitting at the table in Adina's bathrobe, eating a sandwich.

"Oh," Ramón says too quickly to make it sound warm.

Corinna raises her eyebrows. "Oh?"

"I didn't know you were here. Hey." He's still a little ditzed out from being in the beats and melodies zone for the past couple hours.

"That's it?" Corinna demands with a sly smile. "Hey. The fuck's wrong with you, Ramón? Gimme a hug."

He does, not totally sure if he's supposed to or not considering all the back and forth. "Sorry, I'm all caught up in a song."

"Adina mentioned. You gonna play it tonight?"

"Think so. You coming?"

"That's the plan."

"Hey, Ramón." Adina emerges from her room looking, quite frankly, well fucked. "You make me a sandwich too?"

"Naw," Corinna says. "You were sleeping."

"Oh good, then I can have the rest of yours." She swipes the half-eaten sandwich up and makes like she's gonna take off with it before Corinna grabs her and hefts her into her lap.

"Not so fast, girly. We can share."

Ramón chooses to block them out, retrieves a container of Chinese leftovers, and plops in front of the TV, letting his mind go blank to the cawing of telenovela oblivion.

# CHAPTER SIXTEEN

The club is full tonight. The crowd is usually mostly Cuban and Jerseyite, but folks have congregated from all over the tristate area, lured by a winking write-up in last week's *Village Voice* proclaiming North Jersey the new "Havana-flavored" Brooklyn and Luis's club, La Paz, its cultural epicenter. Ramón, or DJ Taza, as he's known, got a special shout-out for his "innovative, edgy, and Latin-tinged" skills. He rises to the occasion, sending up a furious dirty grind of thump-thumping and clack-clacking that has the crowd at full tilt.

Sliding along beneath his skin, feeling those raucous vibrations bounce through him and then back out again, I see that there is not so much space between the orchestra in my sister's hands and the one her son unleashes out of his turntables.

With his left hand, Ramón spins a record and then scratches it to a halt as the other one rotates around to the spot he wants. The beat trundles along beneath, gathering, rising, and then Ramón drops the needle and an urgent attack of electric guitar cackles out, exploding over the drums. Then the beat gets even heavier and so does the guitar, and sure, in sound alone, they are worlds away from my sister's tinkling piano, but the rhythm and melody swerve together in the air, swaying above the dancers just as those notes shimmered and swooped above our heads as we clacked over those linoleum kitchen tiles. And the dancers, entranced, respond, lovingly drawing closer together, closer to Ramón, filling the room with their unabashed revelry.

I take the opportunity to slip into the back room, where Luis Cavalcón holds court over his nightly domino game along with a couple other old heads from the neighborhood. It's tantalizing, how familiar the man seems. But I can't find him in the scattered shreds of my memory. I study that lumpy nose, the half-closed eyes, and billowing gray hair, trying to reconstruct it backward into a younger version. An elaborate mermaid tattoo covers his left arm. Her body twists out of an explosion of waves and crustaceans; her head's turned away, toward some unseen shore. Luis grunts as he plops another ficha on the board, smiles almost imperceptibly.

I got nothing; just the same gnawing certainty I've known him before. I'm close, my breathy nothingness just a few centimeters from his face, and at one point he looks up from the dominoes and right at me and I freeze. Does he see me? Does he understand something I don't? Hold a missing piece somehow? His eyes open wide momentarily and then droop back to their normal sleepy-looking state. Luis goes back to the domino game, grumbling to himself.

"¿Qué te pasa, Luis?" one of the other old guys asks.

"Nada." Luis waves him off gruffly. "No pasa nada."

Nothing didn't happen. Which means something happened. Well, in English something happened. In Spanish, nothing happened even more emphatically. I choose to take the English meaning, double-negative be damned, because I know something did happen.

Something.

I just don't know what.

A collective hurrah explodes from the club and I follow the men in to see what the fuss is about. It's Ramón's new track, intertwining guitar riffs over sneaky beats. The crowd is going nuts and I'm flushed with pride for my nephew. The old men, less impressed, parade back to their domino game but I remain, taking in all the warm collision of bodies and minds that's floating up from the dancers, filling the thick, sweaty club air.

Ramón sends the song off into a record-scratch improv over a shimmering jazz beat. Marcos pitter-patters along beneath him, punctuating with a soft bolero rhythm on the congas. People are going nuts and it's beautiful to watch, right up until the music cuts off. A groan rises up from the crowd; everyone looks around irritably and then the lights come on. It's like jumping out of a warm bath into a cold, rainy day. The club fluorescents burn into squinting faces.

Marcos looks up at Ramón. Ramón shrugs, tries to see past the glare toward the sound booth to find out what's going on. Christian, the sound guy, looks as confused as everyone else though, and he shakes his head at Ramón.

I spread myself. It's nothing I do often because it leaves me groggy and shakes my already fragile sense of self. But I'm curious. And, quite frankly, pissed. I was enjoying the music and if this is what I think it is, well . . . I fill the room with myself. Everything is a little less precise, a little glazed over but I can see the whole club, a global perspective that seems to waver slightly like the world is breathing against it. I'm in the corner next to a sleeping teenager who snuck in with a fake ID and drank more than he could handle. I'm in the middle of the dance floor beside a gorgeous couple in their thirties, still holding each other, still caked with each other's sweat, still breathless with the rhythmic grinding they were deep into when the music died. I'm behind the bartender, an ornery, beautiful matancera who's just about had it with these over-capacity nights and going straight to her day job at the accounting firm.

It's all very benign. I'm about to spring back into my more focused self when I notice the doorway down to the basement. It's ajar. It's never ajar. I'm all in one, collected back into myself and hurtling through the sweat-thick air toward the basement door. But my flow is jacked up from spreading so thin. I keep feeling I've left parts of myself behind, only to spin around and get caught in my own ether. By the time I reach the door, Luis has just stormed through it and Ramón is close behind.

Down a narrow stairwell into a narrower passageway. Luis clicks on the light but it's dim and fragmented, just an open bulb. Up ahead, there's a clattering noise and scattered footsteps. I'm recovered, some-what, and I flush forward, through the gooey thickness of Ramón and then Luis, trying to ignore how familiar he smells, and down the cor-ridor, around a corner, up a small flight of stairs to where a tall guy in a black ski mask is fumbling with the padlocked door. The door leads out onto the streets. The man has a tool kit and an expanding billy club and I have not one single doubt that he's one of the Gutierrez family asswipes.

I congregate my entire being on the padlock. His gloved fingers cover me and I focus myself, allow the first hints of physicality into my being. It shouldn't take much. Disrupting things is pretty easy and I only need a few seconds. He's panting now and his desperation makes him even sloppier, but still he manages to slide the heavy metal bar upright and it'll only take a good tug to pull the thing across the door and break free. Without thinking about it or even really meaning to, I thrust my focus even harder into my hands, my face.

And I appear.

I'm not fully formed, I'm sure; probably just a shimmering, shadowy visage. But it's enough. The man's eyes go wide and he screams at the pair of bluish ghostly hands over his. Then he looks up, glimpses my face, and loses his mind.

He's wailing and slamming his weight against the locked door when Luis and Ramón get to him. "Who the fuck are you?" Luis demands, and I see he is a warrior. Old and hunched over somewhat but still solid in body and fierce in mind and spirit. There's no doubt he's killed men; he's faced his own death more than once. He's certainly willing to again. Possibly right now. I wonder. Ramón stands behind him, less solid in determination but perfectly still and threatening if only for how massive he is.

"The face . . . The . . . !" the intruder whines. "The fingers!"

"The hell is he talking about?" Ramón says.

Luis steps in with one foot and backhands the guy across the face.

He stops writhing and slides to the floor, holding his cheek. Finally he looks up at Luis and it's clear the threat of a solid beatdown overtakes what surely must've been a cruel trick of his terrified mind. Surely. "Ah! Lemme go, man. I didn't do nothing."

"Said the man in the motherfucking ski mask. You gotta be kidding me, son." Luis's accent gets thicker with the thrill of imminent combat. He raises his arm for another blow, but the guy in the mask cowers.

"Don't! Don't! I'm with Gutierrez!"

Luis sighs and rips off the guy's mask. He's not one of the ones that battered on my nephew, which is almost too bad, because I'd love to see them cornered and terrified. No, this is probably one of the brainier guys they keep around for lower impact sabotage like cutting the power to the DJ booth at a nightclub. Pathetic.

"Comemierda," Luis says. He hocks something atrocious from his lungs and releases it on the guy. "What's your name?"

"Pancho."

"First or last?"

"It's just my name!"

"Alright! ¡Ya con esa mierda! Put him in the room." A couple of Luis's heavies shuffle past Ramón and scoop up Pancho and escort him down the corridor and through a door.

"What you think?" Ramón asks as he and Luis pick up the scattered tools and knapsack.

Luis shrugs as I flush past him. "La misma mierda."

"But . . . why? Why tonight?"

"Well, I guess we just have to find out."

# CHAPTER SEVENTEEN

Pancho's already taken a couple of hits when we get there. Nothing serious, he's not even bleeding, but sweat pours down his face and he shivers like a fixless addict. Clearly, this kid doesn't get sent into high-pressure situations very often.

"Why you fuckin' with my club, son?"

"I—" Cadiz the bouncer baps him hard across the face and Pancho makes an *oomf* sound and spits out blood. "The fuck was that for? I was answering!"

"Incentive to answer correctly." Luis shrugs.

"You act all tough but you can't do shit, really. We both know who I work for. You're not going to—" Luis nods at Cadiz and Cadiz wraps his huge arms around Pancho's neck.

"Gutierrez can only do something if they find the body. ¿Me entiendes?"

Pancho nods, gasping. Cadiz lets him go.

"The song," Pancho says, catching his breath. "The one with the rap."

Luis shoots a look at Ramón, who raises his eyebrows and shrugs his shoulders. "What about it?"

"The rapper, Tranq 7." A friend of Kacique's whose words Ramón had laced smoothly in and out of the song yesterday afternoon.

"Yes?"

"He's Cuban."

"We're all Cuban, you piece of dogshit."

"No, he's Cuban from Cuba. Todavía. He hasn't left yet."

Everyone takes a step back. "This is true, Ramón?"

"Yes," Ramón says very quietly. "A friend sent it to me. We've been collaborating through an online forum."

"Shh!" Luis snaps. "Say no more." Cadiz, Ramón, and Pancho are all staring at the old man. Strangely, I have to suppress an urge to hug him. It welled up out of nowhere, an unrelenting tenderness that I have no basis for or understanding of. I shrug it off till it simmers and I can ignore it.

"Jus' so I understand: Your Cuban boss sent you here to fuck with my Cuban club because my Cuban DJ is playing music made by a Cuban, but only the last Cuban part matters, because he is still on the island, and we are not. Is that correct?" There's no way Luis is as incredulous as his voice would have you believe. He's been well aware of the Gutierrezes' extremist political machine and all its associated felonious mischief. He's seen them at work, probably rivaled them for years now. I suspect he's tolerated it this long mostly for self-preservation reasons, and it's probably never come this close to his doorstep before.

"Support for Cuba is support for the regime. You know thi—" Luis himself delivers the blow this time, and it's not gentle. Pancho shakes off the shock and spits out a tooth.

"Don't tell me what I know, traitor."

Things just got serious. *Traitor* is not a word that people who've lived through a revolution use lightly. It's a life-and-death word. And there's fire in Luis's eyes. "You don't get to tell me"—he steps in, raising a fist, and Pancho cringes—"what I know!" Before he can hit, Ramón puts a hand on the old man's shoulder.

"Luis," Ramón says softly. "Wait." The veil of rage lifts some from Luis's eyes. He steps back, visibly struggling to control himself. "Wait," Ramón says again. He steps in front of Luis, looking down directly into Pancho's eyes. "How did you know?"

"What?"

"How did you know I was playing the song tonight?"

"What do you mean?"

Now it's Ramón's turn to get all up in the guy's face, a whole other righteous fury burning through him. "I mean, I only told two, maybe three people I was going to play this song, and you don't know any of them. I've been working on it all day. The only . . . way . . ." Ramón straightens back up, towering over Pancho. "... you could know ..." He's looking up now, putting all the pieces together. Then he looks back down. "You hacked me."

Cadiz sees what's about to happen before anyone else. He's been standing behind Pancho, watching silently, and now he stares at Ramón's face, watches that flicker of rage dance across his eyes and he moves fast, toppling Pancho out of the way and throwing himself forward, catching Ramón just as he explodes. "You fucking hacked into my computer, you piece of shit! You ..." Ramón is swinging, flailing, gasping, and finally panting and stepping away, getting himself together.

When he's calmed he looks at Cadiz and they exchange a nod. Ramón, catching his breath, turns back to Pancho, who's gotten up and sat back in his chair without having to be told to. "How?"

Pancho opens his mouth, closes it again.

"Don't answer. I want to ... I want to talk to Gutierrez."

"He's with the car, a few blocks away."

"No. Not the pipsqueak irrelevant nieto Gutierrez. I want to talk to the elder Gutierrez. You'll bring me to him."

"Wait." It's Luis. He's been simmering by the wall, watching and listening. Plotting, I imagine. When Ramón looks back at him he nods to the door and they step out into the corridor. "I think we might have a play here, if we move cautiously."

"Oh?"

"I don't know this Pancho character, but from what I gather of him, he's not particularly dedicated to any cause but himself."

Ramón peers back into the room. Pancho is sweating and blabbing to Cadiz about baseball. Cadiz just frowns at him. "I could see that."

"He's not a radical or revolutionary. He's just some poor comemierda trying to get paid and not killed."

"So?"

"So, clearly Gutierrez is coming for you. Or me. Us, most likely, for one reason or another. If we go and try to knock heads tonight, first of all, we lose the battle, because he outnumbers us in strength and political pull, not to mention dollar for dollar. Second of all, we lose the war because here we have what could possibly be our one advantage in this entire situation."

"Pancho?"

"Eso mismo." Luis is excited, alive with the joy of some espionage and strategy in what must be something of a dull existence compared to whatever chapter of the war he lived through in Cuba. "We make Pancho our own and así they don't suspect you know you are being watched and they don't estop watching you."

"You mean let them keep hacking my computer, reading my emails, all that?"

"Jus' for a little while, Ramón. Jus' long enough for us to set a trap and flush them out."

Ramón frowns. "What I should really do is call in an ass-whupping from my mom, but I would never do that."

Luis arches an eyebrow. "Who's your mom?"

"Alberto's godmother. He can't say no to her. But I'm not bringing my mom into this. I was just kidding. Keep going."

"Look, I know not doing anything for now isn't a fun prospect from your end. But really, how many emails do you send? Who do you really talk to on the email, Ramón?"

"That's not the point."

"I know. But I want to know what kind of plot is afoot and this is our one and only way to find out."

Ramón grumbles a little and finally nods. "But you keep me informed every step of the way."

"Claro que sí."

"You gonna rough him up anymore?"

"No." Luis wiggles his big eyebrows. "We need him to be our friend now. Change in estrategy."

"I see."

He winks and pats Ramón on the back a little too hard. "Go home, chico. Get some rest. I'll call you in the morning."

Ramón walks back into the club amidst an unexpected swirl of music. Corinna has taken the stage. She looks radiant in the spotlight with a silky scarf around her neck and a flimsy sleeveless top. And she's singing. Marcos is laying down another smooth bolero beat and some old cat from the back room brought up his guitar and Corinna is belting out "Stormy Monday" in a raspy, unafraid voice that makes you want to just sit down and sulk about something. The audience is mesmerized.

Ramón finds Adina, who's dabbing away tears again, and stands beside her while the song unfolds, rises, and gathers momentum around them and then crashes down into a perfect bluesy finale. "I'm such a mess," Adina whimpers when it's over. "What the fuck is wrong with me?"

Ramón puts an arm around her. "Can't really blame you. That girl got magic in her mouth."

"You have no idea."

They bundle into Adina's Volkswagen, bracing against the cold. Corinna rides shotgun and Ramón and Marcos huddle in the back with the congas. At home, they drift off to their respective bedrooms after some quiet simmering over beers and anecdotes, the strangeness of all that just went down at the club. Ramón crawls into bed, curls up, and tries not to let Aliceana be the last thought he has before he passes out.

And me? I take in the length of this strange day and night, the strange thrill of recognizing someone who I don't recognize, and the echoes of that squirming madness—the feeling of being watched, listened to, surveilled. That dirtiness that overtakes you, that sense of violation. I remember it.

I try to shake it off and then begin to unspool a moment of my own life as I slide into place within Ramón's rising and falling chest.

# CHAPTER EIGHTEEN

Isabel, in the flesh.

But only barely. *They got Gómez*, she says as soon as she opens the door to her new hideaway, which looks remarkably like her old one: an apartment high up in one of those Vedado towers, somehow empty feeling even while it's cluttered with supplies, boxes, nightmares. I'm still shook up from our encounter at the checkpoint a few hours earlier, still feeling like the sky might collapse around me at any moment. The old Isabel would've seen the whole thing spilled across my face immediately and forced me to tell her all about it till I felt better. This Isabel doesn't hug me or even seem surprised to see me. Doesn't even register Sebastián, which either means he's been coming around a lot or she's just too far gone to care.

*They showed up at his house and just snatched him up*, she tells us, ushering us in with a nervous glance down the dusty corridor. Gómez the butcher. Gómez, who handed me the too-heavy chicken. Gómez, who gave up everything he had for the revolution, Isabel explains without even offering coffee or cold ration food or a seat or anything. Gómez, who risked his life, left his family's house in Las Colinas to go fight in the Sierra Maestra and then the Escambray. Who took three bullets during an ambush against the guardia and then limped along, watching in horror as the holes in him became gray and then black with gangrene, gulped back antibiotics until there weren't any, and then suffered in silence in the rebel campamientos because if he returned to his home he'd be killed. Gómez, whose sister they killed when they found out he'd joined the rebels. Gómez, who'd gone nearly insane with grief when he found out, who they had to restrain to keep him from rushing straight into La Habana all by himself on some crazed suicide revenge mission.

Gómez.

He'd brought Isabel in, talking to her about the revolution every day when she came to pick up the meat and then when she'd started asking her own questions about it, giving her pamphlets and eventually linking her up with contacts in the La Habana resistance groups. Las Colinas had become a safe transfer point for weapons and information between the guerrillas in the mountains and the Student Directorate in the city, thanks mostly to Gómez and his network of rebel sympathizers.

And now he is a prisoner of the very regime he'd helped sweep to power. Probably dead. And maybe that's for the best. Isabel finally looks up from her monologue, sees me. I think maybe she'll cry again, like she did that day just a few months ago in this same apartment, when the whole world was different and so much the same, on the brink of that great sea change that we're all still reeling from. But she doesn't. She's past all that. She only holds my eye contact for a few precious seconds, this beautiful woman that I will always want to be like, and then she's off and pacing again, as Sebastián and I watch helplessly from the doorway.

She's mumbling about responsibility and guilt. Guilt and responsibility. She won't stop. Sebastián just shakes his head and I walk to the balcony and look out over Vedado. The city is a rippling splatter of pastiche and crumble around and below me, and the unforgiving sea around that. The Malecón will never look the same again, now that I've seen it in the thralls of victory and overrun with a hundred thousand people listening to that man speak for hours on end. It was like he was competing with the ocean itself, who could last longer, and even when he finished he was still never done, it was just a temporary break to catch his breath. The ocean always wins, of course, but still, we're all living in fear and Gómez has been captured. And who knows who else?

It dawns on me, as my own heart fractures at this betrayal, that whatever disappointment and terror I'm feeling must be a hundred times worse for my sister, who fought so hard to make this terrible moment possible. I'm still grasping it all, but she's seen it rot from the inside out.

What do you do when you've already torn down the world to make a better one and the better one turns out to be just as rotten as the one you shattered?

I ask her what she's going to do, mostly because I can't stand the constant muttering. She looks at Sebastián and he shakes his head. *Luchar.*

You shatter the world all over again, I suppose. And keep breaking it until you get one you can name Freedom.

She says it so simply and even with that one word some of the color returns to her face, she stands up a little straighter. *Seguir luchando.* Keep fighting.

✳

Ramón sits up in bed and frowns at his computer. It's catching up to him, the dreams, Old Gutierrez's tightening noose, Aliceana. It's catching up to me too, in a whole other way. In the corner, I fortify myself from the toll the night and its dreams have taken, and brace myself for what the day will bring.

Before Ramón had left the club last night, Luis took him aside and told him not to do anything differently than he normally would. The key to successful counterespionage, Luis said with a twinkle in his eyes, is to not let the other team know you know what they're up to—so you can then reverse it and use it to annihilate them. Ramón had nodded, furrowing his brow.

Now his laptop seems to be staring back at him, an open window. He leaps out of bed and slams the screen closed, grumbles something about Luis, and crawls back into bed. The journal's on his bedside table and he picks it up and idles through the pages till he gets to a blank one and begins to write. Someone's clinking around in the kitchen by the time he finishes, dishes are being put away, and butter is frying on the skillet. Ramón sits up a little more, thumbs back a few pages, humming to himself. I don't think he'd ever read any of the entries up till now, just scribbled them out quickly as he remembered and then gone about his business. But something now has his attention.

Still staring at the book, Ramón fumbles for a cigarette from his bedside table. When there isn't one to be found he looks up, irritated, and picks up his phone instead.

"Ramón?" Adina's voice comes from the other side of his door.

"Yeah?"

"We're cooking breakfast, you want?"

"Absolutely."

He pushes a button on his phone and holds it up to his ear.

"¿Diga?" says a voice that still makes me cringe inside. I'll make sense of this rage one day. I know I will.

"Hola, Mami."

"Ay, cariño. ¿Cómo andas, mi amor?"

"Fine, Mami. Listen, do you remember any of the priests from back in Las Colinas?"

"Of course, there was Padre Eugenio, he always did the Sunday Mass when we were little and . . ."

"Any others?"

A pause, in which I imagine my sister taking off her glasses, rubbing her eyes, and then putting them back on, leaning her elbow on the immaculate kitchen table and massaging one of her temples, noticing a stain, getting up for some cleanser spray and a paper towel.

"Mami?"

"¿Qué, mi vida?"

"I asked you something?"

"Oh, just a minute, Ramón." She's wiping down the table, I'm sure, and then spraying some more, wiping in concentric circles, watching the horrible stain become shiny pure tabletop again, and then making the circles wider and wider till the whole table is shiny and perfect, untouched, immaculate. "Okay, what did you want to know again?"

"Other priests. From Las Colinas?"

"Oh, there was the young one. ¿Cómo se llamaba? Ay, no me acuerdo."

"Sebastián?"

"Yes! That's right. Why do you ask, cariño?"

"Was wondering. I saw Tío Pepe the other day, we were talking about it, is all."

"Ramón, please don't go stirring up trouble with the family."

"He said he misses you—he wants to see you."

"Ay pero vive allá en casa del carajo, m'ijo . . . imagínate." Nilda says this as if him living any closer to what she considers civilization would make a damn difference. She's not leaving the house and she knows it.

Ramón sighs.

"You know, I've told you that people and their memories can be delicate things," Nilda says. "Are you coming over for dinner tonight? Your father wants to see you."

"Sure."

"Okay. Pernil and arroz con frijoles, okay? Okay. Besos."

Click.

Ramón looks at his phone, probably wondering if it's bugged. He growls, puts it on the bedside table, and shuffles into the kitchen for breakfast.

✳

There's a Mexican girl causing something of an uproar in the psych ER. It's odd because she herself is barely moving, has barely said three words since they wheeled her in, but she's sixteen and just shy of three hundred and fifty pounds and covered in blood from a half-assed cry for help. Ramón watches from his post while a battalion of doctors and orderlies stands around her, asking useless questions. Most of them have that bored and skeptical look, but one, a white guy with a fading head of hair and too many pens in his lab coat pockets, is really pushing the *we feel for you* routine.

"Do you want to talk about it, Catalina?" he asks. "Such a pretty name: Catalina."

She shakes her head, looks like she's considering stabbing him with one of those many pens of his, and then she just shuts her eyes and pouts her lips. "The cuts on your arm aren't very deep, Catalina. Maybe

119

you didn't want to kill yourself, is that possible? That you just wanted to maybe hurt yourself a little, or maybe that you felt like you needed to send a message, that that was the only way you know how? Is that what happened, Catalina?"

"Catalina, do you want to hurt yourself or anybody else?" an older doctor demands. He's projecting how unimpressed he is as loud as possible so there's no misunderstandings: *I am not impressed*, his whole slouched body screams. *Don't think I will be either. Seen it all before.*

Catalina stays quiet, frowning, her eyes squeezed shut.

"Do you want to talk to a counselor?" the first doctor says. "Everybody from school is really worried about you, Catalina."

"Alright, we're done here," Unimpressed says. With a sweep of his head he's called off the team and they clamor away leaving only the concerned one with the fwoompy hair behind.

"No, they're not," Catalina says, very very quietly.

Dr. Concerned gets all close, triumphant now that he's had such a quick breakthrough just by lingering behind. "What'd you say?"

"People from my school. They're not worried about me."

"Oh, that's not true. They are. They're very worried."

"No. They hate me."

It's stated so plainly it becomes a fact. Dr. Concerned knows any way he tries to refute it will be shut down immediately. But that doesn't stop him. "I'm sure they don't hate you, Catalina. I know kids can be cruel sometimes, can tease people that they don't understand or that don't look like them. Is that what happens at school?"

"Yes."

"But you know why a lot of them do that? Because they're afraid. Yeah. Or because they don't understand things, you know?"

She's staring straight ahead at a spot just past Ramón. "Would you take off these restraints, please?"

"Well, Catalina, before I do that, I need to be sure you're not going to try to hurt yourself or anyone else, okay?"

"I'm not. That was stupid, I don't know what I was thinking."

"Catalina."

"Really." She finally looks at him. It's not a desperate face, not pleading or vulnerable. In fact, it's almost like she borrowed it from Dr. Unimpressed; she even has the sleepy lids and one raised eyebrow. Like she has an uncanny ability to instantly reproduce other people's facial expressions.

I think that seals it. If she'd tried to go all simpery he might've held out some glint of professional skepticism, might've pushed her just a little further, but the confident, arrogant, even sneer that she just flashed? Finishes off any last resistance Dr. Concerned has. "Ramón?"

Ramón gets up and crosses to Catalina's stretcher. "Whatsup?"

"You can go ahead and undo Ms. Ramirez's restraints." Ramón gets to work on the first one. "Wait." He stops, looks at the doctor. "Catalina."

"Yes?"

"I'm very serious about this. I'm doing you a favor here. I'm trusting you. And I'd appreciate it if you would respect that when we take these restraints off, okay?"

Catalina nods, closes her eyes, and takes a deep breath. Nods again. "Okay, Doctor. I understand."

"Alright, Ramón."

Ramón unbuckles one strap, then the other, and then stands back. Catalina winds up and decks the doctor so hard across the face he's actually lifted into the air and flies a few feet backward before sprawling out on the linoleum floor.

"Gah! Bitch!" he yells through a broken nose. Ramón is supposed to tackle the girl, but she's still on her stretcher. He's supposed to get the restraints back on her, but she's got her fists up, boxer style, ready for him. "What are you doing?" the doctor sputters. "Tie her back down, goddammit!"

"Post three," Ramón says into his radio. "I have a ten-six red, repeat ten-six red."

Catalina cackles, waving her arms around like she's an airplane and screaming: "Ten-six, bitches! Ten-six! Come the fuck get me, you tawdry putos! You think I give a fuck? I don't! Not one single fuck, you little cunt hairs!"

"Listen," Ramón says, one hand up, face straining to look reasonable. "There's about to be like ten guys in here holding you down and they're gonna medicate you and the more you fight, the more of a pain in the ass it's gonna be."

"Go ahead, you fucking perverts! Watch me give a fuck. Watch."

"Catalina." Ramón takes a step toward her and she chucks one of the restraints at him.

"You back the fuck up off me, puto! I will destroy you, you hear me. I will fuck you up so bad, your dead grandparents will cry about it. Don't fucking touch me."

Ramón steps back, both hands up don't-shoot-me style. "Okay. Okay. Just wait, then."

Doctor Concerned has crawled out of the room, cursing and blowing wads of bloody snot out of his shattered nose. As he leaves, Derringer runs in followed by three other security guys and, of course, Aliceana.

"What happened?" Aliceana asks. She already has the tranquilizer drawn up and ready to push.

"Shut the fuck up, bitch! No one gives a fuck what you think!"

"The doc told us to take off the restraints and she broke his nose," Ramón says.

Derringer looks at him. "How you wanna do this?"

"We each grab an arm and then the doctor does what she does. Just watch out—she's got some dried blood on her from cutting herself earlier."

"Fucking right I do. Come get me, bitch parade."

"Bitch . . . parade?" Derringer says.

"The fuck you talking to, fuckboy? You talk when I say you can!"

Ramón puts on some rubber gloves that Derringer passes him. "Alright, c'mon, guys." They move in quickly, two to each one of Catalina's waving arms.

"Unhand me, bitches! Unfuckinghand me!" Catalina hollers. "Perverts! Asswipes! Fuck all your grandmothers!"

Aliceana slides herself between the struggling security guards and pops the needle into Catalina's arm.

"You Chinese whore! Don't fucking . . . Don't!" They wait. She writhes, squirms, fusses.

"Any time now," Ramón mutters.

"You see? You can't just, motherfuckers, you can't just! See? Hahahaha!"

"Might take a second," Aliceana admits.

"Might?"

"Bitches!"

"Maybe hit her with another one?" Derringer suggests.

Aliceana scowls at him. "You a doctor now, Gary?"

"I'm just sayin' . . ."

"Fuck . . . bitches . . ." Catalina is slowing down. Her eyes glaze over and she looks back and forth at the security guys around her. Smiles. "Bitches," she says, and lays her head back down on the stretcher, eyes closed.

"Restraints," Ramón orders. "Now."

They re-restrain her arms and step back, panting and patting each other's shoulders. "Well done, Doc." Derringer grins at Aliceana.

"It's what I do," she says with a smile that almost melts Ramón. "But thanks for your helpful advice on dosage." And then she glances at Ramón, or his chest really, she won't meet his eyes, nods with a confused smile, and saunters off.

"Wow," Derringer says. "So you—"

"Not now, Gary," Ramón growls, taking off after her. His mind fills with words that might bring her back to him, with images, possibilities, grand gestures. None of them make much sense, really, but he's finally going to try. He walks into the corridor and finds her talking to a group of residents, freezes.

For a brief moment amidst the bodies bustling through the

corridor, their eyes meet. I catch my breath. Her gaze is indecipherable. I realize: Against my will, I have become invested. She would be a good partner in crime for my nephew. He would step up his game to match her, and she would develop a stronger foundation for her creative side with him, become more spontaneous. I can see it.

Ramón turns around and walks away.

# CHAPTER NINETEEN

I'm getting better at this. I am. This time I wasn't caught off guard, of course, so that helps, but still: The rage rises in me as I round the corner out of the corridor.

Nilda is in the kitchen, filling it with thick, delicious aroma clouds. I watch the back of her head as she busies herself with chopping vegetables. She's been dyeing away the gray, that much is clear. Her shoulders are relaxed and she's hunched over slightly, head bobbing in time with each cut. *Chop-chop-chop* and then toss the little pieces into a bowl for later. *Chop-chop-chop.* Her fingers tremble and her brow is furrowed in concentration, her lips pursed into a frown, eyebrows arched. Ignoring things is hard work and a lifetime of it is showing in the lines on her face.

I can see myself sliding this untenable amorphia over her face, closing down arteries and vessels until the blood simply clots and then the sudden emptiness within me as her body slides to the kitchen floor.

But no.

I won't.

If nothing else, it would throw Ramón's whole world to pieces if his mom suddenly dropped dead, and I need him to keep it together right now. I need him focused and moving forward. And that's hard enough as it is.

And anyway, somewhere in that shambling carapace, whatever is left of the little girl I once knew and was annoyed by must linger still. Somewhere there is the girl who is a whole orchestra unto herself, whose slender fingers danced across the piano keys. I try to merge this sagging tragedy with the bright child, lips pursed in that know-it-all pout, eyebrows creased. The jawline is the same, that's about it.

And what I see more than anything is the obstinate, fierce girl of seventeen who glares at me across our kitchen table in Las Colinas, barely breathing, barely blinking.

"What do you mean, you're going to see—?" Nilda asked me a hundred thousand years ago, and I shushed her before she could finish.

"No need to tell the entire block," I scolded. "I found her! I've . . . I've been before." This was information I'd been terrified to reveal. I thought she'd be mad that I'd been keeping it, keeping Isabel, to myself all this time. Thought Nilda might even become self-reflective for at least a moment about why, and realize, perhaps, that her own sisters don't fully trust her.

Silly me.

"What is wrong with you, Mari?" Nilda hissed.

"I—"

"You're an idiot if you think—" She stopped, didn't bother, was it even worth it? Clearly no. Sighed instead, a long, irritated release.

"She's our sister," I whispered.

"She's going to get us all killed. Or haven't you noticed?"

I stood, shook my head. "You don't understand anything."

"Mari," Nilda said, but I was already out the door.

*Chop-chop-chop.* It seems to grow faster, more intense, as I watch. Maybe she knows I'm here, can feel me somehow. Maybe the weight of that memory has reached her. Nilda was the last member of the family I would expect to have any spiritual powers. If she did she'd ignore them so hard it would rupture her, file them away with all those repressed memories and feelings, another rusted cabinet, sealed shut.

I wonder if she ever plays piano these days, and the thought fills me with an unexpected warmth. I did love her once. And she did watch over me once, whatever else happened. And she did send those notes simmering through the living room while Isabel and I failed miserably at dancing across the linoleum kitchen tiles. I'm moving backward, watching Nilda toss peppers into the sizzling pan. I'm feeling alright. I didn't kill my sister, for what it's worth. The bar is low for my good mood these days. Then I inadvertently pass over Javier Peña.

Javier Peña is that most skittish of Cuban daemons: a Chihuahua. Technically, he's Javier Peña IV, not by any blood relation to the other three eponymous creatures, but simply by virtue of being the fourth four-pound bulgy-eyed, off-yellow canine that the Rodriguez family has owned. Ramón's grandfather Juan José María Rodriguez gave the first Javier Peña to his dear wife, Angela Cecilia, on Three Kings' Day. Angela Cecilia loved dogs but hated insects and was unimpressed by the tiny keening beast that appeared to be the product of an unholy union between the two. They were about to turn Javier Peña out into the cruel custody of the Las Colinas avenues when little Juan-Carlo, Ramón's father, aged four, got a look at him and fell in love.

After that there were numerous attempts to dispatch the salvaged beast, each one foiled by the ever-vigilant Juan-Carlo. When they dropped him off in the Parque Central all the way in the middle of La Habana one morning while Juan-Carlo was at school, they figured they'd just weather the temper tantrum and eventually the boy would forget the dog and get on with his little life. But Juan-Carlo didn't cry, he startled everyone by locking himself in his room and not speaking or eating for three days straight. On the third day, a humbled Angela Cecilia stepped outside to wait for Dr. Arturo to show up and there, looking slightly worse for wear but still bulgy eyed and concerned as ever, was Javier Peña.

Young Juan-Carlo gave him a thorough inspection, suspicious of the tricks he would later play on himself, and then contented himself that it was in fact the real Javier Peña and life returned more or less to normal in la casa Rodriguez. Javier Peña survived the revolution, the subsequent period of terror, and made it all the way to Miami, smuggled on an international flight inside Juan-Carlo's wide jacket, bought several sizes too big for the purpose of dog storage.

No one knew if it was the culture shock or some change in the atmosphere or perhaps the trauma of leaving, but Javier Peña was never the same again. He became despondent, moped around the house, his little head drooping, barely touched his food, peed wherever and whenever he felt like it. Perhaps, one of Juan-Carlo's cousins suggested before being exiled from the house for six months, Javier Peña was a communist. Nilda, then a newlywed and still stunned from all that had just transpired, probably had it right when she said, *The dog is heartbroken. He misses Cuba just like the rest of us.* And a few weeks later he was simply gone: No body to bury, no mess to clean up. Vanished. Just like me.

So they bought another Javier Peña and he was quickly claimed by Miami traffic and immediately replaced by Javier Peña III, who didn't survive the flight to Jersey and thus came Javier Peña IV—a sniveling, skittish little beast that I just passed over in all my glowing glory. It's an odd feeling, that tiny heart thump-thumping away a thousand times a minute and all those tense little muscles, paws scrambling for purchase against the smooth linoleum floor. Javier Peña lets out a howl and scatters down the hallway. I follow, past smiling graduates, quinceañeras and brides, ignore them, past a hideous painting of a flower rendered all pink and vulvic in the scattered Catholic hyper-sexed imagination of some Boca Raton Marielita and into the heart of Juan-Carlo's household realm: el den.

Javier Peña has forgotten what the fuss was about by the time he arrives, panting and agitated, so he lets out a few desultory yelps on general principle and then settles onto the couch between Juan-Carlo and Ramón.

Ramón is about to ask his father another vague family history question when Juan-Carlo sighs, still staring at the TV, and says: "Ramón, do you know who the greatest actor of all time is?"

"Dad . . ."

"Do you?"

"Will Smith."

"Right. Willsmeeth. Do you know why?"

"Dad."

"Name one Willsmeeth movie. One. That is terrible."

"Dad."

"I'll wait."

"Dad, this isn't even a conversation, it's like a . . . a church sermon."

"Estill, I wait."

Ramón sighs, sits back on the couch. "*Bagger Vance*."

"Ah, well, *Bagger Vance* doesn't count."

"What? Why not?"

"Two thousand was a difficult year for everybody. And golf movies, really, they should've known better. But that's beside the point."

"What's the point?"

"The point is, son, the reason that Willsmeeth is such a good actor, the thing that makes him above all the others, is that he can play any character he wants, and he is still true to himself."

"What does that even mean, Dad?"

"*Men in Black II*."

"What about it?"

"Probably the greatest movie of all time, no?"

"Dad . . ."

"*Wil' Wil' West*."

"Probably one of the most terrible movies in the history of ever."

"Coño, m'ijo, how can you say such things when there are movies like *Snake Eyes* out? Espeaking of which, take Nicolas Cage, for example."

"Okay."

"Never made a single good movie, not once ever in the entire . . ." Juan-Carlo makes a wide arc with his hands to signify the breadth of Nicolas Cage's career. ". . . time. Not one."

"Dad, *Face/Off*'s a great movie. *You* loved that movie."

"But *Snake Eyes* was *so* bad, it cancels out any of the good of his other movies."

"But, Dad . . ."

"Even *Face/Off*."

"That doesn't even make sense. Anyway, what's your point?"

Juan-Carlo shrugs, turns the volume back up on the game. "Pick your battles, m'ijo. That's all I'm saying."

"Dad, what does . . . ?"

"¡A comer!" Nilda calls from the kitchen. Javier Peña, who after eight years hasn't learned that he's not a person and doesn't eat with the people, drops gingerly down from the couch and then flitters off amidst a clickity skittering of his nails against the tile.

Juan-Carlo sighs and says, "Bueno, pues," and heaves himself up, scratches his back, and then saunters into the kitchen. Ramón watches his dad walk away, trying not to notice the slowness of the older man's gait, the back that seems to hunch farther forward with each passing day. Then he thinks of me, the mystery of me, the impossibility: to think of someone you've never met, barely understand. By now, he knows more about me than anyone else; he's closer to me; I'm burrowed inside him; we're damn near one. And one day he'll understand.

# CHAPTER TWENTY

Gómez.

Again.

But this time he's tiny, a hundred miles away, smudge of gray, black, and white, a messy collection of squares overlapping each other that only make up Gómez when I squint. But still: It is him.

The first time we recognized someone on the wall it was Mami's cousin Agustín. I think everyone knew it would come eventually; he'd been a minister of something or other in the Batista government and at family dinners he would rail against the bearded rebels like they'd done something to him personally by cutting the army's supply routes and blowing up the police station at the far side of Las Colinas. I guess in a way they had, considering how everything transpired. When they brought him in he went without a fight, Mami said, and then came the updates: He wasn't eating. He was, but now he was sick. He'd caught a fungal infection, they were petitioning to get him medical treatment. Then he was missing. No one knew where he'd gone. He'd been tortured, broken, put back together again. Tortured.

One of those words that says so much and nothing at all. I had tried not to imagine Tío Agustín tied to a chair or hanging shirtless from a dungeon wall like in the cartoons. Tried not to imagine them punishing his proud face, that smile so big it looked like it was trying to escape the confines of his head. I never liked Tío Agustín much; he didn't look you in the eyes when he spoke and there was something uneven about his manic fits of excitement and rage, but the thought of him bruised and shattered, helpless at the hands of these men that we once called heroes. It haunts me. Haunts us all, I think, and the house takes on an even heavier shadow as the weeks go on and the news gets worse.

Then one day Mami comes home crying, but she's laughing too, says they're going to let him go, he'll be free by the morning, and we all jump up and down, but cautiously, because already the world is such that you never know who's listening, taking notes, remembering, peeking in windows. Already we muffle our words over the phone and the new Cuban code is emerging, a mishmash of sign language, raised eyebrows, frowns, and double entendres. Already, we are perpetually afraid.

And Mami's in the kitchen cooking up the ration dinner later that night when Nilda screams because Agustín's gray and black and white and standing against a wall on our TV and the voices are yelling *¡Paredón! ¡Paredón!* which means they're going to kill him and everyone comes running and we hear the count, the terrible count and then we all gasp and Mami's screaming when the guns all go off. But when I open my eyes Tío Agustín is still standing there, looking harrowed and so alone, this tiny, destroyed man and all of Cuba can see the stain of pee or shit or whatever it is gathering along his pant leg. Not blood because he's still standing, the bullets have torn into the wall all around him and he's crying. Crying in front of our whole country, all the women he's ever loved, his mami and papi, us. Everyone.

They count again and Agustín flies backward as the cracking bursts from our TV; maybe it's louder this time or maybe it just seems that way, because now Tío Agustín is dead. Except he's not. He's still moving, that smudge of gray all mottled and dark on the ground beneath the trickling blood. Someone walks up toward him and the screen goes blank, and then voices are speaking urgently, but I can't understand them over the sounds of Mami wailing.

Nilda shushes her, the neighbors will hear, someone will hear, the wailing is loud, so anguished, but there's no stopping it. Even when Mami finally collapses in the bedroom, the wail doesn't stop. I hear it in my head all through the rest of the night while we clean up the burnt dinner and then go to bed, and in the darkness I hear the wail, crisp and terrible in the empty night air and endless like the ocean.

But this is Gómez on the screen now. Another sorrow entirely. I didn't know him nearly as well, but I liked him better than Agustín, with his quiet certainty. He watched me, not in the creepy way. Watched me like an old oak tree watches the flowers growing around it, bemused and somehow protective. He knew he was putting me in danger, passing those guns on. He knew everyone he touched could be caught, tortured, killed. Revolution asks that its children put not only their own lives on the line, but the lives of all their friends and loved ones as well. It's a wide, sweeping trap, an ever-yawning crevice in the earth.

Gómez knew it, and from Isabel's occasional dispatches about the man's declining health as he slowly rotted away in the mountains, it tore him apart. Every day might bring news of another capture, another killing, another disaster. And then they won and the win was hollow and the whole circus swirled around one man, and it wasn't the man Gómez had put all of his loved ones on the line to be ruled by.

Just like Isabel, Gómez never came out of hiding when the tide turned. He waited up in the mountains, kept a steady suspicious eye at the comings and goings below. Isabel passed him information from her own city hideaway, taking occasional forays into the wilderness; watching, always watching, the two of them, like some heartbroken gargoyles commiserating over the tragic new world they'd midwifed into being.

When the new revolution swelled to life in the Escambray, Gómez joined immediately, although from what Isabel said, he wasn't too thrilled with them either. The CIA had gotten involved somehow, sending money and arms, and we hate those yanqui imperialistas as much as we hate these comemierdas in power, Isabel had told me once. We both spat off her balcony, and watched the droplets fall down down down into the streets below.

And then the government hurled column after column of soldiers into the Escambray, and they caught Gómez and now he's standing there, in front of the same wall so many others have stood and died before on my television. But he doesn't look broken. Old and tired, yes, but still fierce and full of life, like he knows I'm watching, knows Isabel is somewhere watching, the whole country is watching, and we're all fragile and windswept flowers around his great trunk, even the ones who hate him and are yelling *Paredón*, even the ones pointing their guns at him. He sweeps his gaze back and forth at his killers without a shiver and just before they shoot he yells *Me cago en la madre de Fi*—and then it's all crackling rifle fire and he's gone, a messy pile of nothing on the ground beneath the dripping wall. He knew how to make them get it over with quick.

I stand there in the middle of the living room feeling so alive with fury and love and heartache, like all the molecules in my brain are sparkling with a different emotion and they're clacking up against each other, catching fire, exploding. I want to scream, fall to my knees and scream or disappear into catatonia like Mami, curl up and erase myself from the world. But I don't. I just stand there, watching. Voices blurting out all his crimes and offenses against the revolution, how he collaborated with the yanqui imperialistas and is a traitor, an enemy of Cuba, voices condemning, lying, whipping themselves into a patriotic frenzy as the man's body is carried away and the cleaners come in to deal with the splatter.

I don't hear it.

I don't feel it.

I just know everything's different now.

No. Everything has been different for a long time. Now it's me who's different. The fury is a burning cloud inside my chest. If I push it down it'll scald me slowly over years and decades, metastasize into cruel, gangrenous growths.

If I let it out, I will kill someone. The next person I see. Soldier or saint, I will tear them to pieces. It doesn't matter that I'm adolescent and barely over a hundred pounds. Or that I've never laid hands on someone in my life except Nilda that one time. None of it matters. All that matters is that revolution has tumbled down the mountains and into the city, it has filled our hearts and minds, taken root and grown inside of us and when it overflowed it still wasn't enough. We're still yearning for something more, hungry, starved for a feeling beyond all this carefulness—watching our friends and neighbors, family and loved ones shattered across our TV screens. Now it's inside me too, alive and awake and I will cultivate it gently. I will not suppress it or let it burn out in an unruly torrent. I will grow it, nurture it, learn its secret languages of wires and codes, bombs and pistolas. It is rooted in the emptiness in Isabel's eyes and Gómez's guts scattered on the wall and the lines in Papi's face and my mami's impossible silences. Rooted in every time I catch myself before I say the wrong thing or mourn someone I love who has become an enemy of the state.

I will fight.

# CHAPTER TWENTY-ONE

Ramón rises enraged. I am deep inside him today, perhaps too deep. He pulls a chair up to the desk and writes the dream in sloppy letters that spill across the page, stops only to shake out his cramping fingers and then finishes in a frenzy. Another shard of me gone, another step closer to finding out what became of me.

When he's done he looks up. The computer's still on from last night—the screen saver a spiraling rainbow helix—and Ramón growls at it. They're watching him. He knows it. His mind wraps around the certainty that every keystroke he makes will be reproduced and stashed away on some server, where that ridiculous little one-named man will browse over it, weighing out Ramón's allegiances.

With a flick of his wrist, he wakes up the computer and clicks over to an empty email. I KNOW YOURE WATCHING, he almost types but doesn't. IM COMING FOR YOU FUCKERS. He doesn't type that either but it's emblazoned across his forehead. Alas, it's also not true and he knows it. He's not coming for anybody, least of all the mighty Gutierrez family.

No. He's going to work. That's it. Full of a ripening, fiery rage that he can only half understand the source of, a rage he doesn't know what to do with, he puts on his uniform, grunts a *good day* at Adina and Corinna snuggling on the couch, and is out the door and into the cold New Jersey streets, puffing misty breaths at the sky.

And it's an unbelievably slow day. No one to restrain or tussle with. No righteous fuckup to direct his burgeoning anger at. Nothing. It's probably for the best. Ramón is a gentle giant, self-aware enough to be cautious with his mighty limbs, even when provoked by the direst of insults or in breathless confrontations with PCP-addled fury-mongers. But today, I'm not sure how he would use all that unchanneled rage, some of which is born from my memories.

At six, a clutch of young white people enters, the anxious entourage of one of their overdosed brethren. They mill about, bobbing their long pale necks and gazing around with careful nonchalance, exchanging hugs that last too long and medically dubious assessments of their friend's condition culled from hastily browsed websites. But Ramón is exhausted from holding back all day, from trying to name his own sudden emotions and trace their source, and he only halfheartedly waves them off while Derringer looks on, disappointed.

"You not feeling it, Ramón? Normally you'd relish scattering the hipsters."

"I guess not."

"Alrighty, then."

"Mhm."

They stand together for a few minutes, letting the ebb and flow of concerned family members and crackheads swirl around them.

"The big Mexican girl from yesterday?" Derringer says.

"Catalina."

"That one. They admitted her to psych for an extended stay. Dr. Seymour kinda went in on the paperwork, like he really took it personally or something."

"Motherfucker."

"Right? If you take something a teenage psych patient does personally, you got bigger problems than a broken nose."

"I'm sayin'."

"And that guy's an ass. I woulda broke his nose too."

"Mhm."

Derringer lights a cigarette and Ramón cringes, his thoughts aswirl. The girl was wrong to lash out, of course, but somehow the thought of her wasting away in the dingy psych ward for who knew how long sat like a poisonous rock in his stomach. The whole terrible system seemed like a setup sometimes: You crack slightly in the face of a world not built for you, and they load you up with medications till you can't feel anything, then they act surprised when your body and mind rebel and the rebellion is an explosion outward instead of another suicide attempt.

And then you're done: locked away, disappeared, force-fed more meds and trapped in a smiley-faced spiral of *How Are You Feeling Today* and *Let's Talk About What Happened That Day*, and it never fucking ends. It just never fucking ends. The setup didn't have a single thing to do with healing or getting better or confronting the shit that really made life intolerable. It just shut the whole thing down and hoped the tentacles didn't slither from under the carpet. Again and again and again.

"Motherfuck," Ramón grunts, and heads back inside, where Aliceana is waiting. Her eyebrows tilt upward toward each other and her lips are pursed tightly together like she's keeping a deluge in. For a few seconds, they just stare at each other. I think Aliceana might have some speech planned, something courageous and loving that could turn Ramón's whole mood around. Instead, she says in a voice that is almost a whisper: "You're playing tonight?"

"I play every Thursday." Maybe the coolness in his voice snaps him out of it a little, because Ramón then forces a smile and mumbles: "How you been?"

"Fine."

"Cool. You coming tonight?" Struggling not to make it sound too hopeful.

"Maybe. I dunno."

"Okay. Listen, um, I don't know if you sent me an email or were going to, but um, this is a bad time, in my email right now."

"What?"

"I mean, what I mean is, if you have anything to say to me, email is not the best way to do it. That's all."

"Oh. Understood."

"Yeah."

"Alright, I'll see you later, then."

"Okay."

She disappears into the ER and Ramón growls, pressing his palm into his forehead.

※

"Ramón!" Luis's voice is excited over the phone.

"Why did you text me to call you from the pay phone?"

"Because you never know who's listening, man. C'mon. They have a guy reading your email, you think that's it? Anyway, we have a plan."

Ramón rolls his eyes and shifts his weight against the cold. "Oh?"

"It's gonna be great. Gonna lure the mothafuckas out and crush them like the Russians did to the Nazis in World War II."

"Didn't they end up burning half the countryside and having their own people massacred in that particular situation?"

"That's not the point. It's a metaphor, man, don't be so literal."

"What's the plan?"

"I can't tell you on the phone."

"But . . ."

"Listen, you're playing tonight, right? Come in early, we'll talk."

"I got dinner with my folks but I'll come by after that."

"Great, thanks, chico; te veo pronto."

# CHAPTER TWENTY-TWO

It's just starting to rain when Ramón hears the sirens approaching. It's not the usual long wail or occasional yelp that the ambulances use when they pull in; this one's a frantic splattering of sound, machine gun shrieks speckled with sudden resonant blasts. A minute later, Ramón sees why: It's a police cruiser, not an ambulance, and it's zooming the wrong way down a one-way street toward where he stands in the ER bay. It screeches around the small roundabout in front of the hospital, nearly clips an absentminded gynecologist who was listening to music on his cigarette break, and barely pulls to a halt before the doors open and two cops jump out.

"ER!" one of them yells at Ramón. "Where's the fucking . . . ER?" The guy's crying, Ramón realizes as he slides his security card over the laser monitor. The air smells strange, crisp somehow. Another cop comes out of the back and he's carrying something tiny in a blanket. I catch a glimpse of pale, charred skin, see a little plume of smoke creep out from the folds, and it's all I need to see.

"Let me through!" the cop carrying the kid bellows as he rushes past. Then he's gone and only the awful smell of burnt flesh is there, insinuating itself into Ramón's nostrils as he realizes what's going on.

Nurses flood into the ER, grabbing supplies, ushering confused family members out of their way. Ramón passes the cop walking away from the trauma room, his eyes watery and bloodshot. Derringer's voice blurts out over the loudspeakers: "All guests please leave the ER immediately, we have a notification."

Ramón clears a small crowd of drunks and enters the trauma room just as Nurse Dolores screams: "Where's Dr. Nessinger? Did you call a code?"

"He's off today," someone yells from the other side of the room. "And Dr. Barakian is on holiday."

"Get the clothes off."

"I need an IV, people."

"Someone call for cooling fluids."

"What about Dr. Seymour?"

"He's upstairs, but—"

"Page him! You page him?"

"He's—"

"What's going on?" Aliceana appears in the doorway. She sizes up the situation and makes a dash for the bed. The kid is tiny, just what's left of his skin and bones. I already know there's nothing to be done. There's no spirit there, no life. Nothing to save. I think Aliceana knows too, the way she looks down at him, but something else is spelled out across her face too: There are things you *know* and there are protocols and paperwork and lawsuits and anyway, they have to try. It's already in motion.

"Everybody listen to me," Aliceana says. She says it quietly but it works: People slow their frenzy and turn around. "I'm the only resident here right now and we're going to do this right. Page who you have to page, get respiratory ready, fine, but first we need this patient on the monitor and we need to start CPR."

Rosalie, a middle-aged Filipina nurse who is notorious for kicking drunks to the curb, puts her hand on the kid's chest and gingerly pumps up and down. Dolores throws some EKG stickers on those charred little limbs and Aliceana puts an oxygen mask against the child's face and starts squeezing air into him.

"Don't those damn cops know we're not a burn center?" Dolores grumbles. "Don't they—"

"It doesn't matter right now," Aliceana says.

"But we're not even equipped to—" The anxious braying of the red notification phone cuts her off and for a second everything stops.

"Someone gonna get that?" Aliceana asks. "My hands are full."

An orderly named John with crisply trimmed sideburns and horrendous acne picks it up, nods solemnly, and then turns to the room. "There's three more coming in." Groans and gasps. "Two other kids and the grandma."

Ramón looks at Aliceana as the rumblings of shock and dissent rise up from the nursing staff. There's a flash of something in her eyes—fear maybe? But it quickly subsides back to neutral. Then she says, "Get out front, I need you to keep the path clear so there's no trip up. They'll be coming in fast."

Outside, the cop is smoking a cigarette and trying not to cry.

Ramón stands beside him for a few seconds, letting the swirl of sadness and fear rise away from him like steam. "What happened?"

The cop sniffles, wipes his nose. "Fucking electrical fire in a tenement." He's still lit up with all the adrenaline, doesn't even know what to do with his body. "Ol' lady was home watching the kids, I guess, and it was naptime, so they were all caught unawares. The fire guys pulled that one out and there's more on the way with EMS. When we got there there was no buses though, and this kid . . . he's bad, man. So we just, we ran with him. You can't stay, you know? You can't stay. There were so many people. But EMS was coming when we pulled off, so . . . you know. There's more on the way."

Suddenly it sounds like air raid sirens are going off as urgent wailings sing out from the city around them. They get louder and louder and the cop shifts back and forth on his feet and the rain keeps drizzling onto the sleek streets and steam rises from a manhole and it looks like the steam rising off that tiny charred body. The sirens get louder and then two, three, four ambulances zoom around the corner and into the bay. They pull to shaky, uneven halts and doors are flung open, stretchers pulled out, and then the grim parade marches past: first the grandma, arms flailing while the medics try to keep her oxygen mask on and not get scratched, then the two kids, both older—one unconscious, maybe dead, with a tube coming out of her mouth and black char marks on her cheeks. The other is wailing, skin bright pink and peeling, trembling voice lifting up above the hospital.

Ramón swallows the tide of nausea sweeping over him and moves alongside the frantic caravan, sliding the worried onlookers out of the way and then rushing ahead of the first stretcher and holding open the trauma room doors. Aliceana looks up from the tiny burnt child and

142

you can see it takes all her strength not to gasp. "What we got? And where's Dr. Seymour? We need more hands in here now."

The medics run down their list of horrors—body percentages and burn degrees, IVs placed and plummeting vital signs and to top it off the grandma's lungs are filling up with fluid—and then a short Asian lady runs into the room, past Ramón, and starts yelling at Aliceana. "I'm not . . ." Aliceana puts up her palms, shaking her head. "I'm not Chinese, I mean, I'm Filipina. I don't . . . someone tell her I don't speak Mandarin." But no one else does either and the lady's running out of steam. Finally understanding, she sags, and moans, "Baby, my baby . . ." as Ramón sweeps her out of the room and into the embrace of a confused social worker armed with a pile of forms and legal documents.

Chaos erupts in the trauma room again, nurses scrambling around the three new patients, applying blood pressure cuffs and EKG stickers, readying syringes and bags of fluid. Aliceana passes ventilating the baby to a nurse and stands in the middle of the room, her eyes scanning from side to side.

"Does the eight-year-old have a pulse?"

"Thready and fast, but yes."

"The grandma's lung sounds?"

"She's wet all the way to the top."

The old woman lets out a series of moaning coughs and you can hear the fluid sloshing around in her airway with each breath.

"Push one hundred of Lasix and get the intubation kit ready. How's the four-year-old?"

"Stable. Airway uncompromised, lungs clear, vitals holding. Burns look mostly superficial."

The child's crying has diminished to a steady whimper and now he glances back and forth at his shattered family.

"Good." Aliceana rubs a gloved hand on his little head. "Get him out of here for now but keep him on a monitor and keep someone with him at all times. That tube good?"

"The tube is good."

"Where's Dr. . . . oh."

Dr. Seymour appears in the doorway and everyone can see he's drunk. His nose is still red and misshapen from Catalina's fist and he's wavering slightly. "What . . . happened?"

"Where have you . . ." Aliceana quickly realizes the futility of the situation. "Just get out. Get out."

Dr. Seymour slumps his shoulders and slinks away, and the whole room rolls its eyes at once.

"Cooling pads on the kid?"

"Done."

"I need paralytics for Grandma—she's desatting."

The nurses keep bustling back and forth, but they've slid into a rhythm now. They're quick but it's not the desperate rush of the first few minutes: They spin circles and figure eights around Aliceana, barely looking up from their tasks as they call out responses, dosages, pulse numbers. Ramón watches, transfixed, until he realizes Aliceana is saying his name.

"I . . . we need your help. I'm sorry. I know this isn't what you do."

He shakes his head, stepping forward. "Anything. What is it?"

"I need you to do compressions on the kid."

Ramón looks down at the crumpled, lifeless body, puts his hands on the tiny chest as the nurse taps out. It's all the wrong colors: The light parts are bone white and the dark is charcoal-seared black and the flaps of pinkness peel away to reveal bright horrible red. When he pushes down, the sternum gives more than he thought it would and he lets go for a second, horrified.

Aliceana shakes her head. "Keep going. The ribs are broken. Just keep going." It's gentle, a mother's coo, and then she turns. "How many epis we got in?"

"Four," someone yells.

"Where's my paralytics?"

"Coming! We're looking for the narc key."

"Find the key!"

"We're looking!"

"Gloria has it."

"No, Ana María took it before she went on . . ."

"Wait! It's in my other jacket. Shit! Be right back!"

Another collective groan goes up and Ramón keeps pushing up and down, trying to be gentle and still get the job done and not look at the baby's purple lips and glassy eyes. The baby is dead. I think he knows it now, pushing up and down on his useless endeavor. Aliceana asks how long they've been working on him and tells Ramón to stop. He lifts his hands away and finally takes a breath and the air tastes sweet and metallic and everyone looks up at the screen and for a second all you hear is the grandma's raspy, wet gasps and the beeping monitors nearby, but loudest of all that empty, unrelenting drone of a heart that won't beat.

Aliceana shakes her head, looks around at the nurses and they nod their quiet agreement. "Four fifty-six," Aliceana says, looking at her watch. "You get my paralytics yet?"

The nurses put a sheet over the baby and pull the stretcher off to the side. The grandma's flailing again; she rips off her oxygen mask and scratches one of the orderlies trying to comfort her. Pink frothy sputum sputters out from bluing lips. "Push it," Aliceana says, walking up behind her. "And start bagging."

Ramón gets hold of one of her swinging arms and Derringer gets the other, and Rosalie pinches off the IV lines and squeezes in a syringe full of something thick and milky.

"$O_2$ sat still dropping."

"Blood pressure's two-ten over a hundred."

"Succs is in."

Aliceana lowers the head of the stretcher down as the old lady slides into dream state, her gurgling howls dissolve into murmurs, and then nothing at all. "How's the eight-year-old?"

"Holding steady."

"Give me suction."

Ramón watches as Aliceana lowers her face shield and goes to work on the lady, prying open her jaw with a blade and suctioning out gobs of pink froth, then leaning in and sliding a tube down her throat and stepping back, panting, as the nurses scramble to get the oxygen bag attached.

"Sats are coming back up."

"I need nitro hung for that pressure. And I need . . . Respiratory to show up with the vents. Like, now."

"We're on it," Rosalie says.

"The OR booked?"

"OR three is ready for her. And five for the kid."

Ten minutes later, both patients are whisked off in an entourage of orderlies and nurses, beeping monitors and sighing ventilators. Aliceana steps back from the carnage, scans the trash-strewn, blood-splotched trauma room, and takes a deep breath. One of the janitors is spraying some noxiousness around and another squeezes out a mop. Ramón stands in the doorway and for a solid three seconds, he and Aliceana just stare at each other across the room.

She goes to him. He opens his arms to her, but instead of wrapping herself in him, she catches one of his hands, brings it to her face, and whispers: "Come with me."

# CHAPTER TWENTY-THREE

This hideous northern winter has shut out the sun and it's only half past five. The last shards of daytime linger in vague purple splotches on the horizon and New Jersey is a splash of lights breaking up the dark world that stretches out around the hospital. A sign on the rooftop door once warned in all caps that a fire alarm will be triggered, but doctors have long since disabled the alarm and graffitied the sign into oblivion.

They come here to smoke cigarettes away from the endless hum of ambulance engines or watchful, snickering gazes of other doctors or floor supervisors. Here they step away and catch a moment of peace from the slowly dying and the already dead, the gradual suicides and desperate to hold on, the denial, the doubt, the body parts. Here, a hundred thousand deep breaths have been taken, cigarettes smoked, juicy morsels of gossip passed, chewed on, and then passed again. Here they make love, here they argue, check phone reception, and respond to urgent text messages from lovers who don't get it, won't ever get it, can't possibly know what it means to see the inside of a human being, to hold a life in your hands, to watch a heart stop.

Here come Aliceana and Ramón. I came first, because it was obvious where she would take him and because I wanted a moment to purify the space. I expand myself one last time, push out into every congested corner of this strange little cove, and annihilate the stench of stale smoke and medium-income cologne, the clog of uncertainty and arrogance. And then I watch the elevator light ding and the door slide open and the two walk in, hand in hand, children in a dimly lit, empty cement garden thirty-two stories above the earth and lit by the bright lights of the new night in the old city.

There's even a stretcher, complete with implicit understanding that sheets will be changed, spill precautions will be taken, used safety devices properly disposed of.

He flicks off the light. The domed glass roof, remnants of the failed greenhouse plot of a much-ridiculed pediatrician, lets in the city night. It congeals with their breath before they even begin, makes the lights into smudges of color against the darkness.

"I think," Ramón says when they find themselves in the center of the room, which might as well be the center of the sky, arms around each other and spinning in a slow circle to some faraway melody neither of them could describe.

Aliceana shushes him, wisely. And they just rock back and forth for a while like an old drunk couple teeter-tottering along to their marriage waltz hours after their friends have all gone home after a long night of celebrating their lifetime of love. Ramón, eyes closed, beautiful doctor nestled securely in his grasp, does everything to memorize the moment. I can feel his mind turning circles around itself, clutching and clawing to preserve some snippet of the present for the future.

She can sense it too. I'd liked her before, but when she feels his uncertainty, his hesitation, she squeezes him a little tighter, snaps him out of it, and then, I love her. Because she has studied Ramón, in just this flicker of time they've been together, and she has learned. And then he gives in to the moment, to the night and the woman, and he lifts her slightly and she gets on her tiptoes and they kiss.

They'd kissed before but always carefully—not grudging or cold, but certainly not like this. Nothing like this. It's all over her that she wasn't prepared for this at all. She was, in fact, just planning on a slightly confusing but utterly satisfying fuck after such a swirl of chaos. It would be divine, and simple in that impossible way. It wasn't much thought through beyond that—the moment had been severe and they both deserved some loving.

But this: This was not what she had bargained for and for a minute she's dizzy in it, having calmed him. Because when he kisses her he means it, and then she's lost in it. And in order to not blemish the blessing by the sin of overthinking, they lay each other down on the stretcher. And she slides easily out of her scrubs and he lifts her and finds her ready and the city is alive around them and slowly, slowly, the past disappears and then so do I.

✳

Isabel. One last time.

I didn't see her jump, but I can imagine it. Have imagined it, hundreds and hundreds of times. She didn't smile, didn't even pause before plunging. She was never dramatic like that. Never outward or the type to dance around anything. She did. She moved. She was. She fought. So hard, and when the fight emptied her out, she died.

But the last time, she was cruel enough as to offer me a little bit of hope. Cruel because I'm sure she already knew then that there was none to be had. Not for her and not for Cuba, not for us. But she insisted, demanded that our last meeting be some kind of sweet.

She made me coffee and we cracked open cans of things and scooped them onto crackers and I complained about Nilda—I'd tried to get her to come with me, maybe out of some misplaced urge to make us all a family again, maybe because somehow I knew, I knew it was over for Isabel. But Nilda had been Nilda through and through: *She'll get us all killed!*

That obstinate rightness that Nilda radiates. There comes a moment in every argument with her where you can actually see the blinds close over her eyes and it's just over; there's no point in going on after that, you're wasting your time.

Isabel laughs when I tell her the story, but I can tell she's just doing it for my benefit. *You know Nilda,* she says, leaning forward. *I don't know why you even tried.*

*For old times' sake, I guess.* It feels tiny and corny when I say it, but it's all I got.

Isabel shakes her head. *Old times are gone now, Mari. They're gone. We all make our choices, and we live and die with them.*

I know she's right, but right now I don't care about all these high-minded philosophies, I just want us to be us again. All three of us. *I did it for us*, I try. *For the family.*

She blinks a few times, then looks out the window, and I feel bad, like I've just accused her of shattering us even though that's not what I meant to do, but also, she kind of did shatter us. I just know she did it for a good reason, and the world feels gigantically unfair.

I wonder if she'll kick me out for surfacing the impossible specter of our family, when she taps me on the knee and when I look up her grin is back and it's real. *You want some rum? It's the good stuff!*

The heaviness remains but I nod enthusiastically and she plonks the bottle on the table and pours some out into two plastic cups and then we tap them against each other and say *clink!* because it doesn't really make any sound and laugh and drink.

That warmth rushes through my chest and it feels like what love must feel like, a sudden gravity, like the wind getting knocked out of you but in the best way, and I gasp and we both laugh some more, and I don't care why, all I know is that it feels so good to laugh with my sister, to see her face open wide with a smile, a real one, the smile I know Isabel to have, which is at once mischievous and loving, a snicker and a glow.

She smiles and outside La Habana churns and when we settle back down from laughing, I ask her, *Do you regret it?* And her eyes dart away from me, out the window. *Given what's happened*, I say. But there's no need. The code is already established by now, anything that isn't clarified is presumed to be about It. The It that's eaten into our lives and eroded all of our most sacred secrets, that It. Because there's no other, so there's no need. It's defined by our silence about it, a tragedy explained through negative space, and so Isabel just frowns, nods slightly, and sips her rum.

*Sometimes*, she whispers, a few seconds after I've given up any hope that she'll answer. *Sometimes I do, yes.* Then she shrugs, the most Cubanest of Cuban shrugs, adds a slight grimace to her frown, and lights a Popular.

*Tell me*, I say, and without meaning to, I'm begging her. It's one word in Spanish, *dime*, just one letter off from *dame*, give me, because what I want is the gift of her thoughts, her story. Tell me. Give it to me. Don't be a hundred miles away on this, our last cup of coffee shared between sisters in the living world. Tell me before everything falls apart even more, while you're still here to tell. Give it to me.

In this city where everyone is listening always, and our very thoughts are contraband, to tell the truth is an act of rebellion. She told me: about the long nights sleeping under the stars in the Sierra Maestra or tucked away in hideaways and storehouses along side roads and back alleys. About the lice and the diarrhea and the time she was caught and had to let a soldier touch her and then suck him off to get free. She told me about understanding the gun, the heaviness in your arms and the shock of the release, the way it feels like everything's breaking inside the first time you shoot and the way your body gets used to it and the way it feels like everything's breaking inside the first time you kill a man and then the way your soul gets used to it and how that makes it worse. She told me about her friends who helped her along the way, Gómez, of course, and others too, and the men who laughed at her, tried to kick her out or rape her, sneered and spat at her. She laughed and shook her head and told me about the bittersweet victory and the gradual disenchantment.

And that's when I knew, even if I couldn't admit it, it was over for Isabel, because no one in their right mind tells the whole truth in such a place, such a time. No one. That was perhaps the first act of her suicide. So many who'd fought in the revolution were already gone by then, like the movement was eating itself from the inside: Huber Matos, who led the assault against Santiago, had been taken into custody, and Cienfuegos, vanished in a plane crash. So many more. And, of course, Gómez, his last cutoff curse still echoing through all of us, and maybe that's when she decided. When she gave up.

Says she already knew things would spin out of control, even before they did. She'd been watching from the inside, holding whispered consults with Gómez whenever their paths crossed. As the whole multifaced rebellion collapsed into one, singular force and then that one spread out in shock waves across the country, Isabel and Gómez watched, nodding sadly. Then the killings began. One by one the old warriors crumbled, scattered their broken armies, and disappeared into prisons or were lined up against the wall and cut down, their last breaths cursing a single man and his huge maniacal vision.

And some simply fled.

But clearly, there was no stopping the machine. Even when rumors spread of an uprising in the Escambray, Isabel didn't have much hope. She did what she could. Used some of the resources and skills she'd gathered during the revolution to smuggle arms and food along toward the whispers of a new front. But they were just whispers, and Cuba was a giant echo chamber with one booming voice cascading down on all our heads, keeping us up at night, poisoning our dreams, hopes, and fears.

*Entonces*, Isabel says, a placeholder with no place to hold, and I can see there's no hope left in her. *And so.* She lifts the cigarette to her lips, still looking out the window, then she looks at me, right at me. *Entonces*, she says again, and the rest goes unspoken, because it's all around us, it's written on her face. And so: Here I am, a broken woman in a broken country, barely alive with rage for the broken revolution I helped to birth. And not a hope or dream of making it right, a hundred canned goods and ten thousand rounds of ammo around me in this cluttered apartment, a shotgun under the bed and a pistol on the counter so when they come the end will be quick.

She sighs. And so.

And then I leave, making my way through the crowded Vedado streets with tears in my eyes and only half an idea why and already I'm so completely thoroughly alone in the world, in this city that is mine and no one's, that was ours and now is his, that once embraced me and now frowns, cautious, and speaks in code and holds its secrets close.

It's cold, the wind blowing in from the ocean wraps around me and I pull my shawl close and a week later, one year and four months after the triumph of the glorious revolution, in preparation for an imminent invasion at Playa Girón from the yanqui imperialists and their exile army, police go door to door, sweeping up anyone and everyone that has even the slightest hint of subversion in their record so that no uprising will take root. And when they get to my sister's apartment and bash in the door, they just find a cup of coffee on the table, still warm, and a cigarette half smoked in the ashtray and the screen door leading to the balcony open, wide open, and the cool ocean breeze making the curtains dance like spirits in the empty room.

※

She's dressing when Ramón wakes up. He's bleary eyed and heavy with the dream and the joy of sudden sex and the dueling memories of a dead sister and the dead child. Aliceana kisses him on the forehead and smiles at him and is gone and Ramón shudders, alone with his memories and mine too.

# CHAPTER TWENTY-FOUR

There's paperwork to fill out. Boxes to check and straight lines to scribble over. Human tragedies to condense into sweet coded nothings. Ramón walks into the cluttered closet that someone has shoved a desk into and calls the security office. He ignores Derringer's snickers and raised eyebrows and gets right down to it, because he doesn't want to be late to dinner at his parents' house and he's not in the mood for the banter.

"You were gone for a little while."

"Indeed I was."

"You alright? Get shook up?"

"Yes. No."

"Okie-dokie."

Derringer stands there, pretending to read the clutter of bulletin board tirades for and against the union. When he starts whistling, Ramón sighs and looks up. "Are you okay, Derringer? Do you wanna talk about anything or you just lingering?"

"Did you fuck?"

"What?"

"The doctor."

"Which doctor?"

Derringer just shakes his head. "Okay. I can play that game." He resumes whistling and Ramón looks back at his paperwork. The powers that be want to know the exact nature of the incident in question. *Describe*, they insist, *using all possible details and in chronological order, the events as they happened.* And because that might not be explicit enough, they add: *Be specific.*

And all the while, the curtains keep dancing in the wind that swirls through the open window my sister just plunged out of. "Right," Ramón mutters. "Specific."

"Huh?"

"Nothing."

"Did you know Hortense's kid had leukemia?"

"We work with someone named Hortense?"

"Yeah, man, the slim one who only wants to work on the eighth floor? With all the makeup? Anyway, yeah, she's doing a fund-raiser."

"I see."

"So, did you fuck?"

"Hortense? No."

"Goddammit, Ramón!"

"What time is it?"

"Six thirty. Why?"

The paperwork will wait. "'Cuz I have to go."

"Ramón!"

But he's already out the door, half-filled sheets of bureaucratic nonsense shoved deep in his pockets.

"Ramón!" Derringer sighs, turns back to the bulletin board, and starts up his melancholy whistle again.

✳

My sister's suicide is all over Ramón when he walks up the paved path past his parents' manicured lawn. I guess it's one of those things you always wonder about—la tía perdida. A child's imagination can do wild things with death and then all that hush-hush around it. An enigma, and now an enigma with an answer, an image to accompany it. And the image stays with him: Isabel at the table, pulling on her cigarette, looking out the window she would soon jump through. It's me watching her, and then she turns and looks at me, and there's love in her eyes; love and pity, because I'll still have to be here, struggling long after she's a stain on the sidewalk twenty stories below.

Juan-Carlo opens the door. "Ramón." Javier Peña skitters around the corner, yelping and growling and then slides to a halt when he sees there's no invader to fend off.

"Papi." They hug. It's more like a half hug, whatever men have to

155

do to fulfill the cultural requirements and maintain a safe distance, and Ramón shuffles in after his father. "Sorry I'm late. Mess at the hospital."

Juan-Carlo shrugs. "Ya estamos comiendo."

"Smells delicious." And it does. Nilda has outdone herself once again. A magnificent feast is spread out on the dining room table: the lechón glistens, the yucca clumps wallow half submerged in a thick garlicky mojo, the platanos are obviously just crispy enough but still soft and perfect in the middle. It doesn't ingratiate me toward my sister, it just makes me ornery. Nilda stands when Ramón enters. "Ay, m'ijo," she croons. Tío Pepe is here, and Teresa, who shoots a knowing smile at Ramón. There's also a middle-aged couple, someone's cousins, I guess, hopefully from Juan-Carlo's side, because they're unrecognizable to me. They brought their eight-year-old, a squirming, chubby little fellow, and a glowering teenage girl who looks like she'd pay good money to be anywhere else on the planet.

"Sorry, everyone." Ramón puts his bag down, cheek kisses his mom, and waves at the table. "There was a . . . fire. A bad one." He reminds himself this isn't the place for all that messiness and when Nilda gasps her obligatory "Ay Dios mío," he doesn't take the opportunity to elaborate.

"We were just discussing the national tragedy that is contemporary American cinema," Juan-Carlo says, helping himself to more pork.

"Oh, good," Ramón mutters.

Nilda rolls her eyes. "Ay, mi vida, do we have to?"

"Actually," Teresa chimes in, "I think you will find that in a few years, television will surpass the cinema when it comes to producing quality material. I mean look at—"

"¡Qué mierda!" Juan-Carlo thunders. "Have you turned on the TV in the past six years, woman? It's this thing they have, what's it called? Reality TV?" He turns to Nilda as if she'd have never heard of such a concept. "Oyeme, esa cosa, they film people, in their homes, no? And they argue and carry on, every single episode—every single one, mi vida—someone either has sex or gets into a fight. No, no, no. How is that reality? What reality is this?"

Nilda shakes her head. "Juan-Carlo, por favor . . ."

"I'm not talking about reality TV," Teresa says coolly. "I don't know why you watch that stuff. I'm talking about cable."

"But the children are not watching the cable. They are watching basura! Ask them. Cecilia?"

The teen looks up from her cell phone. A jet-black lock of perfectly straight hair veils half her face and her frown is so intense it stops Juan-Carlo mid-rampage. "What?"

"Juan-Carlo was just wondering what you watch on TV, dear," one of her parents chimes in.

Cecilia looks around the table slowly. Tío Pepe is the only one not staring at her; he's fully engaged with the slab of pork on his plate, chewing loudly. "I don't watch TV," the girl says before disappearing back into her cell phone.

"¿Tú ves?" Juan-Carlo demands as if she'd just proved his point.

"I have a question," Ramón says. Javier Peña's under-the-table snores fill the sudden silence. "Why will no one tell me what happened to Tía Marisol?"

A few things happen at once: Juan-Carlo groans and becomes very interested in his food. Nilda lets out an exasperated sigh and tries to put some beans in her mouth but her hands are trembling too much, so she lets her fork clatter down on the porcelain plate and then jumps in fright at the commotion. Tío Pepe looks up, suddenly interested. The chubby eight-year-old defeats some digitized bad guy and the little machine he's holding emits an exalted series of beeps and jingles. Cecilia rolls her eyes.

"Ramón," Nilda says quietly.

"I told you she probably jumped, just like Isabel," Tío Pepe says, shaking his old head.

"But . . . nobody knows? Did anybody look?" Ramón is trembling too now, an inherited gift, I suppose. "Two sisters disappear and nobody tried to find out why? I don't understand."

"It was not so easy, you know," Tío Pepe says. "You couldn't just go poking your nose into people's culos trying to find out things."

Cecilia lets out a stifled laugh and her parents glare at her.

"Did anybody try?"

Tío Pepe frowns. "Ramón, you don't understand."

"I know, that's why I'm asking, Tío. I don't understand. Why did no one look?"

"Because she didn't jump off the building." It's just a whisper. The whole table, even Cecilia, turns to face Nilda. "She didn't jump off the building."

"Nilda," Juan-Carlo whispers. She shushes him and for maybe the first time in their marriage, he listens.

"How did she die?" Ramón asks.

Teresa is shaking her head, her eyes closed.

"She died in prison," Nilda says, looking down at her plate.

Ramón is about to stand. If he does it too fast, if he lets the fury that he, that I, that we feel carry him upward, the momentum will shatter the whole room, send the feast exploding in every direction; it will break the suburban quiet. I soothe him. I don't know why, but I do. It's easier to digest shock when I'm taking care of someone else. I coo a soft lullaby inside him and he doesn't stand, doesn't rage across the house; he simmers. We all simmer. "What do you mean?" he says very quietly but in a voice that brokers no peace.

Nilda looks up. Then at the paintings on the wall behind her guests. They are hideous, rigid off-pink slices across a yellowish cloud. She blinks a few tears away. "They caught her."

"Ju don' know that!" Tío Pepe says, and then he erupts into a fit of coughing. Teresa pats his back, frowning.

Here it comes.

"I do. I . . . they took her away. I couldn't . . . I didn't stop them. And I . . . I thought they would kill me." And? There's more. It's hanging in the air all around her. I can feel it clouding up the room. Its stench forces out the smell of cooling food, eats into us all. It is everywhere.

"I was so afraid," Nilda moans.

What else, my sister? What else happened that day? It's coming back so clear to me now. I can see it all. I remember.

I remember.

"She came back to Las Colinas. She'd been gone such a long time. We'd thought she was dead. Or underground, of course. And the soldiers kept coming back again and again, telling us we had to turn her in, we had to tell them where she was."

Nobody moves except Tío Pepe, whose head is dropped down to his chin, shaking back and forth. "Ay, Nilda," he whispers. "Nilda . . ."

"They were going to take away Mami and Papi," Nilda moans. "If you did not live through it, you don't understand. You can't understand. They said the most horrible things to us, to me. When no one else was home they'd come back, they'd threaten us. That they'd burn down the house, they said, destroy everything we owned. Throw us all in prison. And of course they could do that. They could do whatever they wanted."

"So you . . . she . . ." Ramón doesn't have words. I'm still cooing, but now it's more for myself than him. The way a cat will purr when it's close to death—the innate part of itself lulling the wretched conscious part into a sweet stupor. That's me, because if I don't, someone will get hurt.

Nilda nods her head, tears flowing freely down her face now. "When she came home, I slipped out. Because I didn't know if they were watching or not, and if they were, and she came and no one told them, we all would've been killed. Or worse. Or worse . . ."

"But . . ." Ramón says.

"There's no but. That's what happened. She came in and I slipped out and all it took was a look. I saw one of the young men that came to bother us walking down Calle Septiembre and I nodded. That's all. I nodded. And then I turned around and walked back to the house. And my stomach turned in circles and I couldn't speak or breathe and I went right into the bathroom and vomited everything I had inside me and while I vomited I prayed with all my heart that Jesus Christ forgive me for what I did and that . . ."

Say my name.

"And I prayed that . . ." The word catches in her throat because if she

159

says it she might choke and die, because that's the curse that's lingering on the edge of my existence, waiting to be hurled at her. I don't care that she's partly right, or that she's lived a mostly miserable life because of that day or that she still hasn't forgiven herself and probably never will. I don't.

"Marisol," she finally says. "That Marisol would forgive me, one day. That she'd understand." She sniffles and I think she might shatter at any second.

Ramón breaks the silence. "You're saying . . ." He stops because he's trying to work his mouth and brain around the sentence at the same time and it's getting jumbled.

And then I see past my rage and my devastation and I understand what's got Ramón so caught up.

"Do you even know if she died?" he finally growls.

Nilda nods pathetically, eyes squeezed shut.

"How?"

Nilda shakes her head. "I don't know. A soldier came by and told one of our neighbors, Angelica. It was years later. I had already come here, along with Mami and Papi. He wouldn't say more." She stops to sniffle loudly and catch her breath.

Little Cecilia, who has barely said a word this whole dinner, puts down her phone and stands. "You're saying you were the one who sent your sister to rot in a Cuban prison?"

Nilda just sniffles.

Cecilia glares at her. "Jesus fucking Christ."

Jesus fucking Christ indeed.

# CHAPTER TWENTY-FIVE

Ramón is typing away quickly on his phone while the suburbs whirr past the bus window. I'm trying to keep track of my own splash of emotions and be present in this world too.

At least now I have my *porque*. A strange peace has come with it, although there is still rage and tumult aplenty. At least now I know.

*Aliceana*, Ramón types, *meet me at the club whenever you can. Gonna be there in a few. Need to talk to you. So much is happening I want to tell you about.*

Then he opens up another email and addresses it to Alberto and Old Enrique:

> *Srs. Gutierrez: I regret to inform you I will not be able to perform at your hideous, sociopathic event nor will I rally the masses to your ludicrous cause.*
>
> *All my best,*
> *Ramón*

I suppose that settles that. Ramón hits send. He closes his eyes, smiles, and lets the rhythm of the bus slide him into a gentle nap.

※

Me.

I.

Yo, solo yo.

Alone. Because Isabel is gone now, gone for good. And the truth of that is brand-new, keeps hammering down on me with every breath.

And alone in this moment, surrounded by a hundred acres of nothing and the entire sky pressing down on me. The sky completely pale and ugly on a grayish hideous Cuban afternoon and the sound of bugs and this empty lot in the middle of nowhere, a field on the outskirts of Las Colinas and my pounding heart and my caught breath and my breath won't come and the tears won't come and my words won't come. And I know it's not over, it's not even nearly over, it's nothing but the pure hideous beginning. The beginning. Of the terror. And the sky doesn't care; I have no weapons to defend myself; no saints protect me. I am alone.

It won't rain or even shine the sky is just persistent, dull, unmoved, unshaken. The uncaring gravel digs at my knees. I'm peeling forward, wilted and unreachable, my face in my hands. Sobbing, I let out a moan.

They didn't have to tell me. I never would've known. I could've pretended, ignored the tickling sorrow, moved through my life. Wondered, maybe, where she'd gone off to. But this is Cuba. People disappear. They get lost, especially nowadays. They can come for you at any moment. They can come when you're taking a shit, when you're falling in love, when you're all alone, in a field, outside Las Colinas, moaning. And then you run. Or you don't. Maybe you fall. But there are options; the path has many turnoffs. I could've made up a whole story for her, how she made it to the Escambray, found like-minded hardheaded open-hearted revolutionaries outside the bitter daily politico, outside the bloodshed and backtalk. Away from it all.

I guess she did, in her own way. Because wherever she is, Gómez is surely there with her.

Either way, I'm paralyzed. All alone and immobile, facedown in this field and barely breathing, heaving in great wide gasps and then silent for too long at a time, eyes unfocused, sky bearing down on me; it won't let me breathe.

They told me about Isabel's jump and I ran. Even though I knew already, I still hoped, that somehow somehow somehow, but no. It's a bad time to be running through the streets while your insides turn to dust. Always, yes, but especially now that they're firing the last shots, finishing off the wounded that the tide washed up on the beach at Girón. It's a bad time to be a thinker or a talker or a human being with a beating heart, a bad time to be relentless. And I am: relentlessly alive, relentlessly feeling. My heart is relentlessly broken and my sadness won't stop being the sky that won't stop pushing me down into the sharp gravel.

This is when I'm supposed to scream, but I can't. This is the most alone, the most free I've felt since before everything went to hell, or maybe ever, but still I can't let out the rage. Because what if what if what if a hundred thousand what-ifs, a million unforeseen consequences of a billion tiny actions, a gesture, a scoff, the unintended eye-roll causes offense, raises suspicion, and suddenly your family is under siege and they're waiting outside your door and breathing on the other end of the telephone and smirking at your most sacred memories and then one of us falls and then another, because even to mourn a loved one is an act of rebellion, so whole families get enveloped, suffocate, and die. And so it begins.

When the part where I can't breathe or move or see passes, I stand up. I'm wearing one of my pretty dresses, yellow with white lines, and I wish it were pants. My stockings are torn and filthy, my hands cut. I walk, stumbly and chaotic at first, like a newborn deer, but gradually I straighten up and move with purpose. I have no reason to return home. At this rate, I'll only bring further misery on my family. I head for Padre Sebastián's.

❋

Ramón is also alone, if you don't count me. He's cutting through the streets toward the club, half dazed and somewhere between wrathful and in love; a touch of both. He's full of things to say and keeps having to pull his mind back. It's racing ahead minutes and then weeks and months, guessing and imagining, debating. And then his phone blurts out that drumbeat again, and Nilda's name appears on the screen. We both cringe at the same time.

Ramón blinks at the phone, weighing a million different tensions, finally answers it.

"Ay, m'ijo," comes his mother's shaking voice.

Ramón, a clenched fist, seems to loosen slightly. The power of a mother is tremendous. His voice is ice, though: "Yes?"

"It is impossible to explain," Nilda moans.

Ramón stops walking. "You keep saying that, Mami, but all I've ever wanted was for you to try. Instead you don't want to talk about it, you tell me not to bother with it, you change the subject. All I've wanted was for you to explain."

"¡Pero no se puede!" she yells, and somehow, through the coldness of technology and the frigid night, her rage and anguish reach me. *It can't be done.* She's right. In a way, that yell summarizes my whole predicament. Even with these living memories that inhabit his dreams, he can't understand what it was like. Not really.

Ramón tightens his face against both the winter night and his mother's rebuke. Shakes his head. "But you never tried," he says, and snaps his phone shut.

The silence descends; the clack of that phone closing seems to echo through it. He's never hung up on her before, barely ever chastised her. He shakes away the image of what she must be doing now—bawling, most likely—walks into the club with a curt nod at Cadiz, and finds himself enveloped in a world of sound. Luis—now that I know a little more about my life, I make a mental note to figure out where I knew Luis from; that face is so familiar. Prison, perhaps?—Luis has brought in an acoustic soul group and they're filling every corner of the place with their luscious melodies and shimmering arpeggios. It's hard to think straight, the music is so beautiful, and then the woman starts singing— she's tall with straight black hair and a million tattoos across her bare shoulders and when she opens her mouth the room stops spinning for a minute. Everyone looks up to see where this wondrous noise is coming from. Her voice is deep and raspy, it aches with stories about what might have been. She sings the first little riff, throws back a shot, and smirks into the microphone before letting loose another phrase. People finally look away, return to their dancing, but there's a new sensuality to everything, we're all moving in slow motion and people are dancing closer and closer together; the music won't let their sexual tension stand unacknowledged.

Aliceana is dancing alone though, swaying through a series of simple, graceful steps in a world of her own. She opens a wide smile when she sees Ramón cutting toward her through the crowd. When he reaches her, their hug is a song unto itself. They hold each other, wrapped in music, and gradually begin rocking back and forth and then dancing in tiny, rhythmic pulses against each other.

"Are you okay?" she whispers, pulling his ear down close to her lips.

He looks at her with wide eyes. Nods.

"Do you want to go somewhere and talk?"

They kiss then, a kiss that's born from everything happening around them and the vocalist's raspy truth and the oncoming adventure. It's deep—there's a lot of tongue involved and then it's interrupted by a feeble tap on Ramón's shoulder.

"¡Ay, compadre, *geta rúm*, como dice la gente!" It's Tío Pepe of all people, grinning up at Ramón like a proud father.

Teresa's behind him, shaking her head and mouthing *I'm sorry* at Aliceana. "He insisted on coming to find you guys after everything got stupid at dinner. Said it was high time he go out dancing anyway."

"May I have this dance?" Pepe pronounces each word with exquisite care and bungles them all anyway.

Aliceana laughingly obliges.

At first I don't notice that something bad is coming. How to describe it? A ripple. There are other spirits here—always, of course, especially with such heartbreaking music playing—but I don't mingle or pay much mind to them normally. Now, though, the air is frenzied with shaken shrouds dashing every which way. Whispers, gusts of frantic wind, rumors, and shadows. Someone's coming. Several someones. An attack.

I leave the lovers, swoop out into the night air. Enrique, of course. He could never let such an insult stand, but there's so much happening at one time, and I never thought they'd come so quickly. What form of his illness has the old rebel chosen to inflict on us all now? Which trauma will he manifest outward this time? I flicker quickly through the crowd, don't bother dashing in and out of the pulsing bodies, don't focus my energy with any caution whatsoever. I'm inundated by an onslaught of tangled insecurities and passions, calm precautions, throbbing desires. Sex. This band really has cast a spell on the room, denim grinds hard against swishing skirts like we're all back in school and have nowhere else to go but here, deeper, harder against the fabric, fingertips tracing whispers of what could be along tingling spines, sweat-stuck shirts clinging to chests, pushed to the side, barely there at all, bodies offered up to this haunting, pulsing melody, this woman's rasp an altar.

I let it flush through me, keep moving.

Luis knows. He has his own saints and a soldier's intuition to boot, so he stands stock-still in a side room while his men rush back and forth, preparing for whatever onslaught approaches. He's blinking, like if he adjusts his eyes just so, he'll see it—I almost expect him to sniff the air, but instead he shakes his mane of long, gray-black hair and scowls. "Arturo and Blanco, the back. Cali and Monte on either side. Jorge conmigo." The men nod as he calls their names.

"What about Cadiz?" someone asks.

"He's in front?"

"Ay."

"Leave him there. The man is a wall. If nothing else it'll force the fuckery to one side or the other."

"Want one of us to warn him something's—"

"He'll know," Luis says. "And even if he doesn't, he'll know what to do when it does."

He must've been in the ejercito at some point, this Luis. This is, after all, just a local turf war over a nightclub, but he's running things like they're about to retake the Moncada. "Now go." He says it quietly, almost to himself, but the men immediately hustle off to their respective positions.

Back on the dance floor, the music has shifted. Static guitar comes thrashing down in great ferocious waves and the drummer sounds like he's grown an extra set of arms. Beneath it all the bass rumbles an urgent pulse. People throw themselves against each other, throb and churn, a damn ocean of pent-up everything releasing in peals as the music extends itself around us, through us.

I don't want to find Ramón. If I get anywhere near him he may pick up my own anxiousness. Then he'll try to help, end up outside, and get caught up in the mess. And surely they're coming, in part, for him. No. The boy's safer here, fully immersed in this writhing sweaty mess. Holding Aliceana close, no doubt, smiling from the inside out. I skirt around the edge of the crowd, pass an old man at the bar and a wallflower in a dapper suit gazing longingly into the muck. Near the door a college girl had one too many apple martinis and her friends are escorting her out. All the grace and wonder they worked so hard for at the beginning of the night is gone and they're just wobbly flamingos, little girls unsteady in Mommy's too-big shoes and the dark patches of someone else's vomit decorating their skirts.

Luis was right: Cadiz is not only a wall, he's a wall that knows. His whole body is tensed, eyes narrowed. Some yuppie he wouldn't let in is whining from behind the velvet rope, but the words just slide off Cadiz's broad shoulders. "Quiet," the bouncer says with just enough umph to insinuate grievous bodily harm. The yuppie shuts up.

There are three of them and they walk around the corner talking and laughing like any group of friends out for a night on the town. But Cadiz and I know better. It's nothing you could put words to; an edge to their laughter that lets you know it's forced; an over-assuredness to their stride; one pair of eyes scanning the street a little more than necessary. They cut through the line of party girls and dapper young dudes and get up in Cadiz's face. They're wearing too much cologne and their white shirts are unbuttoned just enough to let some chest hair peek out. The

167

guy in the middle is almost as tall as Cadiz and there's a precision to his movements that speaks of one who aced basic training.

"How much the cover tonight, pato?"

*Duck.* A silly slang for homosexuals. Certainly not used to make friends at this moment.

Cadiz doesn't take the bait. "We're full."

"Oh?"

"Mhm." Then, without breaking eye contact, the bouncer signals the yuppie who'd been simpering in line that he can go in. I'm impressed—a very advanced level of *vete al carajo* being expressed and so few words spoken. The guy in the middle was looking for a fight but he wasn't expecting to get spanked before it even began.

"So you're not full?"

"Now we are."

"Motherfucker, I'm not here to play games."

"Oh?"

"You let us in."

"Are we going to have a problem?"

"If you don't let us in we are."

"Okay."

Then nothing happens, the two just stare at each other, which again was probably not part of the grand fuck-with-the-bouncer plan.

"Yo, fuck this bullshit. You don't let us in, we go in regardless."

As the three start looking like they're gonna pounce, Cadiz taps his ear once and mutters: "Front."

"Oh, you need backup, pato? Need your boyfriends to come help your ass?"

That's when I notice one of the other guys is texting. He clicks the phone shut and disappears it before I can see what was said, but it doesn't matter. Somewhere, some other piece is falling into place. Two huge bodies smash against each other and I hear Cadiz grunt as some blows land against his massive shoulders. The other security guys'll be heading this way, leaving their positions unguarded. Cadiz breaks the other guy's grasp and with a single, effortless shove sends him flying backward against a car. The alarm wails out into the night. People start backing away from the club. Another one of Enrique's men snaps open his billy club and swats at Cadiz. That's when two of the security guys come skidding around the corner from the alleyway. I pitch myself toward them, but what am I going to do?

And then it doesn't matter, because smoke is already billowing in thick angry splotches out of the windows of the club.

# CHAPTER TWENTY-SIX

Even amidst the screams and stamping feet, I can still hear the memory of the bottle smashing a few seconds ago, the sudden reek of kerosene, and then the thrill of the flame bursting out. One second sweet sweet music filled the room. A shattering, a flicked lighter tossed, a roar: Everything changed. Then, from across the club: The same thing again. Smoke billowed out of either side, cascading thick, and then dispersed across over the crowd, exploring every crevice, devastating delicate lungs and tracheas.

Those first few seconds are all still present. They're echoing wildly when I enter, a ricocheting cackle through the panicked nightclub. But now, smoke is the air; the world is gray and the terror is complete, just a few moments later. People hurl themselves at the exits, frightening bodies in unchecked, violent motion. Girls in high heels collapse and disappear beneath the fury of escape. Their friends stop to help them and get sucked in too; the crowd is insatiable in its hunger for life. It doesn't care about sons or daughters, sisters or brothers: It consumes, destroys, carries on in its explosion toward safety, survival its only prayer.

It doesn't take long for the flames to catch the velvet curtains draped on either side of the stage. They're ancient, a holdover from the days when this place was a movie theater, all tassels and fanciness, but now flames dance and devour their creases, burst upward in impossible lashes, unabated, unchecked, sinister. It would be so beautiful if not for the guarantee of death and wave after wave of panic sweeping through me, this room, everyone in it.

I have to find Ramón. There are so many people and they're moving so fast; it seems impossible. If he dies . . . I slow myself. Remind myself that I'm already dead. I suppress the living human instinct to rush in time with the panicked masses. I am still. Smoke pours through me, fire is born and reborn on the walls around me. I am still. Beneath me, bones break and a hundred heart rates accelerate. Lungs struggle to inflate against air thick with carbon monoxide and flame. I am still. I will locate my nephew amidst this mess. Feel his beating heart echo through me. I am still.

Ramón is in the middle.

He's cowering, leaning over. He's holding someone. Someone limp.

Tío Pepe. Of course.

I'm no longer still; I'm a lightning bolt. I'm with them, around them, a shield, but not shield enough. Bodies charged with terror still burst and clutter around us. I whip myself in a furious arc in front of Ramón, sweeping some of the black smoke out of his way. The red exit sign shines through to him and he turns to Aliceana, who's huddled with Teresa, who's wailing and reaching out to Tío Pepe. Aliceana nods.

Ramón pushes through the crowd, dragging Pepe along and Aliceana guides Teresa along in his wake. Someone comes barreling out of the darkness and smashes headfirst into Pepe, who grunts and crumples toward the floor. Ramón pulls his uncle up and then lifts him over his shoulder firefighter style. He only takes another step or two before a column of terrified clubbers shoves into him in a fierce blitz toward the exit sign. Ramón nearly topples but holds steady and then pushes forward, through the crowd. Aliceana has one arm on his back and the other wrapped around Teresa. I'm in front, whipping back and forth breathlessly, slicing smoke out of the way, guiding, holding steady. And then the air is fresh and we're outside in the chilly New Jersey night and Pepe is a barely breathing smudge in Ramón's big arms, face pallid white and eyes unfocused, lost. There are sirens, bright red lights pulsing against us, throngs of crying people and endless endless reams of smoke rising into the midnight sky.

※

There's not much for me to do here. In the cramped back of this ambulance, the paramedics fuss with IVs, monitors, and bandages. The city flies by out the window; the wailing siren blurts out over the ambient city sounds. Ramón sits on the bench, one hand on his uncle's knee. He tries to stay out of the way as the medics do their thing. The older guy, a tall Haitian with a furrowed brow, grimaces from the captain's chair. "He's crashing," he mutters.

His partner just nods and starts to move faster, squeezing a sharp plastic tubing attachment into a liter bag of saline. The beeping heart monitor increases to a furious rush and then starts to slow.

Tío Pepe is not holding on. I don't know why. He's hovering just above himself, a murky, confused form in the bright lights, wavering slightly, eyes closed. I can't save him, can't do anything when he insists on staying outside himself. Perhaps it is his time, as they say. Either way, I have business to attend to.

I flit out into the empty sky above the highway, release myself into a state of almost nothingness, and then surge into the night.

# CHAPTER TWENTY-SEVEN

Enrique stands perfectly still on a hill surrounded by trees. He holds a rifle in one hand, a half-eaten pear in the other, and has ammo belts slung around his shoulder. The sun is behind him, but I can see he's smiling as he chews. His face has finally caught up with that big mouth of his. It's a cruel, playful smile, an exceptional one; it carries secrets. A smile that knows.

And me? I'm disgusting—a rodent of a girl, covered in the filth of two months with no real bed or place to wash up, exhausted and defeated, grimy and in mourning, still dizzy from the loss of Isabel and full of rage at the pigs that took her from me.

I'd seen Enrique Gutierrez a few times already as we marched through the forests of the Escambray. We exchanged pleasantries but hadn't bothered going over the list of our dead in common, our reasons for joining the fight. His new sideburns make him look like the wolf-man, and he doesn't seem to care that the new regime has sent hundreds and hundreds of soldiers, men whom many of these rebels used to fight alongside, into these woods with orders to exterminate us completely, no mercy, no prisoners. He walks like he's bulletproof.

I made contact off a tip from Padre Sebastián. Still aching from the loss of Isabel, still replaying my imaginary version of her death over and over, I found these men and boys, some of whom stormed the Presidential Palace with the Student Directorate back in the hazy midway days of the revolution, and watched their whole movement collapse in a hail of gunfire as the attack fell apart. The scattered remains ended up here in this same forest and most of them never left, sensing the very thing they'd fought for had been betrayed even as the last government garrison fell in Santa Clara and the victors marched in La Habana. Others streamed in from the provinces, bedraggled and exhausted, chasing whispers to this small group that the government called *banditos*.

And I must've looked just desperate and enraged enough to be of use, because they took me in and handed me a rifle. I am filthy and covered in bug bites and wondering if I did the right thing and wondering what else I could've possibly done under the circumstances, because *nothing* was never an option.

And Enrique hasn't looked my way much until right now, when he does, down the hill and right into my eyes. I can tell even through the shadows cast by the setting sun. He's not just looking; he's gazing. Staring even. In a way that would be considered rude in any normal human society. The way he used to stare at Nilda.

And I like it.

*Oye nena*, he calls. *You gonna make it up the hill by yourself or you need help? A concierge, perhaps, to carry your heavy luggage?*

*Cállate, bruto.*

*Bueno* . . . He turns around, then looks back and winks at me. *You're on your own, then.*

A few hours later, I'm sweaty again and the sweat runs in dirty brown beads down my dirty brown skin and I'm thinking I might not be able to make it but knowing I will. And I'm thinking, in an offhand casual sort of way, about Enrique. His smile first, but then my thoughts trickle down his sturdy body, slide inside his open collar, and get lost in the sweat-stained folds of his shirt. Then I imagine his penis. The only ones I've seen have been implied in the folds of a dying saint's tunic or carved in stone, ancient Greek statues. I imagine Enrique's starting as just a sad, droopy thing and then, as his eyes take me in and his smile expands, it grows, rock-hard erect, bursting out his pants for me and only me, and then shattered wood and whizzing bullets erupt all around me as gunfire shatters the still forest and I'm falling into the embrace of the underbrush, wondering if I'm dead or about to be dead, wondering if everyone with me, if Enrique, is dead, if it was all for nothing. But there's no blood when I land, no pain. And then there's quiet, a horrible eerie quiet around us that makes me think maybe I've gone deaf until I hear voices calling from the wilderness, telling us to give up. They're getting closer.

Enrique yells, *Run, fuckers!* and I hear his rifle exploding and more bullets whiz over my head. He's laying down fire so we can get away, this man with the smile that knows things. A few others join him, letting loose blast after blast and then a steady *rat-tat-tat* and I'm crawling on my belly, eating dirt, smelling shit, my insides clenched, my whole body trembling, as fast as I can and praying, gasping, praying, gasping, barely breathing and gasping as I go and I keep moving until I'm somewhere far far away from the echo of tiroteo.

It's getting dark.

I'm alive. Safe even, whatever that means. But I'm alone and exhausted in the jungle infested with government soldiers and who knows what else. I roll over onto my back, stare up at the blue-gray sky, and breathe for what feels like the first time in months. Then I do something else I haven't done in I don't know how long: I smile.

It's a completely true one, not for the benefit of anyone else but me and the sky. It's probably because I'm alive and I actually want to be, finally. I earned it. My whole body clenched with intent, I survived. Took action and survived. I'm still too afraid to raise my head above the tall grass, but I'm not too afraid to laugh, silently, painfully, but it's as true a life as I've ever known, so I let it blurt out of me like a stream.

Maybe I drift off, half slumber. Yes, I do, because at some point it's night and I'm waking up. There are stars above me, beyond the treetops, and the forest is alive around me. I'm itchy and aching, but I'm alive too and I'm still grinning with the wild joy of it when I hear a high-pitched hoot that's too corny to be made by any animal. My heart gets to beating faster and faster and I remember who made that hoot before, a few days ago, as we set out. Enrique, his face tinged with a touch of self-consciousness as he demonstrated the secret code for finding each other and everyone laughed at him. Whatever, he'd shrugged, and then hooted again.

*Just to be clear.* Nesto had chuckled. *Is this supposed to be a very sick monkey or a dying owl?*

175

*Shut your face, gordo.* Enrique tried to say it seriously, but his grin crept out anyway.

There it is again: high pitched and pathetic. I pray it's Enrique, because I am perfect in this moment: disgusting and perfect. I put my hands to my mouth and hoot back. Movement in the bushes; he's not far away. And then I'm looking up at a shadow against the night sky, blotting out the stars. Smiling.

*You gonna lie there the entire night or come back and join your friends, nena?*
*I might just lie here the entire night.*

He nods. *I see.*

*I have to tell you a secret,* I say, and it's easy, like the forest night is feeding me each word before I speak it. I am just a vessel. I release myself to the night, my tired, ecstatic body, I give it over. He approaches, fake cautiously, knowing, I'm sure what's coming; he trusts the night too, in his own Enrique way.

*Dímelo.*

But now he's strayed close enough for me to sweep my legs hard against the back of his knee, so I do. He falls with a little gasp of alarm and then I crawl on top of him and pin both his hands to the dirt. *You have too many teeth,* I whisper, almost directly into his mouth. *And not enough face.*

He stares up at me so hard that for a moment I think this whole game is over—I pushed too far, too fast.

Then that grin erupts in an unruly lopsided curve and he pushes his hips up to mine, and I feel that dick I'd been dreaming of straining through his trousers against me. *Still?*

I nod enthusiastically. *Still.*

*And what will you do with me now that you have captured me?* he asks, almost earnestly.

I lean in close. He smells like the forest and the night and sweat and the danger and drudgery of so many days on the run. He smells like he wants me, to devour me whole and he smells like Man. *Whatever I want,* I whisper.

Then I release his wrists and my back arches as his hands reach around my waist, and I buck my hips against his erection.

*Mmmgh*, he mumbles into my chest. *Gently.*

I want him. The night knows it, curated it, in fact. He does too; his face says so, even louder than the pressure of his hardness against me. I try to imagine the steps between this and him being inside me, the tangle of buckles and buttons coming undone, legs pulled from pants and arms from sleeves, and it all just seems like so much—too much—or maybe I'm scared.

The coarse fabric rubbing between us, I'm not sure if his moaning is pleasure or pain—it feels like there's a brand-new sun being birthed in my pelvis, and it's rising within me, sending rays of heat and light hurtling up past my stomach, through my chest, into my brain, and out into the night.

*I feel*—he starts, still grinding away, but I shush him; nothing can change; it's all so fragile. I will tolerate nothing that will stop that sun from being born. When I close my eyes I can see it.

*I just feel*—he gasps, hands grabbing my breasts through my shirt and then I gasp because now I'm sure nothing at all could stop that sun; it's gigantic, bigger than me somehow, it fills the whole world with light. And I'm sure rays of it are shooting up into the air from wherever we are, terrible, fantastic lights, burning into the dark sky.

Enrique's breaths come faster and he's given up talking, which is good, and instead just pushes harder and harder against his own pants and my pants and me and then he yells and I can't breathe and the sun has risen and the night is alive and bright and all the trees seem to dance.

'*Ñooo* . . . Enrique groans as I roll off him and we both lie there panting and staring at what part of the sky the trees allow through. Everything is filthy, and the crotch of my pants is wet, his soaked, but it feels alright somehow, part of the world, and in a way it just doesn't matter. For a few moments, it's just the sounds of the forest and the murmur of night as we catch our breaths.

*Is it true we take money from the CIA?* I say into the silence.

Enrique scoffs. *Qué romántica.* Then, when I don't say anything: *Probably. We'll take money from anyone at this point.*

Thinking of Isabel, longing for her, I hock a loogie straight up into the air and we both roll out of the way so it doesn't land on us.

*Ay, chica,* he says, still laughing and panting. *I'm not sure if you noticed, but they're wiping us out. We'll make a deal with the devil if it keeps us alive another day.*

*Fuck the CIA,* I say, and roll over into my memories.

Enrique keeps laughing and talking about how only the yanquis can save us now as a deep sadness sweeps over me.

All at once, I feel beautiful and dirty and wild and so alone. I miss my sister. I never got to mourn her, not really. And I miss my parents, whom I abandoned when they needed me most. I even miss Nilda and her sallow face and dancing orchestra hands.

The loneliness grows inside me, a sudden, expanding stain, and I know without a single doubt that I need to go home. Not to stay. I will keep fighting. But I can't keep pretending that the memory of my parents isn't eating me from the inside. I can't keep letting them worry, not knowing if I'm dead or alive. I have to let them know I'm okay. I have to see them.

※

Enrique coughs and sputters awake, clutching his heart. A woman his age sleeps beside him, her eyes covered with a silky light blue mask, her snores outrageous. It's strange, giving these dreams that are memories to someone who isn't Ramón. Being so deep within a whole other body. It's like staying in a stranger's house, nothing is quite in the right place.

Enrique feels more alive than he has in years, even with the lingering memory of a sharp pain in his chest. His breaths come in quick, uncertain gasps but he smiles, lets each one out through a pursed grin. Throwing his legs over the side of the bed, Enrique realizes he has an erection. He smiles even wider, chuckles even. His first in years. More than that, the front of his pajamas are soaked. Not only does he have an erection, he's already come. Christ, he's like a teenager again!

The dream.

The girl.

The forest night.

"¿Enrique, qué te pasa, mi amor?" the woman mumbles.

"Nada, mi vida. Go back to esleep."

She does.

The night.

The girl.

The dream.

Enrique rises, stumbles to the little office he has adjacent to his bedroom, plops languidly at the desk, and clicks on the computer. The screen awakens with a blue light, a series of emails, the terrible back and forth from earlier in the night.

Coño. It all comes swirling back.

The fire at the club. The fatalities. Alberto. Never gets it right. Never. It all seems so pitiful suddenly. So useless. The old man spasms into a coughing fit and is shocked to find his erection is still intact. Marvelous. A miracle. But the club fire is a tragedy. Another in a long series of tragedies that Enrique can put his name to as author and architect. One more horrible night, more lives lost. Enrique sighs.

The girl. Flickers of her brown face close to his, that toothy smile, her eyes rolling back, her mouth open now, gasping for air. His hand finds his own hardness. But the ugly blue light from the computer screen keeps flickering at his attention.

*This has to stop*, he types quickly. *We must make a change. A major change.*

He rubs himself a little harder, feels the length of his fully awake cock in his hand and grins. *We will find a new way to freedom. A new path. One that is about peace. About love above all else. My friends, it is time to make a change.*

The girl. Her nipples hard and perfect dark purple brown in the night, perfect in his fingertips, his lips.

*The change begins now.*

*~Enrique*

He puts Alberto's address in the To box and CCs the entire organization. Then he adds his whole email listserve just for good measure. Why not? It begins now.

Her hips grinding into his. Her shadow above him, riding him in the darkness. Enrique's eyes roll back, his brow furrows. His hand moves faster, slows, moves faster again. Pinpricks of pain erupt along his entire left side and he moans, works himself a little harder. Tiny bursts of light splatter the insides of his eyes and those thighs opening. He blinks and the ceiling gets blurry as her body seems to burst through him, rise up from inside of him, the essence of her alive and ferocious in his gut, his mind, his dick. He bucks forward, suddenly standing, exploding inwardly and out, falls to his knees.

I rise above him, thoroughly exhausted and even more of a flickering wraith than usual. I have to get back to Ramón soon or I'll be gone for good.

Below me, Enrique collapses, gasping, and rolls over onto his back. And there they will find him the next morning, very dead and still grinning with that smile that knows.

# CHAPTER TWENTY-EIGHT

I barely make it back to the hospital, and when I do, I find Teresa and Aliceana watching a flickering TV screen while Ramón sleeps.

There isn't time to pause and take in the peaceful moment. It was foolish, perhaps, to risk so much just to unlock that strange memory within myself, within that old fool. It took so much out of me, to be away from the home that this snoring behemoth has become. I felt my own essence spilling out of me all the way back, whisked away on these icy New Jersey gusts.

I barely made it, I barely made it. The truth of that burrows through me in aching pulses as I collapse over Ramón's rising and falling chest. I am still here, somehow, by the grace of something bigger than me.

A tingling buzz erupts along the edges of my consciousness: healing. The strange non-fabric of who I am rebirthing itself now that I'm safely back to my anchor. I loathe this dependence. I accept this dependence. Somehow, it will get me to the truth, if I can keep from recklessly hurling into oblivion.

Ramón lets out a thunderous snore. I gather myself. Allow some more time to pass, then more. Somewhere down a corridor, they're working frantically and pointlessly to save old Pepe. Nearby, Teresa pretends to be alright, chatting in an offhand way with Aliceana.

It is time. I don't know if I'm fully recovered yet, but I also don't know how long Ramón will stay asleep. And deep within me, I know the nightmare that comes next, at least some shadow-play version of it. I need the rest. I need to get it over with.

Slowly, I seep into Ramón's consciousness; slowly I unravel.

✳

Las Colinas.

Home.

Or it once was. These streets wrapped around me once.

They were broken and muddy, but the faces looking out from the porches and windows knew my name, my parents' names, our lives. Las Colinas raised me.

The name is a lie though; there are no hills in Las Colinas. No one knows why it's called that. If tourists ever came here someone would surely make up a pretty story to go with the name, but they don't. You can look straight down the main avenue all the way past the church and central plaza to the very edge where Las Colinas becomes smaller shacks and then fields and forests. The roads are bumpy, but the land beneath them is flat all the way to the foothills and in the other direction, the sprawling suburbs that eventually turn into the madness of La Habana.

Now I stand in the view outside my bedroom window: a ditch that always turned into a lake, sometimes filled with trash, a weathered old house beside it with a weathered old palm tree out front. Behind me loom the mountains; before me stands the house.

My house.

Or it once was.

I wonder if Isabel ever stood here, in this same spot, and watched us with echoes of an urgent warning in her ears like I have: *Don't do it, girl. You will be captured. Hell, they might be captured too. Is that what you want?*

For me, the words are Enrique's. For her, it would've been Gómez who said it, or some other guerrilla I never knew.

I just know this: I have to see my family again. And I won't get caught.

These are still my streets. I still know their secrets. Certainly better than any bearded soldier from the campo.

And anyway, no one's around, so I walk calmly across the street and up to the door, and then my hand is on the knob, the same knob I turned as a little girl, and then I'm staring at Cassandra's wide eyes and she blinks once and then embraces me, calling my parents and Nilda in.

Nilda comes first and wraps her thin arms around me and what wells up inside catches me so off guard I start trembling. I'd missed her. I've missed her all along and haven't even realized it. And now that she's holding me, all I want is to collapse into her and sob and let her comfort me. Instead, I squeeze back and close my eyes and then she whispers that she's sorry, but she has to head off to get something from the store.

I catch an unexpected sob before it gets out. *But—*

She holds me at arm's length and flashes a strange kind of a smile— it's toothy and too wide and really speaks of fear more than happiness. Her fingers tremble against my skin, like her heartbeat is shooting through them into me. And maybe, if I'd been paying closer attention, that's when I would've known. Instead, I think: *How could she leave when I've only just arrived and been gone all this time?* And don't bother answering the question at all, I just shake my head and let her go, and the door closes behind me just as my parents walk in from the kitchen.

I put my anger at Nilda away and face them, finally.

But something's wrong.

Something's always wrong.

They hug me, yes. They have to, it's protocol. But there's an iciness there that I can't figure out or thaw.

And then they sit across from me in the den while Cassandra fusses with the coffee and hold hands and look like they're anything but happy to see me.

*Why did I come?*

The question settles into me with a splash of panic. Enrique was right. I showed up at the door hoping for a hero's welcome, or maybe just a sense of warmth, and instead I've endangered everyone.

I tried to tell myself, before I came, convinced myself even, that I was doing it for them: They must be worried, I told myself, and they deserve to at least know I'm alive.

But really, I did it for me. I just needed to take a breath. It's only been a few months of life underground, but it's exhausting and terrifying and men I've looked in the eye have been cut down in a flash of gunfire, and death just seems to close in on us with each passing day.

Maybe I came to say goodbye, one last time.

*¿Qué tal . . . todo?* my mother says, hesitating and then punctuating the word *everything* with a wave that sums up the sweeping impossibility of any word describing where we're at.

I shake my head and shrug. *Complicado*, I say with a laugh that must sound absolutely ridiculous.

*Why did I come?*

Footsteps sound outside the door and I jump up, ready to bolt, but then Nilda pokes her head in and I sit, ashamed, heart still sprinting, and laugh that ridiculous laugh again.

I came because I'm still just a girl and the world is even more terrifying than I thought it would be.

Nilda looks sick; she barely smiles, blinks at me rapidly and then makes a direct line for the bathroom, where I hear her throwing up and that's when I know.

*Marisol*, my father says, my name an urgent and hopeless prayer for help that will never come.

*I'm sorry*, I say, rising and stumbling toward the door.

*Mi amor* is the last thing my mom says and then I'm out in the streets, skittering behind the house just as two men in dark green round a corner across the street and yell.

I run until I'm numb and fire rages in my chest and then I slam against a wall panting, but the boots are still clattering somewhere nearby, so I run some more, until I'm somewhere brand-new, away, away, away from my memories and home.

And then: fast footsteps on pavement, a frantic run, the pursuit not far now. Yells in the distance, closing. An impossible clutter of crossroads, alleyways, storefronts. Some unfamiliar neighborhood, and the gnawing sense that one of those streets surely leads to another that leads to another that will bring me to some part of this haunted city by the sea that I do know, somewhere familiar, safe. But no: Instead, the approaching boots get louder and the yells to stop feel like they're right in my ear and I know what's coming, so instead of stopping I run harder and then and then and then

Hard hands on me, wrenching me up from the earth, pounding my ribs, my face, my

❋

Ramón coughs himself awake from the nightmare of my life. The hospital hums around him as the echoes of my capture fade. He takes a sip of the cold coffee in his hand and catches his haunted reflection in the night window. I am a sliver, empty empty empty, but inside Ramón, something solidifies. There is knowing in the head: a grudging acceptance; and there is knowing in the heart: when a thing is simply true. Until now, it had all been an impossible kind of fantasy to him, even in the face of mounting evidence that each of these tiny loves and disasters playing out across the movie screen of his dreams really happened.

That I really happened.

The waiting room is empty; it's four a.m. Aliceana is curled up in his lap, letting out quiet snores and breaking his heart a little bit with each one. The half of his face described in ghostly blurriness against the night looks tired but strangely young, peaceful even.

He will doubt again, but from here out, beneath it all, there will be an underlying certainty. I don't know why, what it was that made it real, but as Ramón blinks out into the brisk New Jersey night, he knows; it's almost like he can see me there in his reflection, blinking back at him.

And I know. Because yes, even I doubted myself, my very existence. I defy all laws of possibility; how could I not doubt?

This, then, is how I died: They line us up against the wall as the calls of *Paredón* ring out and everything is flickery and gray like on TV and then the night explodes all around us, bodies collapse. I'm flinching, praying I don't get hit and knowing I will as I tumble forward amidst more flashes and impossible thunder.

I can taste the memory; the crackle of gunfire is real, not a far-off noise from the television. The collapse into oblivion like giving over to gravity and dispersing, dispersing into nothing.

The decision rises in Ramón, it supersedes the echoes of that panic, that shame. It becomes more clear with each breath.

Inhale.

There are so few things that make sense to do after a month like this, a night like this. I am with him, within him. Every piece of him is in turmoil, but a quiet surety gathers beneath all that mess.

Exhale.

Because nothing can ever really be the same. And acting like they are is just a lie. Something huge has happened inside of him, all around him. Pieces of it have been falling into place all along the way. But still, what exactly has changed feels like some wordless cloudy thing he could never clearly express.

Inhale.

He looks down at Aliceana. She knows. She understands without him having to explain. She showed him that with her eyes when he saw her at the club, her touch up in the greenhouse, her arms around him. She gets it, whatever *it* is.

Exhale.

Putting all the pieces together, turning them around; there's only one thing to do that makes sense. Well, nothing makes sense, but in the crazy mathematics of club fires, long-lost tías, and family revelations, there's one move to make.

Inhale.

The doctors had already come by earlier to let them know things were not good—very bad, in fact—in the cool, precise language of family notifications. Teresa had fallen asleep on the far side of the waiting room. Now the doctors are back, looking appropriately forlorn. Ramón holds his breath as they inform him that they did all they could possibly do and the passing was painless. Teresa stands, wipes her eyes, and nods. She seems to have already understood what was happening. The doctors scurry off. Teresa hugs Ramón and follows them.

Exhale.

Aliceana looks at him as they leave. "I'm so sorry, Ramón." She says his name right, with the slightest roll of the *r* and the gently accented *o*. When they were first getting to know each other and found out the islands they each traced themselves back to, Aliceana had winked and said, "Hey, the 1898 Club!"—the year both nations threw off Spanish rule and got jangled up in American rule—and Ramón had fallen a tiny bit in love right then and there.

"Are you okay?" she asks now.

He nods then sighs and shakes his head. "I have to," he starts, but can't finish.

She adjusts herself, keeping her leg pressed up against his, her hand on his knee. "Talk to me, Ramón," she says. Then, knowing it'll make him smile, "Háblame."

It does, and he says "abukado," one of the six supremely random Tagalog words he'd looked up once to impress her, and she giggles, and it eases the heaviness just enough for him to turn to her and tell her everything.

She listens, eyes wide, and whatever last part of himself he'd been holding in reserve, trying to play it cool, crumbles in the telling. Aliceana nods, somehow taking in the impossible magic of a long-gone aunt invading his dreams, the way the past walks with us, the anomaly of my existence.

She's showing him that he can trust her, a concerted effort, but she doesn't even have to; he already knows. And so the story comes out unencumbered by added boberías like *You'll never believe this but*, or *Don't think I'm crazy*. He just tells it as it has been, as it is, and I simmer in the background, reveling in the truth finally being told.

"I have to go to Cuba," he says finally. "And find out what happened to her."

"You're damn right you do," Aliceana says, her face lit up with the wonder of it, the trust he's put in her, what's growing between them. "And I'm coming too."

# INTERLUDE
## ISLA DE PINOS

# CHAPTER TWENTY-NINE

Me.

Again.

Alone.

Empty-handed.

Once more. This time with these four dingy walls to keep me company. Forgotten. Maybe forever.

The never-ending ache every time I see that last glimpse of my parents: It's subsiding now. Some. A distant thundering behind all this brand-new pain.

During the trial all I wanted was for it to end. Anything to make this incessant madness go away. It didn't even last that long. Just a few short blurts of nonsensical bureaucracy, procedure, the theater of lies and propaganda. I almost prayed for death. Then I did. I wanted it to end even though it terrified me, the thought of standing at that wall, staring down those guns. I wondered how I would do up there, replayed all the possibilities over and over again, considering the different options as if it would really be up to me, as if my stomach wouldn't clench and buckle my knees and betray all my resolve. I could imagine a hundred scenarios, from glorious escapes to Gómez's stolid fearlessness, but in the end I figured I would die pathetic, screaming for my mami, a bleeding, heaving heap of flesh and then nothing at all.

I knew this, convinced myself of it deep down. The image of my groveling, self-pitying end brought a cloud over my every thought as I paced my cell, waited through hours of bullshit deliberations, listened to the indictments of my fellow rebels.

I almost shattered on the stand. It was day two and my parents showed up for the first time. Nilda stayed home, of course; why dare show your face? I heard later she was near comatose for months after betraying me, laid up in bed, an empty shell. Good, I thought. Let the bitch suffer. Meanwhile, the concerned stares from my parents were breaking me down. Here I was, every family's worst nightmare, in the living flesh. And nothing to be done, no heroic rescue in the works, no witty defense lawyer to swoop in and save the day like in the yanqui films. The suicidal had already taken their despondent dives and the ones left over were about the business of living, not getting killed for some sixteen-year-old boba in the woods.

I should've never gone back. Regret chewed through me as the verdicts came down, guilty and guilty and guilty, a traitor to the revolution, an instigator, imperialist bitch. And just a child. A teenager really. They gave me indefinite detention because of my age and gunned down the rest of the rebels caught in the same roundup.

✳

It's the wall and the corner, the sink and the bench. There's too much light and then none. The paint is too thick against the stones. There were moments of *So this is what it's like* at first. I'd wondered. So many had come here, so many dead. I'd wondered. And then I knew. And now I know. Restlessness becomes acceptance becomes restlessness becomes rage. Rage becomes sorrow becomes regret.

Becomes rage.

Whenever a memory of my family tries to creep in, I banish it. This is the one thing I've gotten good at, sending unwanted thoughts far, far away. They always come back, relentless pilgrims, and I cast them out again. The sounds of tortured bodies around me, screams, flesh and bone tearing, shattering. It's awful, but I can take it. The crushing sense that I'll never, never leave—I can take that too.

But memories? Leave me alone. The first glimpse of an image in my mind from home, even after everything went to hell, and some never-ending pit of emptiness opens up beneath and I float in, despondent, unreachable: a ghost. No. I can't think of them. Mami and Papi with their now-so-serious glares. Can't think of their long-gone smiles or what havoc this sorrow must wreak on their fragile bodies.

They had aged ten years when I saw them at the trial. They sat there shattered and stunned, hollow, surely.

And Nilda? I can't. There's time for all that, surely. Endless hours and seconds stretch ahead of me, emptiness. Surely, all this wrath will trickle out along the way. Surely, I will one day be able to see my sister's face without my skin catching fire, my hands clenching around her neck, my teeth gnashing.

I am a monster.

Hours then days pass, pause to find me despondent and emaciated in a drying pool of my own waste, gurgling, gangrening, lost, and then turn to months. I dream of killing Nilda, first slowly, then fast—a hundred different ways. Recount the moment of my capture and each millisecond leading up to it over and over until I'm digging my fingernails into my flesh so hard I draw blood. Then I start again. I dream of Mami and Papi. Padre Sebastián. Isabel. Lose track of which are dreams, which memories, which ghosts. Or are they all the same?

They shove food under the door. Sometimes I nibble at it, a feeble play at life, my eyes closed to ignore the shades of white and blue that bread should never be, throat clenched against whatever evil is squirming, still alive within its crunchy folds. Then I collapse back into my heap and wait. And burn. And wait. Close my eyes and wait.

※

I didn't know what to expect. Didn't know what time meant, nor pain. Didn't know my own body. And now, though it's all I have, this flesh is more like a corpse than anything I know as mine. Someone else's corpse. I think they saw something in me, they saw a fire in me, something that wouldn't break. I wasn't fearless at the trial, but I cemented my face, made it defiant. I had already given over to death months earlier. It wasn't so hard to keep the emotion stored away somewhere.

I didn't lash out, didn't cry. It frightened them. Their eyes were wary, their movements stilted and overly cautious as they shoved me down corridors and into one cell and then another.

Did they know something about this frail body that I didn't? What powers did I hold? Whatever they saw, it landed me in this single cell. The day passes in the marching of feet in the morning, the clinks and clanks of the kitchen and the opening of gates and bodies shuffling through like cattle. And then silence and nothing and my own thoughts and the impossible emptiness of all that lies ahead. And then boredom, despair, heartbreak, regret. Afternoons sometimes bring a strange upliftment. Maybe I will escape. Maybe I will die. Maybe I will catch a guard sleeping and rain death on these useless excuses for humans.

Night falls, snuffs out that little gasp of hope. I pray for sleep, for death, for mercy. When I catch myself whimpering I deep breathe until the sobbing and heaving inside me slows. I won't let them hear me break.

A guard comes in and maybe it's morning, maybe it's night. I've lost track. I don't care. When he gets close enough I spit. I remember fear as the saliva leaves my mouth. I had slipped past caring and then it rushes back fast, the drive the urge the life to be lived. I want to live, but the little globule is already somersaulting through the air between me and the guard and then it's a dark splotch on his uniform shirt. The white part drips down. We both watch it fall. He slaps me so hard it seems like it happened after I flew backwards across the room. His boot finds my stomach and I dry heave onto the floor. I am nothing, a wraith. Terror erupts into my brain, sends frantic messages through all my bones and synapses. An emergency. Suddenly I'm fighting for my life, forgetting that that means certain death. I'm on my feet, my fingernails cut across his face, his neck, his arms. I go in to bite him, thinking if I can get at that jugular vein in his neck it could be all over. Instead there's a flash that starts between my eyes and bursts to the back of my skull and then nothing.

✳

First it was the pain.

A slap across the face. The room resolves, my room, which has become my whole world. I'm tied to something, a chair. And the guard

192

that just slapped me is standing so close I can smell his sweat, see each of the chest hairs peering out from the collar of his dark green uniform shirt. My eyes meet his and they're tight with the determination to look hard, but they're not hard.

*Nombres*, he says again and I realize he's been saying it for a while, even while I was out. *Names.* A demand.

Someone's in the shadows, watching.

I want to fly up above myself. Want to render this moment into nothingness, anything to be outside my body, the wretchedness of being at these men's mercy. I can't though. I can't fight and I can't fly away. I imagine breaking free of the bonds, becoming something gigantic, superhuman, a monster, and smashing the chair to pieces across their faces and their faces to pieces across the walls and then growing even larger until the walls crumble around me and then the whole prison and—

*¡Nombres!* Another hit, this one harder, closed fist, and it brings a flash of light with it that makes me think my brainpan has become slightly unhinged for a moment.

I am not strong. I never have been, but now I've been wasting away for I don't know how long, becoming skin and bones and even if I could smash the bastard, then what?

At some point, I just start babbling. Names pour out of me. Some of them are rebels, sure, others are just people I've heard of, famous actors, radio hosts, saints. Any name I can think of will do.

I stare as hard as I can into the soldier's eyes while I talk, so hard that when he hits me again, this time out of frustration, it feels like a tiny victory.

And then they're gone.

✳

I had wondered if the other one was going to take his turn. I had waited, my eyes closed, willing the moment to end. Praying. Held in all my sobs. Clenched my gut tight so maybe I'd collapse inside myself and they'd find me the next day: just a splash of blood and regret across the dirty floor.

And now they're gone. Maybe my prayers worked or maybe the other one figured there wasn't much information to be harvested from this broken skeleton of a girl, this corpse. Or maybe they're biding their time. In the darkness, the new silence, no shearing blasts of pain, no chest hair, no demands, just my empty body and this empty room—I finally let my family back in. They don't trickle or tiptoe, they flood, the memories.

There we all are on the first day of primaria, Nilda looking smug because she's already been there a year, Mami shooting her a wary glance, Isabel smiling in that distant, sad way, Papi with his most serious face on, one hand around Mami and the other on my little shoulder. My best dress, the one I didn't want to stop wearing even when I got too big for it, with flowers and shoulder straps and little fake pearls inlaid in it. The last time I cherished something so girly, my tiny uncomfortable pantyhose, shiny little shoes. There we went driving in Tío Pepe's automobile, the whole of La Habana swishing past like a real-life movie in full Technicolor, all the glory of the ocean as we speed along the Malecón and the buildings towering above us and the whole city around us, so many people, so many stories. There's Nilda and me, arguing in the kitchen while Isabel rolls her eyes and tries to study. There's Papi getting older, Mami's back leaning forward, her old hands curling around themselves, their two sad bodies creasing into defeat.

Someone is sobbing in a cell near mine. No, it's me. It comes out in sharp, raspy heaves. At first I'm afraid a guard will hear and then I don't care. I can't stop it anyway, it just surges out of me, from a heave to a wail and the wail carries all the dashed hopes all the pain all the fear all the awful of what's just happened and all that lies ahead.

※

In the worst moments, I repeat the mistake over and over and over.

Standing outside my own window like a ghost. I could've turned, could've walked away.

Enrique was right.

I endangered everyone I love.

I lie here, the endlessness of time defeats logic and none of the good reasons I had for lying there make sense and if only, if only. And then what if, what if, what if: an unending cascade of better outcomes, impossibilities, fantasy. They weigh me down, pin me to this pathetic mattress. I can't move, because the possibility I could've somehow done something different is a heavy demon sitting on my chest, laughing at me.

When I do rise, I leave pieces of myself behind; scraps of skin peel off and remain in bloody flesh streaks on the mattress. I stagger to the wall, blink away the pain as I collapse against it. Sweat pours down my forehead, stings my eyes. Maybe tears too. I want to be strong. I don't care if it gets me killed, I want to fight back, or at least have the possibility in my arsenal. Anything to make this constant berating of myself stop. I take a wobbly step away from the wall, my knees buckle, and I'm a pile of limbs on the hard floor, pain pulsing through me.

I lie there, breathing my regret.

✳

My teeth.

In a quiet moment, I run my tongue against them, find they are still sharp, and smile. It's strange to smile. My muscles haven't moved that way in a long time, so it feels like some crud comes loose from the cracks in my face. It's a sudden and secret thing, this smile. It is all mine.

Gently at first, and then harder, I clench my teeth against my tongue. A dull ache becomes a throb, then a piercing shriek of pain erupts as I cut through. The acrid taste of blood floods my mouth and I smile, I smile, because I have a plan now, a plan and a weapon.

Some blood dribbles out of my mouth and down my chin.

✳

They come back.

I don't know how much time has passed since the last time. Maybe days, maybe months. One stands blocking the shard of light cast by the slightly open door. I am again at his mercy, a bag of bones to be tortured and tossed aside. And I am a little deader inside, since the last time; a little more my own enemy.

He steps inside, nods at another soldier in the hallway, and turns around to close the door. It's a small thing, showing his back to me, but it lets me know he has total confidence in his power. I have long, filthy nails and dangling arms. I have knees, but I'm so weak they're not much good for ramming.

He turns back around and considers me, takes a step forward. He is middle-aged, a little younger than Papi. I fight off the onslaught of family memories that threatens to crush me beneath it. He is clean shaven except for a thick mustache and his teeth are unnervingly perfect. There's not much to him; he still wears those months of living jungle to jungle fighting dysentery and diarrhea; it's all over him like a cheap cologne. Those eyes gaze out from sunken valleys, mostly in shadow, and his clothes hang loosely.

A surge of hatred wells up inside of me, this pathetic beast with his hands on his hips, his head shaking. In this moment, if I could become fire and end us both I would do it in a second. I would laugh while his feeble flesh blackened and disintegrated amidst the crackles and screams. I would crow to the night sky for my victory, even as I succumbed to my own flames. I would disperse.

When he takes another step forward, my fantasy shatters and I hate him even more. I pray for a knife, a machine gun, an ax. I pray for mercy, for a seizure, a sudden flood or earthquake. Instead, there is nothing. With all my effort, I stand. And then I fall.

※

Padre Sebastián once told me if you imagine something happening it makes the reality of it bend that direction. I asked him if I imagined myself taller, would it work, and he smiled and shook his head at me, but then he shrugged. *Sure. But you can't expect it to work right away. The universe takes its own time.*

*But then how will I know if it was my mind making it happen or it's just me growing?*

*What's the difference, really?*

*But I was going to grow anyway!*

*That's where faith comes in.*

I scrunched up my face. *What fun is making wishes if you gotta wait?*

But the padre was a wise man. He might not have had this in mind when he said it, but the world has taken many wicked turns since that day. Tied to the chair again and soaking wet this time, I imagine my teeth stretch forward and thicken until they stick out of my mouth like a saber-toothed tiger's.

*¿Dónde?* is the one-word incantation of the day, the one that's supposed to make me divulge some magical rebel hideaway in the Escambray.

As if I could just describe it: the third tree on the left and straight up the hill. As if we didn't break camp every day and restart anew somewhere else.

As if it mattered.

*¿Dónde?* And something sparkling and fierce lashes across me, sends searing explosions of pain along my face, neck, and shoulders.

The pain whisks away all rational thought for a few breathless moments, it whites out the whole world.

*¿Dónde?* And I brace myself for another blitz of agony.

That doesn't come.

*¿Dónde?*

My teeth grow and grow. I retrieve newly fabricated memories of my teeth gnashing through steel cans, machinery, tearing small animals limb from limb and crunching bones. My teeth kill. They were made for this, billions of years of evolutionary mutations have given them special powers and I will bring death with them.

The soldier moves and before I can wince, the wire fizzles across my vision and everything is on fire. There's no air in my lungs, only pain searing from my skin.

Gasping, I tell him to come closer.

He raises an eyebrow—curious. Aroused maybe. I don't care. I can see that soft distended line where his vein reaches diagonally down his neck and as he leans in toward me I open my mouth as wide as I can.

*Ay*, a gruff voice demands from the doorway. *¿Y qué carajo está pasando aquí?*

The soldier whirls around, snaps to attention. *No, n-no*, he stammers. *Es que—*

*Untie her*, the voice says, suddenly calm, magnanimous. The soldier does, his rough hands freeing mine, and then he's gone and I'm left soaking wet and panting and gnashing my giant useless teeth that wouldn't have done a damn thing anyway.

*Are you okay?* the man wants to know.

I'd forgotten he was still there.

He sounds like he actually wants to know, which doesn't even make sense because I've just been tortured, of course I'm not okay. I shake my head, not making eye contact, just seeing his boots and dark green trousers between the dangling strands of my hair. He stands there for a very long time, staring at me, I presume. Then finally he sighs, turns away, and closes the door gently behind him.

✷

His name is David and he comes back the next day. He talks about himself in quiet, unassuming tones and apologizes again and again for what happened. I don't look at him. From the corner of my eye I see he is younger, just a few years older than me, and he has strong, slouched shoulders and a full beard. His eyes are wide to convey openness and his hands hang at his sides like something in him has given up.

I don't speak.

✷

David comes back the next day and sits across from me, talking talking endlessly about his life, why he joined the revolution what happened to him out there in la selva how he almost died what scares him what he hopes for his abuela in Camagüey his cousins in Vedado his mom and dad in Villa Clara and some girl that broke his heart in Pinar del Río. He says her name with a smirk and a choked laugh, brushes some hair off his face, and sniffles a little. I wonder if he'll cry.

I don't speak.

✳

The first time he touches me it's a disaster. He'd been talking and talking and talking as usual. He sits across from me, legs curled in front of him, scratching his beard occasionally and rubbing his eyes when he comes to something sad. He's been sitting closer and closer, and me, I just look away, so I barely notice until one day his hand is on my arm and I'm across the room, screaming and crying and sobbing and screaming. Then he's up, panting, eyes even wider and blue, almost see-through blue. I slow my breathing and shake my head. He leaves. I sit back down, collapse really but he's back the next day, talking again like nothing happened.

He touches me again a few days later. I don't scream this time. I'd felt it coming. I can't tune him out anymore, his whole presence energy voice everything are so invasive, relentless. And now that I bother paying more attention I can just make out the yellowish glow around him creeping slowly slowly along the floor toward me. So when I feel that warm, calloused fingertip on my skin I don't startle. I just look away.

His fingers rub circles up and down my arm. Then he's holding it. Then he rises, adjusts himself, and slides in around me somehow, wraps me in him, and I'm immersed in that man smell and the dinge of his uniform and his heavy breath.

*Rebecca*, he whispers, rocking me back and forth. *Rebecca*. He's crying.

I don't speak.

✳

At first I think he'll try to slide up inside me somehow. He doesn't. His hands brush my breasts sometimes while he caresses me and cries but they don't linger.

It doesn't matter. The violation is just a different color. I don't have any fight in me though. I'm empty. The person who had a family and life and walked outside and made friends and fell in love and railed at the sky and ran off to the jungle; she's gone. Someone else. I'm just a cracked shell, the crinkly bodies the cicadas leave behind, clinging pathetically to a tree long after the symphony is over. I'm just four walls and the smell of decay. I'm more David than I am myself, because he's all over me and his stories his breath his stupid world has invaded mine so completely.

I almost scream at him one day. *You might as well fucking kill me*, I almost yell. The thought of his reverie being interrupted, his startled face, it almost makes me smile. David stops mumbling *Rebecca Rebecca* for a second and looks at me. A few minutes later he starts up again.

But when he leaves, I do smile. It is more than a memory. It is a physical thing; my brain told my face to do it and it did. It reminds me of my teeth. I run my tongue along them again, painting mind pictures of tearing David's throat out.

I smile.

✳

And then one day when the door opens, it's not David. It's someone else, an older man I'd seen once or twice before they threw me in this hole. His beard is streaked with gray and his stiff posture suggests a discipline more regimented than the sloppy mountain guerrilla code. He doesn't smile when he sees me, but that hard face softens ever so slightly.

*Luz Marisol Caridad Aragones.*

I wonder if it tasted dusty in his mouth from so much disuse. Still, even on the lips of my enemy, my name is a scaffolding I can rise up on. I stand, blinking in the new light of the day.

*We are releasing you back in to the general population of prisoners.*

I don't know what this means at first. It just sounds like a jumble of sounds, but then he stands away from the door and I realize I'm to leave. This hole is my home no more. For a terrible second I think I might fall screaming to the floor, through the floor, and shatter, but I don't. I straighten myself and walk slowly, carefully past the captain and into the light.

*This way.* I take a step and then another behind him, down a hallway. There's a breeze coming in from the ocean. Somewhere there's an ocean. There's an ocean and before that is the pine forest, and even the prison itself is alive and vibrant and teeming with new things to show me, new gorgeous things. I am terrified and in awe all at once but I keep it mostly inside and just concentrate on staying in line behind the captain. He leads me through a doorway into a dingy room down another hallway and finally into an open courtyard full of other prisoners, mostly women, some lounging around, some heaving stones out of a ditch, some chopping vegetables.

There's a man in the corner and I don't recognize him at first, his beard is so long and his face so tired, so sad, but when I do I almost fall over myself making my way toward him. I wrap my arms around Padre Sebastián, squeeze him as tight as I can and sob.

Part Two

# VOLVER

# CHAPTER THIRTY

Little has changed. Everything has changed.

I hadn't realized how hungry I was, hungry and terrified to see this place again, to let these warm Caribbean crosswinds caress me, the smell of the ocean finding its breezy way through these decaying plaster castles and all that diesel fuel in the air. La Habana.

New Jersey, in retrospect, seems to glare from beneath an overcoating of gray. There are blues and greens, occasional reds, an orange. But over it all, the gray persists. Even on a sunny day. This is America, perhaps. The layer of dust still lingering from the collapsing industrial wastelands of the great northeast. It gets on you, inside you, taints even the faces, now grimaces, of the good people that flock there.

But here: The sun permeates all. It is unstoppable: It breaches the shade, stays on your skin, wraps around its citizens in warm browns and shining teeth, squinting eyes. It bolsters my shapelessness into something almost real, a cloud, cut through by sunlight, and maybe, maybe alive.

The sun has no shame as it casts stark, afternoon shadows along the wide avenue, the play of darks and lights describing the shifting rooftops, water tanks, and stairwells. An old man sputters past them on a motorbike, against traffic. Three piglets peer out of a cage hitched to the back; they snort suspiciously to each other, aiming their bemused little gazes at Ramón.

"¡Pero mira el camino, compadre! ¿Tú no ves?" The taxi jolts to a stop with a torrent of curse words and ancestor slander from the driver. Two young men in tank tops are stopped in the middle of the road. Between them is a wheeled cart piled high with various household appliances; Ramón sees an oven, two rusted-out refrigerators, and an industrial-sized fan. The driver finishes his tirade, the men trudge on to the sound of squeaking wheels; the taxi grumbles off toward Miramar.

*

"Blah!" Ramón yells. He spits a mouthful of brown water back into the paper cup and scowls. "I thought Cuban coffee was supposed to be the best in the world!"

Aliceana shakes her head. "Not the kind that actual Cubans have to drink though."

"Ugh."

Ramón has his whole mouth under the sink when Aliceana walks into the bathroom. "I'm not so sure you should be, um . . . drinking the tap water so enthusiastically."

He looks up, a yellowish stream dribbling down his chin. "Fuck."

"Or at all really."

He catches the towel she tosses him and gives his tongue a thorough thrashing. "I can feel the malaria setting in," Ramón moans, flopping onto the lime-green couch in the corner.

Adina rolls her eyes. "You don't get malaria from shnarsty tap water, jackass. Even I know that."

"It's true," Aliceana confirms helpfully. "But dysentery for sure, or maybe—"

"Ya, okay, okay, thank you." Ramón disappears into the bathroom and shuts the door.

"What's up his ass?" Adina asks, pouring herself a cup of ration coffee. Probably not much, judging from the sounds coming from the bathroom. "He hasn't been right for weeks."

"I know." Aliceana shakes her head. "He's not sleeping. Keeps waking up shaking, but then he won't talk about it. I mean, he did once, and then clammed up. It's like he thinks if he doesn't talk about it it'll all just evaporate."

"That's actually the Cuban state motto."

Ramón's voice comes through muffled from behind the wooden bathroom door. "You guys know I can hear everything you're saying, right?"

"Good," Adina yells. "Then you can tell us what the fuck is wrong with you."

The two women watch the door for a few moments and then make faces and shrug.

Should I feel bad for torturing my nephew's nights with the shards of my imprisonment? Does it matter if I know I have to? It's another endless ripple of trauma, I know, poisoning a whole new generation, but he needs to understand. Not just see or hear but understand.

This is the truth and Adina is right: We all bury the worst parts so deep inside, praying we'll never be found out, praying it'll just evaporate. But I am that truth, whoever, whatever my life or death has become, I'm the one buried. And the only way to unearth myself in body and mind is through this oversized music wizard fellow that I have come to care about and hurt so much. His stomach is torn up, it's true, but not from the bad Miramar water or ration coffee.

"Can you pass me another roll of toilet paper?" Ramón calls from the bathroom.

Aliceana gets one from their luggage and tosses it to Adina, who places it in front of the door, knocks twice, and then scurries away.

"I'm fine," Ramón says when the door shuts again. "It's just the water or whatever."

"Babe, you've been like this for two weeks." *Babe.* That's cute, how fast they've fallen into each other. The whirlwind of travel documents and family chaos and hospital bureaucracies threw Aliceana and Ramón into a frenzy of late-night cuddling, fucking, and storytelling as they unraveled themselves before each other. But he won't talk about the tiny room that enclosed me, the guard named David. Each time he tries, he just ends up shaking his head instead and getting choked up.

Aliceana and Adina frown at each other as Ramón lets out another grunt. "I'm fine!"

"Adina, would you ask your"—Aliceana makes exaggerated bunny-ear quotation marks in the air—"*tíos* if they have anything that'll settle his tummy?"

"You know if you do that out in the street it'll defeat the whole purpose of the—"

"I know, I know, I know," Aliceana grumbles. "I'm still just getting the hang of things. I'm no good at lying. Especially with my crappy Spanish."

"Better get used to it." Adina flashes a smile as she retreats down the hall but the edginess in her voice is unmissable.

Her "tíos," a middle-aged couple in matching YO AMO A CUBA baseball caps that clashed miserably with the floral dress and tucked-in guayabera, welcomed them with wide open arms and laughing embraces. They carried on amiably all through the cab ride to their little apartment in the Miramar suburbs and once they were all safely inside, Florio, an old work buddy of Adina's cousin, explained the situation in the best English he could muster. "If anybody asks, okay? We are your tíos. Okay? Anybody. Doesn't matter who. Somebody ask who you estay with? Tíos. Okay?"

"Okay, all of us?" Ramón asked, trying not to avoid having to say that Aliceana might have a harder time claiming the very non-Filipino-looking Espadas as family.

Florio was unconcerned. "All of you, sí. Tíos. Even if it is children or abuelas that are asking you: tíos." He looked at Aliceana. "¿Comprendes?"

Aliceana nodded. "Tíos. Got it. Comprendo."

Florio opened up a wide smile. "Okay. ¡Entonces! ¡A comer! To eat!"

✳

"You really not gonna talk about it, Ramón?" Aliceana, at her own peril, stands by the bathroom door. "It'll help, you know."

"Maybe it will. I dunno. Maybe it won't. Maybe it'll make it worse."

Neither of them says anything for a few minutes. "It's just . . ." Ramón says. Adina walks in carrying an ancient glass bottle of something bright red with a peeling label written in excited Cyrillic. She immediately grasps what she's walked into. She places the bottle gingerly on a counter and waits.

"It's just these dreams."

"Your aunt," Aliceana says.

"Marisol. Yeah. It's . . . I see what she saw. I don't know how. I can't explain it. There's no explaining it, I just . . . It's . . ." The toilet flushes and then the sink sputters to life. When Ramón appears in the doorway tears are streaming down his face and his shirt is damp because he used the one towel to scrape his tongue.

"Oh, Ramón." Aliceana is wrapped around him in seconds. He leans over enough to find her shoulder with his face and sobs. Adina watches, teary eyed. "Shhhh, let it out."

"Jesus, I don't know what's wrong with me," Ramón mutters after some heavy snorfling. "It feels good to let it out though, it's true. Shit." He chuckles through all the phlegm and tears and Aliceana squeezes him tighter.

"It's the prison, what you see?" Adina asks.

Ramón nods, sniffles again. "She was in solitary. She was . . . tortured. It's so awful." He accepts a wad of tissues from her and immediately destroys it with a single hork.

"What are you going to do?" Aliceana says quietly.

"Do?" He shakes his head. "I don't know. Kacique said he'd take me by the Ministry of Records, but he says it's a crap idea. Sounded like maybe he had a better idea, but I wanna at least try this first. It all seems impossible and ridiculous now that I'm here, but I don't know what else to do."

"Maybe it's not about what you can find, just that you came." Adina is standing with her arms crossed over her chest, her face scrunched into a pout.

"Maybe." Ramón shrugs. "Still, the thought that she might have just died somewhere . . . alone in a prison cell or in front of some wall torn apart by bullets. It just . . . it's tearing me up. After all she went through. In my dreams anyway. But even if that's not the real story, even if it's just some warped version of my subconscious messing with me: She was in prison. I mean, who knows how it happened, right?"

The two women nod solemnly.

In the corner, I weep.

Florio makes his presence known with a tentative rapping on the bedroom door. "¿Con permiso?"

Ramón pulls out of Aliceana and fumbles on his jeans while she disappears beneath the covers. "¡Voy! Un momento . . ."

"Hay una persona aquí pa'verte," Florio says when Ramón finally peeks out the door. "He is . . . how do you say?" The middle-aged man makes a series of vague hand gestures.

"A mime?" Ramón tries.

"Especial," is all Florio can come up with.

"¡Ramóncito!" a voice calls from the living room. "You come all this way and you don't even let me know when you get here? ¿Y eso? Coño ven pa'ca chico and give me a hug! Mi pen pal de tanto tiempo, 'chacho."

Kacique is a towering, perfectly shaped specimen of a man. His muscles peek out in shiny bulges from his wire mesh A-shirt, his chin line is sharp and outlined with the slightest of goatees. Grinning skulls and Taíno mosaics cover his immaculate brown arms. Kacique takes three long strides across the room and wraps around Ramón, who has to make an adjustment to keep his still fading erection out of the way and then hugs him back.

"You're shorter than I imagined!" Kacique grins, holding Ramón at arm's length to get a good look at him. "But I can see that glint of surly genius lurking around your eyes, my friend."

"Surly, you say?"

"This must be Aliceana." He bends down to kiss her offered cheek. "Ramón composes wonderful email poetry about you, you know?"

I would never have thought to call it poetry, but Ramón has been offloading sprawling torrents of thoughts about his new girlfriend into emails to Kacique. Kacique tends to respond with the smallest wink and nod of understanding, just enough for Ramón to release another spew into the next email, but never any information about his own life on the island.

Aliceana squirms a little farther into the sheets. "I didn't know that!"

Ramón shrugs. "More like a teenager's escaped journal entries than poetry, really."

"It's true he's very anti-grammarian," Kacique affirms with a sly smile. "But in a majestic way!" His English is as impeccable as his body; he seems to pluck and pronounce each word out of the air in front of him with light-speed precision. "If you're nice to me, maybe I will show you some of them."

Ramón growls but Kacique rumbles along without noticing. "Anyway!" He claps once and glides effortlessly into a gentle rumba. Then he stops suddenly. "There really is no correct translation for this word of yours, is there? We have *entonces*, but that's not quite right somehow, yes?"

"It's just a pivot word, anyway," Aliceana says, sliding into a T-shirt.

"Ah! A lover of words! A woman after my own heart! Too bad you are taken . . ." That sly grin again. Then, almost inaudibly: "And a woman."

You can see it dawn on Ramón. His face opens wide for just a second and Kacique nods at him, meaning *Yes, you fool* and also, *No, it's still not a good idea to publicly declare yourself gay on the island of Cuba.* "But, *anyway*, as you say: Tomorrow night is the show, yes? You ready?"

"Of course. You got a crowd coming?"

"Ay, Ramón." Kacique massages his eyes, that smile hinting at the gleeful irony. "You have no idea."

# CHAPTER THIRTY-ONE

"Is it like you thought it would be?" Kacique asks.

Ramón shrugs. "It's not so different. You guys have your high-rises just like us."

"Mhm."

"Chain stores."

"True."

"Advertisements."

"For different things." Kacique nods at a defiant bearded face looking skyward from a long dilapidated wall. "But yes, advertisements are everywhere."

HASTA LA VICTORIA SIEMPRE proclaims the wall. The paint is faded, but no one has graffitied penises or skulls over it like they would've in Jersey.

"Are there security cameras everywhere?" Ramón asks quietly enough that the driver can't hear.

Kacique lets out a little snort. "No, man, that's how you guys do it. We're old-fashioned. Who needs security cameras when you got betrayal?"

"Huh?"

"Eyes and ears," Kacique whispers with exaggerated hand motions. "Listening, watching. All the time." Kacique suddenly reaches forward and pats the driver on the shoulder. "Right, Chano?" he says loudly.

"Eh?" The old driver perks up. "Sí, cómo no. Lo que diga usted."

Kacique shrugs and sits back. "If you have to assume someone is always listening, watching, well, you don't need anything more than that really. We have become our own secret police."

Without warning, the sky opens up and thick, angry raindrops splatter the windshield. The sun persists, shines straight through the sudden downpour and blasts a glorious ray of light over a squad of uniformed schoolkids running past an old cathedral. Their little hands reach over their heads, catching the big dollops, and the squabble of laughter and shrieking rises over the shush of rain and thump-thumping against the taxi roof.

✳

Over a rusted metal bridge, beneath the ever-watchful gaze of a faded brick tower spray painted with revolutionary slogans, through a little field and around some crooked corners, there sits a little one-story stucco building. Palm trees stand guard around its entrance, protruding up from an impressive little city of dangling azaleas, lilies, and cacti. The garden is perfectly tended to, but the gate, once black and shiny perhaps, festers with crumbling light brown flakes. A sun-bleached sign declares this to be the Ministry of Records, Vedado Subdivision VII in the glorious name of the triumphant revolution, etc., etc.

Inside, Ramón and Kacique strike an imposing image, both craning their necks a little to avoid being decapitated by the slow-moving ceiling fans. What Kacique lacks in girth he makes up for in muscles and Ramón is just huge. The tiny graying woman sitting behind the desk in her crisp beige uniform is undaunted though.

She's maybe four foot eight on her tiptoes, but the claustrophobia this woman emits is suffocating. When she gestures at the ugly wooden chairs and asks in a saccharine voice that Ramón and Kacique please be seated, they comply immediately. And me? I find myself once again diminished. It's the barrage of memories, the newness and the oldness, the rising tide of nausea that I have become, here back in the firepit. It's the sense that whatever happened to me, it was not pretty, not a fairy tale or a dashing rescue, not even a glorious, sudden flare-out like Isabel.

The thought that maybe after a tiny life of tragedy and occasional glimpses of courage, I just rotted away, disappeared . . . it deepens my need to know, finally know and know for real what really happened. But I am weak, grow weaker every day.

And I dread the truth.

"Would you gentlemen care for a cafecito or refresco?" the desk maven asks. Her voice is gravelly from ration cigarettes and her hair is pulled so tightly into a bun, it pulls her eyebrows into severe little slants.

Kacique prepared Ramón for this moment as they strolled over the metal bridge. "Take the coffee. If you take the soda she will rule you."

"But why?"

"Ramón, trust me, okay? There is a methodology to even the maddest of madnesses, and communist bureaucracy most of all. The refresco is orange, mostly processed sugar and to accept it is a sign of weakness, understand?"

"Not really."

"You don't have to. Just do what I say."

"How's the coffee though?"

Kacique stopped, put a firm hand on Ramón's shoulder. Beneath them, a dirty little stream limped along between sloping metal panels and trash. "It is a disgrace to the nation of Cuba. But it's not about the taste."

"It's about power."

"¡Eso mismo! It means you won't take her stupid microbrigada excuse for soda. That you have some integrity. That you are a man."

"But if it's bullshit coffee, why not refuse altogether?"

"Oh no!" Kacique laughed and kept walking. "This is Cuba, mi socio. You can't do that."

The tiny woman places two foam cups of coffee in front of a polished brass nameplate that says LT. URRUTIA, stirs too much sugar into each one with a wicked smile, and then clack-clacks back behind her desk. She shuffles some papers while Ramón sips at the café, flinches, and puts it back down. He looks at Kacique, who shakes his head: *Wait.* Finally, Lt. Urrutia looks up, folds her hands in front of her, and smiles. "Now, what may I help you with today?"

I tune Ramón's fumbling explanation out, spend most of it shivering in a corner trying to keep myself from shattering under the crushing presence of this agent of Everything That Had Destroyed My Life.

And then I snap back to some level of engagement when the lieutenant stands and barks a sharp "Entonces." She is actually taller when sitting—apparently it was a big chair—but that doesn't do anything to lessen the impact of her sudden action. "You have described to me a person who was an enemy of the revolución, an imperialist. You said she was *what* to you?"

"My friend's mom," Ramón says, cringing at the one lie in his arsenal.

"Now you have come to this country, to the patria, you say to find out what has happened to the person, and I'm telling you you are paying a great disrespect to the people of Cuba by doing this thing."

Ramón just stares at her, his mouth hanging slightly open. Kacique looks away so the lieutenant won't see him roll his eyes. "Now, where did you say you were staying for the duration of your . . ."—a very wide grin—". . . *visita* to Cuba?"

"With my tíos, in Miramar."

"Is that so?" She leans forward. "How nice. Familia. Write their address down on this piece of paper for me, and then you may go."

"What?"

"Oh, did you misunderstand me? I apologize, Señor Rodriguez. I know your education system is quite secondary. Perhaps if I speak slower?"

"No, I understood you, I just . . . I don't understand. You want me to write . . ."

"Their address. On the paper. And then sign it. For our records, that is all."

Kacique's face holds no answers for Ramón. There are no answers. Every formality is a trap, disaster awaits each step. You can't fuck up because you fucked up by entering the game, period. Lives are at stake, families. A signature on a piece of paper won't alter a single event; it will simply unnerve poor Ramón. And it has, clearly it has. He's sweating and his hand trembles as he copies the Miramar address out of his phone and then scribbles a messy *R* beneath it.

The lieutenant nods at him, opens her grin a fraction wider. "Thank you for your time."

✳

"What the fuck was that?"

"Te jodió, compadre."

"I mean . . . what the fuck . . . was that?"

The bridge again. Kacique is eating a fried doughy yucca relleno from one of the food carts scattered around Vedado. Ramón stares into the pathetic little piss-stream down below. He shakes his head. "I drank the damn coffee."

"I know, but it takes more than that. The coffee just gets you in the door. If she thinks you're telling the truth, it's all over."

"I was telling the truth! Partially!"

"I know. So did she. That was the problem. The system isn't set up to function properly when people come straight forward."

"But that's insane!"

"I tried to tell you, man. You knew this was a long shot." Kacique tosses the grease-stained napkin over the bridge and passes Ramón a ration cigarette.

"How did she get off telling us we *can* leave? We came to see her! She can't dismiss us."

"Ramón."

Ramón takes a puff off his cigarette, looks at it in disgust, and then tosses it into the river. "Will they come for the Espadas?"

"I don't know. But that little piece of paper won't mean a thing one way or the other. You think they don't have all their information filed already? Their favorite flavor of ice cream and their kids' secondario grades? They do."

"Ugh."

"She was trying to fuck with you, and she succeeded. Consider yourself fucked with, a lo cubano. Or a la cubana in this case."

"Ah hell."

"Ramón."

"What?"

"I know this is important to you, but you do realize we have a concert tomorrow night, yes? And it's actually going to be something along the scale of gigantic, something people will remember. Cuba will hear your music, live, for the first time . . ."

"I know, man, I'm sorry. I'm cool, I just . . ."

"And the orchestra is set to—"

"Wait! The orchestra?"

For the first time, Kacique looks put out. "You didn't read the emails I sent you, Ramón?"

"I did, but I . . . you know, I skimmed them."

Kacique shakes his head. "Ramón, Ramón, Ramón."

# CHAPTER THIRTY-TWO

Every second is crisp.

Still diminished, still uneasy and writhing in the ecstasy of all my memories, I slide down the darkening Havana streets. The echoes of that place fill me—the shuffling papers, that rigid, wretched bureaucracy. It was just a simple conversation, but still I feel we barely escaped intact. Out in the avenues, the lanterns barely fend off the night. The sky is unstoppable, and even down these inland side streets, a mile or two from the Malecón, the ocean breathes its impossible hugeness all around, into the cracks and corners, the salty air.

It's quiet.

In slowly shattering apartment complexes, behind peeled-paint facades, families curl up inside themselves. There's an American movie on TV, a white cop and a black cop trade insults and save each other's lives in increasingly improbable misadventures; something from the early nineties, I'd say.

And of course, everybody's watching. As I pass each window I catch glimpses of it: stern eyes beneath a tragic mullet, the cutaway from a sloppy makeout session. "I don't think that's possible," the white cop says. "It'll all be up in smoke soon." The black cop just shakes his head, lights a cigarette.

An old man trudges across the street I'm sweeping along. He stops very near me, smells the air, smiles. Walks on.

Forward, forward, I enter the warm Caribbean wind and let it merge with me. Suddenly, I am not alone: The night is full of ghosts. They are all around me, hanging silently, impossibly still in the empty air. They are sullen, almost comatose. They hold no secrets for me; their mysteries are locked away or gone. I leave them there, sulking mindlessly, forever maybe, in the night. I keep my trajectory toward the sea.

I don't know what I thought I'd find here. More life? My own life, somehow? An answer. There's nothing. A couple kids were playing guitar and singing by the crumbling wall of the Malecón, but they leave soon after I show up. Afraid maybe, or just on to haunt some other corner of town. They weren't great singers anyway. The last of the tourist gift stands has just finished packing away their knickknacks, fake indigenous artifacts, and corny watercolor still lifes of the Capitolio dome, a cartoon santera with big lips and a cigar.

I am alone, every second still crisp. Every answer waiting in the silence and roar of the ocean around me. And still: nothing. No secrets, no lies, no answers at all. I am alone.

✳

Padre Sebastián.

Minus almost a hundred pounds—he was charmingly stocky back in Las Colinas; you wanted to poke his little pudge and watch him giggle— now he's caved in, sallow. But there's a light in him. Somehow, watching him, I understand a thing about what must make a man dedicate his life to God. Sebastián carries something in him that doesn't dull, even here amidst all this concrete and festering wounds and rotting bread. Sebastián's body has decayed, but that light in him is relentless. The church always seemed like such an archaic, confining institution for a man as free as Sebastián, but I see now it gave him something to structure his light around. Focus.

We're in the yard. The sun is an unbearable coating over our skins and the sweat doesn't stop pouring off us and I'm thinking how I wish I knew Sebastián as a teenager, when he turns to me and smiles. *When I am most wretched, I think about the saints.*

It's a strange thing to say because even with the unrepentant sun and mindless stretches of hard labor, this is a relatively good time in our lives at La Isla. I'm still reeling from the joy of not being alone in that tiny room. I feel strangely safe. I'm gaining my weight back. I know some of the guards well enough to get cigarettes or medicine when we need it. The captain leaves us alone. And I don't think about home too many times a day.

*I still feel bad about throwing that book at you*, I say.

He shakes his head with a smile. *One of my favorite moments we have shared. Did you know there are over ten thousand saints officially ordained by the Holy See?*

I put down the rock I was carrying. *That many? Jesus Christ!*

Padre Sebastián's smile shines crookedly through his filthy beard. *Well, technically he's not a saint, no.*

*That's a lot though.*

*And that's only the ones they've made official.*

*What do you mean?* I pick up my own rock and take his too, because he's wobbling beneath its weight. We start toward the half-constructed wall.

*I mean when the Church makes a saint, that person's whole life is a part of the saintliness, no?*

*I guess.*

*Of course! Their struggles with faith, their journey to God, and all the twists and turns along the way. Saint Augustine, who died a bishop, spent his formative years as a street scoundrel. He ran with criminals and loose women. He was a mess.*

*But he's a saint.*

*Through and through. Was he a saint when he was sinning? His whole life is divine: His sins led him to the path of righteousness. All part of the plan.*

*You're saying . . .* I stop because Padre Sebastián has stopped walking. His eyes are closed, he's swaying gently, and I'm not sure if he's about to collapse or start singing. I put down some of the rocks I was carrying.

*What of all the saints that have yet to be beatified? The wait is long, the process fraught with political nuances and gerrymandering that have little to do with the actual actions of the souls in question. What of the truly sanctified souls that don't make the cut? Are they not saints as well?*

He opens his eyes, takes the hand I've reached out to keep him upright, and together we hobble forward. *I don't know. I've never thought that much about it. Just paid attention when the stories got juicy and mostly forgot about the saints except the ones they talk about a lot.*

*Think on it, Marisol.*

✳

Back from my midnight sojourn, I am spread thinly across the room, my breath a faint susurration while the lovers sleep. Everywhere and nowhere, I allow those gentle bodies and their momentary peace to fill me. I won't trouble Ramón with any dreams, not tonight. And anyway, they're stirring, and each small motion resonates and booms into the late-night quiet, their tenderness for each other, their want.

Ramón opens his eyes to find Aliceana staring into them. It's still dark out; some strange birds scream into the Cuban early morning sky. Her skin seems to glow softly in the predawn gray. She's propped up with one elbow against the bed, her hand cupped thoughtfully around her face, and that long black hair, usually pulled back, now tumbles freely down her shoulders and over her chest. One of the straps of her nightshirt has slipped down her shoulder and a glint of light from the lamppost outside catches her collarbone.

Ramón takes her in, resting his eyes on the smudge of brightness against her clavicle, down along the outlines of her breasts told through the creases of her nightshirt. He wants to lunge across the tiny distance between them, spread and enter her again and again a hundred times harder and harder until she's screaming and empty of breath in his ear and then explode. But he doesn't want this moment to end, right here, this soft perfection waiting for him like a holy vision when he shakes off sleep. So instead he reaches out a hand, trembling with the effort of restraint, and traces one finger along her collarbone. She closes her eyes; her mouth becomes the slightest of smiles. His finger glides up her throat, caresses the line of her jaw, lands gently on her lips, and darts away before she can bite it. His whole hand wraps around the back of her neck, beneath her hair, and he pulls her close against him, his hardness pressed up against her soft tummy; one leg slides between hers.

"I . . . I'm sorry," Ramón whispers.

"Ramón, for what?"

"I've just been . . . I'm such a mess, Aliceana. I'm trying so hard to keep it all together, to make things make sense, but they don't, no matter how many ways I turn them upside down or inside out, they don't make sense." His fingertips creep along the back of her neck to the hard surface tucked away behind her ear. "These dreams, and the fire. Tío Pepe . . . my mom. Shit, my whole fucking family."

Fingertips knead gentle circles behind her ear, three times around then back the other way. "I want so badly to just be . . . to be, you know, ferocious. Unafraid. To be sure of what's true and what's not. Like the way Marisol seems like she was, she stood up. She was confused and afraid, but she stood up through all that bullshit and tyranny and did something, you know? And it didn't even seem like a choice to her, like it was just a route of her life that she followed effortlessly and, yes, she paid for it, paid with everything, but . . . but I'm talking about someone I never even met and only know through . . . through dreams, but . . . she's family, whoever she is."

Ramón stays quiet for a few minutes. His fingers keep drawing slow circles just behind Aliceana's left ear, three around, three the other way. He takes a deep breath, looking down at the top of her head, the light line of her scalp showing through where her jet-black hair is parted in the middle. Her forehead, just peeking out like a setting sun from where her face is buried in his shirt. This tiny, phenomenal woman who adores him, who followed him here on a whim and a dream. He puts a kiss on her crown.

"And then you showed up, a love . . . yes, a love because that's what it is, way more so than anything else I've known in my life, even my . . . anyway, yes, this love showed up and I really thought I'd lost you and what that really meant was more than any kind of pain I could look at square in the face, it was bigger than fear or doubt, it was heartbreak, but I never could've said that at the time, because I was too deep in the thick of it, too busy not looking at it, looking at anything else to be able to call it what it was, just like I was too busy looking away for the whole first part of our . . . whatever that was when we were just fucking. I couldn't see you and everything it was because I wouldn't look. Because I was scared. Because I knew I was pretending to just fuck you, I was really really, really what I was was doing something totally different. But pretending felt so good, and it felt safe, safer than really standing back and looking at you, I mean *looking* at you, in a for-real way, and what you did to me. Inside of me. You know?"

He stops his circling fingertips and lifts her face out of his shirt. Her eyes are closed and lips slightly parted, trembling. "Don't . . . stop," Aliceana whispers.

"What, talking?"

"No." You can barely hear her, it's more an exhalation than a word. "Circles."

"Oh." Ramón finds the spot again, circles, as she grinds against his knee.

"I'm listening to you though, I swear Ramón. Just . . ."

"It's okay, babe, I—"

"Uhhh!" Her moan comes out so loud and suddenly Ramón is sure the entire apartment could hear it.

He lifts his thigh a little tighter into her crotch and smiles against her forehead. "Like this?"

"Uh . . . huh."

"I didn't even . . ." He stops because her whole body is trembling and for a second he's not sure if it's a convulsion of some kind. She cranes her neck back, eyes rolled all the way to the side, lips quivering, and you can see the wave after wave of heat, light, sex pulsing out of her body and cluttering up the room around them. She breathes in one time deep, all the way in, lets it out and then pulls in again, body still quaking, and the waves and waves of pleasure burning out of her quicken, become blinding. Her body clenches in his embrace and then she gasps and Ramón feels a shock of pain in his chest.

"Ow! Jesus!"

Aliceana releases the little nip of flesh from her clenched jaw, twitches one more time, and then goes limp in his arms, panting.

"You alright?" Ramón says once she's caught her breath.

"Yes, I'm sorry, babe, I was there with you, that was beautiful, what you—"

"Shhhh." He brushes some hair out of her face and slides underneath her on his back, pulling her on top of him. "It's alright, sweetheart, I just . . . I didn't know you . . . I didn't know that was a spot for you."

"Well, you never tried it before." Her grin is huge as she rubs her pelvis back and forth against his erection.

"Mmgh." With minimal fumbling, Ramón is inside her, all the way. He thrusts once, twice, three times and then she leans forward and catches his face in her hands.

"Listen, Ramón, and listen good."

He raises his eyebrows. The room is perfectly still around them. The morning has come, a hazy gray seeping through the window.

"I heard everything you said. I felt it deep inside of me. You're better at this than you realize, trust me. You think it's all buried away, but I see it, I've seen it all along in you, all those emotions you think you're hiding—you show 'em, you just got weird ways of doing it. But I see you, Ramón. I see you and I love you, okay? I love you."

Ramón nods, then comes silently, gigantically, emphatically inside of her, somehow is standing, on the bed, breathless and drenched, still enwrapped in her, sits back down, then collapses, still breathless, and whispers: "I love you too."

# CHAPTER THIRTY-THREE

Padre Sebastián, his tattered Bible in one hand, the other gesticulating in time to his excited voice, tells me about another saint. But the tower is behind him and I can't concentrate. The tower is always behind everyone, everywhere. The tower is immense, a verb and a noun, ever present. It's a dull yellow, sits square in the middle of the yard where we do our work, right in the middle of the compound, and at the top there's the window where the guards sit. Or maybe they don't; no one knows.

It doesn't matter: After twenty-four hours of wondering you just assume they are, and it's like there are two little bearded men with guns inside your head, watching, always watching. And then slowly they fade away: The brain doesn't want to be in chains; it gradually ejects the intruders. They dissipate; you forget. And then you run outside one day to see what the commotion is about and it's your friend Meelo writhing in a pool of his own blood that keeps getting bigger and bigger. And he cries out, his hands scrambling to stop the flow pouring out of his leg, but he can't he can't and you watch the eyes of everyone standing in the wide circle around, some of them squinting and determined, some wide and wet.

When someone steps forward you know what'll happen before it does and then it does: Another crack rings out and this time it's Miguel, whom you never liked that much—he leered at you and talked too loud about his rich family in Miami and all his ludicrous escape plans—but you never, ever wanted to see the top of his head blown clean off like that, replaced by a sudden burst of pink and red flesh like a watermelon. He drops before the echo dies out. And Meelo is still screaming and everyone's still staring and you're helpless, helpless and useless when the final shot rings out catching Meelo in the right chest, laying him out. He coughs and it's wet; blood speckles the air above him and you pray he dies right now, but he doesn't: His body stubbornly refuses to stop twitching and writhing, his chest rises and falls, faster and faster and then slower and slower and then finally, finally not at all and then, then you never ever forget that the tower is always there, always watching. Even when it's not.

*Marisol?* My name, always a tiny prayer on the lips of a man I love but will never have.

*Santa Cecilia*, I say quickly. *I'm listening.*

*No you're not.* He smiles though, resigned. *It's alright.*

*Padre?*

*Hm?*

*How do you remember all this stuff anyway—about the saints?*

*Ah, some of it they drill into us at seminary.* Behind him, the tower watches and watches. In the yard a few middle-aged women congregate, cigarettes in hand, and trade insults and survival tips. *And I always loved the stories, so I used to stay up all night in my little room at San Bartolo reading them over and over.*

*Fun.*

*And then when I forget stuff I just make it up.*

*Padre!*

*Well . . . Look around you. We have to survive somehow.*

The women in the yard start yelling and Sebastián whirls around. My heart is in my brain, pounding relentlessly, too fast, but then they're laughing and one of them stands a little away, soaking wet. When Padre Sebastián turns back he exhales and turns his face to the sky.

*I feel like I'm disappearing*, he says quietly.

I just nod. I've lost track of time again, as days bled into months, years. My wounds healed. I got some new ones, although none as bad as the first, and those healed too. And that's become the new timekeeper: how long the body takes to replenish in order to prepare for more brutality. One day, I know it won't bother, and we'll all just be walking bruises, bleeding the last of our lives into our broken hearts.

And then we'll be gone.

I know exactly what he means.

✳

Kacique picks them up after a hearty breakfast of café con leche, fresh fruit, and fried eggs.

"Adina, you sure you don't want to come with us?" Kacique says, crossing his arms over his chest.

Adina looks up at the bright Cuban sky. "I'm good." She's over-dressed, wearing sharp sunglasses and a button-down shirt tucked into slacks. And she looks more uncomfortable than usual, out of her element. "I got some long-lost folks to look up too."

"You don't want to join us partway? What part of town you going to?"

"It's fine," Adina says, almost sharply. "It's fine."

Kacique shrugs, looks at Ramón and Aliceana. "¿Listos? You guys look like perfect tourists."

"Thanks," Ramón says. They hop into the same old taxi from the day before and rumble off through the dusty Miramar streets toward Vedado.

"This is your aunt we're meeting with?" Ramón asks.

"Yes," Kacique mutters. "My aunt." His sarcasm is barely concealed. Everybody is everybody's aunt here, I almost forgot.

Old Havana. Crumbling colonial facades and faded murals. Scruffy street dogs roam around in packs, scatter at the slightest hint of trouble. Puddles pockmark the uneven streets; a little kid pees on the curb while his mom looks away. The taxi pulls to a halt. Ramón pays and then Kacique leads them through a huge wooden door to a shadowy atrium inside an ancient row house.

"It's called a solar," Kacique says. "This design with the balconies around an inner open area, yes? People who grow up in these apart-ments all know each other, they are each other's families, both literally and because they share a space together."

227

Aliceana and Ramón nod. "Which one does your aunt live in?" Aliceana asks.

"Oh, she doesn't live here."

"But—"

"Shh."

They stand still for a few minutes. The quiet churn of the city comes and goes like breath, the plants around them stir gently. Somewhere, a baby cries and a woman yells for Mercedes to get the milk off the stove, ya. There is a constant drip-dripping, the shuffle of feet, and the soft murmur of a radio announcer, punctuated by rhythmic bleats marking the passage of time. Somewhere not far away, a rooster calls.

"Okay," Kacique says. "Vámonos."

They step back out into the open sunlight and proceed up a narrow side street. "It's about a ten-minute walk from here."

"Why didn't we just—" Ramón starts.

"Because then the taxi guy'd know where we're going, man," Aliceana says.

"Ah," Ramón says. "But, if you don't trust the cabbie, why hire him twice in a row?"

"Because I don't trust anybody, but I still need transportation to get my friends the yanquis places, no? And Chano is mostly deaf and entirely stupid and very horny. I know how to keep him happy and confused."

Aliceana's eyes go wide. "You mean you—"

"¡No, coño! ¡Ay, qué horror! No, I buy him how do you say? Magazines? Girly? Girly magazines?"

"Ohhh!"

"They're very hard to come by, you know." It's true: All along the mercados and causeways of Havana, old books and the state-run newspapers glare out, but there is not a bikini-clad woman in sight.

"Up this way." Kacique leads them up a stairwell between two buildings that look like they've been collapsing in slow motion for at least a century. Maps of peeling paint savage the sun-soaked stucco walls.

Kacique pokes his head out into the street at the top. It is empty. He motions them briskly to a gated entranceway and hits the buzzer. A kid opens the door—alright, maybe he's twenty-one or -two? He has a bright, wide-open face and a gray Mets T-shirt that is way too big for his lanky frame. When he sees Kacique he grins with half his mouth and narrows his eyes in a way that seems somehow self-effacing and sarcastic.

"¿Los yanquis?" the boy says.

"Cállate, coño, Catabalas, and open the damn gate, before the whole of La Habana gets to be in on our conversation."

Catabalas smirks and rolls his eyes, fumbling with the metal lock, and then makes an exaggerated welcoming gesture. Kacique waits until the massive wooden door is shut before making introductions. "Ramón, Aliceana, this is Catabalas. Besides knowing much more than anyone ever should about computers and things, he is perhaps the biggest pain in the ass the Cuban government has ever known."

Catabalas cheek kisses Aliceana and gives Ramón a pound. "It is an honor to meet you, Ramón. Your song 'Mechadrome'? I play it while I watch the pirated German pornography and listen: perfection. Understand? It's like you were in the room when they were making the films and matched each beat to a thrust."

"Oh. Uh . . . thank you!"

"No," Catabalas says sincerely. "Thank *you*. Now come. Kacique here tells me we have business to discuss."

This place, it's comfortable. The front room opens to an inner garden; two short palm trees keep watch over a menagerie of lilies and daffodils. The next room is shadowy, but the wide windows let the breeze in from the garden. Wind chimes glistening in the doorway sing out a constant shimmery tinkle like the flow of water. It takes me a moment to adjust and then a strange sense of home comes over me. Family portraits dot the cracked walls. There's a small cabinet in the corner and a nightstand beside it. At the far end of the room, an old woman lies perfectly still in a wooden bed.

The room breathes in and out with the garden breeze, the soft murmur of the wind chimes. The woman may as well be dead. Catabalas nods at her as they pass. "My tía, Adriana. She's one of the famous Damas de Blanca you may have read about in the newspapers, eh? Or maybe not, I don't know."

"Is she . . . okay?" Aliceana asks.

She is, but only barely. I'm just inches from her sallow face. She's not so old as I'd first thought, but her frail body is collapsing piece by piece.

"She's on a hunger strike," Catabalas says. "To demand the release of my mom, Argelina Malcatrán? I don't know if word gets out or not over there. We try to keep the international press informed, but there's not much breaking news to someone being in prison for another year, so it usually gets buried underneath more important stories like Eddie Murphy getting divorced."

"Eddie Murphy got divorced?" Kacique blurts out. Catabalas punches him in the chest.

"You okay, Tía?"

Adriana nods ever so slightly. For a moment, we merge. Her life force pulses so languidly: a feverish, thready beat every now and then. A sorrow that I remember well drenches the emptiness between each pulse: loss. The uncertainty of one left behind, the urge to live mingled with the stench of regret. Starving brings physicality to the emotional loss.

"How long?" Aliceana asks.

"The fast? Twenty-one days now."

"But . . ." Aliceana struggles for the words, comes up empty.

"I know," Catabalas says. "I know."

"There are some Americans here, Tía. Cuban Americans. My favorite DJ is here."

"Bueno." It's a whisper, a croak really. "Mira, ver si quieren refresco."

Kacique rolls his eyes, flinching as Catabalas pops him again. "¡Hola, Tía Adriana!"

"Ay, Kacique. Ten cuidado, mi amor, ¿okay?"

"Okay, Tía." They pass into the next room. "She says that every time," Kacique mutters just before the door closes.

I feel peaceful here. Adriana struggles between holding on and letting go; the room is tainted with her sorrow, but it is home to me somehow and I find myself dispersing into the empty space above her bed. I wonder if I knew her. She may be about my age, I think as I become thinner and thinner in the air. The family photos reveal no familiar faces, but I could imagine one of her people may have been in prison with me, no? Cuba is a small world; subversive Cuba even smaller. Claustrophobic even.

It doesn't matter. Something in this woman's mourning is also mine. We have both lost a sister, even if hers is still alive. Or maybe she's what I imagine Isabel would be like if she'd lived.

I don't want to leave. I don't want to leave, but Kacique seems to think the Catabalas fellow has the key to finding out what my fate was. Particle by particle I reunite, then breathe a few moments. I can't heal her—she is at war with herself. But still I radiate the best of myself with each breath, all the peaceful moments of my life I can find, a prayer made from memories, and then flutter off to find the others.

# CHAPTER THIRTY-FOUR

The light in Catabalas's cramped hacker den is tinted green and shrouded over by various drapes dangling from the ceiling. Thrasher metal grinds out of a speaker system that seems to sprout out of every corner. Mostly naked, improbably busty cartoon women strike poses along the walls beside a glowering black light portrait of Malcolm X.

"This is nice equipment," Ramón says, running his finger along the soundboard.

"Yeah, the CIA gave it to me."

Ramón's eyes go wide.

"I'm kidding. If the CIA were to give me one cup of coffee the dipshits upstairs would put me away for being an imperialist. Anyway, I hate those pigfuckers too."

"Oh. How does everybody speak so freely here?" Aliceana asks. "Everywhere else we've been so far it's all sign language and subterfuge."

Kacique puts an arm around Aliceana's shoulder. "This is why I love your girlfriend, Ramón. She notices things. You should be grateful that I am a no-vagina zone."

"You can't imagine how grateful. Along with all the other straight men of Cuba, I'm sure."

Catabalas shakes his head. "You don't even know, hermano."

"Anyway." Kacique squeezes Aliceana one time and then releases her. "Catabalas has rigged the place with antibugging devices, the most sophisticated there are. And he scans it every morning after his cafecito."

"Damn," Ramón whispers into an exhale. "It's really that deep here, huh."

"Correct." Catabalas lights a cigarette, further murking up the already hazy air. "Sorry, I farted. Now, let's talk business, eh?"

As Kacique and Ramón run down the basic premise of the visit, I circle past the drapes to the ceiling. For all its physical clutter, the place is pleasantly free of other ghosts or unnecessary energies. There's no spiritual mess clogging up the upper corners of the room, no lingering demons or echoes of nostalgia. I feel crisp here, fresh, and I suspect the young hacker keeps a babalawo around for regular cleansings.

"This woman fought against the regime. She went to prison. She disappeared. Yes?"

"From the best we can figure," Ramón says a little sheepishly.

"What are your sources?"

"It's, uh . . . complicated."

I suspect this boy wonder would be open to the dream narrative, but Ramón is too shy about it. It doesn't matter; he has more pressing concerns. "But you said the very mention of this situation rattled the lady at the ministry of peepeecaca, yes?"

"To the core," Kacique says. "You know they don't want any gusanos coming back looking for their long-lost rebel tías, come now. They were put out. Started throwing threats and paperwork around the office as per standard operating etc., etc."

"Mmm . . ." Catabalas pulls out a piece of paper.

"So it irritates the hell out of the Cuban government." He checks off a box. "Does it help out a committed ally or friend of the movement?"

Kacique raises his eyebrows at his friend and cranes his neck forward.

"Okay, then. Check. Is it a problem that can be feasibly tackled with the resources I have on hand? Well, obviously. And finally, does Catabalas come out somehow on top in the end?"

Kacique snickers. "Well, that's a whole other type of—"

"No, of course, of course," Ramón cuts in. He's shuffling awkwardly through his pockets.

"No," Catabalas says. "That's not what I meant."

Ramón frowns at him.

"Well, I'll take some of that too, but more importantly: Her name is Yaniris."

"Listen," Ramón says, palms raised. "I don't know what you heard..."

"I just want a chance to talk to her. I... she doesn't even know I exist."

"Why don't you just—" Aliceana says.

"And, you're her favorite DJ, Ramón. She is crazy for it, every time we have an opportunity to pirate more of your music."

Ramón shrugs. "What do you want me to—"

"She is so beautiful!" Catabalas spins around in his chair and starts clicking away at his desktop. "You see?" A girl's face pops up on the screen. She looks alarmingly like Catabalas, even has the same wiry glasses, but her face is framed by long, curly hair that drapes down around her shoulders. She wears a wily smile and glares at the camera like it just said something slick about her. One of Ramón's beats erupts from the sound system and a fluttering of animated doves bursts out over her face.

"Whoa," Ramón laughs. "You made a little digi-shrine for your love? That may not be the way to—"

"I was going to show it to her, but..." Catabalas shuts off the music with a click and navigates to another page. "I got shy."

"She's cute," Aliceana says. "What do you want Ramón to do?"

"Somehow, to give me a chance. That's all. I don't know how. You figure that part out. But this"—he clicks open an official-looking website with the Cuban flag on it—"I'll do whatever I can to get information about your tía."

Kacique sighs. "I don't think this is what Ché meant when he said all revolutionaries come from love."

"You shut up," Catabalas snaps.

※

I walked here. Both as a child and later, in much more troubled times, with fists clenched, praying I wouldn't be noticed. Very little has changed. The Gran Teatro de La Habana is the same towering gray relic;

still filthy and obtuse. Its pigeons and pigeon-shit-covered statues still loom over the park, where old men still tease each other about American sports teams and beautiful women.

There are more tourists here, that's all. Last time I passed this way it was only a year or two after the revolution. A few adventure seekers straggled through, but nothing like this hustle and bustle of pasty, flashing-camera desperation. Here's a German family, crisp tight pants unrolled from cramped suitcases, having a minor fallout over whether to head to the Capitolio or call it a day. The late afternoon sky menaces more rain. There go some Spaniards, teenagers, wild and frothy on their first romp overseas. A middle-aged man in a suit strolls along the busy throughway arm in arm with a young Cuban girl. She's maybe thirteen and reminds me, with a pang of sorrow, of Nilda; she has her eyes and that proud, defiant lift of her chin. They're careful not to brush against a filthy beggar lurching past on crutches.

And here comes Ramón, making his way through the crowds alongside Kacique. He's his own peculiar brand of tourist: The jineteros and beggars aren't sure what to make of him. He *looks* Cuban, yes? Certainly has that whatever it is that we see in each other, some nuance of his facial structure or a rhythmic tic invisible to the conscious eye. But his clothes are not quite right. The tall, unabashedly effeminate, perfect specimen of manhood that walks beside him gets stares for a whole other reason. They don't blend in, but it doesn't matter: Before anyone can ask too many questions they've ducked down a small stairwell along a side wall of the Gran Teatro and are gone.

❋

"What is this place?"

"The basement." Kacique hits a switch and a splash of Technicolor lights blinks to life, chasing each other across a stage at the far end of the room.

"They do shows down here?"

"On Wednesdays and Fridays they have some old cha-cha-cha and

235

danzón cats play and all the viejitos come out and swing around the dance floor a couple of times. It looks like they all crawled out of Colón cemetery and have to hurry back into their graves by midnight or they'll turn to dust."

Ramón just stands at the doorway, speechless.

I don't know what's so great about this place except it's a big empty hall. You can barely see anything because the stage lighting only reaches so far into the darkness. I suppose for a DJ it's all you really need, the music will do the rest, no?

Ramón hasn't moved. I'd launched into the great open middle area, but he's still frozen with his mouth open. I return to him, first thinking he's disappointed somehow, typical spoiled American, doesn't realize what kind of massive wrangling it must've taken Kacique to secure a spot such as this.

But then I pay attention. This place, at this moment, has always existed within Ramón. To come perform in some ancient hideaway, dusty and legendary, to be anxiously awaited by an adoring fanbase, to be in the midst of it all: the fluttering pigeons and bustle of the street, the whole world of it spinning madly around this central cathedral-like monument to music—he had imagined some form of his homecoming to the home he'd never been so many times, and this outshines them all.

"It's . . . it's perfect."

I slide into his skin. What promise does an empty hall beneath the Gran Teatro de La Habana hold for this man-child? What secrets can he see here that even I can't fathom?

Joy. It's the simplest kind—not sullied by uncertainty or fear—uncluttered joy. It radiates from his core in easy-moving waves, overtakes the darkness around us with flashes of what will be: bodies clustered together, moving as one to the music, the sweet swelling music. No, it's not a vision of the future, I realize as I turn slow circles in the pulsating club scene of his imagination. Before I came along and interrupted his late nights, Ramón dreamed of this.

What is mythical to me because of my own memory is a whole other kind of adventure to Ramón. He has heard stories all his life, he's wondered, thought, doubted, and, of course, dreamed. And it hasn't been real until this very moment: Kacique's gift, this place.

"Do the theater people mind that we're using it?" Ramón asks, once he's collected himself some.

Kacique is on the other side of the room, fussing with some wiring. "To mind they would have to know, yes?" He hops up onto the stage and grins out at Ramón.

"Um . . . won't they hear the music?"

"They had an early show and already finished up for the day, Ramón. Anyway they're doing *María! La! Fucking! O!* again." He punctuates each word of the zarzuela's name with an angry pelvic thrust. "¡Basura! Anyone would be pleased to hear your music over that comemierdería anyway, but that's not the point. The only people around will be security, and they . . . let's just say they don't mind, yes?"

"So we don't have a permit? Doesn't everything need to ha—"

"Ramón. Be quiet. There are other ways of doing things than the right way, and believe me when I tell you, if they don't want you to do something they won't give a . . . what's the expression in English? They give a dick? They don't give dick?"

"It's *fuck* in English."

"Whatever, the permit, it doesn't matter. Not at all. They want to shut you down, they shut you down. Se acabó. The permit is designed to further tie down people who are already by the book with bureaucratic knots. ¿Comprendes?"

"I guess. It's just . . . I've always wanted to play here."

"Here? In the Gran Teatro?"

"No. Not exactly. Yes? I don't know. Cuba, I mean. We're not even supposed to consider coming here, you know, us . . . gusanos. It's not an option on the pull-down menu. But . . . yes. I've thought about it many times. Many, many times."

"Well . . ." Kacique lunges slowly into some kind of yoga position on the stage, his muscular arms wrapped impossibly behind his back and underneath one leg, his chest bulging out. "Ahhhh! Here you are!"

"You okay, man?"

"Yes, just stretching. You know, Ramón, that this party tonight is special, yes?"

Ramón cocks an eyebrow, then wiggles it. "Because DJ Taza has finally made it to la patria?"

"Ha, of course," Kacique guffaws. "But also because it's rare *we, mi gente*"—he makes a gesture Ramón doesn't understand and I don't quite catch—"get to have a fiesta just for us. You understand?"

The gay community of Havana is throwing itself a ball, and Ramón gets to DJ. Excellent.

Ramón nods slowly. "The Gran Teatro dance floor is gonna be a whole other world from Jersey, huh?"

"Oh yes," Kacique says slyly. "Anyway, we're also borrowing something from the Teatro they might be even more upset about than their basement."

"Oh?"

"Yes." Kacique opens up his winning grin, great big teeth reflecting the dancing lights of the stage.

"That's where you got the—"

"¡Hola, Kacique! ¿Cómo andas?" A triangle of light opens from somewhere along the wall and a dark-skinned bald man in a tuxedo walks in. A tall slender woman and two more tuxedoed, middle-aged men enter behind him. And three more behind them. They're carrying instruments: violins, a cello, a French horn. They're all chatting amiably about some celebrity who's in town and might be coming tonight.

"Jesus, man," Ramón gasps. "You work miracles."

"Eh, minor miracles, but I'll take it. Anyway, there are some drummers coming as well, Orisha people. For the last track we worked on."

The orchestra musicians are setting up folding chairs around the stage, talking quietly to each other. "Cinco," the first orchestra man says, extending a hand to Ramón.

"Ramón."

"I know. We have been working on your tracks for the past month. I believe you'll be pleased with what we've come up with for the orchestration."

"I'm . . . I don't know what to say."

"Then shut the fuck up!" Kacique chuckles.

"Shall we run through them?" Cinco says.

Until this, Cuba has been a series of quiet suburbs, bureaucracies, and passing street scenes, tangled with the many myths passed along throughout his life. Ramón has barely had time to catch his breath, he's been so busy trying to find . . . me.

I'm flushed with shame.

This, though—this is his. This belongs to Ramón: the music, the space. The people. I've occupied his dreams, replaced his aspirations with nightmares, insinuated myself into all of his most intimate inner shrines. And why? To goad him into finding my own corpse? To close some absurd, meaningless loop, end an already closed chapter . . . What right have I?

The orchestra begins setting up, the first strains of their instruments filling the hall. I've seen enough. Blistering with an unnamable mix of shame and pride, I disappear into the night.

# CHAPTER THIRTY-FIVE

The ocean swells beneath me.

A few minutes earlier I swept south over vast stretches of campo and then out across the water. The sky is blue gray and the sea is dark. Off to the west, a dim yellow haze marks where the sun dipped below the horizon. A few clouds linger just above the water, their light purple cut with a dramatic crimson.

And I am free.

Doomed, perhaps—I can already feel myself coming undone, the immediate result of pulling that invisible thread to my nephew to breaking point. It happens faster now, but it's not just being away from him physically—it's something else. I had always planned on returning to him the other times I'd left. I had seen our fates and struggles as one, somehow. But maybe only because it was easier to see it that way than the truth: That I am a parasite.

I speed faster across the ocean, pass snarling waves, some fish burst up into the air near me and collapse back down; seagulls dive. A few fishermen smoke and chat with each other, gaze at the dancing lights marking the edge of water, and begin turning their rickety boats around for the journey home.

Parasite. Been so caught up in maintaining my own life force I hadn't realized I was draining his. Or had I, and just not cared? I thought somehow the truth would be a blessing to him, after all that caustic silence my sister raised him with. Thought even the horror story of my life would somehow set him free. But I was wrong. All it's brought him is family drama and diarrhea. And for what? An off chance at finding some truth.

It's not enough.

I see the wall of pines rise over the horizon and speed forward. I am close.

I am a gust of wind through the towering trees. Darkness envelops me, branches shudder as I breeze past. They blot out the empty sky, go on forever in every direction until I'm past them, flushing fast along a dirt road, past a row of quiet buildings out into an empty field.

The towers loom ahead of me, shadows on the dark blue sky. I am . . . back. Somewhere I never imagined I'd return, a place I emptied all my prayers into wishing myself away from.

It's empty now: a museum and mostly in disrepair. The buildings are shabby, rusted; the streetlights shed a pale, deadish glare on the walls that once kept me in. I don't know what I thought I'd find here. Maybe a final resting place. An answer? It's just a skeleton now. I open myself wide in the night, disperse, and then enter the wall, feel the angry prickle of concrete and steel pipe passing through me, and then I'm inside.

The whole world is very, very still.

Immediately, I know where I am. I haunted these corridors for years, with only slightly more flesh and bone than I have now. I am home. This hall wraps around the center atrium, where we played, chatted, and died, where the tower always watched. But the moon is the only all-seeing eye left, and the moon doesn't care.

With a flicker I'm out in the courtyard, surrounded by myself, a hundred thousand aching memories and all those faces staring back from each room. Here I stood beside Padre Sebastián while he delivered a sermon made for one on whichever the saint-of-the-day was, here I watched Paco bleed to death, here it was Simón. Here I stood for hours on end one day, refusing to work, refusing to eat. It was after Constancia died, a guard had raped her and she'd gotten pregnant, then paler and paler as her body burned and finally she was gone and I couldn't move. I memorized all the angles of the walls across the sky, the tower against the sky, and the shifting shadows as night fell. They came to beat me but something in my eyes warded them off; they knew to stay back and anyway, a riot was already brewing over what had happened with Constancia.

And then, without having meant to come here, I'm back in my cell. I know it's mine because I etched each crack and imperfection into the inside of my brain. I know it better than I know myself. I am in my cell, as if the all-seeing eye were still there somehow, implanted forever deep inside me and this is where I will always land, back here, in this impossible little box. Padre Sebastián is with me. He's dying. I remember this. I am still so young here, so damaged and broken, but I am flesh and blood and this man, this man who saved my life so many times is a quickly emptying shell in my arms. He's barely there.

This is a memory I want so badly to turn away from, but I remain, splayed like a spotlight over my younger self. She runs a finger down the broken priest's face. He's soaked in sweat, eyes far away. There's a wound in his leg and it festers. I don't remember how he got it; there are so many ways to die here. She, we, wants to die too. It would be so simple, she thinks, eyeing the sunlit atrium outside the cell window, the tower.

Sebastián was the pillar of peace after the endless nightmare of solitude. He was the antidote.

There's not much left in him now. He'd been burning with fever for days, but now his skin shines with a shivering, clammy chill. He writhes as the festering leg sends throb after throb of dull pain through him. *Listen*, the priest says in a voice so harrowed and raspy it still shudders inside me all these decades later. *Listen*.

The girl that I once was leans close to him, her face so near his, doesn't flinch from the death that decorates him. I close around the memory, a cloak keeping out the world; it's crisp before me, realer than the prison walls that kept us in. It happened right here, right here.

*You don't have to be confined. Remember what I taught you, mariposa. Remember everything I taught you, eh?*

She shakes her head. Her long hair hangs in curtains, makes a tunnel between her face and Sebastián's, blocks out the world. *No*, she whispers.

*Remember you are never alone, you never have to be alone. Not if they put you back in the hole, not if you escape and live in the woods, not in a room full of strangers; never alone, mariposa.*

*That's not true. When you go . . .* Tears slide down her nose and land on his face.

*Shhh . . .* the priest murmurs. *You have to understand what I'm saying to you. Listen to me.* Sebastián rallies, lifting himself onto his elbows. *Stop crying and listen to me.*

Marisol sniffles a few times. Tears still tease the edge of her eyes and she won't look the man in his face, but she shut up at least.

*I need you to understand this before . . . what happens next.* He coughs; it's wet and thick. *I have given you what you need to survive. To escape. These walls cannot confine you, Marisol. Marisol.*

She looks at him. Her name, my name, a prayer.

*These walls cannot confine you.* He touches her face, his hand cool but no longer trembling. *These walls.* His finger sliding along her cheekbone, her jaw. *Cannot confine you. Marisol. Do you understand me?*

She nods.

Does she?

My god.

Herein lies a tiny miracle. The secret, perhaps, perhaps, perhaps, to my escape.

And then, for just a flickering moment, I know: She will. She will understand him. She will find a way out of the walls that are her skin and then the walls that are this prison and then, somehow, get free.

Perhaps, perhaps, perhaps, this is how I became me. Which means . . . *You decide, when you're ready to move beyond them.* He searches her face for understanding.

She shakes her head, lets out a snot-laced laugh. Wipes her nose.

*Are you just agreeing so I shut up and die already without bothering you anymore?*

"No," she laughs, crying again. *Stop it.*

Satisfied, Sebastián lies back down. The pallor overtakes him again. Which means.

*One more saint?* the girl asks. I want to shake this young me. I know it's not fair; she's living in a world of pain and about to lose her one ally through it all. She's in the mud. But I want her to know there's more, there's so much even in what she has. She has bones and skin, muscles that do what she tells them to. She is of the world, whole. And she has the secret of my existence dying in her arms; I need more information. I need to know. But she wants to hear another fairy tale from the doomed.

Sebastián shakes his head. *No more saints.* Each rattly breath gets further and further apart.

*You said there were thousands, Padre!*

*No.*

*But...*

*There are millions. Sometimes you have to squint to see them, but they are everywhere. Scattered. You make up your own, eh? It'll keep you busy for a while, if you stop and think about it.*

I can't see any more. Padre Sebastián closes his eyes as I release the vision into the cool night air. I am surrounded by these same walls.

... which means, which means, which means, perhaps, perhaps, perhaps ...

Out in the yard, I glide in steady, solemn circles. Gradually I realize there's a noise coming from me. I don't know if it's real or not, or audible to anyone besides myself, but there's no one here, so I suppose it doesn't really matter. It's a low hum I discover as I circle another time around the tower. A quiet melody, something familiar and so far away. It is beautiful, to make a noise after so much silence; I hadn't even realized. It is a reckoning, a song of hope—three tiny, tinkling phrases, each starting with one note and then leaping to an even higher one. *Quizás, quizás, quizás.* Because it is all real. Not that there'd ever been doubt, but to be here, to witness it, this most physical of reminders, this hard concrete world I inhabited.

My circling song fills me up with moments of my captivity, my solitude, my torture, healing, friendships, losses, loves, rage, my slowly unwinding self. My song encompasses even the songs of others, the dead that linger, voiceless, in recesses of each other's memories, and it keeps getting louder, fuller, fiercer with each building note. This night, this memory, has birthed something new in me. I am alive. I live. Even if my body is broken and buried, even if I'm dead, I live. Wherever I was, whatever I did, I decided it was time. I breached these walls, that body, cumbersome flesh. I moved beyond it. Yes. Yes, it's worth it. Yes, I need to know.

And if I can reach Ramón before I fade away for good, if I can get through to him, then just maybe . . .

*Quizás, quizás, quizás . . .*

I'm moving quickly back through the pine forest. Don't know how much time has passed but I know I need to find Ramón; I don't have much left in me. We are so close. Our destinies are entwined already; it's no mistake.

I flash out over the ocean.

# CHAPTER THIRTY-SIX

What is this music?

The empty room is full: full of sweating, moving bodies, of course, but more than that, full of a sound so crisp, so layered and raw I can only hold still when I first glide in over all those jostling heads. It's one of the songs Ramón had been working on, I know, but I barely recognize it. Cinco has taken what was a standard string arrangement, a staticky mess of a recording, held true to the melody, and orchestrated it into something much more grandiose, something alive. The violins dance up and down a dizzying, slightly off-balance scale, now falling quiet, now sheer with menace. Ramón works his beats across this ululating landscape, leaving long gaps of sudden, breathless space between each deep crash and bringing that clacking in suddenly with an echoey cackle of the snare.

But it's the guitar that pulls the whole thing together. Ramón and the orchestra have fallen into a steady vamp; the crowd pulses accordingly on the shuffle. The guitarist is an absurdly tall, slender fellow, cheekbones sunken in, graying hair pulled back into a ponytail, eyes closed and light brown brow furrowed. He lets loose a fury of flamenco-inflected riffs, pauses to let the music swell beneath him, and then unleashes again.

The music is building, building, growing around us, an angry, decadent creature inhaling and exhaling and expanding with each breath; each note, every new cycle of the beat brings us deeper inside.

I have found Ramón now, so I'm fortified some and I take it in. The vision at Isla de Pinos is still with me, the flesh I escaped so near, the will to live and the hope that somehow, maybe . . . I did.

And this music—it speaks my language. Without meaning to, without even realizing it's happening, I disperse myself across the whole room in the space between the crowd and the ceiling. Así. Each note is reborn inside of me, the whole audience's churning reaction, their presence, enthusiasm, all the wild emotions this song opens up with them—I take it all in, expand further, and release the whole mess of it into the ceiling, past the ceiling, and empty theater seats and past the plaster angels dancing across the upper echelons of the Gran Teatro, straight into the sky.

There's a celebrity of some kind in the crowd. His entourage parts a small berth around him. He's short, with slicked back hair, sunglasses, and an impeccable white suit. Someone international; a Spaniard probably. The swirl of acoustic guitar and gathering storm from the orchestra has rendered him irrelevant though, for probably the first time in a while. All eyes stay with the miracle unfolding on stage. The clatter of strings, beats, and cackling guitar phrases reaches a manic peak, at once perfect and dissonant, it aches to resolve. Instead, everyone cuts out at once and in the sudden silence the crowd takes a collective breath.

Down below, the audience is enthralled. In the dark corners, men suck each other's faces as if gasping for air, and surely that's not allowed in this state built on the myth of machismo. But then, this is an underground affair, and I imagine that foreign celebrity adds some bit of invincibility to the event. Now that I notice it, more than a few men in the audience are holding each other close, some grinding, some just looking into each other's eyes, some arm in arm. Kacique has turned this space into a brief sanctuary from the world outside, a private concert for those who must live in the shadows.

And the silence brings me gradually back to myself. As it stretches longer, I return to this slender nothingness lingering above their heads. After a tantalizing few moments, Ramón lets out a scratchy saxophone phrase from his turntable, cuts it out, and zips it back in again, letting it play almost to the end and then shutting it off suddenly. We're all of us glued to the sound, eyes closed, hanging on to what'll happen next like the reveal at the end of one of those detective movies they used to play at the Royal. No one even yells out, we just wait, breath bated. He lets the saxophone moan again, all the way through this time, and a single violin comes in beneath it. On the far corner of the stage a group of men all in white, the santeros Kacique had mentioned, bring in a gentle guaguancó on their congas. It starts down deep, raises up like two questioning eyebrows, and then drops again. Repeats to infinity. Ramón waits a few measures, then drops his beat around them. Another violin joins the first as the saxophone phrase scratches back in, almost finishes, and starts again from the beginning.

Something is happening to me. Each gathering element of this musical storm brings a new weight to my spinning facade. I am buffeted on the currents of it, but more than that I find I can hold it inside of me. Just glimpses at first: a note. A short stanza. Moments. But they stay. They build and then, like a net, they draw more. I concentrate. It's easy to stay focused on the swirl of hundreds of years of culture connecting in the air around me. I inhale and bring in the notes, the rhythm, everything; I don't release it. And then, I am. More than a desperate glint of something, more than a mourning specter, a pathetic hallucination: I am. A thing. Real, I have breached through and I linger above the crowd: a woman described in light and color, buoyed by the music.

The guitar player is the first to see me. I'm slow-motion spinning directly in his sight line, reveling at my sudden entrance into this world. He looks up from his fingers that dance across the fretboard, sees me, stops. It's just a momentary pause. He squints, as if to confirm, then smiles just so. His fingers find the strings again, dance. His eyes stay on me, my spin. Some of the other musicians notice his gaze and follow it. The orchestra stumbles, but Ramón keeps the beat thrashing along beneath, effortlessly covering up their fallout. Soon the crowd starts looking up, pointing, mouths open, eyes wide.

The music doesn't stop though; it swells. This is Cuba; apparitions come with the territory. Ramón is the only one not gaping at me. I focus all of myself, all my light, my whole tiny universe of concentration converges on the man standing on the raised platform behind his record decks. He looks up, freezes, mouth hanging open. His expression barely changes, but there's a tiny loosening as shock becomes acceptance and then, beautifully, recognition.

To the crowd, I am a miracle, the Virgen de la Caridad del Cobre perhaps. To Ramón and Ramón alone though, I am Luz Marisol. An entirely different, personal miracle. I watch it all travel across his startled face: the incredulousness, understanding, and relief. He is no less crazy than the three hundred other people there and much, much less crazy than he'd been thinking he might be. He smiles.

And I smile. It feels strange, to do this thing. This sacred act I hid away like an illegal prayer for so many years. We smile at each other, and then all the amplifiers cut off with a sharp crackle and the orchestra falters. Only the guaguancó keeps churning for a few more measures, the santeros far away in their circling rhythms. As the last couple beats tap out I feel like I'm being torn out of my own skin, my brand-new skin. This sudden solidness—I was *something*. Something physical—pieced together and filled by the organization of all that perfect sound and now I'm scattered in this new silence.

There's a general groan from the crowd, some worried muttering, and then a man yells, "¿Qué carajo pasó, coño?" and everyone laughs. The overheads flick on, cruel fluorescents after all that darkness. I'm everywhere, a pathetic scattering of shards that will never make a whole. Watching from the corners, the doorway, ceiling pipes: I'm broken, dizzy. When the plainclothes cops come crashing through the door, the shock almost ends me completely.

They're so young. They have new sideburns and their first mustaches and they have curly black hair and angry, scared eyes. The first few carve straight into the crowd, lashing out with their fists and wooden sticks, yelling *maricón* and *pájaro* as they go. I see a tall black man cracked across the face; he falls forward, blood pouring out of his mouth, and gets trampled beneath the sudden rush of bodies.

They're laughing. It's from fear or excitement, it's from adrenaline and the freedom of being turned loose on a helpless crowd. All that young rage just bursting out, a simple matter of aim and release. They fall in packs on stragglers, pin them down, cuff them, and toss them into corners like crumpled-up scraps of paper.

Ramón is gone. The stage is empty. There must've been a back exit somewhere.

I know what has to happen: I have to collect myself, find some wholeness in all these scattered fragments, and I have to find Ramón.

The shards of me culminate in my uneasy sojourn. By the time I'm three quarters of the way across, I'm almost a whole spirit again. I have to find Ramón. I have to make sure he's safe, but what can I even do if he's not? I'm even more barely there than usual.

I bring back the room around me; it's in shambles. Trash and broken bodies scatter around. The cops have flanked out to all the exits; they confer while keeping edges of their eyes on the prisoners. Memories reach out to me, demons. What will prison be like for these young people? They're curled up and crying; they're stony faced and some are unconscious, blood-crusted hair on the floor. I can't. I can't free them I can't dwell in their future misery I can't get caught. I can't lose myself, not now. Not after all I've seen, how far I've come.

The curtains waver slightly as I pass through them: a good sign. I'm down a little corridor, up some stairs. Out into the night.

# CHAPTER THIRTY-SEVEN

The streets of Havana are empty.

Everyone must've scattered to their own predetermined hideaways as soon as they got out—it's only been a few minutes. The Gran Teatro looms over a park. The ancient crumbling alleyways of the old city stretch out around me. There are no cars, no tourists, just an old blind man sitting on a bench across the street, tapping his cane against the cobblestones. And a stray dog sniffing through some trash.

I've lost Ramón.

Somehow, he's just gone—untraceable.

And without Ramón . . . all of that hope that rose in me begins to crumble as I flush forward through the dark streets.

But he is part of me. I found him once in this giant, fucked-up world. I don't know how, but I did. And I will again. Surely our connected spirits can call out to each other in the night. I rise above the musty statues adorning the theater, gaze down from the starless sky at the wild labyrinth of La Habana Vieja.

My call pulses into the night. *Ramón*. It blasts down alleyways and around corners, pauses in doorways, peers through windows. *Ramón*. My call sweeps along rooftops, skirting around illegal satellite hookups and corroded water tanks, dips into hot cluttered apartments where fevered bodies clutch each other against the night.

My call pauses at the ocean and whirls back again through the streets, now frantic, a wailing terror, harsh night zephyr, catching in the tobacco-stained throats of old watchmen and upsetting wind chimes into a senseless jangle.

*Ramón*.

And then it stops.

Somewhere, not far away, it stops.

I flash along the path of that racing heart, its call pulsing through me. I cross rooftops, flood forward into the streets, breeze past a window display of photography books for tourists, around a corner, and there's Aliceana. She has her back against a wall, it's a closed-up tobacco shop. Cartoon Indians turn their gloating smiles out from the window display. Her breath comes quick and unsteady, eyes dart back and forth.

Ramón must be close. His pulse is a frantic beacon, bleating along much faster than it should be. He's so close. But someone else is close too; their boots clomp through the streets toward us. Aliceana catches her breath, her eyes scan the walls for a window to crawl in, an alley to disappear into. But the old city is shuttered. She looks like she's about to crumble, so I enter along her spine and allow our selves to intermingle. It's startling at first—what are soft edges to Ramón appear to Aliceana as jagged lines. Her emotions and fears tumble through in free open spirals; even her darkest thoughts flow, whereas Ramón's tiny inner ecosystem trips over itself, gets clogged up on a whim, shudders in the unsteady gait of uncertainty.

Ramón. My call answered, but still no Ramón. I thought maybe he was hidden nearby, wounded perhaps or just terrified; his racing heart still thunders in my ears, but we are alone. For the moment anyway. I doubt whatever would happen to Aliceana in the hands of these child cops would be worse than what'll happen to the Cubans picked up at the Teatro. Aliceana has her American passport with her, and international incidents can't be good for anybody's agenda these days. Still, the frenzy of this sudden burst of power, these long-fingered power mongers with wily eyes and a thirst to subdue the world to their will—there's no telling what could happen.

The echoing clatter of boots and yelling gets louder.

Aliceana and I move as one. We hurl out from the tobacco storefront into the street. It feels like being suddenly naked—the shadows of the wall gave at least an illusion of protection. I spin my vision in a wide arc as we cross. It's unsteady—I'm still getting used to Aliceana's small, easy-moving body—but it seems the police haven't broken into our crossroads yet.

We're charging down a narrow, dusty side street. Balconies with dangling plants and barred windows frame the sky. Aliceana's furious pulse mingles with Ramón's now. I want to stop, cast my Ramón net again, but there's no time. Everything now is escape.

We turn onto a wider avenue. The ocean is close now, I can feel its impossible hugeness infringing on the edges of the city. Lion statues snarl from a dark pillared building next to a dilapidated solar. I've been here, came as a child once with Papi. His hand was warm and huge around mine, guiding me through the crowds and into a market, a thousand crashing smells of life and death, the pungent tang of still-alive fish, fresh vegetables, soil, body odor, perfume, the crush of bodies haggling for the right price.

But now the plaza is dead. The ocean wind tumbles crumpled paper plates and a few leaves through it. Maybe in the morning, that same market will open up again, all these years later. Aliceana's foot slides on a rotten red pepper, painting the street with an icky stain. When we turn down another alley I realize the doctor actually has a plan. Here I'd been throwing myself into the singular project of Away, but Aliceana was following an internal compass. I hadn't even realized. I burrow deeper, try to block out the still urgent SOS call of Ramón's tachycardia.

Aliceana has her passport and wallet nestled in a pouch slung beneath her T-shirt. Its gentle irritation against her skin whenever she moves gives a comfortable reminder that it's still there. She's got a shimmering image of Ramón painted against the back of her chest; flickering in and out with her worry. An illustrated encyclopedia of numbers, ratios, normalities, and monstrosities, angles of approach, pathologies, ways to die—it's all wallpapered behind the visage of Ramón, it's all over her, coloring each tiny move and decision. It's a miracle anyone carrying around this much knowledge can move with such ease.

Beyond all that, there is a destination and map. We're moving still, darting along the shadows past a closed-up bar, now a spiraling hotel, now a school. We're turning, hurrying up some stairs, and finally I understand: Aliceana has brought us back to Catabalas's place.

Kacique's face is pulled tight when he answers, like he's bracing for a blow. Aliceana had whispered her name over and over while she knocked, tiny sobs escaping with each breath, but all trust has evaporated in the wake of the attack. Still, once he sees she's alone he reaches those long, sculpted arms out and envelops her in them, lifts her body off the ground, and slams the door against the ever-watching street.

"What happened?" Aliceana gasps when Kacique finally puts her down.

"Come." He takes her hand, brings her through the front room. We were all here just hours ago. Everyone was cracking jokes and getting to know each other; a brilliant night was in the works. Aliceana trembles as we enter Adriana's room. The old woman is sitting up in bed, scribbling something on a yellow notepad in the flickering light of a seven-day candle. She looks up, her face mostly in shadows, and hits Aliceana with such a penetrating stare—those sunken eyes—that I'm sure she sees straight through all that Aliceana and into me. Me, Marisol. Yes, she sees me. Death is so close to this woman.

"I'm sorry," she says.

Before Aliceana can ask why, Kacique says something sharp under his breath and herds us into the next room. Catabalas's place is treacherous to navigate with the lights on. Unruly piles of magazines, crumpled clothes, and assorted post-adolescent detritus dominate the place. And now they're keeping all the lights in the place off except Adriana's candle. Aliceana trips, catches Kacique's shoulder before crashing into the nerd vortex of Catabalas's den. Kacique holds her up with one hand and clutters through the darkness with the other. Something grinds—gears? And then a terrible whine breaks the quiet. It's just an old door hinge creaking, but we're all so on edge it might as well've been a child screaming. Kacique's shadow disappears into something, a stairwell, and Aliceana tiptoes after him, feeling along the wall to keep balance.

"Aliceana is here," Kacique announces. In a dimly lit room, several people stand at once: Catabalas, Adina, Cinco the conductor, another tuxedoed dark-skinned man I don't recognize, and Catabalas's dream-girl, Yaniris. Adina crosses the room first, wraps around Aliceana, and starts bawling. Rainbows and smiling clouds cavort along the walls. This place is or was a play area. There are still toys stuffed into shelves along the wall and construction paper animals dance across the plaster ceiling.

"What . . ." Aliceana's saying, wiping tears away. "What happened?"

And I hear another heartbeat. It's slow. And then I understand.

Catabalas steps to one side so Aliceana can see the cot behind him. Ramón is laid out on it, his head swathed in a bloodstained bandage. He's unconscious. I flush forward, am beside him and then within in seconds.

It is a very deep sleep, this one. I can't tell if he'll wake, but everything else seems to be in working order. He's not *gone* gone, but he's very thoroughly knocked out.

I release myself back into the room. Ramón's heartbeat still plods along its slow march inside of me, an occasional gasping. But that other pulse, the one I'd thought was his, the one that led me to Aliceana, keeps racing along beneath it, a puppy running circles around its tired old owner.

There is a new heir to this lineage now; she is tiny and her heart is strong. I flatten against Aliceana's inner walls, slide down, and then pour all my love and strength into becoming a cocoon around this dot of new life that is my family.

# CHAPTER THIRTY-EIGHT

In a park in the teeming heart of Havana, there is a famous ice cream stand. You would wait in line for hours, a line that stretched all through the park and out onto the sidewalk, but you would feel lucky just to be in that line, because all around you are people who are going about their business and not even getting ice cream any time soon. You, though, you are baked by the sun, assailed by mosquitoes, annoyed by obnoxious older sisters who don't know how to appreciate the glory of the day—and none of it matters, because every passing minute brings you closer to the guy who will ask what flavor and smile with missing teeth, sweating through his T-shirt, and reach his magic scoop into the bucket and carve out a perfect curl of ice cream. Sometimes, on the most inexplicably perfect days, he opens up a brand-new vat just for you; he'll peel off the top and reveal the untouched surface of all that goodness. In the moment he takes to put cream in cone and grab a napkin, you pause and notice the empty space he's created in the middle of that smooth swirl. You almost feel bad, being the one to ruin that sweet unbroken ocean, but then he hands you the cone and nothing else matters except you and the ice cream in your mouth, on your face, dribbling down your neck.

At some point, I must've been that smooth a surface. Even this far in, after all that had happened, I had managed to hold on to some bit of grace, some joy. But Sebastián's death reopened all the wounds, the loss of one sister and betrayal of another, the impossibility of ever knowing freedom again. It tore open an irreparable gap in me, and soon I will be empty.

I don't know how long I've been sitting in this same spot while the sun rises and sets through the wired window behind me. I don't know how long it's been since Padre Sebastián died. I only know I've had enough.

I had taught myself to fight off the ghosts of the two guards. They came to trouble my last waking thoughts and then my dreams. First I sweated and writhed beneath the weight of them night after night—one my interrogator, the other believed himself my savior somehow, a more insidious kind of torment, a haunting. And then slowly I learned to tame them. Padre Sebastián taught me to take hold of my imagination and I did. I made them shriveled, pathetic pig-men, children, worms. The power terrified me at first: The visages became mutants and they were furious; in their fury they attacked harder. And then gradually they fumbled, their slippery hands slid from my skin. Still they returned, but feebler each time.

Now my friend and protector is gone and all my nightmares are back. It's not just the torturers. My family. I had become an expert on erasure. Wiped my brain clean of all of them. Until now.

Now.

I sit perfectly still, still in my own filth, still and devoured by insects, rot, my own starvation. Consumed. I sit perfectly still and endure wave after wave of these phantoms. Sometimes they are guards or other prisoners, come to poke and prod me so that I eat; I've lost track of which ghosts are real. I sink and sink closer and closer to the floor and hell beneath it. I burn with fever, then shiver inside my broken bones and then one day for no reason I can fathom, I stand. My legs are shaky, withered, but they hold me. I step out into the terrible sunlight, it's mid-afternoon and burning hot and I'm a strange new animal, rebirthed from my own shit so many times I've lost count. I take a deep forlorn breath and accept this life that will not tear itself from me no matter how hard I pray for it to.

※

"We have to . . . we have to get him to a hospital . . ." Aliceana is flailing her arms when I emerge from the gray haze of Ramón's broken subconscious. Only a few seconds have passed. I settle in an upper corner of the room, nestled between two shelves full of colorful alphabet books and board games. "He could be . . ."

Kacique is shaking his head before she even finishes the thought. "They will arrest him and all of us. They know the people from the club will be trying to get treatment."

"But he . . . he needs to get checked. We need X-rays, bloodwork, a surgeon maybe."

"I know," Kacique says quietly. "And believe me when I say it's worse for him if we try to get him out of here. He will end up in prison. At least here he's in our care. Your care."

"But I'm . . . I have nothing. I don't even have gloves. What can I do, Kacique?" Aliceana veers between sorrow and frustration, her eyes darting around the room for something to make sense of all this.

Adina stands beside her, puts a hand on her shoulder. "They have some supplies here. They've been keeping a first-aid kit stocked up to take care of Adriana. There are bandages and . . ."

"He doesn't need bandages." Aliceana steps away, shrugs off Adina's caress. "He needs a hospital. You guys don't understand. He could be hemorrhaging, he could seize, he could go into cardiac arrest. You don't understand."

Catabalas stands. "No, we do understand. *You* don't understand."

Aliceana glares at him.

"This is what life is here. This is the resistance. We do what we do on the edge of what's allowed and any moment, they can take us away. They already have, again and again, Aliceana. They did tonight, they will tomorrow. We don't know why they do one time and not the other, but we still do what we do to be alive because that's the only way to be alive. We're barely out of the Special Period, barely scraping by. Tonight, we threw an illegal party for all the gays in Havana! *In* the basement of the Gran Teatro. Do you realize the sheer amount of illegality in that? The *only* reason we were able to make it happen at all is because that famous foreigner was in town with his entourage and the government knows if they lay a finger on him it's an international incident that they don't want. And then he left, and here we are. Ramón, no offense, is not quite so famous yet. Now they are escouring the streets for people who had anything to do with that party, and Ramón is one of those people. In fact, he's the most public one, because he was the DJ. They don't have his name, but they saw him, they hit him. If we take him out of here, he will get picked up and so will we all. Ramón they'll maybe let free in a day or two, because he is American. Me? Probably ten years if ever, given all I've done. Kacique maybe they kill on the spot. Okay? Can we make it more clear to you?"

Aliceana nods slowly. "I know all that. I do . . ."

"You are afraid. You care about your man," Kacique offers. "We know this too. The best we can give is what little supplies we have. In the morning, the streets will be clear and we can do what we have to do. *If* we lie low tonight."

"And Yaniris is a nurse," Catabalas says, smiling for the first time since we've arrived.

"Ay, no, Cati, por favor." Yaniris's hair is locked and pulled behind her head. She wears frameless glasses and a white button-down shirt so ginormous she practically swims in it. Maybe it's her father's. She stands up but stays partially shielded by Catabalas, her skinny shoulders slouched forward, long arms waving away the idea.

"Really?" Aliceana asks.

"I was . . . in school . . . for medicine. But I had to leave."

"Do you know how to take a blood pressure?"

The girl brightens a little; her eyebrows raise as she nods. "Of course, yes!"

"Come on, then, I guess we gotta start somewhere. Let's get vital signs and see what we got, yeah?"

Somewhere in the midst of all that arguing, Aliceana made the slightest of pivots inside herself. It was so smooth I didn't even catch it. She had been Aliceana the Worried Lover; now she is Dr. Mendoza, on scene to assess her patient. It's probably for the best that she doesn't know she's carrying his child yet. The boys are right: There are no other options. She has every right to let her sorrow collapse her, for a few minutes anyway, but she's also the only medical care Ramón's going to get for a while. We need her.

Yaniris's slender brown hands tremble as she wraps the cuff around

Ramón's arm and starts squeezing it tight. "Tranquila, mami," Aliceana whispers.

The girl nods but doesn't look any calmer. "Ciento-cincuenta por ochenta."

Aliceana looks at the ceiling. "Pulso."

Yaniris puts two fingers up to Ramón's neck.

"Take it at the wrist," Aliceana says. "La mano."

A moment passes. No one in the room seems to be breathing at all. "Setenta y ocho," Yaniris finally says.

Aliceana allows herself the tiniest of smiles and everyone else sees it and exhales. "Not bad," she whispers. Then she looks down, directs her full attention to Ramón. I'm across the room in seconds, slipping along the surface of her back and then entering, careening through all those synapses and vesicles, past avalanches of anatomical sketches and equations and then I'm watching Ramón's chest rise with each breath, studying the tension in his face, asking tiny, indescribable questions of each detail of his body.

"Stay with us, Ramón," Aliceana says, kneeling beside him, and I silently repeat the words to myself, over and over. It is a prayer made from both love and selfishness. I have come to adore this lug of a nephew; and not just because his beating heart pulled me like a lifeline from the abyss. He is a profound and soulful beast, and I wouldn't trade him for anyone.

And without him, I'm sure I'll disappear forever, a never answered question.

# CHAPTER THIRTY-NINE

The first time it happens, I'm in my regular spot in the center of my room. The large crack still creases in a long arch down the wall and splits into four smaller ones. The sun is about to set, paints the room orange. My mind carries the echoes of laugher; Guillermo and Roca Sanchez were doing another comedy routine in the yard and the whole world had stopped to watch. Guillermo put on the affect of a guard and goose-stepped in circles while Roca Sanchez mimed taking a shit and then offered it up as a tasty dinner to Guillermo. Total, perfect nonsense. Also, a terrific way to get shot, but crowds of laughing prisoners make it harder to tell what's going on from the tower. And anyway, we need laughter. Need it so badly that a silly mime routine, replayed over and over with almost no variation, somehow becomes more hilarious with each identical repeat. Gruff, uncertain glares become smiles and then giggles. Because we are hungry. We are in need. We are dying. And this is something altogether different. At first, my body didn't recognize that strange trembling, the noise coming out of my open mouth, the sudden release. Then I looked around and everyone else was doing it too. Laughter.

The memory of it stays plastered across my face in a lopsided grin hours later. I'm still tingling with it when I assume my position in the center of my cell. And there are the cracks, dipping wide and splitting; there's the part where the wall bulges outward slightly, fading sunlight glints off the top, a gentle shadow below.

The demons always come first. I have accepted that. Today they are the same ones as usual: faceless, bearded soldiers, the judge from however many years ago, my beautiful family—also without faces. They crowd around me and next comes the part where I destroy them all—its own kind of nightmare, because I take no pleasure in their annihilation.

261

It is a grim duty I must perform; a nightly rite of passage to get somewhere peaceful. And I do and I do and in tatters they slink back to their dark corridors, leaving only the hoarse echoes of their promise to return.

The next nightmare is the depths of loneliness. This one took longer to move past than the demons. I still cry for what must be hours, allowing all that emptiness to roar up inside me. First it's everyone I've ever loved and the knowledge of how far away and unreachable they are to me. So if you ever wonder what we, the disappeared, dream of in our darkest hours, know that it is you: those who remain. And we dream of each other, catalogues of the dead and forgotten; we wonder which are still out there in some tiny hole, praying for death or praying for life, dreaming of us, fighting off demon memories and then supreme loneliness.

And then.

And then.

Something happens.

There is a place beyond all that.

I learned that sometimes, when I sit with it long enough, when I allow it in, the sadness of being alone dissipates. It wants to have its say, wants to be given its due. When I fight it, it stays, but not fighting means balancing on that thread-thin precipice between uneasy peace and falling over the deep into infinite unfathomable sorrow.

Today I get there. I think the laughter buffeted me through; I brought it with me, an unruly crew of angels into the pit of hell. An easiness comes over my body, even the ache that pulses forever down my back and through my hips, it's a familiar, comfortable pounding now. A reminder of my body. I accept it. I accept it and I accept the lengthening shadows across my wall, the dull haze night casts on my room, the cracks and subtle indentations that vanish in the darkness. I accept it.

I close my eyes, and when I open them, I see myself.

It is not a perfect image. The contours are ragged, incomplete lines. As it resolves, I am horrified. What a slender husk of a human being I have become. Are there any parts of me still left from my childhood? The chin. My chin still juts out just so—defiantly, a teacher once told me, like Nilda's, if I'm honest with myself. My favorite part of Nilda. Another phantom I can't get distracted by. My hair is raggedy, cropped short. My clavicles pop out from my chest, you can see them beneath the filthy shirt I wear.

Surely, I am dreaming.

I accept.

It's so much more pleasant than the hells I'm used to, this dream, which is perhaps not a dream at all. To continue my inspection: I'm pleased how straight my spine is in spite of it all. I'd imagined myself hunched over and decrepit somehow. Also, a few bruises speckle my arms and legs, some of them I know to be from at least a year ago. They persist, but so do I, it seems. Something else: I am worn to the bone, yes, but the air still moves around me with deference; my lines slide gracefully into each other, form angles that sit just right on my skin. All these parts of me, all I have lived: They combine to form a rather elegant whole.

Perhaps this is not a dream at all, no more than anything else I've lived through. Perhaps, perhaps, perhaps.

I accept.

✳

"What do you think?" Kacique and Aliceana sit in two chairs that are clearly designed for people much smaller than them. They're sipping ration coffee that Cinco had made upstairs and brought down on a tray to much fanfare and applause.

Aliceana rubs her eyes. "I don't know. Could be so many different things going on inside him. I don't know." She looks up at him, smiles. "Kacique, listen, I'm sorry for earlier, I was being an ass . . ."

The big man silences her with a wave of his hand. "Tsh! Stop. We are all terrified in different ways, all for good reasons. And you, Aliceana, you are out of your element, of course."

"Of course. I just meant . . . Thank you."

Kacique rolls his eyes. "De nada."

"I guess one person got his wish, at least." Aliceana nods at the far corner of the room where Catabalas and Yaniris are curled up together inside a giant womb-shaped chair.

"It's about time that boy got some action." Kacique chuckles.

"When do you think it'll be safe to move Ramón?"

A dull thump sounds from upstairs. Kacique leaps to his feet, crosses the room in three long strides, and taps Catabalas.

"¿Qué pasó, carajo?"

"La puerta."

Catabalas shakes sleep off as he fast-walks up the stairs. He pauses at the landing, frowns down at Yaniris's curled-up body, and trades a solemn glance with Kacique. Then the door closes and he's gone.

Kacique crosses back to Aliceana. "Adriana taps her cane on the floor when someone comes to the door. It's the alert. That's all. Could be anyone."

They sit, sip at the dregs of their coffees.

Adina must've woken up when Catabalas rushed past the couch where she'd been sleeping. She pulls a child-sized chair up beside Aliceana's. "What's the plan?"

Aliceana shrugs. "I don't know. We gotta get him out of here soon."

"Clear," Catabalas says from the top of the stairs. "Ya se fueron. No fue nada, un vendedor. A guy that sells things, is all."

He walks slowly down the stairs, careful not to creak them too loudly, and snuggles up around Yaniris.

Aliceana turns to Kacique. "And now?"

"We wait till mid-morning. Then we assess." He looks away for a second and then meets her eyes. "I am sorry."

"Don't be." Aliceana stands, puts her hand on his shoulder. "I'm sure you saved his life."

She walks over to the bed and nuzzles up against Ramón's unconscious body.

# CHAPTER FORTY

Alone in my cell, hovering just above my body, I remember Padre Sebastián's words. These walls cannot confine me. I cannot be confined.

It's been what? Several months? Yes. At least three full moons have passed since that first night. Since realizing it wasn't a dream. And even that knowledge—having a sense of time, a connection to something besides these same dead cracks in the unchanging walls—this is a sign of my triumph. Everything is different now. I have to be cautious because the others will notice the extra something I carry with me and I don't want that kind of attention. It's still like a shiny new gift and I need time to think. Time to plot.

Yesterday a guard was staring at me. Not like he wanted to carry me off—those wide eyes weren't hungry. And it wasn't suspicion either. Those are the two kinds of elongated looks we get from guards. This was different. His eyebrows were both raised, his mouth slightly open. He was so young, with pretty brown eyes and a gentle goatee. When I caught him staring he didn't look away, just closed up his face into a pout.

I almost smiled at him. In my imagination, this is what people who are free do. A cute boy is caught off guard by the sunlight reflected off a pretty girl as she passes. His mouth drops open because, more than just sexy, there is something about her, something unbridled, that radiates with life. She sees how his young eyes drink her in, the sway of her hips, her neckline, and she favors him with a delicate smile. It reveals just enough, this smile, like the light blouse she wears that reveals the tops of her breasts: a hint. A secret. And then the moment is over and the girl struts along down the causeway and the boy goes home to write poetry about her and drink wine and masturbate.

But this place and that freedom know nothing of each other. I pushed the smile away from my face, didn't even allow a coy nod. I can't afford the risk, not now especially. So I turned and as simply as I could, I walked away.

It was the saddest moment I've had since I learned how to separate myself. Mostly, I wander in strange, impossible circles through the prison, learning my limitations. When I stay away from myself for too long, I feel my already barely there presence begin to fade. It's like being in an ocean, miles from shore, and feeling yourself become gradually too tired to swim. The first time I barely made it back before evaporating completely into the ether.

But still, a strange joy pervades me.

Tonight I lift away from myself, through the prickling resistance of concrete and out into the sky. I settle in a cell where there's some quiet chatter. Edgardo Gil and Tesoro Milán. I don't like either of them much; they used to clown Padre Sebastián during his sermons and not in the funny playful way. They were just assholes. Their cells are next to each other and they are muttering from their windows.

*Is it settled?*

*It is.*

*Do we like them?*

*Eh . . . They are acceptable.*

*If it is true, when?*

*Next week. I will have word for certain.*

*I am skeptical.*

*You should be. But . . . we don't have much choice, you know.*

*I know.*

A few moments of silence pass between them.

*Alright.*

*Okay.*

*Tomorrow, we'll see what we see.*

*Hm.*

When I'm sure they're done, I swoop up through the ceiling, past the second, third, and fourth levels, out into the night, above the tower even and still higher until I feel the edge of emptiness creep over me.

Ramón blinks twice and the world comes into focus around him. I had felt this coming: His body shuddered and creaked back into normal working condition a few minutes before his mind did. First his heart sped up and the suddenness of it broke me out of my memory-dreams. It's so much more powerful than that other bleating cycle of life inside Aliceana, who lies huddled up against Ramón. The heart thump-thumped out of its slow delirium and his blood flushed with new vitality through each vessel, pumping life into the tiny veinules that curl and rivulet across his inner flesh.

The spark rose up inside and then Ramón opened his eyes and now he's smiling, trying to figure out why there are children's paintings on the walls around him and stroking his hand idly through Aliceana's straight black hair. For a moment, I revel in this small victory. Ramón is alive. He is awake. This matters more to me than I was prepared for. Inside him, I shudder, blissful at his consciousness but horrified by how close we came to losing him. This man whom I have inhabited the inner world of for months now. This man who barely knows me but knows me so well. We live.

"Ramón!" Aliceana whisper-shouts, pulling herself up to his face. "Are you . . . what do you feel? Are you okay?"

Ramón nods. "I think so. My head feels like it's under a truck though."

"Ay, poor baby. Come let me see your eyes."

He obediently opens one wide and then the other while Aliceana gets all up in his personal space examining them. Then she lays her head on his chest and nuzzles. "I thought you were gone."

"Me too. What happened?"

"Kacique says one of the policía smacked you with a billy club. Do you remember?"

"No. Are you okay?"

Aliceana nods. "I ran. We got separated. And Ramón . . ." Aliceana

267

sits up again, her face goes blank. "There was something . . . I don't know how to describe it. I saw something, at the club, I mean."

Ramón lifts himself onto his elbows and furrows his brow at her.

"A woman . . . she was . . . above all of us, above the crowd, but . . . it wasn't just me, everyone saw her. She was there. I think it was, I think it was Marisol."

"It . . . was." He nods. "It was. I remember that. That's the last thing I remember, actually. She was there. She is . . . she's with me." He throws his legs over the side of the bed. "And . . . We have to find out what happened."

"He lives!" It's Catabalas, calling from the top of the stairs. "And I bring information." He tromps down, followed closely by Yaniris, who's carrying a tray of cafecitos. "And coffee."

# CHAPTER FORTY-ONE

That file in Catabalas's hands carries my truth. Some semblance of it anyway. But then, it's probably a government document, no? Since everything here is. And what do government documents know about the truth? Nothing.

And still.

I spread across the room and then swish back into myself, simply because I don't know what else to do. Just moments earlier, I was reveling in the memory of having been seen, of Aliceana and Ramón's shared moment. And now I feel like I've been scattered across the city from sheer anticipation.

That gentle song of hope dances through me, teasing: *Quizás, quizás, quizás.*

"Catabalas." Aliceana narrows her eyes. "We still have to get Ramón to a doctor. He needs X-rays."

"I'm okay," Ramón says.

"Ramón."

"X-rays can wait." Catabalas sits in one of the tiny chairs and Yaniris stands behind him, her delicate hands on his shoulders, like they've been married for years. He puts a file on the bright red picnic table and grimaces. Ramón sips his coffee and leans in. "What you got?"

"Before we begin, I have to tell you that none of this is all that conclusive, but I'll get to that." Of course. *Of course.* Nothing is ever conclusive in this pit of lies.

"The first thing is this: documento uno." Catabalas lifts a single sheet of paper with a rough photocopy of an old court document on it. "Your aunt, one Luz Marisol Caridad Aragones, was in fact a tried and convicted rebel against La Revolución Cubana, captured not far from her house in Las Colinas and sentenced to an indefinite term at the famed Isla de Pinos, and spared execution only because of her young age at the time of her imprisonment. She had not yet turned seventeen."

Aliceana's hand is on Ramón's knee, squeezing. Ramón puts his hand on hers. "In prison, she was at times a notoriously badly behaved prisoner. She went on several hunger strikes, did a number of months, possibly years in solitary, the records are murky. Intelligence officers report she was particularly close with a priest from her province, one Padre Sebastián Enchaustegui, who initially supported the revolución but later helped run guns and apparently even was something of a munitions expert, although that's all a little unclear. Enchaustegui died in prison from an infection, according to records."

"And Marisol?" Aliceana asks. I'm startled by her concern; she's leaning all the way in, her fingernails dig into Ramón's leg.

"According to this . . ." Catabalas takes out an old copy of *Granma*, Cuba's state newspaper. "There was an attempted jailbreak in 1981, not long after Mariel. Seems more than a few of the prisoners thought they'd be released along with the slew of petty criminals and mental patients that were unloaded on the US during the boatlift. Of course, the regime wasn't about to free a bunch of unruly political prisoners and rebels. So a small cadre took it upon themselves to break out, including your tía. A boat was arranged, someone's cousin smuggled messages back and forth, maps and weapons were brought in; a very elaborate plan."

Aliceana has had just about enough of Catabalas's penchant for storytelling. "And? What happened, man?"

Me? I'm quiet. I'm still. Whatever happened, I am here. Here in this simmering in between, but there is a clear progression ahead. There is more to me than I've ever known, and I accept it. I occupy the space just behind Ramón's head; I am a curtain, the cautious embrace of a warm breeze, the tingle of certainty that a warm day brings after a long winter.

Catabalas leans forward. "A disaster."

Aliceana exhales like a punctured balloon.

"Someone ratted out the conspiracy. The guards let the plan go through just far enough for them all to make it outside the walls and down to the beach. Then they massacred them."

Yaniris squeezes Catabalas's shoulder so hard he flinches. "Díselo ya, coño," she whispers.

"According to this, your tía was listed among the killed." Everyone lets out a long, sad breath.

"The would-be escapees were catalogued, meticulously, in fact. Their bodies brought back, names published in the paper, all of this. Hoopla to annunciate the theater of good and evil, the all-powerful state, dissidents be warned, etc., etc."

So that, finally, is how I died.

A hail of gunfire, but not against a wall. By the sea, probably.

Inwardly, I nod, accepting it. At least I made an attempt. Whoever I had become after all those years locked up, I still craved freedom. I was cut down in the pursuit of it.

I accept.

And now I will begin the process of fading away; this time for good. It will be peaceful, I think—a relief to release this strain of holding on and holding on and holding on.

Perhaps I have done some good in this world while I was here. Maybe this second chance of mine served others more than me.

So be it.

I accept.

Ramón, less so. "Why do you sound like there's something else going on?"

Catabalas lifts one shoulder, then the other. "I'll just say this as a precaution, but I don't want to overcomplicate things or get your hopes up unnecessarily, so I'm hesitant to say it at all."

"Yes?"

"The *Granma* lies. I mean, of course it does, yeah? It's a state newspaper. The records about these things are almost impossible to access unless you're actually a government worker, even for me. Unreachable, really. As in, I couldn't reach them."

Yes, the *Granma* lies, but there is nowhere else to turn now. And I am exhausted, depleted. I don't have much choice but to accept. If it's not the truth itself, it's probably something close. A tainted caricature of the truth, but the larger pieces of the puzzle remain intact.

"This is all I could bring you really," Catabalas says, holding up the yellowed newspaper, "besides the original court documents detailing her detention."

"Which was *a lot*," Ramón says, clearly still reeling. He stands. "Thank you. Seriously, I . . . Thank you."

Catabalas waves him off. "Be that as it may, there's nowhere else to turn really. Not to be . . . well, yes to be arrogant, but if I can't access something, then no one can access it."

"I know, I just . . ." Everyone in the room raises their eyebrows at Ramón. His gut is clenched, fists too. He shakes his head. "I need to keep looking."

Another long collective exhale. I can already see the strain building in Aliceana. She's exhausted and filthy and terrified and all she wants is to go home. "Why?"

"For what?" Kacique asks.

Ramón strides across the room, rubbing his face. Returns. "Something else . . . a source that isn't a liar . . . some goddamn *truth* in all this!" The room goes deathly quiet. "Something besides all these dreams and propaganda."

I want to scream: *It's over*. He found what he needed to know, all that's left now is just for me to fade away peacefully. But not if he can't let me go.

✳

Tesoro Milán.

An unlikely sort of savior; he is a thick man with explosive side-burns and a mass of curly hair crowding around a perfectly round bald spot. He stands very, very still in the darkness of the trees. We surround him, ravaged, frightened pilgrims, just shadows really, each tasting the uncanny freshness of air outside those walls for the first time in years. In the middle of the yard, close to the tower, the stench of shit and rotting flesh dissipates some and you can sometimes catch a whiff of pine in the early morning breeze. But of course, you are near the tower and therefore all the easier to gun down. Here, in the forest, all we smell is pine, pine and soil, soil and life, rain, the tiny formulations of dew preparing themselves for the break of day, the gentle churning of trees, the murmur of life all around us. I inhale and almost topple over from the sheer joy of it. Almost.

But there is something else too: terror. Because we have only just made it out through a raggedy hole they've carved through someone's cell and because at any moment we could be dead or captured and suddenly, after so many years of craving death, of settling into filth, of giving over to the mindless acceptance of degradation, suddenly being alive matters very, very much.

Tesoro Milán shakes his head, meaning we aren't to move yet. The forest gives up no answers, no rattling gunships, no rush of bootstomps, just the sheer shush of nature, wind, trees, life. I try not to let myself get distracted, but it's a chore; every breath of air offers new wonders, new joys. Somewhere, not far away, the wild ocean lets itself be heard. I hunger for it; it's a new frontier of freedom. Suddenly the forest isn't enough. Out there in the darkness, a boat waits. It must. It must.

Tesoro nods and we move. He wasn't happy to see me. They hadn't included me in the plot and my presence hinted at a conspiracy that had slipped out of their hands, worked its way, like all secretes do, in whispers across the prison yard, cell to cell. A morbid sign. Still, he had no choice, and besides my friendship with Padre Sebastián, Tesoro bore me no ill will.

The forest breathes in and out, chortling softly as heart rates soar, hands tremble, muscles clench. A tentative freedom, so sudden it's violent: an assault on the senses, and so conditional. The drive, in all of us, is to just burst through the trees aimlessly, to act in accordance with the graceful whims of the night. But we're a disciplined lot. And what we truly crave is a freedom less fragile than this. We crave the lasting kind. So we move steadily, if not silently, through the prickle of pines, the seductive caress of wind unsullied by shit and death, the occasional glimpse of the moon through the trees instead of framed by ugly walls. We move fast, it feels like it because I'm running out of breath and wonder how much longer, but how fast can it be if we've been moving all this time and still not found the ocean? The ocean had seemed so close, its snarl surrounded us, beckoned.

And now it's gone.

Panic wraps around me, squeezes. Tesoro has his directions confused, he's a spy, he's gone mad. A million possibilities. I will die before we reach the boat, of heartbreak or the shock of actually still having a heart. Or of a bullet, which will break the skin just above my clavicle and enter my flesh, forcing tissue and blood vessels out of its way and bursting through my lungs, destroying, devouring and then collapsing luxuriously in the chambers of the heart I hadn't even realized I still possessed until milliseconds before it was shattered.

They will turn on me, my fellow escapees. This sudden freedom will make them mad with lust and what unspoken rules we'd lived with inside those walls will crumble, I can already feel it happen, and they will take turns destroying me like I always feared the guards would do. They will . . .

I stop. We all stop. Because the ocean is back in our nostrils, unmistakable, gigantic. She is bigger than prison, bigger than fear, bigger than hope even. The ocean doesn't care, but she's there, she's there and that's all that matters.

※

"Ramón?"

"Eh?"

"You dozed off. We're here."

Here is the Passports Ministry, a cluttered oven of a building that looks suspiciously similar to the Ministry of Records. Ramón and

Kacique get out of the cab and make their way inside, and I flush ahead of them, still nursing my despair.

I linger in the lavishly decorated upper corners, amidst the slow turn of ceiling fans and far away from the mountainous paperwork files. "This is not a good idea," Kacique says as they take their seats. He has his arms hugging protectively around himself; it's rare for him—he usually projects his chest out, hands wandering small, demonstrative orbits to accentuate the excessive importance of some point.

"Nothing I've done has been a good idea." Ramón shrugs, stubborn. "And look where it's gotten me."

Kacique actually laughs out loud, mostly to defuse the tension, I think. One of the studiously disinterested ministry trolls glances up from his paperwork and frowns. Kacique wraps back around himself. "It's gotten you to Cuba, where good ideas come to die."

The irritated bureaucrat stands, suddenly gracious. "Buenas tardes, señores. How may we help you today?"

Kacique and Ramón approach the desk. The man is positively swamped in towers of paper, folders, photographs. The nameplate on his desk says SR ALVAREZ. An unfortunate comb-over does little to keep his shiny head out of view, and his uniform is rumpled and several sizes too big. He peers out at them like a very dull fish from an aquarium, misery barely concealed behind a thin smile.

"Ah, originally I had planned to just come here for a few days," Ramón says. "But I'd like to extend my visa."

Ramón glances at Kacique, who just shakes his head and looks away.

"Ah, no se puede hacer," Alvarez says.

"What do you mean?"

"It cannot be done."

Ramón grunts a laugh. "No, I know what *no se puede* means"—a silent but implied *asshole* hangs in the air between them—"I mean what do you mean it can't be done? *Why* can't it be done?"

The bureaucrat lets out a long, steady sigh. "Because the original term of the visa has not expired yet. You understand?"

"Absolutely not."

"What you will have to do, in order to get a longer visa, is this, I'm going to explain for you, yes?"

Ramón narrows his eyes at the man. "Okay."

"You must wait until after the period of the original visa has expired, yes?"

"Wait."

"And then return to this office and submit form siete-jota-jota for a longer duration of stay, perhaps, okay? And then await response."

"But won't—"

Alvarez clasps his hands together with a self-satisfied smile. "When the ministry responds to that request, if it is in the affirmative, then you may stay for the extended period of time. You understand?"

"So I'm allowed to overstay my visa in order to apply for a longer one?"

Alvarez turns suddenly stern. "Certainly not."

Kacique looks away and squeezes his mouth shut. Ramón just shakes his head. "Let me ask you a question."

"Anything, señor."

"HOW AM I SUPPOSED TO RETURN TO THIS OFFICE AFTER MY VISA HAS EXPIRED IF I'M NOT ALLOWED TO BE IN THE COUNTRY?"

Alvarez smiles wider. "Ah, that! That is for you to figure out. I, desgraciadamente, do not make the rules. May I see your original visa?"

Ramón glances at Kacique, who shrugs.

"Mm." Alvarez reaches for the visa and Ramón passes it to him. He clacks away at an old desktop computer that looks like it could overheat at any moment. "There's a note in your file, Señor Rodriguez."

Ramón looks up. "What?"

"Seems a Lieutenant Urrutia in the Ministry of Records placed a note in your file."

Now Kacique is paying attention too. I don't know what this means, but it can't be anything good.

"She did some investigating," Alvarez says, sounding almost fatally bored. "And based on her findings the state of Cuba would prefer it if you not be here at the time being."

"I'm being kicked out?" Ramón gasps. "Why?"

Alvarez looks up, suddenly very present. "That's not what I said, señor. That would be . . . er, complicated, yes?" He cringes slightly, then relaxes. "From an international relations perspective. I said that according to your file and the research done by Lieutenant Urrutia, we would prefer it if you leave, based on your association with a known exile."

A known exile.

He must mean the Gutierrezes—their activities are renowned and certainly they are enemies of the state here. But how—

"Who?" Ramón blurts out.

Alvarez checks his computer screen. "Luz Mari—" is all he can get out before Ramón stands up so fast the old wooden chair he was in falls backward, clattering to the ground. Alvarez looks up, alarmed.

"It says exile?" he demands.

Kacique wraps a calming hand around Ramón's wrist and picks the chair back up. Ramón sits.

Alvarez watches them both and then returns to the screen. "It says here her official status is *Desaparecida*, vanished. But according to the documentation, she is presumed to have escaped to the United Estates following the failed prison break at La Isla de Pinos."

Everything seems to have gone very, very still.

Slowly, I allow myself to slide down from the ceiling.

"But she was reported as killed by the *Granma*," Kacique says, because Ramón is just sitting there with his mouth hanging open.

Alvarez cranes his neck forward and blinks at the screen for a few seconds, during which I'm sure neither of the men across from him are breathing.

"Des . . . a . . . parecida . . . ," Alvarez reads aloud. "Ta ta ta, fulano mengano, no sé qué y no sé cuánto, ah . . . aquí. A ver." Then he cringes again. "Yes."

"Yes *what*?" Ramón says, clearly fighting the impulse to overturn the desk and see for himself.

"Yes, that is what the *Granma* reported. The official documents tell a different story, as is sometimes the case." He smiles, peering over his glasses at Ramón. "I'm sure you understand."

Ramón stands, sits back down. Shakes his head.

I hold perfectly still, terrified I'll somehow ruin the moment.

"What story do the official documents tell?" Kacique asks.

Alvarez shakes his head and makes a poofing gesture with his hands. "Desaparecida." Then he shrugs. "Would you still like the paperwork you'll need to extend your visa, Señor Rodriguez? I will remind you that the official—"

Ramón is already halfway to the door and I'm already out it, into the sun-strewn streets, the wide and beautiful world. "No, thanks!" Ramón yells. "I'll be leaving tonight!"

# CHAPTER FORTY-TWO

The Malecón: the edge of the world. Here is where I drove with Padre Sebastián and before that so many times with Papi, staring out the window each time, taking a moment to pay homage to the giantess crashing again and again against the crumbling walls of the city. I swirl up above them to take it in. A row of faded plaster palaces watches the water from behind us, peeled paint forms crude maps across their facades, open windows and dangling laundry and beyond that all of La Habana stretches toward the teeming suburbs. Night lets itself gently down on the city one block at a time; the ocean still radiates orange streaks and a sudden gash of red emerges from the violet haze where the sun once was.

And maybe, just maybe, I survived this island.

A tiny sliver of a possibility, but at least according to the official records, I vanished and am presumed in exile. *Desaparecida.* There are so many ways to vanish, really. So many meanings to that word.

But it doesn't matter.

A surge of joy has been rippling through me since that frumpy little bureaucrat pronounced me an exile, but also a brand-new urgency. Because still, I am fading. My time is almost up. Even when I replenish, it's not enough, like there's a leak somewhere, and every bit of energy I acquire surges right back out. And I don't think I have more than a few memories left to give before I'm simply gone. But I'm so close, and somewhere, somewhere there is an answer to the riddle that is my life, my maybe death.

Some kids finish up their messing around down by the rocks, smack the water from their soaked T-shirts, and chase each other, all giggles and cursing, up the stairs to the street.

"I know this is a possibly very stupid question," Ramón says.

Catabalas laughs. "You're allowed three stupid questions and you already used up two of them, so choose wisely."

Kacique rolls his eyes. "There are no stupid questions, Ramón. Only ignorant privileged ones that have no business being asked."

"Great. Is there anything, uh . . . I can do . . . to get either of you . . . out?"

It's a worthwhile question, my awkward nephew, but I already know the answer.

Both Kacique and Catabalas laugh some more before shaking their heads. "Ay, Ramón. We're stayers. You didn't know? We stay. Like your tía."

"Didn't do her much good." Ramón cringes a little when he says it, but hey, he has a point. "And she didn't have much of a choice."

Catabalas shakes his head. "It's part of it. Part of staying is knowing that we might disappear too. That we're disappearing a little bit, every day. From ourselves, from you. Part of leaving is having to watch us disappear." He shrugs.

"I guess. But . . . thank you? I guess that's what I was trying to say."

"Then just say that," Kacique says. "You gusanos are so overcomplicated."

"I consider the whole event a net gain." Catabalas tries to put an arm around Ramón, but he only comes up to his nipple line and his arm doesn't even reach halfway across the bigger man's back. He gives up and shoves his hands in his pockets. "I irritated the regime, found out some new methods of e-intelligence gathering, hacked into a whole new ministry server, and got a girlfriend. Plus that cash you slipped me. So thank you, mi hermano."

"It was my pleasure," Ramón says. "I'm happy for you two."

"How's your head?"

"Still throbbing."

"Adina found her tíos?"

"Yes, but apparently they're less exciting than mine. She sounded relieved. We're picking her up there on the way to the airport."

Kacique reaches his long arms to either side and makes a grunting noise. "What a beautiful night! Alright, mi gente. Time to go, eh?"

"Pero qué dramático tú eres."

"Cállate, Catabalas. Ramón, you ready?"

Ramón takes a last look at the fading light over the ocean. "Ready."

✳

Now that I have the basic details, the rest comes back in a rush. No sleeping vessel needed to filter this memory; it's just there:

Our feet touch the rocks, the rocks nestle into the sea, the endless sea. We are shadows on the shoreline, tiny beneath the greater shadows of the trees. The trees that reach into the soil, the soil that slopes beneath the rocks into the sea.

I'm crying. I don't make any noise. The tears stream down my face, and my body heaves every now and then. Out there in the darkness, three lights blink on and off, on and off, on and off. That's it. Three lights, three blinks. Then darkness, unending. We are saved. Tesoro Milán lets out a breath so long and loud I think he'll collapse when it's done. *Coño*, he mutters under his breath.

Edgardo Gil had been waiting for us here, just like in the plan. He was anxious, Edgardo. He hopped up the rocky shore to greet us, let loose a slew of curses in his shrill whisper, hugged Tesoro. We all looked out to the darkness of the sea and waited, became shadows on the shoreline and then the three lights blink and Tesoro Milán exhales and a strange birdcall comes out of the forest. And then it comes again. It's a ridiculous imitation really, almost as terrible as the one Enrique did back when we were children playing soldiers in the Escambray, all those years ago. As we're looking at each other, there's a splash. Edgardo Gil. He's jumped headfirst into the water. Which is so silly, because the boat hasn't arrived yet and it's too far to swim to. But the birdcall, the birdcall.

The sign.

The black water is cold against my thighs. The words flash across my mind as I dive forward. The birdcall, the sign. The black water breaks around me, catches me, swallows me whole. On the shore, men are yelling. And then the night explodes all around us, bodies collapse. I'm flinching, flinching, praying I don't get hit and then I remember I'm in the water just as the shadows strut out of the woods toward us amidst more flashes and impossible thunder.

I sink and kick myself away from the shore. When I emerge again, flashlights dance against the rocks, over broken, bleeding bodies. I sink, trembling, and wonder if I should bother surfacing again.

When I do, a raspy voice is yelling from somewhere between me and the shore. *All clear?* Edgardo Gil, who betrayed us. I wonder what for. *¿Ya?* I see his dark form rise out of the water. There's movement on the rocks, something I can't make out. Edgardo yells, *But!* Three more bangs crack across the night and he disappears beneath a splash.

I'm panting already, swallowed between darkness above and darkness below.

All of them are dead. I am alive.

Nothing more than a speck, but alive. A survivor. I outlived everyone and I don't even know why. I'm still crying. Tiny saltwater tears dribble down my tiny cheeks and become a part of the huge ocean.

And then I swim, because there's nothing else left to do. The boat is an impossible distance from me and surely they're scattering to figure out what to do next. A motor growls over the rush of waves, but it's not from the boat ahead of me. A light breaks across the surface of the water. It's another ship, farther away but getting closer by the second. The first boat revs its own motor, cuts a wide circle, and then charges directly at me.

My arms wave from the ocean, my voice a high-pitched, pathetic wail in the night. I don't care. It has to be louder than the engine or they'll zoom right past. I yell and yell, my voice hoarse from suddenly being put to so much use after years of near total silence. But I have a voice, I have a voice. I scream, splash, cry. The getaway boat slows as it nears me; I hear its engine stutter.

*Please*, is the only word that comes out. *Please*. And then it's closer, close enough for me to reach, even as the Cuban Navy boat's roar grows louder. I stretch my arm across the night over the ocean toward freedom, however uncertain. And then strong hands wrap around mine, lift me out of the water, and the motor growls to life as I collapse onto the wooden bench, the wind catches my hair. And any second bullets will shred me, angry hands will pull me back into the gaping hole of all those memories, any second.

There's a man smiling at me. A boy really. His were the hands that plucked me out of the ocean. It's so dark but I can see creases of concern in his thick eyebrows, the lopsided smile. The night wind whips through his long hair; he has my shoulders in his hands. *Mermaid, you are safe*, he says, barely audible over the motor and the rush of air. *My name is Luis.*

# Part Three
# RE/VOLVER

# CHAPTER FORTY-THREE

Over and over, I try to draw him across the inside of Ramón's mind. I trace lines along the face I remember: that crooked smile, wide forehead, and bushy brows. The way his gray eyes always seemed to squint just so, like those cheeks were made a few sizes too big for his face and everything else had to adjust to make room. I don't know how I missed it, how I could be so close to this man, all along, all along, and not know. Even now that I do know, it unravels slowly for me, piece by piece, our life together.

Ramón is stubborn. Stubborn and exhausted, but too wired to sleep. On the plane, he watches the sky slide past, Aliceana's head on his shoulder, their hands interlaced. But anyway, I don't have it in me to dilute his dreams with my memories. I just have one message: Luis. It's a simple one, but somehow beyond my power to convey. I have been weakening every day, with each passing hour. What once seemed easy now requires incredible effort. I am dying. Perhaps for the second time. And I don't know how many memories I have left to give before I'm gone for good.

Then there's the slow flurry of customs, unloading, claiming, form-filling, and box-checking. The whole process still trembles with new ferocity from the terrorist attacks a few years back. There are so many frowning soldiers, big guns, tight eyes, and doubting questions. We've been regurgitated out of one iron-fisted bureaucracy into the mouth of another. Painted murals on crumbled walls espousing the glorious revolution give way to shiny posters demanding passengers say something if they see something, and praising the noble commander in chief. Then the never-ending carpeted labyrinth of JFK, escalators, elevators, a gliding walkway, and all the while the unceasing nag of advertisements, their slick coercive whispers and shouts. Then the air tram and her pointed announcements, other passengers ragtag and irritable after hours of monotony, then more gates to push through, elevators and tickets to be managed, the A train, a bus from Grand Central, more troubled thoughts through stop-and-go traffic, and this ever-present feeling of fading, fading.

Within Ramón, the pulsing uncertainty about his mother casts a long shadow. They've barely spoken since he hung up on her, and the memory of that sudden silence, the mix of guilt and triumph—it still pounds through him. He called the next day to check on her, but she was busy making arrangements for Tío Pepe's funeral and then it was one thing and then another, but the truth was: Something had broken between them, and Ramón knew it. He'd put away most of the roiling nastiness of it during the trip, but now he's back, and there's so much to do, to say, and the impossibility of all that lies ahead sits on his shoulders, smirking.

That woman haunts me too, in an entirely different way, a new way, but right now, I am painted with only Luis.

All the while, Luis.

I can see us now, the two of us. It happens as this bus slogs through a dreary rain-soaked traffic jam into New Jersey. Ramón glares out the window; Aliceana writes in her journal; Adina sleeps. I hover by the air vents, almost impalpable to even myself, lost in everything we've found.

Escape was a sudden gasp of air, then came landing and processing and explaining. But I couldn't. I had to move slowly; sudden jolts would shatter me. I drifted off that boat up onto the beach and into the lights of Miami and I barely spoke. Luis guided me along like I was an old crazy woman, the others kept their distance. In the safe house, I collapsed, disappeared into a storage closet for days because small dark rooms were the only thing that made sense. There was a comfort in the terror that the shadows brought. It was familiar, even if it shredded me.

We creep along the highway. Industrial wastelands stretch out beneath us. It hasn't changed much, now I realize. I have been here before, long, long ago.

"Ay, nena," Luis said to me. I had fallen asleep in the passenger seat of his beat-up Chevrolet. In my sleep, I'd dropped my guard and found his shoulder and made a home there, and as I drifted back to the surface I made peace with his musky body odor and the last traces of some cologne.

"Nena, despiértate. Estamos en Jersey." I still hadn't told him my name. I had barely spoken. My open mouth on his T-shirt was the most I'd touched him. I could tell he wasn't moving any more than he had to, trying to hold tight to the moment.

Factories churned around us, their smokestacks gushed angry gray prayers into the angry gray sky. "Welcome," Luis said gravely, "to the Garden State."

I lifted myself from his shoulder. Smiled. Parking lots reached toward some distant huddle of skyscrapers. The Garden State. This man who pulled me out of the ocean had a sense of humor. I exhaled, and a little hiccupy gurgle of a chuckle came out.

The bigger joke: being alive and in a strange car with a strange man in this strange new country. All that finally worked its way through the layers of sorrow and fear and the impossible shock of sudden freedom. And it was hilarious. Laughter poured out of me, a torrential downpour. I had no name no home no degree. And for a moment, it felt just right.

Luis put his hand on mine, smiling at the highway as the lights came on around us. "You don't have family somewhere you want to look up, see if they're alright?" The laughter caught in my throat. My parents had died while I was locked up. A guard had informed me, months after the funerals. Nilda, I wanted to look up, yes, but not to see if she was alright—to make sure she wasn't.

I took my hand away, watched night cover the city out the window. "My family is dead."

❋

"How was it?" Marcos wants to know, wrapping his arms around Ramón.

How was it. Ramón smiles, hugs back. "A fucking mess."

"How's your head?"

"Concussed, according to Aliceana." Ramón puts down his bags, plops on the couch. "She keeps saying we have to X-ray it, but I'm alright."

"Your aunt?"

Ramón shakes his head. "Long story, man. There's rum and cigars in the bag by the door."

Marcos starts unwrapping his gifts and I'm out the window, embraced by the gathering night. This place looks different now: It's like I'm seeing double. The present is a thin veneer over the Jersey I once knew. The trees remain the same, some of the pavement. A building here, a shred of dusty architecture I must've strolled past once. Nothing resolves fully until I round a corner toward downtown. Here, two-story family houses with mild-mannered front lawns give way to a larger throughway. A pizza place is shutting down for the night; the neon sign blinks off and chairs go up on tables. Beside it, the beauty supply store and Laundromat have already closed. Farther down, large windows take up a whole storefront. Faded gold letters spell out the owner's name with elegance: SERRANO'S. Beneath that a less thoughtfully rendered barber's pole stands a little off center. New cardboard displays adorn the window: a walk to cure something, a teeth whitener, but beyond them, in the semi-dark perfect stillness, sit the same old chafed maroon cushions and ornate brass chairs.

I enter.

All these faces, staring back at me through gray tones and glass. Luis is everywhere, that serious glare he used to put on for the world, but I ignore him for now. I have to concentrate. I might be here. Here's Maceo, tall and burly and hairy: a poet. Here's Benigno the boxer and his Colombian boyfriend, Eliazer, who never bothered to learn English. Their smiles say it all, just a few inches apart, leaning into each other just so, but they never said a word about their love. Here are José Luis and José José, best friends, matching 'fros and Puerto Rican flag T-shirts, undaunted ease in both their grins, pants too tight, and little Serrano himself stands between them, arms crossed over his chest, his face a pockmarked frown: the perennial badass, even with that silly bow tie he always wore.

And Luis, Luis, Luis, all throughout. Serrano was his best friend, I now remember; they'd come up in Santa Clara together. Radicalized when Eddie Chibas offed himself on national radio, they stormed side by side through the jungles with Huber Matos right up until nothing turned out to be what it seemed.

"And then," Luis said to me one day long, long ago, and both his hands slapped the bedsheets. "Well, you already know." He looked away, went inside himself for a few moments, and we sat there in the wavering light coming in from the kitchen and took stock of the dead we'd brought with us. There were so many, so many lost saints, but Padre Sebastián was always the first, because the hole he left in my heart is wider than all the rest. Even Isabel had become the faraway kind of ghost by the time I lost Sebastián. Isabel came second, then Gómez, with clandestine meat packages and the bloodstained wall. My parents. Altagracia, a sad, obese woman I used to sit quietly with in the courtyard beneath the tower; they blew her head off. Santos, starved to death. Echeverria flung himself from the wall, landed on the other side with a wet thud. Miguelito from Camagüey, vanished one day without a trace, but we all knew. Juan-Pedro whose brains scattered across the gravel and left a sopping, chunky stain for months.

"¿Nena?" I had gone deeper than Luis, buried myself beneath the mountain of dead that I carried. "¿Adónde fuiste?"

He didn't touch me. This was early still; he'd learned the hard way not to touch me without asking. But his eyes wouldn't let me go, that harsh glare, furrowed brow. "Come back, nena."

Bartolo died so slowly; became skin and bones and then every week we thought would be his last, but he kept going, torturing all of us with that rattly cough that sounded like Death laughing through his ribs. "¡Nena! Oye." Daniyana's little cousin smuggled in some powder that she used to make an explosive. They shot her as she approached the tower and she lay there, sprawled out and alone on that great empty stage, a hundred eyes on her, the growing stain on her shirt. And then she detonated: a clap that snapped across all our skulls, burned the flash of that day into our eye sockets. We kept finding pieces of her in the crevices and imperfections of the building, and in the yard they said she'd won, in her own way, she'd won. And we shook our heads.

"Coño carajo, mujer." Luis's voice, a hundred miles away.

Once I'd cycled through the saints, the demons would come: David the prison guard and all his faceless friends. That great big yammering skull with a beard and dark green cap whose voice boomed across the whole island, the world. And of course, Nilda. Nilda's final, shivering hug and whispered excuse. Nilda with her satchel of music paper and places to be. Nilda with her lies, her betrayal. She went up out of her way to find those soldiers, to destroy me. It wasn't just a passive thing. She made the choice, followed through, broke me.

My hands would one day find her neck, I decided, and close around it. I won't look away either. Won't flinch. I'll make the choice and follow through, and close this hateful loop.

"MARISOL!"

I looked up. Luis sat on the edge of the bed, panting from his own battle against his own ghosts. He shook his head and lowered it into his waiting hands. Selfish, I'd gotten lost in my own trauma just as he was letting out some of his. Stupid. Two damaged people cobbling together a life out of what? The shrapnel of their old ones? It was like trying to glue a smashed bottle back together. And all these ghosts vying for attention. The urge to simply no longer exist roared up, filled the room. I'd come all this way. We'd come all this way. Separately. Found outrage and the insurmountable will to live amidst so much death. We'd made it. And now we were broken, couldn't even find solace in each other's sorrows.

*I want to die*, I almost said. The words remained in the space just behind my teeth. The truth, but not the whole truth. I kept it back, sealed my jaw tight, waited. *I want to die.* Softer this time. Luis's head still in his hands, not crying, not moving. *I want to die.* A whisper. I swallowed some saliva and took the words down with it. Opened my mouth to see if they had really gone. Nothing came out. A metallic taste in my gums. Luis's back was big, speckled with hairs and a few zits, a long red frown stretched across it from when they beat him with the electric cord.

I reached out my hand. The room was so still. The light from the kitchen buzzed and flickered, buzzed and flickered, made a line of brightness along the brown skin of my arm, my hand as it touched Luis's back. *I want to die.* But still just a whisper, and then gone again. A cackling reminder that it will return.

"Luis." His name a tiny prayer, just like mine. It was the first time I'd said it out loud. He looked up. "Luis." I reached my other hand through the dimness, across all those miles of pain, the tiny bedroom, the flickering, buzzing kitchen light, and then wrapped my whole self around him. "Luis."

I tugged him, the gentlest of tugs, like when you're dancing and the man lets you know it's time to switch it up, that tug. It's time to lie down, my tug said. Come. It's safe now. I've put away my ghosts, now you can put away yours. We lay back, and his face became a fist, his breath heavy as he fought and fought and fought and then released, in a low, scratchy wail, just a tiny bit of all that was inside of him.

It's his sleeping face I see behind all those pictures of him though. The face he made that night, after the release, after holding me, the face that meant he'd found a little scrap of peace. In these photos he's tensed up, always ready for a throwdown. I remember that Luis, the public Luis, but no matter how tough he mugs for the camera, what I see beneath it is the sleeping man beside me who knew how to be so exquisitely patient even while fighting his own living nightmares.

# CHAPTER FORTY-FOUR

Ramón's bags still lie by the door. Empty bottles and full ashtrays on the coffee table suggest a long night recapping the trip for Marcos. The beginning of day creeps over the building-lined horizon and into Ramón's open window. He knocked out without even shutting the curtains, clothes still on, face plastered into the pillow like he was trying to burrow through it.

Hovering just above him, I watch his body rise and fall, match my own breath to his. Luis holds the key to whatever happens next. All I need to do is paint the full picture, let the memories unravel through Ramón's dream state like I always do. But which ones? Where to begin? Suddenly back and now armed with the knowledge that I've been here before, that I lived beyond the prison walls, beyond the ninety miles of water, beyond even the treachery of entrances and exits—I feel like I'm drowning.

There were years here, I now realize. Years of my life that I settled into the way normal people do; the cracks in the pavement and particularities of the trees, the smell of hair salons, the corner stores: They became my friends. At some point they ceased to jump out at me, rude, each time a surprise, and became simply true.

Still, I pulsed with memories. Still the urge to hunt down Nilda and make her pay for what she'd done burned through me over and over like the ever-circling ray of a lighthouse. Still I thought about the life I left behind me that day I stood outside my own window in Las Colinas.

But I was fully alive. I was present.

One night I reached my hands over my head and let Luis pull my T-shirt over them and stood before him with all my scars showing and let him slowly, gently, hold me. One night I waited until he fell asleep and then took off all my clothes; slipped beneath the covers, and nuzzled into his heavy grasp.

And when I asked him to, he uncoiled those tightly wound muscles and, tears sliding down his face, told me. It took him forever to actually start, because he kept being afraid his words would erupt inside of me and send me off, away and away and never to return again. But finally I convinced him I was strong enough now, I was ready, so he told me about growing up in that far eastern corner of the island, a town not far from Santiago, and those heady adolescent days he'd spent dodging bullets in the Sierra Maestra, the gradual disassembling of his trust in the world he himself had helped create, the quiet feeling of madness that followed and his arrest in the run up to the Playa Girón invasion, the same roundup that sent Isabel plummeting from the top of the trampoline of the dead. He told me about the torture, a hunger strike, his eventual release and exile and how he fell in with a militant Miami group that terrified and excited him at the same time, and led him to the doomed rescue mission that saved my life.

And when I asked him to, he lay quietly with me in that hot dingy apartment, and we listened to songs we knew we'd never hear the same way again from an island we swore we'd never see again.

And when I asked him to he took my clothes off, slowly, lovingly, carefully, and lay back so I could ride him. And when we asked them to, sometimes our ghosts and night terrors would stay away for a few hours and let us have some privacy and unbroken sex.

I should give one of these to Ramón. Lord knows I've invaded his privacy plenty, but I can't. I need to build a shrine inside myself of things that are mine and only mine. Even if it's unfair; I know. The boy has had no such opportunity since I've been around, but what really matters is the simple, clear arrow pointing directly at Luis.

Another night, the fear roared up inside of me as I lay awake in his arms; I was going back to prison, filth seeped from my cells and fouled up the fabric of everything I touched. Everything I touched became a prison.

"Breathe, nena," Luis said, waking up to my gasps. "You're not breathing."

I exhaled, sent the shit out with it; waited for it to rise again; fell asleep waiting.

I can't give Ramón these memories either. They're mine, and so very few things are. Having invaded the darkest corners of my nephew's life, I become greedy over my own. Mine. I have shared myself too; placed so many hideous intimacies on his mind. These I will keep.

Big Maceo, Benigno, and Luis in Serrano's. José José in the chair; Serrano leaning over him with the razor, eyes sharp but mouth wide open. "Because, comemierda, you don't get to demand one standard of freedom in one place and not another."

"But it's not that simple, primo," Benigno said. "You're not taking a global perspective."

"Fuck a global perspective."

General shouts and curses erupted. No one noticed me standing in the doorway until Luis looked up from his newspaper, crossed the room at a bound.

"This is the mysterious Marisol you keep telling us about?" Serrano said. José José turned to see me, and Serrano manhandled him back into place.

"La una y unica," Luis said. "What's up, nena?"

*I couldn't stay in the apartment for another second because the walls close in on me unless I keep turning around fast enough to hold them back. And my brain had caught on fire from thinking too hard, from fighting demons and waking myself up out of recycled nightmares about pig-faced men dressed as prison guards shredding my naked body with their talons. And my body crumbles every time I wake up too suddenly; my muscles become shards of granite and I am a landslide, then dust.*

"Nada, Luis. Everything's fine."

"You look sad." A whisper, away from the prying ears of his homeboys.

*I look sad because disappointment has become a spider in my gut and it lays eggs, hundreds of thousands of them and when it died, instead of fading it calcified into a cobalt fist, has me shitting rivers for weeks.* "No, Luis, I'm okay."

"Alright."

"You are from La Habana, Marisol?" Serrano asked. His gentle way of fishing me out of my hole and inviting me into the fold.

"Las Colinas." I managed a smile.

"Ah, my cousin Ediberto was from there. He went to Santa María's."

"I went to Santa María's."

"Ah, you see? Come sit. You must've known Padre Sebastián, then."

The smile hardened against my face and then shattered.

Serrano saw it all. Luis put a hand on my shoulder and I shrugged it off.

"He was a good man. A hero."

I nodded. Fought off the scream that rose up inside me. Found a seat next to Big Maceo. Nodded at Luis to sit beside me. "He was a good man," I said.

There. Ramón can have that one. That should do it. I'm still hovering just above his sleeping body. Memories stream through me like I'm an open wound, a flickering, hemorrhaging catastrophe. I try to stem the tide and finally do, barely, barely.

I hold the barbershop and their banter in my mind, let it seep through me and then, lovingly, release.

# CHAPTER FORTY-FIVE

I'm going to kill my sister.

I decide this as we wind through the Jersey suburbs toward her house. Ramón, headphones on, gazes out the window. It's midday—pale frosty sky above and manicured gardens all around.

Once there was a young woman who made it to freedom, and she had one wish in the world: to make her sister see what she'd done to her. To make her pay. That, if nothing else, requires honoring. Perhaps that's why they sent me back.

I was mad before and didn't know why. Then I found out but didn't know the depths of that betrayal, what I had lived through.

Now I know.

Now I know, and what's more, somehow, I survived. I survived prison, and the island and who knows what else, and even if I'm dead now, I am armed with the truth of her betrayal. I've seen it, felt it, all over again, and all the terror that followed.

I'm not sure how to do it, though. When I took out Gutierrez it was more like helping him along than anything else. That train wreck old heart already careened toward collapse; the sudden rush of memory, the jolt of sex in loins long useless: I devised a perfect storm for my old lover and as he rattled toward his climax, I waited, watched, and then reached in, ever so slowly and in the perfect stillness before explosion, I pushed.

I know how to push. And I know how to wait.

Nilda's heart isn't feeble the way Gutierrez's was, but she trembles like a dry leaf that will easily crumble to dust if disturbed. I know how to disturb. And I know how to wait.

Ramón adjusts in his seat, frowns at his phone, changes the track on his little music player, turns his frown out the window to the passing lawns. He's preparing himself for a confrontation too. I was alive, at some point anyway, and forgotten. If this woman had found it inside herself to do something, to look for me, maybe . . . maybe.

His fists have been clenched since he woke up. The revelation of Luis, my presence in Jersey, the truth of my disappearance and rescue: It all jostles the burning embers of his rage. I, whom he never knew, live so bright in his mind he's ready to fight for me.

And I'm ready to kill.

✳

I'm practicing a series of motions, swooping appendages through the air in some vague cutting gesture, imagining Nilda's frail body split in half around my arms, which have become machetes.

But then I stop.

Very suddenly I stop, because we've exited the bus and approached the house and something is different. No. Something is the same. How did I not see this before? Ramón walks ahead, up the path to the front door. I linger beside a tall bush. Frost sprinkles the top of the grass on their front lawn. A few weeks ago, Juan-Carlo mounted a ladder and fastened a rainbow of blinking lights across the roof. Today, the air smells of snow and when it snows, it will cover the lawn and the lights will reflect in it, winking colorful shadows of themselves, and the world will seem both perfect and perfectly still, for however long you stand there in the night, watching each breath become a ghostly shroud and then vanish.

I know because I saw it, however many years ago, as I stood right here. My fingers, seeking warmth inside flimsy jacket pockets, wrapped around the switchblade I'd stolen from Luis. The steel burned in my hand; I massaged the indentation where you could press just so and make the blade appear. I had practiced in front of the mirror many times while Luis was at work. I had become an expert.

It would be simple. Here no record contained me, my fingerprints, my hair, my life. I had never arrived. And in Cuba? Dead. Drowned. Even Luis didn't know my full name; I was simply Marisol: a phantom.

I could murder and leave no trace and vanish and then I could stop hating and hating this woman, this last shard of family I had left. I could move on.

The front door swung open and I almost yelled. A boy ran out, ten or maybe a tall eight. He burst down the steps and went crashing into the snow like he was on fire and then lay on his back, staring up at the night, watching each breath become a ghost and then vanish, become a ghost and then vanish. Snow had started to fall—I hadn't noticed, so deep in my plots—it cascaded and spiraled slow, carelessly, and wherever it landed it landed gently, with grace.

"¡Ramón!" Her voice quivered even when shouting. The boy's head perked up from the snow. "¿Dónde estás, m'ijo?"

Ramón flattened again, watched each breath become a ghost and then vanish. The door opened, slowly this time. My fingers tightened on the knife handle, teased the release button. She stared out into the night, silhouetted by the warm glow from the house. The snow picked up, swirled into a frenzy, and spun out across the sky. Nilda watched her son, smiled. "Come inside, m'ijo, you'll get sick."

*I can't take this boy's mother from him.*

That's how it started. A very simple thought. A true one. I didn't have to look for it; it was right there.

Nilda had betrayed me, sent me to my doom. And I had betrayed her too, by coming back, by leaving in the first place maybe. Betrayed them all. To exist in a regime with its foot pressed against your throat is to constantly be in a state of betrayal. If I had not left, I would've been betraying myself, Isabel, what I knew must be done.

There was no right answer back in those hazy, hot days of the revolution. There was only despair and betrayal, which led into each other in a never-ending loop. Nilda chose one and I the other and we both ended up in the same place: fucked. But Nilda got out, somehow, and so did I, and here we are.

But her son had done nothing, knew nothing of our crimes.

A strange feeling washed over my body; my muscles unclenched.

The hand around the knife felt like it was on fire until I let go, the last part of me to release, and I did.

I did.

Somehow, without meaning to, I let go. It was the boy. He was outside of it all: a brand-new thing. My blood. What had been a closed circle, never ending, never advancing, and always always repeating, was suddenly wide open. I hadn't considered this new generation of us. Surely Nilda had invested some of her own trauma and guilt in him, her bullshit too. But this child looked so free. His movements weren't constrained; he had flung himself with such ease out the door, into the snow. A Cuban child, born in a land of snow, outside of the debilitating fear and clenched stomachs, away from the gnawing certainty that someone somewhere was about to betray you, once again once again.

This boy was what we had all fought so hard, in our own wretched, insidious sometimes glorious ways, to get to: freedom, beyond our sorrow. There he was lying in the snow, watching each breath become a ghost and then vanish.

"Okay, Mami," the boy said. My sister stared at him for a few more seconds and then, satisfied, went back inside. I counted five more phantom breaths rising into the air before Ramón threw his legs over his own head and tried to flip himself into a standing position. It didn't work; he landed flat on his back with a thud that would've been painful if it hadn't been cushioned by all that snow. He said, "Oof!" like the wind was knocked out of him and then laughed so loud and long that Nilda peered back out the door and yelled at him to hurry up, coño. He finally stood, still laughing, panting, coughing and laughing again as the snow came down in sheets around him, covered up all our sadness and sin.

✳

I came back.

I didn't mean to do that either; wasn't going to. But then one night Luis and I had gotten into it over absolutely nothing, some petty bullshit that's code for we're both heartbroken people, still having to find all the pieces of ourselves and put them back together each day after so many nightmares. We fought each other because we trusted each other and no one else, and knew as hard as we screamed and as horrible as the curses we could come up with would become, we'd always find our way back. And we fought each other to stave off that cool empty feeling of defeat, having fled, having left so much behind: the feeling of nowhere to turn. So we turned toward each other, sometimes with rage, mostly with love.

It was the TV that time, some telenovela I wanted to watch and he was sick of. I was already working at the Laundromat on Sixth, Consuela's; we'd both had long days, it was summer and the air clung to you, impossibly heavy and thick, even at midnight. I launched out into the sizzling streets, past catcalls and sirens, walked without knowing where until I found myself back in that same bush, now adorned with a perfect, still explosion of yellow teardrops, forsythia I think it's called, and before me stood the dark house of my sister.

I checked and yes, I had still forgiven her and forgiveness seeped like a balm down my tired body, slid beneath my skin and shushed these muscles, each a clenched fist; forgiveness made them gentle with themselves. And then I remembered: I was magic.

It seems, maybe, like something you would never forget. Since leaving that place I'd concentrated all my energy into being away from it. The shadows would draw up around me, the cracks in the walls, the peeling plaster, and I'd fight fight fight and finally the crisp New Jersey air would be true again and I could breathe and the tower, the smell of rotting flesh, the fear would abate. I pushed it all out, including the magic, Padre Sebastián's magic. But I had it in me somewhere, I must.

I closed my eyes and concentrated with everything. I breathed, tried to remember what it was I had done that made me able to slide outside myself like that, but it wouldn't come. When I opened my eyes, the night hung thick and sticky around me and a single light illuminated a window on the top floor. I froze. Had I let out a noise of some kind while I was in my trance? A face looked down from the window. The boy.

Ramón. He looked right at me. For a few seconds, neither of us moved. Then I waved. He waved back.

And inside myself, I made a tiny pact. I would not take this child's mother away. Rage had seethed through me again since that first night I'd seen Nilda. It had receded, risen again. It would recede and rise, probably for the rest of my life. But I would not take this child's mother away. I wouldn't be party to continuing this endless cycle, so far away from where it started.

I smiled at the boy, turned, and walked away.

✳

That pact carried me, I remember now. It fortified me. Forgiveness came so easily, caught me off guard, and I thought: If I can effortlessly forgive one that did me so wrong, I can do anything. Surely, that simple thought carried through the darkest hours between me and Luis. It came to me when I wouldn't let him touch me, lay sweat-soaked and shuttered on the floor fighting memories. I had forgiven, effortlessly forgiven. I still had some magic, even if I couldn't escape my own body anymore.

And now:

Soon it will snow. It's so many years later; the urge to take a life rose inside me but the memory of forgiveness once again eclipsed it and here I am, sobbing softly in this forsythia bush, barely a shadow. Without thinking, I slide across the lawn and into the house. I expect to enter a shouting match—instead I find Ramón in the den, standing across from his mother, both of them frozen.

"What do you mean, you don't think she died in Cuba?" Nilda says very quietly.

"I—"

With some rasp now: "What do you mean, Ramón?"

"Exactly what I said." You can hear the strain in his voice, the shout that's about to erupt.

"Pero," she whispers, her gaze far away. And then she slumps down into the plastic-covered couch, and for a moment I think she's passed out and a mix of emotions swarms me, but mostly: sadness.

"Mami," Ramón says, rushing to sit beside her.

"I don't understand," she moans, her forehead pressed into one palm, eyes closed.

"I don't either," Ramón admits. "I'm just . . . I'm trying to figure it all out, Mami."

She looks impossibly tiny; she must've shrunk three inches in the time we were gone. She's sobbing. Sitting on that perfect pink couch and sobbing like a baby and Ramón rubs her bony back and shakes his shaggy head and whispers, "Shh, Mami, shh. We'll find her. Or we'll find what happened to her, I promise. Okay?"

Nilda nods. "I'm just . . . I'm so, so sorry. I don't understand. She was here . . . she was in the States and she didn't . . . she didn't . . ."

They have no idea how close.

"I know," Ramón coos. "Shh."

"Pero of course not, after what I've done. I didn't . . . I didn't have a choice. I know it seems simple from where you stand, but I didn't have a choice, Ramón."

"It doesn't seem simple." Ramón is tearing up too now, but he pushes it back down. "Nothing seems simple, Mami. I know you're not a bad person."

She looks up, and finally, after what seems like years of blinking and glancing everywhere else: She looks at her son, takes him in fully, and even manages a smile. A genuine one. "Ay, m'ijo. You don't know what that means to me."

He nods. "And I'm . . . I'm sorry I hung up on you."

She laughs into the tissue she's blowing her nose on. "Ay eso no importa, mi amor. I don't care about that."

Ramón exhales. It might be true now but definitely wasn't then. Either way, it's not what matters.

Nilda blows her nose again and continues: "I did what I did because I thought I was saving my parents' lives. That's all. I never thought, I mean, I should've known, but you know, I never thought she'd be gone *gone* like she was. I never thought I'd never see her again. Even though I should've known, I know I should've known." Her feeble fist bangs her knee with each word, until Ramón wraps his big hand around her little one and stops it.

"Shh, Mami, shh."

"You will find her, Ramón."

"I'll do my best. I'll find out what happened."

I watch her body heave up and down and then the heaving slows and she horks into a tissue and then laughs a little bit. "What are you going to do?"

"I have to talk to Luis," Ramón says. "I think he knew her. You know Luis?"

"Luis . . ."

"Cavalcón. He runs the club I play at sometimes."

"Ah, sí. I think I know who he is. Troublemaker." That's the one. "He knew Marisol?"

"I think so."

"How do you know, m'ijo? Where are you getting your information?"

"It's . . . it's hard to explain, Mami. I can't really get into all that right now."

Within Ramón now, I simmer and open myself to his turmoil. My own anger had taken over, become all I knew, and I'd missed his. He's been thrashing through an ongoing state of wrath and forgiveness for a long time now. And his anger is already slipping away, barely there.

I look at Nilda, my sister, through his eyes. See the woman who raised him, who shoved through her own traumas, ghosts, and demons to make this boy into the man he's become.

Without meaning to, I forgive her once again. And then again. It feels like a miracle, and I'm suddenly wild with it, a strange, desperate kind of joy, a deep breath.

Nilda cocks her head at Ramón and then smiles. "Okay, m'ijo." She blows her nose again. "Do what you have to do."

Ramón stands.

"Do what you have to do."

# CHAPTER FORTY-SIX

"Do you have a plan?" Adina asks when Ramón climbs into the back seat of her beat-up Ford.

"Hi," Ramón says, dispensing a cheek kiss to Adina and a mouth peck to Aliceana.

"Hey, babe," Aliceana says. "Do you want to role-play?"

"I mean . . . yes. But right now?"

"Shush, man! You know what I meant."

Adina zips off. I pretend that we're not speeding toward the man who pulled me out of the ocean and reminded me I'm alive. I pretend that I don't care. I hover in the farthest back corner of the car, amidst Adina's forgotten paperwork and crushed iced-coffee cups.

Gradients of gray on gray streak the sky; the whisper of oncoming snow. And then that thaw will come. I don't know if I'll be around to see it though, with or without a body. Somehow, this matters. It weighs on me. I want to see the season change from winter grays to spring green, feel that first splash of sunshine on bare skin after so much frost. I do, I want it. I haven't always, but something's broken in me, once again. Being in Cuba unlocked something. I lived again, after all that. It was hard, walking these streets with all those memories and ghosts, but I did. I released one or two every day, like sandbags off a hot-air balloon. And they came back and I hurled them over the side again.

My God, I was a powerful woman.

Ramón shrugs. "I'm just going to say what I told my mom just now, that I had some information about Marisol and that I know she lived here after she escaped Cuba."

"How'd that go?" Adina asks.

"I mean . . . she cried a lot, but it was cool."

"I think this is gonna be different," Aliceana says.

"Why?"

And he must be a very powerful man, this Luis whom I have known and loved and forgotten. He must be, to put up with me and all my ghosts and my long journey back to the surface of life. I don't remember much. But this man remained by my side all the while, that I know. He caressed me when I needed it, was quiet when I needed peace. He challenged me, told me the difficult things I didn't want to hear, cried when I hurt him and even more when he hurt me. He stayed away when we learned how to communicate without having to talk and I let him know I needed to disappear for a while.

"I just think this is different," Aliceana says. She exchanges a glance with Adina. "I mean, I don't know any more than you, Ramón. Way less. But this dude, this is the dude that your aunt was with, after everything. And whatever happened, it was probably intense. And who knows how he's gonna react? That's all I'm saying."

Who indeed.

Ramón retrieves the journal from his shoulder bag. "I brought this. Might help."

"The dreams?" Adina asks, raising her eyebrows in the rearview mirror.

That book holds my entire life. Each guardian angel that helped me along the way, and a few demons too. Everything that matters. The sum of me. Interpreted through the broad strokes of a twenty-six-year-old security guard who never knew me; his dreams of my memories. So many lives and deaths. Padre Sebastián's prison philosophies. The rumble of history, revolution, survival. Love. Seems like it should be heavier, but they're only words.

Adina shakes her head. "Well, I'm sure Luis will be happy to read that you've been dreaming about the love of his life."

We turn onto the highway, watch the Oaks fade as New Jersey becomes a nondescript industrial park and then the 'burbs again. Without warning, the city rises up around us. Commerce and decay compete for attention as Adina merges to the right and down a ramp that wraps beneath the overpass into the heart of the city.

I'm tiny.

The buzzer buzzes, the trio marches upstairs. I linger outside. Luis lives in a newly renovated building surrounded by run-down row houses. A bodega, two hair salons, and a pizza place take up the rest of the block. A gigantic housing project looms nearby, beyond that you can see the highway disappear between skyscrapers. This isn't where we lived together. He's upgraded, if only slightly. I'm happy for him. I want everything to be wonderful for him, I almost even want him to have settled down with a nice woman, have kids. Almost. Sometimes the human heart is an asshole.

No. I have to let him go.

I can do that. I've let go of everything else, even my own body. I can't carry all my expectations and hopes up there with me, because I doubt I'd withstand them being crushed. Anyway, I am nothing. Barely a phantom.

I enter.

Glide up the three flights. Ignore the pulsing that won't stop within me. I've already seen him in this new modern time. I know who this man is. I shouldn't be nervous.

"¿Café?" Luis calls from the kitchen as I enter.

"Claro que sí," Adina says. Ramón fidgets on the leather couch. Aliceana puts a hand on his knee. It's a comfortable place; someone has put love into decorating it. The walls are painted a warm stucco orange, decorated with protest signs and posters of different rock bands and poets.

Luis has so many books! I don't remember him being this much of an intellectual. Or maybe they're not his? I almost get lost sliding along the labyrinth of book spines: folktales, Orisha stories, post-colonial studies, basic business owner guides, the Nuyorican poets, some dime-store novels. Hours, days, years of literature.

"It's almost ready!" Luis says. There's a click and some salsa group from the seventies blasts from the kitchen. "Have you guys seen this Napster thing?"

"What Napster thing, Luis?" Ramón asks.

"No, Napster. This thing that is Napster. Amazing!"

Adina coughs back a laugh. "Yes, we have seen Napster, Luis. You just jumping on that bandwagon, viejo?"

"Coño, Adina, listen, but they have everything! I mean, there are songs on here we used to listen to back in the day but way back in the day! I didn't even know . . . I mean!"

"You are hilarious, Tío."

"Adina." Luis appears with a tray of coffees. "Don't mock your elders."

I leave. I can't be here. He looks the same as he did a few weeks ago, of course, but now he is someone new. Someone new to me. I move quickly past the bookshelves and a wide-screen TV, down a narrow hallway and around a corner and into a little side room the size of a large closet. And then I stop. Because I am staring at many, many smiling pictures of me.

# CHAPTER FORTY-SEVEN

We had already taken over the streets when they killed Maceo. We'd taken them and lost them a few times, in fact. We knew the smell of tear gas and the thrill of an open charge after holding the line for so long. We'd tasted our own blood, healed each other's cracked ribs and blackened eyes.

We had no national aspirations, no political savvy, no platform. We simply got fed up one day, of the trash not being collected, the elevators being broken, the ambulances never coming, the filth accumulating, the highway cutting straight through our homes, the police sneering as they murdered us, the schools crumbling, the shoot-outs, the boarded-up shops, and maybe more than anything else, the way it was all so different just a few miles over, in the Oaks.

We didn't know the nuts and bolts of why, but we knew enough to be enraged, and that a letter to the editor and a bake sale didn't mean shit. We were Cubans, Puerto Ricans, black Americans, and a few scattered Angolans, Nigerians, Senegalese. An Ecuadorian, a Colombian, a family of Mexicans. We weren't in denial.

The Cubans, Luis and I and Serrano, Maceo, and a few others, knew enough to recognize brutality and repression when it leered at us; we'd seen it all before. That our wealthy compadres and comadres in the Oaks not only turned their back on it but openly supported it only made us fight harder. The irony, the sick, demented irony of escaping one kind of prison only to slip into the grasp of an entirely other one—it festered inside me, inside all of us, and then boiled over one hot day when they tried to bulldoze an abandoned lot we'd made into a community garden.

One sit-in became a showdown and then another and another and then, one day, they shot Maceo.

Maceo would do these street poetry marathons: He'd set up

somewhere on Grayson Avenue at sunrise, in front of the abandoned candy store across from Corridor Park, just a stack of books and thermos of coffee, not even a microphone. He'd open a book, tiny in those big Sasquatch hands of his, and he'd look something near ridiculous standing there all burly and gigantic in a huge T-shirt and cargo pants, cap turned backward and wraparound sunglasses—but then he'd open his mouth and some glory would come out, some old country glory. He'd start with Martí, and then work his way through Lorca, Piñera, Arenas, Dulce María, and some time around noon he'd put the book down, pour himself another cafecito from the thermos, and then launch into his own poems.

They say when you love someone, all the things that seem crazy about them are just normal to you, and that's what it was with us and Maceo. It was crazy, what he did, but we never blinked. He formed part of the natural landscape of our community; people would stop and listen as they walked their kids to school, bring their lunch and camp out on a park bench for hours. Lovers would make out under a tree nearby; sometimes Maceo would cede the spotlight to some teenagers who had their own poems to unleash.

In the year of protests and street fights with the cops, the politics of public space caught fire. Maceo yelled his poems; a new raspy wrath had entered his voice, new rage in his arsenal. The cops had demanded he move, they had berated and bullied him. Maceo kept on strong. When they shot him, they said he had a gun. We poured out of our houses and shops, teeth clenched and fists high. Maceo having a gun was crazier than Maceo yelling poetry at the sky from dawn to midnight on a sweltering summer evening. Maceo ain't have no gun. You want to see brown people with weapons? (They didn't.) Hold on, we'll go get ours. (We did.)

※

The newspaper articles tacked to the wall chant alarming warnings about that day. BLACK RIOT, TERROR ON MAIN STREET, VIOLENCE WOUNDS 4 IN NEW JERSEY SLUM, they yell. Maceo's death erased. One grainy photo shows

Serrano, brow creased, charging a cop. Behind him, Luis reaches out, mouth open, but he's getting bodied by two other cops. And there, there beside him, a grainy splotch that resolves into a face, barely visible over the burly shoulder of that cop. That's me, I'm sure of it. I remember that day: It felt different. Maceo's murder did something to us; we weren't just angry anymore. We were ready for war. The cops felt it; they bristled, moved in quick.

We carried clubs and broomsticks. A helicopter buzzed overhead, cops or news crews, I couldn't tell which. Didn't matter: Surveillance is surveillance. We marched halfway up Grayson before they charged us.

Here's Maceo's obituary. It's from one of the local papers, so they actually didn't make him out to be a lunatic or a gangster, just a poet and a friend. Here's a poster from the rally: JUSTICIA it says in bright red letters. Here's another poster, from the next day. It's a wrinkled piece of paper with the word MISSING on top and a picture of me in the middle.

"I said what the fuck are you talking about!" Luis's voice bellows from the other room. Ramón says something; it's just a mumble through the wall.

"¿Pero cómo te atreves?" Luis again.

My name is beneath my photo, Marisol. Just Marisol. I never used my family name after I escaped, because I had no family. Just Marisol. Here's the same poster, this one sun-bleached. And here's another. They form a circle on the wall: the posters and newspaper clippings and photos. The circle is a halo, in the middle sits a small table with a white cloth over it, a white candle, and a little plaster statue of a mermaid. It's kitschy, probably from some tourist shop in Florida, but it's me. I know I was his mermaid, pulled from the sea, tattooed forever across his arm.

"You don't know a single goddamn thing about my life or what I've lived through, Ramón. You don't know..."

The day I vanished. The day I vanished again. My life has been a series of deaths and resurrections. Maybe this was my final death. I remember the cops surging at us, helmets and shields, an unstoppable onslaught, and I remember not caring. Other times I'd had that same jittery tingle I'd get in skirmishes in the Escambray. That day, nothing. I became a rock and stood solid as they flooded through our ranks, demolished us.

"Vete de mi casa." Luis's voice. "You can't just come here and tell me these fantasies that you have no basis for, just boberías that you made up!"

That's all I remember.

A glass shatters in the other room.

"Luis, no!" Adina's voice.

Something huge crashes against a far wall, probably Ramón, and the building shudders. A word catches my eye as I spin. It's in one of the articles about the street fight that day. It's longer than the other words and definitely Spanish; it jumps out and tangles my vision, a centipede among ants. A name. I slow, return to the article. Skim.

Gutierrez.

Councilman Gutierrez.

"I don't see any inconsistency in the police reports. They took the necessary action against an angry mob and defended the people of New Jersey," said Councilman Gutierrez. "That's their job. If some rabble-rousers got hurt in the process, they will hopefully learn that armed demonstrations and disturbing the peace are not the way to get things done in America. This isn't Cuba; this is a democracy."

Gutierrez. I can see it so clearly: the monstrosity of documents tucked away in that file cabinet in his cozy Oaks mansion. He saw it all. Watched the whole movement rise and crumble.

Surveillance.

"Let me explain!" Ramón pleads, his voice finally a roar.

"There's no fucking explanation."

Gutierrez's files. He had the answers. The answers are somewhere.

I spin back into my circle, the same one I spun along the inner walls of my prison; faster now. The newspaper articles, photos, and posters blur into a slosh of black and manila and red. That song emanates from me, the same spinning song, quizás, dammit, quizás, but it's not enough, they can't hear it over their own yelling. I spin faster, let my charged molecules accumulate, burn, and rupture, and get reborn even hotter, heavier, angrier inside me—then dip my trajectory ever so slightly down, collide head-on with the glass of water on the altar. The glass tumbles, knocks over the mermaid. The mermaid lands in two pieces in a puddle. The glass rolls along the surface of the table and then over the side, shatters.

A moment passes as I recover myself from the exertion.

Footsteps approach and then Aliceana stands in the doorway, one eyebrow raised. She walks in and her breath catches; the shrine room instantly makes sense to her. For a moment, she's lost in the clippings and photos.

I wait, a wisp of a shadow and fading, always fading. Down the hall, the argument rages on.

Aliceana's eyes travel down past the MISSING poster, to the empty table, the water, the broken glass. She crouches, picks up a piece of the mermaid. Looks up. She's not looking at me, I'm in the corner, but I know she understands. I move myself to where she's looking. She still doesn't see me, I'm so close to gone, but it matters to me. She blinks twice, smiles ever so slightly, and I realize she knows she's pregnant.

"Ramón!" Aliceana yells, still crouching. "Luis!"

The argument doesn't stop. She grabs up the other piece of mermaid and runs out of the room.

# CHAPTER FORTY-EIGHT

Luis's face hangs slack. Sweat shines off his tan skin. His shirt is ruffled where Ramón must've grabbed him back. He's panting and scowling, but he knows, he knows. He has to know.

"What do you mean it just fell?"

"You heard the glass break," Aliceana says.

"And it was . . ." Luis crouches by the table, puts a finger to the wet floor, ". . . this?" He's still so bulky, a solid man after all these years. I remember in street fights he would break out of the line like a cannonball and all that girth moving so fast would have cops scattering. I remember all that thickness being around me, devouring me, holding me up, holding me down, cocooning my nights.

"This was my . . . this is." He looks around and it's like it suddenly dawned on him that strangers have entered his temple. "She's . . . I already let her go for dead. I don't understand. I looked for . . . so many years."

Ramón lets out a sigh from the doorway. He clutches the notebook to his chest. "I know, Luis. I mean, I don't know, but I understand. My whole family barely speaks of her. But . . . the dreams are real. I couldn't make them up if I tried. She's . . . she's with me."

Enough of this. I don't have the luxury of these slow-to-realize-the-truth living folks. I need answers, if nothing else so I may vanish this time with some peace and end this terrible cycle. Gutierrez has answers. Or he did before I ended him. But that house—up in that house there's a file. One of them has my name on it, or Luis's maybe, and inside there must be answers.

"Marisol," Luis whispers, his head lowered. "Te esperaba."

I know he waited. I see. And now I need him to move, this man of interminable action. I need his body and his weight and his brain. And

315

I need my nephew. I need them to understand this last piece. It's not in me though. I hurl myself at the wall where the article is, claw at it, direct all my waning strength to the far edge of myself and batter against it, but I'm spent. That last spin pushing the glass emptied me.

"What happened?" Aliceana asks. "What happened at this rally?"

Fading, always fading. I hurl myself at the wall again, almost make purchase with a folded corner of the newspaper but slide off instead.

"They killed a poet we loved. A . . . friend," Luis says. "Maceo, his name was. We took to the streets once again as we had been doing all summer that year. They came heavy, crushed us, shot tear gas canisters directly into the crowd. Marisol was by my side like she always was and then everything was that impossible white and she was gone. When the world came back to normal I was bruised and my eyes were burning, but I was okay. Marisol . . . gone."

"Did you . . . ?"

"Of course I looked. For years, I looked and looked. I scoured public records, wallpapered the city with her picture; I fell asleep at the courthouses, wading through red tape and political backwaters."

Ramón steps beside Luis, who suddenly looks very old. My nephew reaches down, wraps his hand around my old lover's shoulders, and helps him up.

"I searched," Luis finishes. "Until I nearly had a nervous breakdown and they sent me to Puerto Rico for a year to recover."

Nobody knows what to do with their hands, where to look. I lean hard against the newspaper article, achieve only a vague breeze. No one notices.

"Then I came back here. I opened the club and I went on with my life." Luis looks around. "Mostly."

We are not alone. With nothing having changed, the room seems fuller, the air thicker. I see Aliceana cock her head to the side and look around. I feel them surround me like a sudden forest; I am full of them, enraptured. Luis looks up, blinks through the tears he'd been holding back.

There are so many of them, a perfectly still tidal wave materializing in its own fine time.

And then I see Gómez, and I understand.

Ramón still cradles the notebook under one arm. The book that contains my life, the lives of so many others. A tremendous feat of conjure work, the act of remembering. Isabel stands beside Gómez. She wears a white dress, her beautiful shoulders bare for all the world to see, a cigarette in her hand. I thought I was just remembering for my own sake, to save myself, but I brought so many with me. Papi and Mami linger in the back, holding each other close, their faces drawn and serious. Prisoners from Los Pinos appear, first one by one and then in clusters. Miguel and Meelo. Altagracia, Echeverria, even Tesoro Milán.

Luis made this room a shrine. A shrine to me. And now we've brought into that sacred place a book full of all the stories that made me who I am, the people who helped me get through. Of course, a certain alchemy would commence. They are everywhere. And then, together, we move toward the far wall. Together we reach forward and as one, we swipe the article from where it was tacked. And together we watch, the living and the dead, as it dips and glides through the air and lands at Ramón's feet.

He bends down, retrieves it. The whole room stares at him.

"Councilman Gutierrez," Ramón reads. He looks up. "As in, Enrique Gutierrez?"

"Of course," Luis says. "That hijo de puta. What about him?"

# CHAPTER FORTY-NINE

I remember the cell. Thinking how much brighter American prisons were than Cuban ones. I missed the darkness, even for all the nightmares it concealed. That penetrating, forever shine of this place would destroy me even faster than the caverns of Los Pinos did. The brightness was all I knew though. They didn't wash the pepper spray from my eyes, so I lay there, sobbing in a ball and blind, and waited.

"Okay, te quiero," Ramón says into his mobile. He rolls his eyes. "Sí, Mami, claro. I know how to handle myself." He ends the call, shaking his head. "My mom wants us all to be very, very careful."

"What are we going to do when we get there?" Luis asks. He's giddy, almost laughing now, but his hands tremble.

"I'm not totally sure," Ramón says. "I just know . . . I know this is where we're supposed to go."

Aliceana nods, keeping her eyes on the road. "I felt it too. There's no question. There's something at the house she . . . they . . ." She takes a deep breath. "They want us to find."

The spirits linger. They surround the car, a solemn entourage, a few stragglers pick up the rear. They don't speak, barely look at me, but I feel them inside myself, their love and sorrow. I wonder where Padre Sebastián is. Been wondering since they first showed up. I'd waited. Hoped.

"I think," Ramón says, "I know what we need to find."

✳

Something is wrong. It can't be this easy. We were let immediately through the gates. The guards are all gone, a single smiling butler in their place. The Gutierrez mansion is a spiraling stucco monstrosity. But it is almost entirely empty.

"Hello?" Ramón calls into the massive front hall. His footsteps ricochet through the corridors. The butler has vanished. No one answers.

"Maybe we just go ahead in?" Luis suggests. He moves slowly, eyes darting back and forth. The warrior will always be ready to strike.

"Hello?" Ramón yells again.

Aliceana shakes her head. "No one's here?"

The spirits fan out and stream through the corridors, up to the rafters, out into the courtyard.

None of this makes sense. The old political wrangler sent out his final cryptic email and died and who knows what happened after that? His silly overzealous grandson probably picked up the reins, but to what end? Did he run the whole family fortune into the ground in such a short time?

"Ramón?" Alberto appears at the banister of an inner balcony. But he's changed. His doufy blond hair has been shaved off and he's smiling. His smile appears . . . genuine. It's disconcerting. "So glad you could come through! I was wondering how your trip to the motherland was."

The motherland?

"The motherland?" Ramón says. "Alberto, what's going on?"

"Come, we'll discuss. Coffee? Tea?"

❋

"Anyway, the whole thing, it just . . . it changed me." Alberto smiles again and sips his coffee. "I think my abuelo really did die peacefully." He has no idea how peacefully. "Having had that revelation, I mean. But I realized that even if it was, in a way, too late for him, it wasn't for me. And if he had done the single powerful act of changing me before dying, and I dedicated my life to something worthwhile, to peace and reconciliation instead of war and terrorism, well . . . what better way to honor his dying wish, no?"

"That's beautiful," Aliceana says. Luis and Ramón just nod, speechless. We're in the same sitting room that old Enrique received and threatened Ramón in just a few weeks ago. The walls are bare now, no more awards and gloating photos with right-wing politicos. No more war memorabilia. I hover near the ceiling, trying to keep track as all the spirits from my life float past.

"Anyway, what can I help you folks with today?"

Ramón shakes off the puzzled look. "I believe your grandfather has a file that we need to see."

"Oh?"

"The night you kidna . . . the night I was here, shortly before he passed, the councilman mentioned that he had kept ties on the left-wing activities going on downtown for the past few decades."

Alberto closes his eyes, takes a deep breath. "My grandfather did have a very complicated relationship with morality, didn't he?" This boy still possesses the slipperiness of a wet toad, regardless of what side of the political line he's slinked over to.

"He was a . . . ," Luis begins. Then he coughs and settles himself. "Okay."

"My aunt Marisol was a political prisoner in Cuba and then came here, but she never got documented and at some point she disappeared. We think she may have been arrested. I think your grandfather's records might be able to lead us to her."

The spirits have gathered again. They've found what we need; they bristle with it. Time slides past, wasted on this young clown.

"You still run the club, yes, Mr. Cavalcón?"

Luis nods curtly. "We reopen next month." *No thanks to you*, he doesn't say.

"And you still command a fairly large audience when you DJ, correct, Ramón?"

Ramón balls his fists. "What are you getting at?"

"I've retooled my grandfather's organization into something positive, peaceful. But we're starting from scratch, in a sense. What do you say we strike a deal?"

Luis narrows his eyes. "You want to hold a party at the club and have Ramón DJ, for your organization?"

"Yes, but more than that: I want to use your club as a center for community building. It's a perfect spot, and we can—"

Ramón stands up, knocking over his coffee cup. "No." Everyone looks at him. A black stain seeps into the couch. None of them had been buying Alberto's bullshit, but the suddenness of his switch up must've tipped Ramón's finally fed-up meter over the edge.

Alberto's eyes go wide. "What?"

"I said no. No more bargaining, no more politics, no more bullshit. If you're leveraging information we need to find my lost family member to get your organization a home, especially with all the money you have, then you're just as full of shit as the assholes trying to play me for more visa money or the corrupt pricks that imprisoned my aunt. You're just as fucked up as your twisted grandfather."

Alberto stares at him. The spirits hover around us, perfectly still.

"What makes you think you can barge into *my* house, insult me and my family, and then tell me what to do?"

I feel Ramón brace himself for violence. It's a battle he would win, but it would make getting what we came for much harder, and we all know it.

Then a voice from the doorway says: "He can't." Everyone spins around to gape. "But I can."

Nilda.

Nilda, wearing her favorite purple parka and a stylish silky scarf.

Nilda with her hair perfectly coiffed, her eyes blinking furiously behind her tinted drugstore glasses, her little, trembly hands clenched into fists.

"Madrina," Alberto gasps.

Nilda, bowed and worn but undefeated after all these years. Nilda, who made it out. Nilda, who set off a new generation of us. Nilda, who saved our parents from my mistakes.

And this is when I realize that the book of lost saints never stops being written. Every day, there are new saints who step into our lives out of the blue, who have been there all along. And if they became a saint one day, then they must've always been one, even when they betrayed you and almost got you killed.

Even when they were selfish and showed up back at home, risking their whole family's lives.

Even me.

She steps forward, Nilda, who carries a whole orchestra in those little hands, or once did. Nilda, my lost saint. "You are going to let us look at the files, Alberto Rafael San Pedro Echeverria Gutierrez. And then Luis is going to do lo que le dé la gana con su club. And that's all there is to it. ¿Me entiendes?"

Alberto nods. The spirits nod too.

# CHAPTER FIFTY

This is what I remember:

The cell had only partially resolved when the guard came in. It was gray. Thick gray paint; I could feel it against my calloused fingers; the paint had congealed in sloppy frozen dollops. The crushing weight of so much concrete and misery around me once again, and the panic welling up inside, calming back down, rushing up again. And then the metal bars clang open and a figure stands there. I can't make out what his uniform is, is he Cuban? A soldier of the revolution? No, I'm in Jersey. He's just a blur though. And for all I know, they sent me back. I don't know how long I've been unconscious.

This is what I knew: I wouldn't be a prisoner again. Not for a minute, not for an hour. I wouldn't be held down, abused, touched. Not ever. In my head, I kissed Luis goodbye and then I banished him from my thoughts, just like I'd learned to banish my family. I said goodbye to the memory of Padre Sebastián, whom I would soon meet on the other side.

When the guard stepped inside, I tore the seat off the toilet and broke his face with it.

The last thing I remember is a hundred hands holding me, grabbing me, a fist finding my face and then a much heavier, duller catastrophe exploding across the crown of my head.

Then nothing.

And nothing.

And more nothing.

※

Ramón.

The last of my lost saints, for now anyway.

He walks in the middle. Luis and Nilda on one side; Aliceana and

Adina on the other. An orderly accompanies them a few steps behind. I am with Ramón, always with Ramón. Behind us, the slowly marching souls of the past flush forward through the present, stern, unflinching, to be part of this one last act of grace, whatever it may be.

Linoleum footsteps echo down this corridor. Black tiles and pink walls. A water fountain. A picture of flowers in a vase. The doors have windows with wire mesh over them. Inside, TV screens flicker over tiny still lifes of lives lived in almost perfect stillness: an old man sitting up in bed, a woman alone in her rocking chair. Vacant stares.

"Here it is," the orderly says. "B-201. Jane Doe." This is where the paper trail ends. At some point, in the confusion of prison hospitals and trials in absentia my name vanished and I became Jane. Gutierrez always had his eye on me though; he hadn't forgotten our time tumbling through the Escambray. It's his signature on the transfer from the prison to this hospital. A deranged act of mercy, perhaps; I'm beyond caring. Ms. Doe's file hid among a stack of photos, documents, and court orders in the old man's archives—all about me.

Luis swallows back some saliva. Aliceana squeezes his arm and smiles up at Ramón. Ramón closes his eyes, breathes, and opens the door.

Inside, a woman sits in an easy chair, staring at the space just above the television.

"Jesus," Luis says. "Jesus."

She is me.

She is me.

My hair is gray brown, and dark bags weigh down the skin just beneath my eyes and I look so gray, so sallow and gray. My eyes, so distant. But she is me. I have a body, skin, and bones. Through prison and shoot-outs and across the sea, and more prison, I survived.

Ramón just stands there staring. Luis crosses the room, drops to his knees. Me, my body, she doesn't respond, just stares.

The old man shakes his head. Ramón frowns at Aliceana. His eyes say that he doesn't know what's supposed to happen now, after all this, now that they've found me and I'm a shell.

But I know.

Luis sobs quietly into the chair. I cross the room. Pause to take in the moment from the outside, one last time. That dress they put me in is floral print and hideous; I would never wear it by choice. It'll have to go.

I gather myself. Slide along the edges of my arms, inside the skin, feel my feet find my feet, my ribs my ribs, my heart my heart. I settle into my face, these arms my arms, these hands that I have loved with, killed with: They are mine.

Compared to the others whom I briefly inhabited, Ramón felt like somewhere I was meant to be, at least for the moment. But he was always just a rest stop along the way. This—my spirit fingers fill these flesh fingers and they both flex together, now as one—this is home.

This beating heart is mine. It beats for me, to keep me alive. It's been beating all this time, faithful.

I must've slept for a hundred years. When I crane my neck down, the man I love is sobbing into my lap. So I lift my hand ever so slowly and put it on his furry head. I look up and there is my nephew, this great big man full of love and courage and he's smiling. He watched my eyes click into focus. He wraps his arm around the woman he loves.

Across from him is another man I love. Padre Sebastián's quiet smile hangs in the air just in front of me; his essence covers this room. He has been with my body all along, cuidando. Taking care of this empty shell while my soul wandered the world. He begins to fade and then Ramón appears in his place, puts his hand on my shoulder and looks down at me with tears in his eyes. Aliceana stands beside him, one hand on her tummy. I find Ramón's face with the tips of my fingers.

"Marisol." He says it like the prayer it is, my name.

I smile. It is a strange thing to do, lifting my cheeks to either side, but it's something I could get used to. It's natural, even if I haven't done it in ages.

And this is how I will die, one day, many years from now: surrounded by my loved ones, finally at peace after a very, very long journey.

# ACKNOWLEDGMENTS

I was taking a walk through Bed-Stuy with my best friend, astrologer Samuel Reynolds, one autumn afternoon, trying to figure out what I would write next. Sam said, "You know, sometimes I wonder what happened to the spirits of the people who died at the Isle of Pines . . ." and it was such a striking thing to say, because those spirits had been dancing through my head for some time, maybe always—not just the ones from that prison specifically, but the many voices lost in the tumult of the revolution. And perhaps that is the haunting that every child of a diaspora, every descendent of war, carries; and sometimes it's a burden, and sometimes a blessing, but right then I knew there was some work to be done to let those voices out. I went home and started preparing to write the book you now hold. So first and foremost, I want to thank Sam, whose words led to an avalanche.

Secondly, I want to thank my family, who survived so much and came through with their souls intact. This book is not about them, it is not based on them, but it is deeply inspired by them, and especially my mom, Dora Vázquez Older. She is a light in dark times, a teller of difficult truths, a fierce and loving soul who I am blessed to know. I hope to one day be as wise and compassionate as she is.

Very special thanks to Tananarive Due, who I have always looked up to both as a writer and human and who was instrumental in helping *The Book of Lost Saints* become the book it is today. I wrote the first draft of this book while attending Antioch University's low-res MFA program in Culver City, where she was my mentor, and I'm very grateful to her and all the teachers and classmates there who gave their thoughts on early drafts in workshops and meetings, especially Gayle Brandeis, Alistair McCartney, and Jervey Tervalon.

Thank you to my editors, Rhoda Belleza and Erin Stein, for believing in this story and lifting up this voice. As soon as I met Rhoda at a book festival in Cambridge, I knew she would see this book for what it was, and I'm so honored that she took it on.

Thanks to the whole team at Macmillan, especially Weslie Turner, Molly B. Ellis, Brittany Pearlman, Katie Quinn, and Allison Verost.

To Eddie Schneider and Joshua Bilmes and the whole team at JABberwocky Lit: You are wonderful. Thank you.

The great Raysa Madeiros provided notes on various points of Cuban history and those particularly Cuban Spanish phrases. Thank you, Tía! (All mistakes are mine, all mine, and probably there on purpose.)

Thank you to early draft readers Kimberly Banton, Shanae' Brown, Brittany Nicole Williams, Sorahya Moore, Marc Older, Zahira Kelly, Cheryl Chastine, Christina Lynch, Anika Noni Rose, and Carolyn Edgar.

Thanks to Brian White and the Fireside Fiction crew for publishing an excerpt of this book in the form of a short story called "Stay."

Thank you to the Speculative Literature Foundation for helping me get to Cuba for research.

Many thanks to Leslie Shipman at The Shipman Agency and Lia Chan at ICM.

Thanks always to my amazing family, Dora, Marc, Malka, Lou, Calyx, and Paz. Thanks to Iya Lisa and Iya Ramona and Iyalocha Tima, Patrice, Emani, Darrell, April, and my whole Ile Omi Toki family for their support; also thanks to Oba Nelson "Poppy" Rodriguez, Baba Malik, Mama Akissi, Mama Joan, Sam, Tina, Jud, and all the wonderful folks of Ile Ase. Thank you, Jason Reynolds, Jacqueline Woodson, Anika Noni Rose, Akwaeke Emezi, Jalisa Roberts, Lauren Chanel Allen, John Jennings, and Sorahya Moore and fam.

And thank you, Brittany, for everything. I love you.

Baba Craig Ramos: We miss you and love you and carry you with us everywhere we go. Rest easy, Tío. Ibae bayen tonu.

Carmen Gonzalez, in your tower by the sea with your pups and sci-fi books: I still think of you and lift up your name. There is so much of you in this book. Ibae bayen tonu.

I give thanks to all those who came before us and lit the way. I give thanks to all my ancestors; to Yemonja, Mother of Waters; gbogbo Orisa; and Olodumare.

# DISCUSSION GUIDE

## THE BOOK OF LOST SAINTS
### BY DANIEL JOSÉ OLDER

1. Marisol initially struggles to understand Ramón, but by the end of the book, she grows to love him as family. What events or realizations do you think bring about this shift in her feelings? How would some of your relatives (living or deceased) perceive your current life if they were with you every moment? Which relative(s) would you be happy to have with you? Which relative(s) would you never want to share your life with in this way?

2. Nilda chose to turn Marisol in to the authorities. Can you sympathize with what she did and/or with her silence about it for so many years? Would you find it easy or difficult to forgive her as Marisol learned to do? Do you see any parallels to current events in the choice Nilda was faced with? If so, what are they?

3. Marisol urges Ramón to write down his dreams. What is the role of written history in the story? How does it compare to the role of oral history? What role do written and oral history play in your own family history?

4. What are some of the parallels you see between Marisol's and Ramón's relationships to their family?

5. What role does music play in the book? What role does music play in the lives of Marisol and Ramón? How are music and memories linked? What songs or types of music are associated with specific memories for you?

6. Marisol and Enrique both feel that the new generation needs to learn about Cuba's turbulent history. What are some similarities and differences in their views of that history? Do you see ways that Marisol's perspective might influence her decision to kill Enrique?

7. What drives Aliceana and Ramón apart, and what then rekindles their relationship? Do you see any particular parallels between their relationship and Marisol's story line?

8. Marisol eventually forgives Nilda and deems her one of the "lost saints." What other characters in the book would you consider "lost saints" in both Marisol's and Ramón's lives? Who do you consider "lost saints" in your life?

9. The relationship between trauma and healing is crucial to this novel. In what ways do each of the characters find their own ways of healing? How are they similar? How are they different?

10. How does family history affect our sense of self and identity? How do previous generations affect the next generation of a family?

## ABOUT THE AUTHOR

Daniel José Older, a lead story architect for Star Wars: The High Republic, is the *New York Times*–bestselling author of the young adult fantasy novel *Ballad & Dagger*, the first book of the Outlaw Saints series; the sci-fi adventure *Flood City*; and the monthly comic book series *Star Wars: The High Republic Adventures*. His other books include the historical fantasy series Dactyl Hill Squad, the Bone Street Rumba urban fantasy series, *Star Wars: Last Shot*, and the young adult series Shadowshaper Cypher, including *Shadowshaper*, which was named one of the best fantasy books of all time by *Time* magazine and one of Esquire's 80 Books Every Person Should Read. He won the International Latino Book Award and has been nominated for the Kirkus Prize, the World Fantasy Award, the Andre Norton Award, the Locus Award, and the Mythopoeic Award. He co-wrote the upcoming graphic novel *Death's Day*. You can find more info and read about his decade-long career as an NYC paramedic at danieljoseolder.net.